ROY HORNIMAN
KIND HEARTS AND CORONETS

ROBERT (Roy) Horniman, novelist and playwright, was born in Southsea in 1872, son of the distinguished sailor and Paymaster-in-Chief of the Royal Navy, William Horniman, and an aristocratic Greek mother.

He was educated abroad, then at Southsea Grammar School, and at the age of 19 went on the stage. For a time he was tenant and manager of the Criterion Theatre, writing many original plays and adaptations of his own and others' novels. In later life he wrote and adapted for the screen, and after his death his 1907 novel *Israel Rank* (also known as *Kind Hearts and Coronets*) became the basis for the 1949 film *Kind Hearts and Coronets*.

In World War I he served in the Artist's Rifles. As well as his professional work Roy Horniman devoted much time and energy to various causes, especially anti-vivisection for which he often spoke eloquently in public. A contemporary characterised him as 'a well-to-do bachelor who knew what did and what did not suit him, marriage being in the latter category, the social round in the former'.

He died in London in 1930 at the age of 62.

ROY HORNIMAN

KIND HEARTS AND CORONETS

DEAN STREET PRESS

Published by Dean Street Press 2020

First published in 1907 by Chatto & Windus

Cover by DSP

ISBN 978 1 913054 75 5

www.deanstreetpress.co.uk

A PRELIMINARY NOTE

THERE is an old saying, 'Murder will out.' I am really unable to see why this should be so. At any rate, it is a statement impossible of proof, and one which must always remain a matter of opinion. Because certain clumsy criminals have placed themselves in full view of that dull dog, the Law, we are asked to believe that crime is invariably awkward. The logic is not very obvious. I am convinced that many a delightful member of society has found it necessary at some time or other to remove a human obstacle, and has done so undetected and undisturbed by those pangs of conscience which Society, afraid of itself, would have us believe wait upon the sinner.

ISRAEL RANK.

CHAPTER I

It was the close of a bleak, autumnal afternoon. All day long in the chill and windy atmosphere the dust had been driven helter-skelter along the shabbier streets of Clapham, whirling with it the leaves which had fallen from the depressed trees in the gardens of the innumerable semi-detached villas. Here and there, fragments of torn paper rustled spasmodically along the gutter as the driving gust caught them, or—now that the dusk had fallen—floated spectrally for a few moments in mid-air, like disembodied spirits, essaying an upward flight, only to be baulked by a lull in the wind and to come suddenly to earth again, where they lay until the next gust of wind caught them.

Among the dismal streets not one was more depressing than Ursula Grove. As if to deprive it of the least trace of individuality it was but a connecting link between two more important residential roads running parallel with each other, and even these were not very important; hence it is obvious that Ursula Grove was humble indeed.

Each house had a yard or two of front garden entered through cheaply varnished wooden gate-lets, which announced in faded gold lettering that should anyone enter he would find himself in Seaview, or on The Riviera, as the case might be. Provided the name was inappropriate there appeared to have been no initial objection to its being anything. In fact, those responsible for the christening of these desirable residences appeared to have acted on the same principle as the small builder, who, erecting houses at too great a rate to be able to waste time in seeking appropriate names, was accustomed to choose them haphazard out of the newspapers, and thus christened two small stucco atrocities joined together in semi-detached matrimony, the Vatican and the Quirinal, because these two names appeared in the course of the same leading article.

Each house had a little bow window which belonged to the drawing-room. If these bow windows could have been removed and all the little drawing-rooms placed, as it were, on exhibition they would have presented an extraordinary likeness. There were the same three or four saddle-bag chairs, the same saddlebag sofa, the same little bamboo occasional table, and the same little gilt mirror; all luxuries that were rewarded, apparently, by their own virtue and a sense of their own unique beauty, for it was seldom that their owners enjoyed them. In the summer the blinds were kept down for fear the sun should spoil the carpet, which it certainly would have done if it had been allowed a fair field and no favour with the gaudy little stiff squares of cheap Kidderminster. These front rooms, although infinitely the largest and most convenient in the house, were never degraded to the level of living rooms, however large the family. Sometimes in the winter a fire was lighted on Sundays and the inhabitants sat round it, but by Monday morning at breakfast time all traces of this revel had disappeared, and the fire ornaments were back again, trailing their gilded and tawdry finery over a highly polished grate, glittering out on the darkened, frosty room, that suggested nothing so much as the laying out of a corpse.

These chilly arcadias were the pride of their owners' hearts, and if, when about their household work, they heard the door of the sacred apartment open they were immediately on the alert.

"Willie, what are you doing in the drawing-room?"

"Nuffin', mama, I was only havin' a look."

"Then come out and shut the door immediately."

Willie, old enough to be troublesome, but not old enough to go to school, would do as he was bid, at the same time impressed by his mother's admonition with a sense of the splendour of the mansion in which it was his privilege to dwell.

The family always lived in the smaller sitting-room—an apartment rendered oblong by the exigencies of the staircase. These rooms were invariably furnished, as were the drawing-rooms, with a depressing similarity: two horse-hair arm chairs with the springs in a state of collapse; six ordinary dining-room chairs to match; some framed *Graphic* Christmas numbers on the wall, an untidy bookcase, and the flooring a waste of linoleum with a little oasis of moth-eaten rug before the fire.

I mention these facts because the atmosphere of my childhood is important in view of my after development.

It was on such an evening as I have described—at least, I am credibly informed that it was so—that my father descended from his 'bus two or three streets off, and, after threading his way through the intervening maze of semi-detached villadom, entered the depressing length of Ursula Grove.

An unusual though not astonishing sight met his eyes. The blinds of the first-floor-front of his own house were drawn down and a bright light from within glowed against them and streamed from under them. It could not be his wife dressing for dinner, for they did not have dinner, and had they been in the habit of dining neither of them would have thought of dressing. Their evening meal was tea; it might be with an egg or it might be with ham, but it was certainly tea.

My father hastened his footsteps. The cause of this phenomenon had suddenly dawned on him. He opened the wooden gate-let with unwonted gentleness and without letting it swing to, which was the usual signal that he had come home. Then he went round to the back and softly let himself in.

He walked along the passage and paused at the foot of the stairs. There was borne down to him from above the wail of an infant. He was obliged to catch hold of the bannisters, for his heart leapt into his mouth and nearly suffocated him.

He sat down on the stairs to recover himself, while the tears of joy and pride welled into his tired eyes and flowed down his faded cheeks.

The doctor on his way downstairs nearly fell over him.

"Come, come, Mr. Rank, you must bear up. 'In the midst of life we are in death.'"

Apparently the doctor was condoling from force of habit. The speech was certainly alarming, and my father whitened.

"But my wife?"

"Mother and child, Mr. Rank, both doing well. It's a boy."

The alarm disappeared from his face. He was a father at last. "An Isaac was born unto him."

"May I go up?" he asked timidly.

"Most certainly, but be careful not to excite the patient."

My father went upstairs and knocked nervously. The nurse opened the door holding me in her arms. It is to my father's credit, however, that he hardly cast a look at the desire of their married life, but crossed at once to the bed.

My poor mother looked up tenderly and lovingly at the dowdy little figure bending over her, and smiled.

"It's a boy," she whispered, and then added: "We wanted a boy."

My father pressed her hand gently, but remembering the doctor's instructions not to excite the patient kissed her lips and stole gently out to look at his first, though somewhat late, born. A puckered face, to which the blood rushed spasmodically, clouding it almost to the suggestion of apoplexy, was all he could see. My father looked down at me and saw that I was dark. I could not well have been otherwise if he were to believe himself my father, for he was Jewish from the crown of his well-shaped head to the soles of his rather large feet.

If my mother is to be credited, he was when she fell in love with him a singularly handsome little man, but at the time of my birth the physical blight which falls on nearly all men of our race towards middle age was upon him.

She possessed a small cabinet photograph of him, taken when such things were a novelty. In early years I was accustomed—misled by the out-of-date clothes—to regard it as a very frumpish affair indeed. When I grew up I came to think otherwise: for one day, placing my hand over the offending clothes, there looked out at me a face which, granting the wonderful complexion which my mother always insisted he possessed, was singularly handsome and very like my own.

I only remember him as a faded little creature, who had run to stomach to an extent which was absurd, especially when it was contrasted with the extreme thinness of the rest of his body. He was a commercial traveller, and always attributed this inharmonious excrescence on an otherwise slim form to the amount of aerated waters he was obliged to mix with those drinks the taking of which was indispensable to his calling.

My mother was dark too, so it was little wonder that such hair as I had when I was born was of the blackest imaginable hue, as likewise were my eyes.

"He's a beautiful baby; a bit small, but beautiful," said the nurse.

My father, who could not at the moment dissociate my appearance from Mr. Darwin's theory of the origin of species, tried to believe her, and stole downstairs, where he made his own tea and boiled himself a couple of eggs. A meat pie with the unbaked crust lying beside it suggested that I had arrived quite unexpectedly, as indeed had been the case. This perhaps accounted for the fact that as a baby I was weakly.

Before the first year of my life was over, my doting parents had gone through many an agony of suspense, and my father had more than once slackened his steps on returning home after his day's work, fearing to enter the house lest my mother should meet him and weeping inform him that the tiny thread of life, by which I was alone prevented from flying away and becoming a little angel, had snapped.

But by dint of the greatest care from a mother, who, whatever may have been her coldness to the outside world, possessed a burning affection for her husband and child, I was brought safely to my first birthday.

Sitting here during the last few unpleasant days with nothing to entertain me but the faces of ever-changing warders—whose personalities seem all to have been supplied from one pattern—I have had time to think over many things, and I have more than once reflected whether I would not rather my mother had been less careful and had allowed the before mentioned tiny thread to snap.

My present nervousness, which even my worst enemy will find excusable, tempts me to regret that her extreme care was so well rewarded. My intellect, however, which has always shone brightly through the murk of my emotions, tells me—and supports the information with irrefutable logic—that I am an ignoble fool to think anything of the kind. I question whether Napoleon would have foregone his triumphant career to escape St. Helena. The principle involved in his case and my own is the same. I have had a great career; I am paying for it—only fortunately the public are asking an absurdly low price. It is only when I have smoked too many cigarettes that I feel nervous about Monday's ceremony.

One thing I trust, however, and that is that my mother will not in any way be made unhappy, for should her spirit have the power of seeing my present condition, and of suffering by reason of it, it would give me the greatest concern.

But to resume. My arrival must have been an immense comfort to my mother even more than to my father. His business frequently took him away from home for a week at a time, and although he rarely failed to be with us from Saturday till Monday the shabby little Clapham house had been very dull till my shrill baby cries broke the silence of his absence.

Until I arrived to keep her company my mother had been thrown almost entirely on her own resources, and the reason of this loneliness is also the reason of my strange career. They are inseparable one from the other.

My mother had married beneath her. Her father had been a solicitor in a fair way of business, blessed with one son and one daughter. They were not rich but they were gentlefolk, and by descent something more. In fact, only nine lives stood between my mother's brother and one of the most ancient peerages in the United Kingdom.

My mother's maiden name was Gascoyne, and her father was the great-grandson of a younger son. Her father's family had for the last two generations drifted away from, and ceased to have any acquaintance with, the main and aristocratic branch of the family. Beyond a couple of ancestral portraits, the one of Lord George Gascoyne, my mother's great-grandfather, and the other of that spendthrift's wife, there was no visible evidence that they were in any way of superior social extraction to their well-to-do but suburban surroundings.

My father and mother were brought together in this way. My mother's brother belonged to a cricket club of which my father was also a member. The two struck up a friendship, although at a first glance there could appear to be very little in common between the successful solicitor's heir and the junior clerk in a wholesale city house. My father, however, had a gift of music which recommended him strongly to his new friend, and, as my mother always said, a natural refinement of manner which made him a quite possible guest at the quasi-aristocratic house of the Gascoynes.

"Perhaps I was sentimental and foolish," my mother would say, with that quiet, unemotional voice of hers which caused strangers to doubt whether she could ever be either, "but he had such beautiful eyes and played in such an unaffected, dreamy way. And he was so good," she would add, as if this were the quality which in the end had impressed her most. "He might have been much better off than he was, only he never could do anything underhand or mean. I don't think such things ever even tempted him. He was simply above them."

My father became a great favourite with the household till he committed the intolerable impertinence of falling in love with Miss Gascoyne. From the position of an ever welcome guest he descended to that of a "presuming little Jewish quill-driver," as my uncle—whose friendship for him had always been of a somewhat patronising order—described him.

In fact, my uncle was considerably more bitter in denouncing his presumption than my grandfather, who, his first irritation over, went so far as to suggest that the best should be made of a bad job, and that they should turn him into a lawyer, urging his nationality as a plea that his admission into the firm was not likely to do any harm.

But my uncle was certainly right in receiving such a proposal with derision.

"He hasn't even got the qualities of his race," he said—although this very fact had been, till their quarrel, a constantly reiterated argument in my father's favour.

My father and mother were forbidden to meet, and so one Sunday morning—Sunday being the only day on which my father could devote the whole day to so important an event—my mother stole out of the house and they were married before morning service, on a prospective income of a hundred a year. As mad a piece of sentimental folly as was ever perpetrated by a pair of foolish lovers.

The strange thing was that they were happy. They loved one another devotedly, and my grandfather—though quite under the thumb of my uncle—surreptitiously paid the rent of the small house where they spent the whole of their married life, and which after a time, still unknown to my uncle, he bought for them. My uncle, whom even when I was a child I thought a singularly interesting man—and the estrangement was certainly one of the griefs of my mother's life—had a great opinion of himself on account of the family from which he was derived.

He made a point of having in readiness all proofs of his claim to the title in case the extraordinary event should happen of the intervening lives going out one after the other like a row of candles. His researches on the subject enabled him to show a respectable number of instances in which an heir even as distant as himself had succeeded.

My mother's unequal marriage caused him to make all haste in choosing a wife. He might not have betrayed nearly so much antipathy to my father as a brother-in-law had not the Gascoyne earldom been one of the few peerages capable of descending through the female line. Thus, till he should have an heir of his own, his sister and any child of hers stood next in succession.

He chose his wife with circumspection. She was the daughter of a baronet, not so reduced as to have ceased to be respectable; and the main point was that the match would look well on the family tree. To his infinite chagrin his first child died an hour after birth, and Mrs. Gascoyne suffered so severely that a consolation was impossible. It thus became inevitable that should the unexpected happen the title would pass after himself to his sister and her children.

He drew some comfort from the fact that so far my father and mother had no child.

Whether it was the disappointment of his own childlessness, or a natural disposition to ostentation, I do not know, but from this time my uncle's mode of living grew more extravagant.

Through the death of my grandfather he became the head of the firm. He left the suburbs where he had been born, and he and his wife set up house in the West End, where they moved in a very expensive set, so expensive, in fact, that in less than five years my uncle, to avoid criminal proceedings—which must have ensued as the result of a protracted juggling with clients' money—put a bullet through his brains.

He was much mourned by my father and mother, who had both loved him. He was a fine, handsome fellow, good-natured at heart, and they had always deemed it certain that one day a reconciliation would take place.

Inasmuch as my parents had never met my aunt she could not become less to them than she had been, but evidently to show how little she desired to have anything to do with them, she allowed their letter of condolence to remain unanswered. Those who were responsible for winding up my uncle's affairs forwarded to my mother, in accordance with his wishes, the portrait of my ancestor, Lord George Gascoyne, together with an envelope containing a full statement of her claim to the Gascoyne peerage. My father, who was certainly more interested than ever my mother was in the documents that constituted this claim, took charge of them, and I believe that at my birth not a little of his elation was due to the fact that he was the parent of a being so exalted as to be only nine removes from an earldom. In time he came to regard himself as a sort of Prince Consort whose claims as father of the heir-apparent could not fail to be substantial.

I don't think there ever was a child more devotedly tended than I was. Arriving late, and being the only one, my parents were able to afford positive extravagances in the way of extra-quality perambulators and superfine toys, and in my earliest years it would have been quite impossible for me to guess that I was other than the child of affluence.

I was christened Israel Gascoyne Rank. From my earliest years, however, I cannot remember being called anything but Israel, and in my childhood if I were asked my name I was sure to answer "Israel Rank," and equally sure to supplement the information by adding, "and my other name is Gascoyne—Israel Gascoyne Rank."

I suppose that it is due to my sense of humour—which has never deserted me and which I trust will not do so even at the last trying moment—that I cannot help feeling just a trifle amused at the idea of my saintly mother and my dear, lovable little father carefully bringing up—with all the love and affection which was in them—*me*. It must be admitted to have its humorous side.

I played about the dingy house at Clapham during my happy childhood and was strangely contented without other companionship than my mother's. I certainly betrayed no morbid symptoms, but was, on the contrary, noted for a particularly sunny disposition. My mother declared that my laugh was most infectious, so full was it of real enjoyment and gaiety.

I have always attributed my psychological development along the line it afterwards took to a remark made to my mother by a woman who used to come in and sew for her.

I was playing just outside the room with a wooden horse, when Mrs. Ives remarked as she threaded the needle preparatory to driving the machine: "Lord, mum, I do believe that boy of yours gets handsomer every time I come. I never see such a picture, never."

I was quite old enough to grasp the remark, and for it to sink deep into my soul, planting there the seeds of a superb self-consciousness. From that moment I was vain. I grew quite used to people turning to look at me in the streets, and saying: "What a lovely child!" and in time felt positively injured if the passers-by did not testify openly to their admiration. My mother discouraged my being flattered—I suppose from the point of view of strict morality, with which I cannot claim acquaintance. Flattery is bad, and yet at the same time it always seems an absurd thing to talk to and bring up a child of exceptional personal attractions as if he or she were quite ordinary. If he be a boy, he is told that personal attractions are of no consequence, things not to be thought of and which can on no account make him better or worse, and then, whether girl or boy, the child finds on going out into the world that it is as valuable a weapon as can be given to anybody, that to beauty many obstacles are made easy which to the plain are often insuperable, and that above all his moral direction and his looks stand in very definite relation.

It was of no use telling me that I was not exceptionally good-looking; I grasped the fact from the moment of Mrs. Ives' flattering little outburst.

My father was immensely proud of my appearance; I suppose the more so because he could claim that I was like him and that I did not resemble the Gascoynes in any way.

I was dark and Jewish, with an amazingly well-cut face and an instinctive grace of which I was quite conscious. I have never known from my childhood what it was to be ill at ease, and I have certainly never been shy. I inherited my father's gift of music. With him it had never developed into more than what might give him a slight social advantage; with myself I was early determined it should be something more, and was quick to see the use it might be in introducing me into good society.

CHAPTER II

WHEN I was about seven years of age my father died. I think the cause was aerated waters, although I remember that on being shown his body after death it looked so small that my mind hardly established any very definite relation between it and the weary, kindly little man with the abnormal waist whom I had known as my father.

My mother must, I am sure, have sorrowed greatly, but she spared my tender years any harrowing spectacle of grief and set herself courageously to the task of keeping our home together.

My father had been insured for some five hundred pounds, which brought my mother in a tiny income. The house fortunately was her own. She immediately dismissed her one servant and let the front rooms, so that we were not so badly off after all. My mother, who had hitherto superintended my education, was now no longer able to do so, as the house took up most of her time. Certainly, the school I was sent to was a very much better one than a boy circumstanced as I was could have expected to attend. It was patronised by a great many sons of the comparatively wealthy in the neighbourhood, and was by no means inexpensive. I went right through it from the lowest form to the highest.

My masters pronounced me quick, but not studious. Personally, I don't think highly imaginative people are ever very studious in childhood or early youth. How is it possible? The imaginative temperament sets one dreaming of wonderful results achieved at a remarkably small outlay of effort. It is only the dull who receive any demonstration of the value of application.

My mother was careful that I should not be dressed so as to compare unfavourably in any way with my schoolfellows, and managed that I should always have a sufficiency of pocket-money, advantages which I hardly appreciated at the time. How she accomplished this I do not know, but I can honestly say that I never knew what want meant, and although my mother did all the work of the house herself, and cooked for the gentleman to whom our front rooms were let, we never lived in the kitchen or descended to a slovenly mode of life. We had our meals in quite a well-bred manner in the dining-room, which was also our living-room.

Our lodger was a mysterious creature who always brought me a handsome birthday and Christmas present and declined to be thanked.

The first time he saw me he pronounced me to be too good-looking for a boy.

He was gruff and abrupt in manner, but the incarnation of deferential courtesy to my mother, whom I truly think he worshipped. I believe that his prolonged residence in our front rooms was not entirely due to their comfort or to my mother's cooking.

I am sure he embarrassed her by his chronic efforts to spare her trouble. By degrees he took to dining out nearly every evening, although his arrival immediately after the dinner hour showed that he had no engagement anywhere else.

I have every reason to believe that he made her an offer of marriage, but if it were so he did not allow her refusal to drive him away. He remained, and continued to treat her with even greater deference than before.

Apart from the memory of my father, which she held sacred, her devotion as a mother would, I think, have kept her from the remotest contemplation of a second marriage. She lived entirely for me.

I was early made acquainted with the story of the Gascoyne succession, and it was with a quiet smile of indulgence that my mother told me of the interest with which my father would watch the ebb and flow of the heirs that stood between his wife and the peerage.

The idea, however, seized my vivid imagination. I got my mother to bring out all the papers and I set to work at once to see how far my claims had advanced or receded since my father's death.

I was obliged before I could completely determine my position to have recourse to *Burke's Peerage*. I was surprised to discover that I had come appreciably nearer to the succession. There were still six lives between myself and the peerage, but two branches which had formerly barred the way had become extinct. Perhaps it will be as well to give a tree of the succession from the point where the branch to which I belong came into existence. It must be understood that I do not give those branches which had died out, or the names of individuals who did not affect the succession.

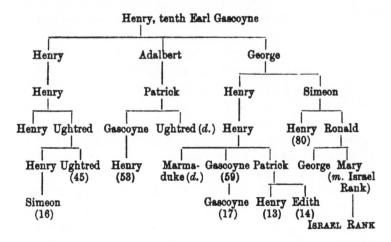

It will thus be seen that there was by no means a lack of male heirs and that my chance was remote indeed. In fact, on going into the question, so little prospect did there seem of my ever standing near to the succession that I gave up taking an interest in the matter, at least for the time being.

In looking back at the development of my character, I am not conscious of a natural wickedness staining and perverting all my actions. My career has been simply the result of an immense desire to be somebody of importance. My chief boyish trait was a love of beauty, whether in things animate or inanimate. People who have possessed that intangible something which is known as beauty—that degree of attraction made up of always varying proportions of line, colour and intelligence—have invariably done something more than merely attract me; they have filled me with a burning desire to be obviously in their outlook, to move for a time within their circumference, to feel that I had left an indelible impress on their memory, and it was my early appreciation of a capacity to do this that perhaps fostered my egotism, till it had become an article of faith with me that I must be someone. I looked upon the possession of rank or renown as a useful weapon for drawing attention to myself, of increasing the number of individuals brought under my personal influence.

I was greedy of importance, because of the beauty it might bring into life. Naturally the beautiful things in life vary according to temperament. Romance was to me the chief thing. After all, it is the salt of existence. Not that I believe romance to be necessarily conditioned by rank and wealth. A real artist may create it for himself out of very humble materials. One of the most complete romanticists I ever met was a coal-heaver, who had a list of experiences that sounded in the telling like the Arabian Nights entertainment. At the same time, rank and wealth fascinate as much as precious stones. They glitter, and they have value. The Israelite is probably less of a snob in these matters than the average Englishman, but as an Oriental he appreciates their decorative effect. Nevertheless, I doubt very much whether he is ever so far dazzled by them as to forget his own interests. I most certainly was not. I should have liked to be Earl Gascoyne. It would have meant grasping the lever to so many things, and this fact dawned on me more and more as I grew up.

My distant relationship to the Gascoynes was the cause of some humiliation to me at school. There was a boy whose father had just been made an Alderman of the City of London, and he was rather boastful of the fact.

"Bah! what's an Alderman?" I asked.

Instinctively the other boys felt that it was not right that one of Hebraic extraction should make such a remark. They had the intuition of their race that a Jew is after all a Jew.

"Shut up, Sheeny," said one.

"Now then, old clo'," said another.

I was not the possessor of Jewish blood for nothing. Where an English boy would have struck out I remained Orientally contemptuous of insult. I merely wondered if the time would ever come when I should be able to remind Lionel Holland—the last boy who had spoken—of his insult.

"If six people were to die I should be Earl Gascoyne," I said grandly.

There arose a shout of laughter.

"Pigs might fly," said Lionel Holland.

I flushed. The only impression produced by my grandiloquent speech was that I was a stupid liar. Even my bosom friend Billy Statham shrank away from me. Such a useless lie offended his sense of propriety.

I was only twelve and had some difficulty in keeping back my tears.

"It's true," I asserted.

"How can it be true?" demanded Holland. "You are a Jew and your name is not Gascoyne."

"It is—my name is Israel Gascoyne Rank. My mother's name was Gascoyne."

But whatever I said they declined to believe in the possibility of such a thing. The incident taught me, however, to hold my tongue on the subject of my noble extraction, and that was a point gained.

I don't think I was unpopular at school, but I suffered the penalty of all marked personalities; that is to say, I was very much liked or very much detested. I was not in one sense of great importance in the school life. I should have been untrue to myself if I had been. There is perhaps nothing more remarkable than the false estimate held by boys of character. Their giants are as often as not the pigmies of after life. Our school captain at the time I am speaking of was a boy called Jim Morton. He had a pleasant face bordering on good looks, and the body, so we thought, of a young Hercules. The basis of his popularity was a sense of justice and a reticence in the display of his physical strength. He was most certainly worshipped by the entire school, including myself, although I was by no means prone to idealise those in authority. For Jim Morton I had a veritable respect, although in any case my Jewish blood would have taught me to simulate deference until I was in a position to betray my true estimate without danger to my own interests. To my imagination as a small boy he seemed to possess something Titanic, to tower above everybody else in the school immeasurably. I met him in after years, an insignificant looking man with a ragged moustache and a slouch. It was quite a shock, and I waited for him to open his mouth, sure that his power over my juvenile imagination must have been a question of intellect. I talked to him for a long time, hoping for some echo at least of a lost magic. I can safely say I never met anyone more destitute of ideas, and it seemed impossible that he could ever have had any. Perhaps had he lived among savages the primitive virtues which had made him supreme among boys—and boyish communities are psychologically similar to savage races—would have developed, and he would have remained a force. It may be so; I give him the benefit of the doubt. I am inclined to think, however, that there never had been any personality in the true sense of the word.

Billy Statham, a boy a year older than myself, I loved. Where my affections are roused—and I have very strong affections, however much people may feel inclined to doubt it—I cling like a leech. I am supremely indifferent to defects in those I love, even when they affect myself. The only thing I ask is marked characteristics; I am incapable of concentrating myself on the colourless.

Billy Statham was certainly not colourless. He was gay, emotional, and beautiful as morning. He was brilliant and indolent. In many ways he seemed to be the most backward boy in the school, but to accuse him of being ignorant would have been preposterous. I never knew him tell a lie, and I never knew him do a dishonest thing; and yet once when a boy in the school who had been discovered in a flagrant piece of dishonesty was by general agreement sent to Coventry, Billy Statham was the one person who treated him as if nothing had happened. I really think his was the most Christ-like nature I have ever met. He always seemed to hold on to the intangible something in people which is above earthly stains. Evil had at times a bewildering effect on him. I have seen him look quite blank—when a curious look of wonder did not come into his face—as other boys were discussing matters which properly belonged to a more adult stage. The impending complexities of sex into which the other lads were always taking surreptitious peeps attracted him not at all. It seemed as if he must have possessed some inward consciousness that his body would never be called upon to take part in the sterner struggle. When he was fourteen he contracted rheumatic fever, and was returned to us after a few months with the roses blanched from his cheeks and the consciousness of a weak heart. One day he told me that he had heard the doctor say to his parents that if he had rheumatic fever again he would die. On a damp afternoon in late autumn we were caught in a heavy downpour and I left him at his front door shivering. I did not see him alive again, and I have never known boys so profoundly moved by the death of one of their number. It seemed as if they realised that something spiritual and valuable had gone from them in their corporate capacity. He left behind him the recollection of a nature entirely unspoilt.

To me his death was a profound grief. I have never experienced so great a friendship for anyone since. At the time, I was unable to understand why he chose me as his Jonathan, excepting that, as I have already said, he had the instinct of great minds for grasping the essentials in human nature and allowing a man's actions to remain a matter of opinion. He seldom argued with me. He was content to influence, and in this he displayed another trait of great natures, which let fall here and there a truth, but are not prone to discussion. I have often thought that he might have been the remnant of a great consciousness, having somewhat, but not a great deal, to expiate in human form. His goodness seemed to stretch out, invisible, beyond himself.

When he died I was fourteen, and the firmest of friendships are not at that age sufficiently strong to leave an inconsolable grief. My next great friend was a boy of very different character. Grahame Hallward was the son of a fairly well-to-do City man. They lived in comfortable style, albeit they were a somewhat uncomfortable family. Wherein their uncomfortableness lay it would have been difficult to say. They all had a more than usual share of good looks, and this possibly was their first attraction for me. Indeed, two of them, Grahame and Sibella, were quite beautiful to look upon. The family constituted a very aristocracy of physical gifts, and, despite their peculiar natures, I was always at my ease among them. It is true that they were inclined to patronise me, but the qualities of my race enabled me to endure this without resentment, and even with dignity. It was, however, only natural; for although I was always neatly dressed, the position of my mother was well known, and had it been otherwise, the house and street in which we lived would sufficiently have revealed the truth. In matters of this sort I was not a snob; besides, I had too quick an instinct for things well-bred not to realise that my mother was gentlewoman enough to hold her own with the very best.

One day I took Grahame Hallward home to tea. I think he felt a little nervous, wondering if tea in the house of such poor people would be a very uncomfortable affair. I realised from the way in which he accepted that he was a little surprised at the invitation. He always had beautiful manners, and he said that of course he would be delighted to come. The two words "of course!" were a mistake, however, and I resented them, although I was secretly amused.

He came one day after school, and when we reached the house my mother was already seated before the urn. There were flowers on the table, and the linen was spotless. There was a silver teapot and sugar-basin given to my mother by our lodger on the occasion of his having completed two years' residence in the house. His ingenuity in finding occasions whereon it might be considered suitable to make my mother and myself presents was quite remarkable. I was entrusted with the task of calling him in the morning. Hence it became necessary for me to have a watch, entirely, as he explained, to suit his convenience. In the same way a piano arrived one day—our own had been sold at my father's death—and our lodger explained that it had been left to him by a distant relation. I gazed at it longingly as it disappeared into his sitting-room. After a day or two he said that he believed it would be spoilt unless it were played upon, and asked me as a favour to do so. Then, having come home once or twice as I was practising hard, he declared almost irritably that it was inconvenient and that he really thought considering the time he had been with us we might oblige him by having it in our sitting-room, but that of course if my mother objected there was nothing more to be said. He would have sold it had it not been in his cousin's house for so many years. Needless to chronicle that the piano stood henceforward in our sitting-room. Our suspicions were somewhat aroused when the man who came to tune it gave as his opinion that the instrument could not be more than two years old, if that; in fact, he should have said it was brand-new.

My mother was pleased for my sake that she was able to greet my friend from behind a silver teapot and sugar-basin. I was secretly conscious of the effect she produced on Grahame. He had, I am sure, believed—despite all my assurances to the contrary—that my mother was a Jewess, and he was not a little surprised to find a well-bred Englishwoman with a reserved and quite distinguished manner. Tea being over my mother kept us seated, whilst, almost unobserved, she placed every article from the table on the tray. She was full of manoeuvres for minimising the bustle consequent on the want of a servant. I was rather nervous of the moment when she would rise and bear forth the tray. I had set her on such a pinnacle before my friend that I could not bear that he should see her otherwise than enthroned. I was painfully conscious that there is no snob like a boy. My mother, however, had foreseen everything.

"Israel dear, Mr. Johnson has brought home a beautiful old Chinese cabinet. I am sure Mr. Hallward would like to see it."

Mr. Hallward—barely fifteen and a half and very flattered at being referred to as Mr. Hallward—ex-pressed himself as most anxious, and we adjourned to the front room.

Short as was the time we were gone, on our return all signs of a meal had disappeared, and my mother was seated before the fire as if she possessed ten servants instead of her own ten fingers.

Then I played. This was not entirely a novelty; I had often been shown off at the Hallwards' house. Indeed, my musical abilities were, I fancied, often made an excuse when the Hallwards felt that the presence of my humble self in their mansion occasioned surprise. In Clapham, residence was everything, and the leading families were a little suspicious of anyone who lived in a house as small as our own. Had they been generally aware of the lodger they would have considered themselves entirely justified in deciding that I was not socially eligible!

I walked part of the way home with Grahame Hallward.

"I say," he burst out, "your mother is ripping."

If Grahame Hallward said so I knew he meant it. His chief enemy in life was his tongue. He always had an uncontrollable habit of speaking his mind.

Sibella Hallward exercised an irresistible fascination over me from the first moment I saw her. She was undeniably lovely even at an age when most girls are at their worst. Her hair was deliciously silky and golden. Her eyes were large and blue, with dark-brown brows and lashes. Her cheeks were the petals of a blush rose. Her mouth was perfect and petulant, and the one imperfection with which Nature invariably salts the cream of the correct was her nose; it was a little tip-tilted, and seemed to have been made to match her voice, which was curiously childish and treble, with an acerb complaint in it that was indescribably delightful. She allowed me to play at sweet-hearting with her, and then one day when we quarrelled called me a horrid little Jew. I was possessed by my love for her from that day. My obsession has never been defensible. She was no excuse for any man's love excepting that she was beautiful, and I loved her because such beauty would confer distinction on the man who won her.

She was vain and shallow, but with a will of her own which was somewhat remarkable, combined with her other characteristics.

I was constantly at the Hallwards' house. I was always quarrelling with Sibella and declaring that I would never visit them any more, but she invariably managed to lure me back without in any way apologising or admitting herself to be in the wrong.

At this time she was a shameless little flirt and permitted me to make love to her, which I did with all the precocity of my semi-oriental nature. Her parents were a good-natured, indulgent couple, and they usually alluded to me as Sibella's sweetheart.

It was not a household where principles counted for much, and most of the inmates possessing, like Sibella, very strong wills the result was chaotic. At the same time, they were sympathetic in an egotistical way. To anybody who like myself was able to hold his own, and also to put up with them, the household was tolerable and enjoyable. Woe, however, to any luckless person who found them too fascinating to avoid and too strong-minded to be battled with! Such a one was ground to powder by the sheer weight of their egotism.

I suppose it was this egotism that made Grahame Hallward somewhat unpopular at school. He always bore himself with an extraordinary pride; not aggressive, but the sort of innate aloofness and condescension which might have been expected from the member of a reigning house. It was natural to the family, and even shallow Sibella possessed it. At times it gave one the impression that she had dignity, when in reality it was only an aspect of her vanity.

Amongst other things which Grahame Hallward and I had in common was a dislike of Lionel Holland. We had both suffered from his superior physical strength, and with Grahame even more than with me this was an unpardonable offence. Lionel Holland was not deficient in head; he had great intelligence of a certain kind, and almost a genius for displaying his mental wares to the best advantage. It was commonly reported that his father had begun life as a newspaper boy, and certainly his son's wit and repartee were of the gutter order notwithstanding their veneer of middle-class suburbanism. He was slightly older than either of us and of an altogether stronger type. We found a means, however, of putting an end to his tyranny. We engaged in a defensive league, not verbally agreed upon—Grahame would have been much too proud to admit that such a thing was necessary—but we got into the way of standing by one another when he commenced to annoy us. Candour compels me to admit that he was almost a match for both of us, but we managed to inflict sufficient punishment to make him consider that the entertainment of baiting us had its risks, and finally he left us alone.

It was Lionel Holland's ambition to be captain of the school. He considered that his brilliance at certain sports entitled him to it, but somehow he never reached the position he aimed at. The boys did not trust him. He was deficient in those very qualities that make a boy's hero, and they were not to be deceived by the easy insolence of his manner. I never knew success in the cricket and football field carry a boy such a little way into his comrades' hearts. He was a handsome lad enough, embryon of the flashy, brilliant brute he afterwards became. I think, but for Grahame and myself, he might have been elected to the post he coveted. He had more money than any other boy in the school and spent it freely where he had an object in view. My friend and I, however, were determined that so unsuitable an election should not take place. The captain of the school had large powers, and we had no mind to see ourselves in Lionel Holland's hands. Our brains were more astute than his when it came to a real tussle of intellect. We discredited him in every way possible, and he endured the humiliation of defeat. A psychologist would have been interested in noting how, when Lionel Holland's defeat was an accomplished fact, the different characteristics of Grahame's nature and my own displayed themselves.

Grahame, having attained his object, was sorry for his antagonist. I was unfeignedly glad, and rejoiced in his humiliation to an extent which was very unpleasing to my friend. We had quite a quarrel over the matter; and Grahame, whose plain speech never failed, told me that I was exhibiting the worst faults of the Old Testament, in that I showed unsportsmanlike exultation over a fallen foe. I ought perhaps to mention that Lionel Holland had attempted to win me to his side by asking me to go with him to the Crystal Palace and there treating me to all the side shows. I enjoyed the outing but took the liberty of continuing to distrust him; another method of which Grahame disapproved most strongly. Certainly Lionel Holland would never have attempted to bribe Grahame. The crudest of perceptions—which his was not—would at once have seen the futility of such an attempt.

I fancy that I was constantly disappointing my friend, and he was impatient of any point of view which he was unable to sympathise with. It was therefore the more remarkable that he should have remained so staunch. I think that at times his friendship for me was living on his capital of loyalty, of which he possessed an inexhaustible store. His loyalty tended to make him very inelastic in argument, but he was altogether an unexpected person and would on occasions display a susceptibility to logic which was amazing in one so young.

He was, what most people who knew him superficially hardly suspected, sensitive to an extraordinary degree. His impassivity deceived them. He had a horror of death, and Billy Statham's end affected him more as a practical example of the inevitability and ruthlessness of bodily extinction than with regret at the loss of a schoolmate whom like all of us he had really loved.

He did not believe that my fear of death was not equal to his own, and concluded that my indifference was affected and mere bravado. In after years when I explained to him that without having any particular religious opinions, I regarded this body as a more or less useful vessel in which to perform part of the voyage of mental evolution, I found him quite unable to follow me and still possessed by just the same dread of death. The mere idea terrified him. The sight of all dead things, even when they happened to be the corpses of quite low forms of life, filled him with repulsion, and the idea of making him a doctor, which his father had entertained during his childhood, was abandoned.

I used to find a certain satisfaction in raising the question of death in order to see the colour fade out of his cheek. He was too proud to say that it frightened him, but it did. Fear was so little in his character that

I came to the conclusion that it lay partly in the extraordinary value he and his family placed on personal appearance, and that in addition his terror might have its roots in some such cause as made Catherine de Medici faint when she saw an apple, even if it were a painted one in a picture.

As a boy I forbore to make him a confidant of my passion for his sister. Perhaps I realised that he would resent it. I think he believed that his sisters were fit matches for the most exalted, and was secretly astonished and disgusted when the eldest married a struggling young solicitor.

Once, when Sibella had taunted me and teased me past bearing, I threw the Gascoyne pedigree in her face. I shall never forget the silvery and maddening laugh of disbelief with which she received the announcement. She did not even ask me for proof but went on laughing till I could have struck her. At the moment I hated her. It was on a half-holiday. I had been asked to tea, and was making love to her in the schoolroom, waiting for Grahame and his brother to come in from football.

"When you laugh at me like that," I said tersely, "I feel as if I could kill you."

"And when you tell stories like that," she said, mimicking my intonation in her childish treble, "you are simply ridiculous." She took another chocolate from the bag of sweets I had brought her. I used to save up my pocket-money for two or three weeks until I had sufficient to buy sweets worthy of her acceptance. It is very certain that had she considered them other than the best she would have told me so.

"Yes," she continued, "you are simply ridiculous. Just as if you could ever be a lord. I don't believe it! If six people died!" she concluded, with a laugh which made me feel what I was capable of. I could have killed her where she stood but for the consequences.

If I held human life cheap I was still possessed of the caution of my race, and even at that age I loved her. Even at that age indeed! Looking back at my boyhood I am astonished at the insanity of passion of which I was capable. There is nothing more narrow than the scepticism with which older people treat the love-sickness of the young. Boys love even better perhaps than men ever can. Romeo was, I am convinced, not more than seventeen or eighteen—that is to say, as Shakespeare conceived him.

I felt humiliated by her disbelief. I had been anxious to give myself some importance in her eyes, and instead she treated the whole thing with absolute derision. That day was to be in every way one of bitterness. She was standing at the schoolroom window drumming on the glass, when suddenly she gave a little shrill cry of surprise.

"Oh what fun! Grahame is bringing someone in to tea, and father is with them."

I looked out and saw to my annoyance Lionel Holland accompanying Grahame and his father up the drive. What was the meaning of it? Surely Lionel Holland had not succeeded in winning Grahame to friendship! It was hardly likely.

"And I do believe it's that good-looking boy who won all the prizes at last year's sports," continued Sibella. "Yes, it is!"

I had, even at the age of sixteen, a very genius for the analysis of character—although analysis is hardly the word. Characters have always had a way of displaying themselves before me at a bird's-eye view. From the first I mistrusted the effect of a handsome and confident piece of physical splendour on a nature like Sibella's.

In the hall I could hear Lionel Holland apologising for his mud-stained appearance, and Mr. Hallward's breezy voice laughing away his scruples.

"Nonsense, my boy, nonsense, I like to see it. It shows you have been enjoying yourself in a fine, manly way. Grahame, take your friend upstairs and let him wash his face and hands."

Mr. Hallward always took pleasure in the display of jovial hospitality. In reality he was a somewhat bad-tempered man, but when he was in the mood for a little display of amateur histrionics there was no one more genial or hearty.

Sibella was flushed with excitement and I was inwardly fuming.

"What is his name?" she demanded, turning to me as Lionel Holland's voice died away upstairs.

"Lionel Holland," I answered, as cheerfully as I could, determined that, if possible, I would not betray my annoyance.

"Do you like him?"

"Oh, he is all right." I might just as well have said plainly that I disliked him, for Sibella was not deceived. She had a Jezebel's gift for detecting antagonisms between those of the opposite sex and playing upon them. I believe this characteristic invariably differentiates the woman who uses her sex power for evil from the woman who uses it for good.

"You don't like him," she answered at once. "You are jealous of him."

"Jealous! Why?"

"Because he plays games better than you do."

I laughed. It was the last thing that was ever likely to make me jealous. She saw that the taunt had failed and tried another.

"And also because he is so much better looking than you are."

I laughed again. From Sibella the absolutely untrue was not convincing.

But Sibella had a way of thrusting till she thrust home.

"You needn't laugh—because it's quite true, and you are also jealous because he is so much more manly than you are."

I knew what she meant. Lionel Holland's flamboyant animalism and sex assurance stood in her eyes for prime qualities. She was superficially feminine and loved a brute. The woman of delicate upbringing, who astonishes her friends by her inexplicable infatuation for a boaster who is obviously a cad and a bully despite his physical advantages, is twin sister to the lady of the slums who worships the brute who blackens her eyes and kicks her as an amusing conclusion to the week's work. The poor slut flatters herself that it is evidence of a strength which he would not fail to use in her defence, forgetting that a bully is only occasionally a brave man.

I saw what was coming and grew sick at heart. One thing comforted me; Sibella was a snob, and despite his riches she would never be able to taunt me with his superior caste.

"I shouldn't show my jealousy if I were you," she concluded.

I looked at her quietly.

"You ought to be killed."

I said the thing I knew would bludgeon her into silence. She shared Grahame's fear of death, but in her case it was more ignoble. I believe if Grahame had been condemned to death his pride would have overcome his fear. I could imagine Sibella whining and fawning at the executioner's feet.

She looked at me with distinct apprehension, and at that moment Grahame entered the room accompanied by Lionel Holland. Sibella immediately began to exercise her fascinations and to concentrate the attention of the visitor on herself. I have often thought since that Lionel Holland must have manoeuvred his invitation to the house, for he seemed already to have made up his mind how to proceed with Sibella. He flattered her vanity, said that he remembered her perfectly on the day of the sports, and declared that he should certainly not have tried so hard had she not been there.

The younger members of the Hallward household had tea in the dining-room, and on Saturdays were privileged to bring in their friends, so that there was generally a large gathering. The tea itself was a sumptuous affair, and as the elders were seldom present it was as a rule very enjoyable. Cynthia Hallward, one year older than Sibella, poured out.

Lionel Holland seemed supremely unconscious that Grahame was not very pleased at his presence.

I was of course unable to express my displeasure until I was given a lead. Grahame lingered a minute or two in the school-room with me.

"I wish the Guv'nor would mind his own business," he said sulkily.

"Didn't you ask him?"

"Is it likely? He insisted on walking home with me, and just as I was saying good-bye to him the Guv'nor met us and said 'Bring your friend in to tea.' Friend indeed!" And Grahame snorted.

When we reached the dining-room Sibella had arranged so that Lionel was on her right and a girl friend of her sister's on her left. I verily believe she wanted me to sit opposite to her in order that she might enjoy the spectacle of my chagrin. She should have known me better. I betrayed not the least sign of the hatred and wounded vanity that were surging within me. I was measuring my chances against Lionel Holland. I was better looking than he was, but not in the way likely to appeal to Sibella. He was rich; I was far cleverer. It appears to me on looking back that I quite understood, even at that early stage, that the incident was the prologue to a drama which would develop itself in after years. Most boy and girl romances might be ephemeral, but ours had the promise of permanence. This was the more curious in that two out of the three, Sibella and Lionel, were entirely superficial.

I joined in the conversation and laughter with very fair success, but Sibella was in her most aggravating mood. Cynthia Hallward asked Lionel Holland what he wanted to be. Apparently he did not quite know, but some cross-questioning from Sibella elicited the fact that his only definite ambition was for riches.

"My father wasn't always rich," he announced; and, to do him justice, his pride in the fact that his father was self-made was the pleasantest trait in his character. "He began without a shilling, and he says that money is nine-tenths of everything, and he ought to know. I wouldn't give twopence to be anything which didn't bring in money."

"Wouldn't you like to be a lord?" said Sibella, looking at me mischievously.

"It's quite easy to be a lord if you're rich enough," said Lionel.

"Oh, but Israel is going to be a lord. That is to say, when six people die," laughed Sibella. And there was that peculiar quality in her laugh which when it was turned against myself made me feel cruel towards her.

Lionel Holland laughed too, delighted to assist Sibella in teasing me.

"Israel is always telling us that at school," he said.

"I've only said so once," I answered, keeping my temper by a violent effort of self-control, "and it's perfectly true." I think there must have been something in my voice that warned them to desist, for the subject was allowed to drop.

After tea we adjourned to the school-room. Sibella's appetite for sweets was insatiable, and she took the most comfortable seat by the fire and proceeded to finish the box of chocolates I had brought her.

"Do you like sweets?" I heard Lionel ask. He was sitting by her side. She handed him the box and he helped himself.

"Awfully." Sibella's English was extremely slipshod.

"I'll send you some. What kind do you like best?"

"Chocolate nougat."

"Very well. I'll send you a much bigger box than that."

Sibella laughed appreciatively. "That will be jolly of you," she said, perfectly aware that I could hear. She was evidently entirely dazzled by her new admirer, but was too much a born flirt to let me go even if I had had the least intention of retiring from the contest.

Just before I left the house she sidled up to me.

"You're not angry, are you, Israel?"

I made a faint attempt at a smile as I answered:

"Angry? Of course not. Why should I be?"

Finding me inclined to fence, she assumed her most childish treble.

"I don't know, I'm sure, only you have been looking so dreadfully cross."

I very nearly shook her.

Lionel Holland left the house a few minutes before I did. Grahame walked with me as far as the gate.

"I say, Israel, what's that about your being a lord some day?"

"Nothing. I don't want to go into the matter. Everybody is so beastly rude about it."

"Is it true?"

"Of course it is. I'll show you the papers if you like."

"I don't want that. If you say it's true, of course I believe you."

But I was secretly determined that Grahame should see the papers, and I took the earliest opportunity of showing them to him, for I knew that though he liked me too much to say that he disbelieved me, he felt that there must be a mistake somewhere.

I explained the whole thing to him and showed him our genealogical tree.

I fancy he was more surprised than he appeared to be, for although he had always been very kind to me there had been just the faintest suspicion of patronage in his manner. It was perhaps only natural. A semi-Hebrew lad, in humble circumstances, with no prospects to speak of, was not in the ordinary course of things the most natural companion for the son of a successful city merchant.

I knew he told Sibella, for she condescendingly informed me that I was not such a story-teller as she had thought, adding, however, that it wasn't very much to boast of, as the six lives between me and the peerage would probably be sixty-six before very long, and it was quite evident that the Gascoynes did not even know of my existence. She became quite friendly again, but when I tried to kiss her she refused to allow me to do so; or rather, she attempted to prevent it and was really furious when I did so by force. I detected in her resistance that I no longer occupied her thoughts. Indeed, I was soon made aware that I was expected to be content with the place of an ordinary friend. Lionel Holland managed to be constantly at the house. Grahame had expressed his disinclination to bring him, but Sibella and her sister evidently had an understanding by which they were to meet him by appointment on Saturday afternoons and bring him back to tea. Mr. and Mrs. Hallward were too easy-going to notice these manoeuvres, and would have treated them quite good-naturedly even had they done so.

The Hallward children were allowed to do pretty well as they liked, with the result that careful mothers of the neighbourhood, resentful of their extreme good looks, made Cynthia and Sibella the subject of much spiteful gossip and whispered innuendoes which I verily believe had little truth in them. Compelled to stand by and watch Lionel Holland's triumph, I suffered terribly, and my mother grew quite anxious at my appearance, but attributed it to overwork.

Once, and once only, did I implore Sibella to have pity on me. She laughed in the most silvery manner, and frankly said she was tired of me. I recall my abjectness with humiliation. Lionel Holland's was a nature quite devoid of sympathy for his own sex, and where another lad might have decently veiled his triumph from his rival, he displayed it on every possible occasion. His manner was insufferably self-complacent. He had the natural contempt of all Westerns for anything Jewish, and he had not the breeding to disguise the fact. He told a mutual friend that 'it was just like a beastly little Jew to make up to a girl like Sibella.'

I affected indifference because I knew the remark had been repeated to me with the object of goading me into fighting him; and that was a matter which required thinking out. At the same time I planned the first attempt of my life to deal a secret blow at an enemy. It was crude, but youth and inexperience must be my excuse.

Lionel Holland was training for a mile handicap, and I knew that in the evening he used to go to the school sports ground, with a friend to time him, and train till after dusk.

The track, half a mile in circumference, ran round the entire ground, skirting the backs of houses, and bounded at one part for the length of about a hundred yards by a hedge. I conceived the idea of throwing him as he was running. The track was hard, and he might hurt himself seriously or not at all. There was at any rate the chance of a full retaliation.

I chose a spot about midway along the hedge opposite, where on the inner side of the track, just upon the grass, and facing the cricket pitch, was an iron seat firmly fixed to the ground.

One evening I followed Holland and his friend to the sports ground and, having seen them go in, reached the back of the hedge by a circuitous way. There was an aperture just large enough for me to crawl through. I waited. In about ten minutes I heard his measured stride on the hard asphalt. He passed me going at a good pace. As he disappeared in the dusk I crept swiftly through the hedge, passed a cord I had with me round the upper part of one of the legs of the iron seat, and, holding both ends in my hand, crept back.

In a few moments he came round again. I pulled the cord as tight as I could. He tripped, fell full length and lay still. I hauled in the cord and stole away.

My sensations are worth analysing. At first I felt a certain elation at having thrown an enemy. Then I experienced disappointment. What I had done was somewhat pointless. Unless I had spoilt his looks—which was hardly likely—I could not be said to have scored any advantage, unless—I stopped, and my breath came quickly. Was it possible I had killed him? I had heard of people dying from as slight a cause. I felt terribly uncomfortable. I grew afraid of having the cord in my pocket. I went swiftly home and burnt it, a small piece at a time, lest my mother should come in and find it being destroyed. Afterwards I was ashamed of my want of nerve. Even if he were dead nobody on earth could connect me with the accident. I had always heard that murder will out, but I was strong-minded enough, considering the circumstances, to doubt whether it was possible in this case.

Anxious as I was to know the upshot of the affair I slept quite well and started for school not a minute earlier than usual. I was in the same class as Holland. When school began he had not arrived and neither had the boy who was his time-keeper. Five minutes late the latter walked in with a note in his hand.

"Holland has had an accident, sir." He handed the note to the master.

"Indeed? I am sorry to hear that." He opened the note and began to read, his face growing more serious as he read on. "Concussion of the brain! Mr. Holland does not quite seem to know how it happened."

"It was on the cricket ground, sir. It had just got dusk and I was timing Holland for the mile. The second time he did not come round, so I went to see what had happened and found him lying on the path insensible. I had to leave him there whilst I went for help."

"Has he recovered consciousness?"

"Yes, sir."

"How did it happen?"

"I can't think. He must have tripped. The doctor says he is not to be asked any questions and that he is to be kept quite quiet for the next few days."

"Quite so. I suppose you will be going round there, so you can let us know how he is getting on."

"Yes, sir."

The boy went back to his seat. The class had been listening intently. The master looked up and caught sight of my face.

"Why, Rank, you have turned quite pale."

Everybody looked at me in surprise. The lack of friendliness between Lionel Holland and myself was generally known, and it certainly astonished them that I should have turned pale out of sympathy for him.

He came back to school in about a fortnight looking none the worse for his accident. He was as confident as before and as irritating to me as ever.

I heard him explaining the incident in the playground afterwards.

"I'll swear," he was saying, "that something caught me just above the ankle. I don't see how I could possibly have tripped otherwise."

"What could it have been?" asked Grainger, the boy who had been timing him.

"I can't think, I am sure, but I'm certain something tripped me up all the same."

"I expect you turned giddy," said a member of the Lower Fourth.

"Giddy? Never was less giddy in my life," and Holland turned a withering glance upon the small boy that made him retire into the background.

He had a way of twisting the arms of small boys, and holding their elbows while he brought his knee sharply into contact with a soft but sensitive part of their bodies, besides many other little devices for making them wish it were possible to grow up suddenly into a strong man with a strong fist.

I have always resented cruelty for cruelty's sake, and petty tormenting with no object in view has invariably impressed me as being supremely silly. It is quite another matter when one is obliged to take a strong step in support of a logical line of action. The end must justify the means. The Jesuits are quite right. All around, Nature teaches us the lesson. An infinite amount of apparent evil is being done that good may come, and even if the end be not a particularly elevated one that surely is a man's own affair; especially if he be prepared to pay the penalty of supporting his own opinion with action which is against the moral sense of society in general.

Sibella's solicitude during Lionel Holland's illness was an ample revenge for the latter had he known it. It tortured me. At one time I calculated my chances in a stand-up fight with him supposing I should train for the event. I decided after careful thought that the odds would be against me, and I had no intention of fighting for honour's sake with the prospect of leaving him more triumphant and complacent than ever.

CHAPTER III

I WAS now sixteen and a half, and my mother had kept me at school much longer than her means had warranted. I think that at one time she had some idea that I might gain a scholarship and go to Oxford or Cambridge, but my progress, though respectable, never suggested that I might achieve honours. I think, as a matter of fact, that I could have done so had I cared to, but I had no ambition to spend the best years of early manhood in a torture chamber, and it is obvious that to a youth of imagination, who has no means of joining in the recreations of his fellows, and is expected to justify himself by brilliant scholastic success, a career at the 'Varsity can be little else.

The question of my future was a very serious one. It was not possible for my mother to pay anything towards giving me a profession, and without influence the outlook was not hopeful.

Unknown to her I conceived the idea of writing to Gascoyne Gascoyne, a distant cousin who was at the head of a large stockbroking firm. I pointed out our relationship and asked if he could possibly find room for me in his office. He replied in a type-written letter saying that he had no knowledge of the relationship. He did not deny it, it might be so, but at any rate he had no vacancies nor was he likely to have any. It would therefore be of no use for Mr. Rank to trouble him again.

I kept his letter, but I did not run the risk of a second rebuff from any other member of the family.

Mr. Johnson came to the rescue. He had, it appeared, a great friend in the City who employed two or three clerks and who had a vacancy. I was interviewed, approved of, and engaged at the salary of fifteen shillings a week. From circumstances which afterwards came to my knowledge I believe that Mr. Johnson paid something in the way of a premium. My mother was delighted. It was a start in life, and in her eyes a good start was everything. Personally, I thought it a deplorable beginning, and only took it because nothing better offered. I was determined, however, not to stay longer than I could help.

With the best intentions in the world Mr. Johnson was quite incapable of grasping my character. He talked to me of a youth of application, a middle age of strenuous endeavour for a living wage, and an old age of decent competence. The prospect appalled me. It sounded inexpressibly grey. I gravitated towards wealth and luxury as the needle to a magnet. I remember his saying:

"By the time you are thirty, Israel, you should be able to keep your mother in this house and have it to yourselves."

I had much ado to restrain a scornful laugh. By the time I was thirty I was determined to have established my mother in a house fully ten times the size.

I soon realised that the office I was in did not even afford a starting point for a career, and could not be a recommendation to anything better. I had no friends in the City of my own age. I instinctively avoided those youths whom in the natural course of events a person in my position would have associated with. The school my mother had sent me to had put me out of sympathy with them, and—what was more to the point—they could not be of any possible use to me. I was bitterly envious of those boys who entered their relations' houses of business on advantageous terms, with sufficient allowances and smart clothes. My poverty appeared to me extreme. I was not in the first few months ever sufficiently in pocket to be able to go to theatres and places of amusement as other young men did, and yet I found myself with tastes equally expensive and with an abnormal love of pleasure. Of my fifteen shillings a week I gave my mother eight, and out of the remainder I was obliged to find my lunches and fares to town and back, a condition of things that reduced me to chronic discontent. I saw that the great point was to have rich friends and make use of them. I also grasped the cardinal maxim that for success in life it is essential to avoid the unlucky and the necessitous, and above all not to be led away by the fact that in themselves the latter are probably the most entertaining sections of society. If a man wishes to be rich he must live among the rich, and how to do this on fifteen shillings a week was the problem.

A Semitic appearance, however superior, is not the best recommendation to society. In the Western it rouses instinctive antagonism. At the same time, and because the laws of compensation are inevitable, it is this antagonism that makes the Jew what he is. His powers of resistance are automatically developed by it, and it encourages his virility. The greater the odds a man has to fight the greater his ultimate skill of fence. That man is fortunate who has the world against him.

At sixteen and a half, however, my philosophy was not equal to the annoyances of the situation. I wasted a great deal of valuable energy in useless complaining. Sibella seemed lost to me for ever. Even had she promised herself to me I should have placed no faith in her staying power. I was quite sure that my humble start in life must have brought home to her the difference in our positions as nothing in our boy and girl relations had ever done. To Sibella, luxurious, pleasure-loving and flippant, the junior clerk in a third-rate business house was an altogether inferior and impossible person. The shabbier I seemed, the smarter Lionel Holland must have appeared. He was blossoming into a complete dandy, and had all the means at hand to gratify his taste for fine clothes. I had spent a year under these depressing conditions when I made a friend.

Godfrey Twyneham was the son of a rich man with whom our firm did a certain amount of business. He was about eighteen months older than myself, and there was nothing very remarkable about his personal appearance except a pervading air of gentlemanliness. He had been coming in and out of our office for twelve months before I realised that he was inclined to take special notice of me. One morning as I was on the way to my contemptible lunch he joined me. We walked a few yards together, I painfully sure that he must be very anxious to be rid of so shabby a companion. To my surprise, however, he asked me to lunch with him. I was on the point of refusing, but he linked his arm in mine in an altogether friendly and unpatronising manner, and I yielded.

He had evidently taken a great fancy to me and insisted on my lunching with him first about once a week, then twice a week, and finally every day. He also insisted on my going to theatres with him, and grew quite offended if we did not spend our Saturday evenings together. In vain I protested—not very vehemently perhaps—that I could in no way make any return. He laughed the idea to scorn. Why should I? We liked each other. He was well off, I was not. That was a mere accident, and we should be small-minded indeed if we allowed it to interfere with our intimacy. He insisted on lending me money, declaring that I was sure to make a fortune, and when that day came I could pay him back. He was certainly the most generous person I have ever met, and, though I have not paid him back, he has never mentioned the matter to me. I don't think he allowed the question of money to come between himself and his friends. At the present moment he is in South America, and just before the trial I received quite a heartbroken letter from him, declaring his belief in my innocence, and in case I should need it, placing a large sum of money at my disposal. Poor Godfrey! I suppose he forgot that Earl Gascoyne is a rich man.

Before I met him I had all the inclination for pleasure and indulgence, and his generosity had the effect of making me feel that I could never again endure life unaccompanied by a certain amount of excitement.

I was hopelessly unfitted by temperament for the dreary, sordid life of shabby suburbanism that lay before me. I dwell upon these facts because I think they may serve to show that I was impelled by all the forces of my nature to make some attempt to rescue myself by decisive action from the mire in which it seemed only too probable I was destined to wade all my life. Godfrey Twyneham, with the best intentions in the world, and from motives of purest friendship, succeeded in making our house at Clapham appear ten degrees more shabby and my position in the City infinitely more humiliating. He introduced me to his tailor, bootmaker, and hosier, and lo! I found myself well dressed. I dined at his father's house in a decent dress suit, and was introduced to a circle of his friends who gave me a very good time indeed. The Twyne-hams lived at Highgate, and I constantly spent Saturday to Monday with them. I think my mother missed me, but she never complained and seemed only too glad that I was enjoying myself. I was compelled to invent some plausible excuse for being able to afford clothes so very superior to anything I had been accustomed to. I explained that Godfrey Twyneham had been able to put me in the way of some private business and that he had introduced me to his tailor, it being neces-sary that I should be well dressed in order to follow up my opportunity. Godfrey was one of those good-natured souls with no such strict prin-ciples as prevented his telling a small fib to oblige a friend. My mother and he took to each other at once, and it flattered my vanity not a little that he seemed to like coming to us and sharing my humble tenement bedroom apparently as much as I liked visiting their luxurious house at Highgate.

I think the only occasion on which I was tactless enough to cause him to disapprove of me was when I began to apologise for the poor-ness of our household. I think I detected the faintest suspicion of a scornful surprise in his face as he said:

"I don't think those things matter, do you, except to snobs?"

The rebuke was severe, but it did me good and I avoided such mistakes afterwards.

Even now I recall with pleasure the look of astonishment on Sibella's face the Sunday afternoon I called at the Hallwards' in my new finery. I felt that I had reason to be satisfied with myself. I knew that I could do justice to my clothes and that I need not fear comparison even with Lionel Holland. In fact, his smartness invariably had something of the dressed up shop boy about it, while I had reason to believe that in spite of my half Semitic origin I conveyed an impression of distinc-tion. At least, Godfrey told me so, and I knew he was to be relied on in such matters. The drawing-room was full of people when I entered, and Sibella said in a confidential tone of approval:

"You do look smart, Israel. You will make Lionel quite jealous."

Lionel Holland was also taken by surprise when he came in a few minutes afterwards. Sibella, true to her character, and feeling that Lionel had perhaps received enough encouragement of late, osten-tatiously permitted me to be her favoured cavalier for the afternoon. She was unable to control her desire to set men at each other's throats. Had it been anyone else I should have managed her properly and not permitted myself to be played fast and loose with. Sibella, however, was the exception in my life, and she was always drawing the unexpected from my character.

I heard her say to Lionel in a voice intended for me to hear:

"Doesn't Israel look nice, Lionel?"

"He's been robbing the till, I suppose."

Sibella laughed a high, silvery laugh. The reply was sufficiently spiteful and showed that she had succeeded in deepening an animosity already bitter enough.

The sneer had truth, in that it suggested the disparity between my apparel and my income, and consequently I hated Lionel Holland the more.

Mr. Johnson might have proved a most awkward inquirer as to the sources of my apparent prosperity, but just about this time he died. He was found one morning sitting in his armchair, in front of a fire which had burnt out hours before, dead, and clasped in his stiffening fingers was a portrait of my mother in a little leather case. He had evidently had it secretly copied, for she had not given it to him. He had no relations, and the only person who appeared on the scene to take charge of things was a local solicitor, who informed my mother that she had inherited through her late lodger the sum of one thousand pounds and all his personal effects. I think she was glad for my sake as much as for her own.

"You see, Israel, with the house, which is our own, and a thousand pounds properly invested in addition to what I have got, we can never come absolutely to want, and if I can only get another lodger who will pay well we should be quite comfortably off."

The prospect failed to dazzle me. My ideas of what constituted comfort grew daily. We discussed the manner of investing the thousand pounds endlessly. My mother would not hear of anything but gilt-edged securities, and would have been quite content with a miserable three and a half per cent., whereas I declared it was a matter of no difficulty to obtain a safe five or even six per cent. Before the matter was decided my mother died and I found myself alone in the world.

The event plunged me into the deepest dejection, for I had loved her dearly. I took stock of my position and decided that whatever happened I would resign my clerkship. My resignation was promptly followed by the offer of a rise in salary, so potent a lever is independence to progress in life. They were unable, however, to make me any such proposal as tempted me to remain.

At first I made all sorts of good resolutions, which I might have kept had not Godfrey Twyneham, whose advice was always practical, been called away at this moment to South America. His father had a branch of his business at Buenos Ayres and Godfrey was destined to manage it, the control of the London house being reserved for the eldest son. He was anxious for me to accompany him and even went to considerable trouble in finding a post for me. I could not, however, bring myself to give up Sibella and at the last moment declined to go. Poor Godfrey! I don't think he ever quite forgave me, and since then we have not seen much of each other.

My fifteen hundred pounds soon began to dwindle. From day to day I salved my conscience by assuring myself that, though I was spending my capital, I was making friends who could not fail to be useful to me. Inwardly I knew perfectly well that the class of young men I was mixing with could never help me to a livelihood. I shut up the house at Clapham and took rooms near Piccadilly, and eighteen months of my life were wasted in unprofitable lounging. I seldom rose till late, and when I was dressed strolled round to a luxurious bar near Bond Street to meet several boon companions and spend the afternoon in tippling. In the evening I frequented those theatres at which the more frivolous pieces were played, and afterwards hung about the stage doors. I soon found myself led into extravagances in the way of little suppers and small presents of jewellery, which made my capital disappear at an alarming rate. Like countless other young men before me, and no doubt since, I was unable to pull up, although I could feel my financial bark throbbing with impending disaster and could hear the roar of the rapids growing nearer and nearer. I shut my eyes and went ahead, hoping for a miracle. Somehow I obtained a reputation for riches for which there were no reasonable grounds. I managed to hold on for a year at high pressure, then for another six months with difficulty, living on the credit that twelve months' ostentatious solvency had secured me. Then ensued a few months of decline, and on the morning of my twenty-third birthday I found myself heavily in debt and penniless. A few borrowed fivers kept me afloat for a short time and then Lionel Holland put a spoke in my wheel and sent me headlong. I had been asked to a supper given by a friend of mine who had just come of age. He had partaken frequently of my hospitality in my prosperous days, and, having some sense of gratitude, had not omitted me on this important occasion.

To my annoyance, I found that Lionel Holland, with whom I did not know my friend was acquainted, was of the party. We welcomed each other with outward civility, but I saw danger in his eye.

The supper passed off pleasantly enough, and afterwards we took hansoms and drove to my friend's rooms. I escorted a chorus-girl from the Frivolity, a particular friend of mine, with whom I was making desperate attempts to keep on terms of intimacy. Our hansom broke down, and my little friend, nervous and hysterical, fainted. I carried her into the vestibule of a well-known club, where, with the aid of brandy, she was brought round, and after ten minutes or so declared that she had no intention of going home, but asked me to take her on to join the others. We found them wondering what had happened to us, and in the excitement of detailing the scene I did not notice that the manner of the others had perceptibly changed towards me. As soon as I detected a certain coolness I realised that Lionel Holland had been saying something to my detriment. The women were especially distant, and I know no class who can make a man feel so unpleasantly that he is not wanted as the sort of female whom my host was entertaining. They have a genius for being cruel to anyone who is going under, and after all, it is not to be wondered at. They themselves have risked too much to care about increasing the odds. In such a mood, however, they are dangerous, for no considerations of breeding restrain them. My own particular friend was taken out of the room by one of the other women, and on her return I could see at once that she had had repeated to her whatever Lionel Holland had said. Her manner became suddenly insolent and aggressive, as if she felt that it was she who had been wronged. Inwardly I quaked, for I knew what she was capable of.

She had taken more wine than was good for her, and was by no means mistress of herself.

As usual, I was in charge of the piano, playing accompaniments for anyone who would contribute a song and filling in myself with snatches of music hall ditties, or florid pianoforte arrangements of the most popular tunes of the day.

I had even successfully accompanied Lionel Holland, who had rather a nice voice, and had managed with great skill and tact to put him in high good humour with his performance. I was nervously conscious that it was necessary for my own dignity to make the evening pass off smoothly.

My little friend was then pressed to sing, and I hastened to join in the request. Though she had an exceedingly pretty voice she was one of those people who become vocally helpless if in any way under the influence of alcohol. Her voice sounded weak and tremulous; she was unable to keep to the right key, and, feeling that she was making an exhibition of herself, lost her temper more and more at every bar. In an absolute panic I did everything I could in order that her song should pass off successfully, but to no purpose. She forgot her words, and I ventured to prompt her, which seemed to irritate her the more. To make matters worse the others laughed.

Suddenly she stopped and laughed too, an unpleasant laugh with little mirth in it.

"He's a nice pianist, isn't he? He'd be more at home blacking the lodger's boots, instead of pretending to be a gentleman on his mother's hard earned savings."

She herself was a plumber's daughter, but in her case that was not to the point.

With commendable presence of mind I pretended not to hear, and commenced to play something loudly on the piano.

She was, however, transported with rage at her own failure and determined to make somebody pay.

She shut the lid of the piano down violently, and I only just managed to save my hands from being crushed. To such a female, in such a condition, it is not a long way to hysterics.

"Get back to the lodgers!" she screamed. "What do you mean by coming here and pretending to be a gentleman? You ought to be horsewhipped. You—" Here followed a string of epithets intensely humiliating to have to listen to under the circumstances. The other ladies present proceeded to take her part and to treat her as a highly injured female. They crowded round her as she lay sobbing and gurgling and swearing on the sofa, and deluged her with sympathy.

"I really don't wonder at her being upset," said one.

"Such a thing to find out. Enough to make her feel small," protested another.

"It is indeed," said a third, and turning to me added with a comic attempt at hauteur, "You cad!"

I felt terribly uncomfortable. I quite saw the sort of character Lionel Holland had been kind enough to give me. I felt like breaking a champagne bottle over his head, only it would have done no good, and vengeance should always bide its time if it is to be effective.

He too looked uncomfortable, as if he had not expected the mean part he had played to be brought home to him so obviously and so soon.

As my presence seemed to make the lady grow worse every moment I suggested that I should go. My host, a youth with every instinct of good breeding, would not hear of it, but several of the other men were growing a little tired of the scene. They had only met me in such society as we were now in and it did not matter to them what my origin was. They would not be called upon to recognise me in a legitimate social way.

"Good-night, your lordship," said one of the women mockingly, as I left the room.

It was no haphazard gibe. Obviously Holland, in order to heap further discredit upon me, had revived the boast of my schoolboy days. I went up to him before I left the house and said quite quietly, so that no one else could hear:

"You will be very sorry for this, and I want to assure you of the fact."

I cannot describe the intense conviction I managed to throw into the words. I felt they would come true. He tried to laugh scornfully but the failure died upon his lips. He was frightened in spite of himself.

CHAPTER IV

THE NEXT morning I had a stormy interview with my landlord. He would wait no longer for the arrears of rent. He gave me three days to pay or to find other rooms. In the meantime he would detain my things. My little skiff had decidedly reached the rocks.

I went down to the house at Clapham, which I had failed to let. The blinds were drawn and a weatherbeaten notice board leant in an intoxicated manner over the shabby railings. I had not been near it for months, and as I opened the front door the place smelt damp and reminded me with a shiver of the deaths that had taken place there. I almost heard the whisper of my mother's voice in my ear.

Curiously enough, I had made no attempt to sell the furniture. I seemed to have had a premonition that the house would yet be a home for me. I went over it, drawing up the blinds and letting in the dreary February light. Every now and then I paused and listened. I seemed to hear someone moving about the house. The garden, which had been my mother's hobby, was in a most desolate condition, and a dead and decomposing cat lay across the threshold of the back door. The atmosphere of the whole place seemed tuned to the key of my own depression, and I must admit to sitting down in the forlorn parlour and shedding tears. Even the most self-reliant character must resent being absolutely alone in the world, and I felt terribly alone. I suppose those who have listened amazed to the story of what they are pleased to call my crimes would scarcely believe that I have a craving for sympathy. True, it must be sympathy on my own terms, but I crave for it. Personally I do not at present ask for pity, but were the comfortable classes given to psychological analysis—which they are not—it might astonish them to discover in how little they differ from the practised enemy of society, the criminal. Many a highly respected member of society whom prosperity has prevented from feeling the incentive of crime is a criminal in embryo. For myself, I have achieved my object; I shall die Earl Gascoyne, and my child will bear the title after me. My descendants will belong to the ruling classes, and I shall be handed down to posterity as an interesting study. The British snob never wholly deserts a lord, and will consider the scaffold to be not a little honoured by my patronage. I am sure that there are thousands of worthy people who would sooner the whole matter had been hushed up; I for one am of their opinion. I could have dispensed with a niche in history between Gille de Rais and Madame de Brinvilliers. The fame of posterity always asks too heavy a penalty in this life.

I realised that I should have to do the work of the house at Clapham myself, so I decided to lock up all the rooms except the sitting-room, a bedroom, and the kitchen.

I engaged a woman to come in for the first few days and light fires and clean up. Then, handing her the key, I returned to town.

I owed over sixty pounds at my lodgings which I had not the least prospect of paying. I had my landlord's word for it that he would not allow a thing of mine to be moved out until my debt was discharged. I had no mind to lose my stock of wearing apparel, which constituted a very valuable asset. Removing my things during the night would be a very difficult business, and the slightest noise would rouse the people of the house and prevent my ever getting them out at all. I walked about the whole afternoon thinking the matter over and evolving one scheme after another, only to throw them all aside as impracticable. My chambers were on the second floor, which increased the difficulty. The only possible thing was to bring my clothes down loose and put them in a four-wheeled cab and then to remove my travelling bags empty. To carry down heavy luggage would have been impossible. I secured a four-wheeler and conceived the idea of telling the driver exactly what I was about to do, promising him a sovereign if he would help me. Never was money better spent.

I told my landlord to call me early as I had a certainty of obtaining a hundred pounds in the morning. So cheerful and optimistic was my manner that I am sure he was deceived, for he executed my order for a chop with alacrity. At about eleven I went to bed and, ringing my bell, asked for some whisky and hot water. This was in order that the servant might report that I had retired for the night. Three o'clock was the time my cabman was to make his appearance, and at half-past two I rose, dressed, and looked out of the window. There he was, and the street was clear of policemen.

I put on my fur coat and, carrying as many things as possible, crept downstairs. In an incredibly short space of time I had placed my first instalment in the cab. Half a dozen times I crept upstairs and down again, with my heart in my mouth, till my belongings were bursting from both windows of the cab. To my infinite delight, I rescued everything, down to my boot-trees. There was hardly room for me in the cab, but I managed to squeeze in and we drove away. Robinson Crusoe returning to the island with his raft covered with useful articles from the wreck was not half so elated. We trundled away to Clapham, and at about four in the morning I had my belongings safe and sound in my own house. Their loss would have been a terrible blow, and as I retired to rest I breathed a sigh of gratitude. My landlord would, I suppose, declare that he is revenged, now that he has had the felicity of reading how an unfeeling judge gave me certain details as to the way in which the law proposed to deal with me. The death sentence has always sounded to me a most undignified and vindictive snarl. I have most certainly never been impressed by it, and never less so than when I was directly interested in its pronouncement.

It was very clear that I was now called upon to earn my own living. I did not doubt my ability to earn enough to keep me, but I shuddered at the prospect of days of hopeless drudgery in the City that other men might grow rich. For eighteen months I had lived in comparative luxury. I was spoilt for playing the part of a slave. Five times the salary I was ever likely to obtain seemed to me mere poverty. I strolled about the City day after day for some weeks without any definite result, and the very few pounds I had managed to scrape together were disappearing fast.

Grahame Hallward was now in the City and as friendly to me as ever. He would, I was sure, lend me money if I asked him, but a very natural feeling prevented my exposing my parlous condition to Sibella's brother. In fact, I did everything possible to give him the impression that I was prosperous. Sometimes he would come in during the evening and smoke with me, and I invariably kept from him the truth that I did the housework myself, complaining bitterly of the incompetence of the imaginary female who came in to cook and put things straight for me. There was only one person from whom I could borrow money, and I felt a very natural diffidence in writing to Godfrey after the way I had treated him. Shipwreck, however, was too imminent for such scruples to prevail, and in reply to my request the kind-hearted fellow sent me twenty-five pounds, saying that I was on no account to allow pride to stand in the way of asking for more. As to my not having fallen in with his views, surely I had a right to manage my affairs my own way.

When alone in the evenings I used to draw out the genealogical tree of the Gascoynes and study it. Whilst living in London I had made a good many inquiries and had found out exactly where I stood. That is to say, I had collected a great deal of information as to the habits, health, and chances of longevity of the members of the different branches that stood between me and the succession. The table I have already given had not altered materially. The Earl at that time was twenty-three years of age, holding a commission in the Guards, and had been married some months before to an American heiress. They might have any number of children, so that it was strange that, though I was in no way lacking in common sense, I should persist in dreaming of myself as finally attaining the rank of Earl Gascoyne.

It was at this time I came across a book which interested me exceedingly. It was a record of most of the celebrated poisoning cases in history, but the author had the gift of vivifying whatever he touched with rare qualities of imagination. He was able to fill in the bare outlines left by mere chroniclers with an atmosphere which carried singular conviction, and he could weave a tale of interest from the most meagre details. Given the crime and the historical characters, he followed them all through the different emotions which led up to the catastrophe with faultless instinct. He possessed a breadth of mind in dealing with assassins which was unusual, and pointed out that great criminals are as a rule so far removed from other men that it is presumption to measure them by the same standard. The courage and fortitude with which they almost invariably face death, he cited as a proof that probably most of them had reached a philosophic elevation of which they themselves were perhaps unconscious, and from which death hardly seemed so terrible an event. He was not interested in the commonplace criminal. The Borgias, Madame de Brinvilliers, the Earl of Somerset, and Thomas

Henry Wainwright, were the aristocrats in crime who roused his curiosity and seemed to him worthy of psychological analysis. A criminal in his eyes might be great, just as any other man might be great who lifted his profession out of the common rut by the magic of personality. He deprecated, for instance, the unreflective execration which historians pour out on those who have removed Kings and Emperors. Most of them, he held, were men who had everything to lose and nothing to gain by their act. They could look for no immunity. Ravaillac, torn to pieces by horses, Gerard, tortured to death for having done what he considered his duty in removing William the Silent, seemed to him to have missed their share of commendation. More dignified a hundredfold they seemed to him than the egotistical apes who sat in a mockery of the judicial mind in judgment on Charles I. For the latter at least there was every chance of escape and no personal courage was required.

Not that he had anything to say in actual defence of secret poisoners. If they chose such a line of conduct, they must not grumble when the day of reckoning came. At the same time, he paid all deference to their courage, for the risks of murder are always enormous. I cannot say when first the book began to exercise an influence over me, and to turn my mind in a certain direction, but as I grew more and more depressed with my failure to obtain a means of livelihood, an idea gradually formed itself which, though I dismissed it with a laugh at first, returned again and again, assuming more and more of a permanent character each time.

The loneliness of my life, for with the exception of visits from Grahame Hallward my days were solitary, encouraged morbid reflections. At first I entertained the idea as an abstraction. I clothed the Gascoyne family and myself in fifteenth-century garb, and placed the scene in a medieval Italian city. I wove plot and counterplot. One by one I removed them all from my path, and till the end walked unsuspected, doing my work with caution and precision.

Each day I had a new set of subsidiary characters whom I moved hither and thither according to the exigencies of my mimic conspiracy. The game became a mania with me. I read every book I could discover that had to do with secret crimes.

For a while I walked with the grim shadows of the past and would have no companion but the shades of murderers. Caesar Borgia whispered in my ear as we paced the gardens of the Vatican, and the scarlet bow of his mouth twisted sardonically when he told me in a low, musical voice of how Giuseppe died.

Lucrezia intoned as in a trance her secret deeds, telling me how she had killed her boy husband and taken her brother for a lover.

I bore Nero's cup of poison to his victims and watched their vain efforts to grapple with unconquerable agony, or their final look of terror as the growing paralysis of death crept over them. There was in the long list of poisoners, ancient and modern, a French abbé who in particular interested me. His crimes had been uniformly successful, for he had discovered a drug which left no trace, but a gradual terror took possession of him and, though unsuspected, he confessed his guilt.

Recorded poisoners have necessarily been the clumsiest. To be detected is to confess oneself unskilled. Pretty, dainty Madeline Smith, sitting imperturbable and charming through the long days of her trial, must have reflected that the thing could have been better done and that eighteen is a little young to begin.

Madame de Brinvilliers and the French poisoners in the reign of Louis XIV, were fascinating. The crime drew a meretricious charm from the daintiness of the period, even if the punishments were barbaric. It was certainly unlike the porcelain manners of the time to break a lady, an aristocrat, on the wheel.

CHAPTER V

ONE DAY it struck me that I had never seen Hammerton, the magnificent Hampshire home of the Gascoynes. It was the most important of the half-dozen places that went with the title, and I wondered that so far curiosity had not impelled me to visit any of them.

I made up my mind to see them all, beginning with Hammerton; and so, one exquisite day in June, I got on my bicycle early in the morning and rode out of London. The bicycle probably strikes a jarring note in the telling, but I have no doubt that their emblazoned chariots, caparisoned horses, and luxurious barges, were to my great prototypes as little romantic.

As I rode along the level Roman road, the only figure in sight, I felt a great exhilaration. I was the adventurer setting forth, the hero of the story going to claim his own. The towers of Hammerton rose ever like a mirage on the horizon, and once or twice I was obliged to check myself, so far had my fancy roamed. I reflected seriously that my plans, if romantic in the after telling, should be practical in execution, and that it must be left to the poet and dramatist to mould them to poetic fancy. I doubted not that I should at least achieve a name worthy of their notice. Romance, however, was my master, as it must ever be of the imaginative. She is the mistress of the secret ways, and the touch of her finger-tips is superior to the very lips of my Lady Commonplace.

I breakfasted at a wayside inn, my table set in a garden which was a melody of roses, while beyond, on fields and pasture-land, the growing sun drank up the morning mists. By the time I was on the road again the day had become tropical and I was fain to ride easily.

I had chosen, for an excellent reason, apart from a human weakness for fair weather, a fine day and a Saturday. Hammerton was a noted show place and on such a day there was likely to be a considerable number of visitors, and I should most probably not be noticed by the person whose duty it was to take the visiting parties round.

Hammerton lay some way from the main road and some thirty-five miles from London. I struck off into narrow lanes where the trees arched overhead and the sun streaming through their branches made lacework of the shadows beneath. An intense stillness lay about these bypaths, and it was but rarely I passed anyone. Here and there I saw little patches of red, violet, or white in front of me which when I overtook them turned out to be cottagers' children, and invariably there was a thatched dwelling near nestling by the road. I was too entirely town bred to be able to identify the countless species of birds that piped and warbled as I rode among them.

At last, after having descended a steep lane where the ground was so broken as to make riding impossible, I began to ascend, and finally emerged on the brow of a hill and on to another high road. Some three miles off, crowning another hill which was a mixture of rock and grass land, stood Hammerton Castle, lordly and feudal. At the foot of the hill on which it was built a river wound its way through the pasture-land, and, about its base, nestling beneath its shadow as if for protection, clustered the little township of Hammerton, red-roofed and mellow. I looked at my watch. It was barely twelve o'clock, so I went into an adjacent field and lay down in the grass, amidst buttercups and daisies, and from the shadow of a great elm surveyed the home of my ancestors at leisure.

It was indeed a noble dwelling. The glamour of a great past was about it. Its majestic proportions and lordly turrets told of traditions which were little less than royal.

It was from these walls that a Gascoyne had flung defiance at King John, following it by so stout a defence that that amiable monarch had been compelled to pass on gnashing his teeth, only to meet his rebellious Barons at Runnymede.

A Gascoyne had held Hammerton for Edward of York. It had been a favourite with Queen Elizabeth, whose condescension had impoverished a couple of generations. Later, it had stood a siege from one of Cromwell's generals, and so stubborn had been the defence that the only military tyrant England has ever known hastened to its reduction, and was after all compelled to grant an honourable capitulation. Even now as I lay and dreamed in the morning sunlight I could see the shattered garrison emerging from those gates, drums beating, colours flying, while the Puritans, who never had a chivalrous word for their foes, looked sourly on.

I lay gazing over the intervening landscape at the castle till well on into the afternoon. I wove it and its surroundings into one day dream after another.

It was four o'clock when I arrived at the main entrance and stood with a small group of excursionists waiting for a guide. The great gates opened on to level lawns, and, large as the castle looked from without, I was amazed at the space of ground its circular and battlemented walls enclosed, even though it was broken up by buildings, some of them quite modern. I stepped after the guide with a distinct feeling of pride in the knowledge that even if far removed I was in the line of succession to all this magnificence. There was among us the usual historical authority who kept on stopping the guide to ask him some irrelevant question. The latter, however, had a very effectual manner of dealing with such tactics, and always began the particular description he was engaged on all over again. We were shown the spot where Lord Gascoyne, hero of the memorable defence against Cromwell, fell mortally wounded. In the banqueting hall there was a superb collection of armour, which included a coat of mail worn by Richard, the Lion Heart, and the sword used by Henry at Agincourt. It was the picture gallery, however, which interested me most, and I had barely scanned half a dozen Lelys, Reynolds and Gainsboroughs, before I saw how entirely my mother had been a Gascoyne.

She might have sat for the portrait of the celebrated Anne, Countess of Gascoyne, whose picture occupied the post of honour. My mother had possessed the same curiously deep blue eyes. The nose, just a little too large, was identical, as were the oval of the face and the turn of the head. I lingered behind the others to look at this picture more closely, and when finally I tore myself away I found the guide droning over the description of the most remarkable portrait in the gallery.

It was true that most of the Gascoynes were dark, but Ethel, the sixth Earl, was more like a Southern Italian than an Englishman. The name sounded curious as belonging to a man. He must have had singularly fine eyes, and yet the painter, with rare perception, had painted them half closed. To have done otherwise would have been obviously wrong. There was not a feature or a point in the portrait which did not suggest subtlety. Since that day I have often sat and gazed at the picture. It has a fascination for me which never palls. I intended to have had my own hung by the side of it. Indeed, I have left orders for a portrait to be done.

In common with most people who walk their way in secret he had apparently a love of green, for though the picture is slightly disturbed by a note of scarlet, in this again the artist showed rare judgment. He had rightly felt that the composition, to be characteristic, required it. The figure in the picture wears emerald earrings, and his sword, belt, and boots are embroidered with jewels. The guide book tells us that he secured the title by treachery. He was more than suspected of poisoning his eldest brother, and was known to have killed in a duel another brother who stood between himself and the earldom. He spent, so the guide told us, a great deal of his life in Italy, where his doings were reported to have been of unfathomable infamy. Late in life, long after the period of the emerald earrings, he returned to Hammerton, and if his youth had been prodigal he compensated for it by a penurious old age. He shut himself up in a tower and left the remainder of the castle to go to rack and ruin. He had one companion, reputed to be an Italian magician. The countryside told awful tales of the secret rites and horrors practised by these two, and the guide-book mentioned a village maiden spirited away by supernatural means and compelled to bear them company against her will. True, another chronicler of the time confidently asserted that the self-same maiden was afterwards seen in a neighbouring town in very undesirable company, but this latter historian was a Gascoyne and obviously biased.

I was in dread lest a most extraordinary coincidence should strike the guide or the excursionists. I at once noted the great likeness between the portrait and myself. The features were Jewish and so were mine. This was the more curious because in this respect we had no common ancestor. He must have been about my build and height, and the eyes seemed to meet mine with a slightly mocking smile of recognition and a subtle under-glance of sympathy.

I do not know whether the picture is all I fancy it to be, or whether my imagination, fired by its likeness to myself, gives it its atmosphere, but to me it is extraordinarily suggestive. Whenever I look upon it the life of this exquisite passes through my brain like a painted procession. He was obviously one of those born to the worship of beautiful apparitions, and his life had been passed at the extremes of joy and bitterness which that apparently exoteric, but in reality deeply esoteric, cult involves. It was a face that could never have known the lethargy of mediocrity. When his spirit slumbered it must have been the sleep of satiety. I am glad I never saw a picture of him in old age. That face, stained with the vices of an intoxicating youth and torn by the humiliation and agonies of middle and old age, could not have been pleasant. I am convinced that there were no looking-glasses in that solitary tower where he and his mysterious friend died and were only found when the rats had half eaten them.

But to me the great point was that he was impatient of dullness, and had stretched out his hand to take what he wanted. The guide-book said he was without natural affection. How little the world understands men! As if an egotist of character might not slay the mother he loved for a dear purpose.

Morally, Ethel, Earl Gascoyne, was a matricide, the family chronicles deponing that his mother had died of grief at his crimes. He could not have been entirely destitute of natural affection, for he was apparently overwhelmed with sorrow at her death, as the inscription on the stately tomb which he erected to her memory in Hammerton chapel indicated.

I wandered after the gaping, chattering group hardly hearing what was said. How was it that I was so like this Gascoyne who was so singularly unlike his kinsmen, and who had put into practice the dreams I had dreamt? He had been right. Hammerton had been worth risking something for.

We visited the lonely tower where he was supposed to have spent the haunted evening of his days in searching for the elixir of life, and where the rats had left him a hideous, obscene corpse. The trippers seemed infected by the gloom of the story, for in silence they tramped through the spacious, echoing, upper chamber, where he was reputed to have studied the stars, and to have sold himself to the Evil One.

This old man who found it so difficult to die—he was nearly a hundred when the end came—spent his last years in a debauch of mystical speculation, remaining interesting to the end.

As we crossed the grassy lawn on our way out a carriage and pair drove in through the great gates. It in were seated a young man and woman of a surprising distinction of appearance. The young man was dark, but not as Ethel, Earl Gascoyne, had been dark. The hair, eyes and moustache were dark brown. The face itself was almost feminine in its delicacy of colouring. The flush of the cheeks and the redness of the lips might have been envied by a young girl. The suggestion of effeminacy, however, was negatived by the iron determination of the mouth. I don't think I have ever seen so firm a face which did not suggest obstinacy. The eyes were keen, and looked out from beneath the finely pencilled eyebrows with a winning expression of kindliness. The face, however, was too sensitive to be designated by so stodgy an expression as good-natured.

The guide touched his cap, and turning to the group who stood waiting, said impressively: "That is his lordship."

The excursionists gaped after the carriage as if my lord and my lady were a show.

I rode back to London in the cool of a perfect summer evening thinking deeply. I had seen enough of the world to be quite sure that luck or capital were the only two things which could bring wealth while a man was still young enough to enjoy it. The first could in the nature of things only come to one man in a thousand, and the chances of a stroke of luck really worth having were even more remote. As for capital, I had none, nor was there the least probability of my obtaining any. Therefore, unless I was content to work hard to make some other man rich I must step out of the conventional path.

I was unknown to all my aristocratic relatives. Should mine be the unseen hand which was to remove them from my path? And if so, was such a thing possible without risks disproportionate to the gain? It was a stupendous enterprise. The career of a murderer was not to be undertaken lightly and without reflection. The more I thought about it, however, the more convinced I became that I should decide on making a struggle for the Gascoyne title and the Gascoyne millions.

After all, the family was nothing to me. The member of it to whom I had appealed for assistance had refused even to see me, and should I persist in my design this would have been as well.

From the study of poisoners I proceeded to the study of poisons, and in this way I spent the remainder of the summer.

CHAPTER VI

WITH the help of Grahame Hallward and a strict economy of the money which Godfrey Twyneham had sent me I managed to get through the summer fairly comfortably. I visited the West End but rarely, and was spared the indignity of being cut by my former acquaintances.

I gathered from what Grahame Hallward let fall that Lionel Holland had given him an idea of the humiliation I had undergone in his presence. Grahame was much too chivalrous and sweet-natured to wound my feelings by any direct allusion to it; I doubt, indeed, if he realised that he had ever given me a hint of his knowledge.

Sibella had no chivalry, and when I called could not forbear to make pointed allusion to people who passed themselves off for being what they were not. Again I left the house hating her, and still my dreams were tormented by thoughts of her.

By the autumn I had quite made up my mind that I would try and clear my path to the Gascoyne earldom. I tabulated the lives it would be necessary to remove. They were as follows:

Simeon, Earl Gascoyne,	aged	25
Ughtred Gascoyne,	,,	55
Henry Gascoyne,	,,	62
Gascoyne Gascoyne,	,,	68
Gascoyne Gascoyne,	,,	27
Henry Gascoyne,	,,	22
Edith Gascoyne,	,,	23
Henry Gascoyne,	,,	89

It was strange that there were not more women, and it was somewhat of a relief. The killing of women is not a pleasant task, believe me. I have learnt so much from experience. The great question was, where to begin. The old gentleman of eighty-nine might be left out of the reckoning. It was highly probable that by the time I brought my operations to a conclusion, he would be beyond the need for attention.

I debated with myself the alternatives of beginning near the head of the house, or with those members who were furthest removed. After much reflection I decided that it would be better to begin where there was likely to be the least suspicion of foul play.

Gascoyne Gascoyne was the son of the man who had snubbed me so unmercifully when I applied to him for introductions. He was twenty-seven years of age, and I had absolutely no knowledge of him beyond that fact. I knew that his father was on the Stock Exchange, and the Red Book told me that he lived in a house at South Kensington. I wandered about in its vicinity for several evenings and gathered that young Gascoyne lived at home with his father and mother. It was hardly likely that the young man who came home every evening at the same time and only went out again at irregular intervals would be other than the son of the house, and I was assured that he was the man I was looking for by his entering a carriage one evening with the master and mistress of the house and being addressed by them as Gascoyne. The time had come to formulate a plan of campaign, and I went home and shut myself up with French cigarettes to think.

My study of poisons had been profoundly unproductive of suggestion. The vast majority of them were thrown aside as ridiculous. To use them would have been suicidal. Corrosives, for instance, with their obvious evidences, could never be employed except by the most thoughtless and ignorant. I even disliked reading about their symptoms. I would certainly as soon have dashed out the brains of my victim with a sledge-hammer.

True, there are, I believe, on record cases where poisoning by arsenic had passed undetected, but it was far too slow a medium; I might not always have sufficient time at my command. I studied the irritants with an equal feeling of dissatisfaction, and the neurotics filled me with a sense of the hopelessness of the task I had undertaken. I was firmly convinced that there must be a poison somewhere in which the chances of detection were infinitesimal. Copper, and the possibility of its being administered so that its presence in food might appear accidental, detained me some time and cost me a great deal of thought, but how to manage it was not very apparent. At any rate, I mentally registered the idea; I was determined that on no account would I commit anything to paper. I have at all times considered the carelessness of criminals in this respect most curious. I reflected that it would be an excellent thing to devote so much time every evening to a retrospect of the day's work and if possible to destroy all evidences as I went along.

My sinister resolution had been taken so imperceptibly that I found myself engrossed with the details before I was quite aware of how far I had travelled in the matter.

About this time I picked up a book on reincarnation, and I began to wonder if after all I might not be Ethel, Lord Gascoyne, come again. In default of being able to prove the contrary I came to the conclusion that I was. The fancy pleased me and I would indulge it.

In my search for a good medium I was confronted with the fact that the secrets of the best poisoners have died with them. Confession does not recommend itself to the strongest intellects even when *in extremis*. Now and then of course the vanity of a great artist has led to inconvenient death-bed boasting, as in the case of Philippe Darville, who, imagining himself about to die, gave an exhaustive and circumstantial account of his crimes, and recovering, was brought to the block, only his sense of humour supporting him through the trying development.

I continued my search for the medium I wanted, and in the meanwhile made myself thoroughly acquainted with the habits of young Gascoyne Gascoyne.

In appearance he was tall and athletic, and his character seemed to be that of most young men about town with natural instincts and without too much imagination. He patronised the lighter forms of theatrical entertainment, and I recognised him as having been one of the habitués of the Frivolity Theatre. Further inquiry elicited the fact that he was being assisted to sow his wild oats by a young lady of the chorus with a snub nose and with that in her which can only be described as "devil." She appeared to be genuinely in love with him and had proved it by declining to allow him to marry her—an offer he had made in the first days of their acquaintance. He was busily employed in the City all day, and, being an only son, his parents seemed to expect more attention from him than would otherwise have been the case.

The house they lived in had gardens at the back which opened on to a quiet road. Having no very clear conception as to how I was going to act I derived a certain satisfaction from hanging about this road, and was surprised one night by almost running up against young Gascoyne Gascoyne as he emerged from a private gate which he locked behind him with a pass-key. I watched him walk swiftly into the thoroughfare, hail a cab and drive away. It was barely eleven o'clock, and when I returned and looked at the house all the lights in the lower windows were out. That, however, in what I had by observation gathered to be his bedroom was alight. Evidently he was not sufficiently emancipated from parental control to go his own way openly, or his secrecy was due to consideration for his parents' feelings.

I ascertained that as a rule when he spent the evening at home he left the house as soon as his parents were in bed, and if in time called at the theatre and drove his infatuation home. Sometimes he did not return to South Kensington till daybreak. It seemed such a daring proceeding that at times I wondered if his father might not be cognisant of it. The girl's name was Kate Falconer. I don't suppose it was her real name, but as such she figured with a couple of dozen others at the bottom of the play bill.

Since her attachment to young Gascoyne she had dispensed with the attentions of all her other admirers.

I was sorry for her, as it meant that she was wasting time. She lived in a flat in Bloomsbury, three floors up, and once her front door was shut she was as secure from any observation as if she had been living in the moon.

The problem was a difficult one. It was essential that I should not be acquainted with either of them. Put brutally, the task I had set myself was how to poison a man to whom I was a perfect stranger, and to whose food-supply I had absolutely no means of access.

Whichever way I looked at the matter I was forced to the conclusion that there could be no success without a certain amount of risk, and I had not yet accustomed myself to the idea of risk. It seemed inevitable that I must make myself acquainted with young Gascoyne somehow or other, but I left this as a last resource, and I am glad I did so, for fate assisted me in a most remarkable manner.

One Sunday afternoon I found myself wandering in the neighbourhood of the Bloomsbury flats where Kate Falconer lived. I had become so tenacious of my purpose that whilst thinking out some definite scheme I enjoyed feeling that I was in the vicinity of my intended victim. I knew that as a rule he spent Sunday afternoon at the flat. A sudden curiosity impelled me to enter the building, and, passing the hall-porter as if I had business, I climbed to the top. It seemed likely to have been an aimless proceeding, but as I was descending I heard Miss Falconer's door open on the landing just above me, and recognised her voice in conversation with young Gascoyne.

"I shan't see you till next Saturday then?"

"I'm afraid not; my father and mother will want me every day till they go away. I shall call for you on Saturday at eleven. Our train leaves Waterloo at eleven-thirty."

"Just fancy a whole week at the seaside together! It will be perfect, won't it?"

There was a silence eloquent of an embrace. I waited, anxious to know where they were going.

"You don't mind a quiet place?"

"I should have minded it a year ago. I like it now."

"Well, Lowhaven is quite quiet, and at this time of year we shall probably have the hotel to ourselves."

There was another embrace, and, conscious that the interview might draw to a close any moment, I stole downstairs.

I would go to Lowhaven and stay at the same hotel. It might lead to something. In thinking the matter over I had arrived at the conclusion that I, having apparently no motive in young Gascoyne's death, could use means which would be unwise on the part of people upon whom suspicion would fall as a natural consequence of their crime.

Supposing unseen I dropped aconite, or some such poison, into a whisky-and-soda, how could suspicion possibly fall on me? At any rate, it was worth while going to Lowhaven. I could not quite make up my mind whether to travel by the same train, or to precede them, or to follow them. Even such minor details required careful consideration. It was impossible to say which method of procedure might not leave a clue to the acute mind of Scotland Yard.

Discovering that there was only one hotel at Lowhaven, I decided to go down on the previous day.

Lowhaven turned out to be a mere village, at which I was somewhat sorry, as every new arrival became at once an object of attention. The hotel was situated at the extreme end of the tiny parade. Such walks as I took were all in the direction that led away from the town.

Whether I should write my own name in the hotel book or not was a question. I was undecided about it up to the last moment. I reflected that it was quite possible that a smart detective might take the trouble to find out all about the only visitor to the hotel if anything should occur. As a matter of fact, there were three other visitors in the hotel, a mother and two daughters, who as a rule kept to their rooms, only emerging to go for walks or drives.

Gascoyne and his companion did not come by the train they had settled on, and I began to wonder whether after all they had changed their minds and gone somewhere else, or whether circumstances had prevented their coming at all. I was far too cautious to ask or seek information even in the most round-about way.

I studied the time table in the privacy of my own room. There was another train which would bring them down about five o'clock.

I established myself in the vestibule with some afternoon tea in front of me, and a little after five they drove up looking deliciously happy.

I grew quite sentimental over them, and was compelled to take a long walk to cure myself.

I had, before I left town, decided that aconite would be the best thing I could use if I chose to run the risk of a poison which left evidences. Aconite essentially knows its own mind, and the struggle is not a long one.

After tea I went for a long tramp, and on my way back met them walking along the edge of the cliff. They were entirely engrossed in each other and barely noticed me as I passed, although there was not another soul in sight. The day had been perfect, but a gale sprang up as soon as the sun went down, and the rioting wind shook the little hotel as if it had been matchwood. There were six of us in the hotel dining-room at dinner, and with true British aloofness we had placed ourselves as far apart as possible. The lady and her two daughters dined in silence, as if it were a solemnity too deep for words. I sat alone and surveyed the reflection of young Gascoyne and Kate Falconer in the mirror in front of me. A bottle of champagne decorated their table, and between the courses they gazed into each other's eyes in an ecstasy of happiness. After dinner the widow and her two daughters disappeared. Young Gascoyne smoked a cigar and took coffee and liqueurs in the vestibule with his chair pushed close to Kate Falconer. By half-past ten everybody in the hotel had gone to bed, and I lay smoking innumerable cigarettes and thinking deeply, while the storm howled and raved without. In the morning when I awoke there lay before me a panorama of foam-crowned waves, driving furiously to the shore or tossing tumultuously and flinging their spray into the air.

It was Sunday, and despite the terrific wind the widow and her daughters went off to church, disappearing up the winding path of the cliff with super-human struggles against the wind. I was late, and watched them from my bedroom window.

As I passed down the corridor on my way to the dining-room I met a servant carrying a breakfast tray. It could only be for Gascoyne and his friend, and I would have given a great deal to have had five seconds with that teapot undetected.

It disappeared into bedroom No. 10, and I went downstairs to a solitary breakfast in the dining-room. The day passed quite uneventfully. The two lovers appeared to a late lunch and spent the afternoon in a bow window in the hall. Young Gascoyne smoked cigarettes which

Kate Falconer lit for him, a proceeding contemplated by the elder of the widow's two daughters—who, apparently a little wearied by the company of her relatives, had descended to read a book in an armchair—with a tightening of the upper lip. Kate Falconer's bringing-up, however, had trained her to the disapproval of the more respectable members of her own sex.

I suppose the day would have been very dull but for the state of suppressed excitement I was in. Once I almost thought my chance had come.

After tea the lovers parted for the first time since they had arrived. She went upstairs and he went to the reading-room. I strolled out into the garden and glanced in at the window. He was seated at a table writing letters. After a few minutes I returned to the hotel. As I entered the door a waiter was carrying a whisky-and-soda to the reading-room. I sat down in the hall and waited, not imagining that I should be able to reach the whisky-and-soda but determined not to lose a chance. In a minute or so the waiter returned to the servants' quarters, and in a few minutes more Gascoyne came hurriedly out of the reading-room and ran lightly upstairs. I walked slowly into the room. The whisky-and-soda, untouched, stood on the writing-table by a half-finished letter. Unfortunately there was a glass door between the reading-room and the hall, and it caused me to hesitate. The next moment Gascoyne was back again in the room and the opportunity was gone.

He and Miss Falconer, who seemed to have recognised me, had evidently more than once made me the subject of conversation, but had been too wrapped up in each other to take any further notice. Finding ourselves alone, however, he became quite companionable. He had charming manners and a singularly pleasant voice. I took a fancy to him from the first, and keenly regretted that our acquaintanceship must be so short.

I was compelled by the exigencies of the situation to avoid anything like actual friendliness, which I could see young Gascoyne was perfectly ready to display.

I had five days in which to do my work.

Monday passed uneventfully. It was a glorious day, and Gascoyne and Miss Falconer went out early in the morning and did not return till dinner-time. There was nothing to be gained by impatience. The only thing was to watch, and to seize the opportunity should one occur. Tuesday and Wednesday went by, and on Thursday I heard Gascoyne tell the manageress that they would be leaving the next day. It seemed as if my visit were to be in vain.

I had ascertained that Gascoyne and Miss Falconer had two rooms on the same landing as myself, Nos. 10 and 11. On Friday morning, the day of their departure, as I was on my way downstairs I saw a breakfast tray for two on a chair on the landing outside their room. The breakfast was untasted. It was obviously theirs, and the waiter had most probably gone back for something.

There was not a soul in sight. I looked over the staircase. There was no one to be seen in the hall below. In a second my resolution was taken. Swiftly I took the tiny phial containing the aconite from my pocket and dropped a few grains into the teapot.

As I descended the stairs I met the waiter returning, breathless. He held a sugar basin in his hands, which he had evidently forgotten. I went on to the dining-room. To me the hotel was already full of the ghosts of pain. I was haunted even in that moment of stress by the one weak spot in my scheme. Aconitine is not instantaneous, neither does it rob the victims of their intelligence, which remains clear and undisturbed till the end. Should either of them be asked if it had been suicide the reply would of course be in the negative, and that would be an awkward factor at the inquest.

In a few minutes the hotel was in a state of excitement. This was what I had expected. The doctor was telephoned for from the village. Before he arrived, however, all was over and an awful gloom descended on the place. I felt severely the disadvantage of not knowing all that had passed in the death chamber. It appeared that the widow lady thoroughly understood nursing, and had at once ordered anyone who could not be of use out of the room. I was certainly not likely to pretend to any medical knowledge, so I remained in the hall asking eagerly for news from anyone who came down from the sick room, the widow's two daughters, all their reserve banished, keeping me company.

It was their mother who brought us word of the tragic ending.

In a few minutes everybody in the hotel was gathered in the hall discussing the affair in hushed voices, and it was at this moment that the doctor bustled in.

"I was not at home when you telephoned," he said.

The manageress explained that the people he had come to attend on were dead.

"Surely not, my dear Miss Worcester. Let me see them at once."

The widow stepped forward.

"I have been a hospital matron, doctor, and I have no doubt about it." She commenced to lead the way upstairs, the doctor and the manageress following her.

In a few minutes the manageress reappeared.

"Telephone to the village and tell them that someone is to come from the police-station at once."

This was unpleasant, and I must confess to a dismally nervous feeling, but I was somewhat reassured by hearing the manageress say in conversation with the widow:

"I think it must have been suicide."

"They seemed very happy," said the widow.

"Lately married, I suppose." And the manageress raised her eyebrows and looked at the widow interrogatively.

"One must not judge, but I fancy—" the widow stopped. She did not look the sort of woman who would take the least pleasure in scandal.

The doctor sent down again in a few minutes instructions to send a messenger for another medical man. The driver of the hotel fly mounted a horse and rode off in hot haste. We wondered whether it was possible that after all they were not dead. I scarcely knew which I hoped for. I was not sufficiently hardened to be without a vague desire that they should be alive. At the same time, it would be a terrible nuisance to have to do the work all over again.

Our doubts were soon set at rest. When the doctor came down he announced that there was no longer the least doubt that life was extinct. Gascoyne's card-case and his town address had been discovered, and his father had been wired for, who replied that he would be down by the next train. At the time he was expected I went out. A nameless horror came over me at the idea of seeing the father's face in its first grief and despair.

When I returned to the hotel the coroner had arrived. The postmortem took place that afternoon; the inquest was held the next morning, and I attended.

Mr. Gascoyne first gave evidence, formally identifying the body of the man as that of his son. He was marvellously self-controlled, but his face was ashy. So far it had been impossible to communicate with any of Kate Falconer's relatives, but in the course of the inquest a telegram was received by the coroner from a sister, who stated, however, that she had not seen her for two years.

The evidence of the waiter who carried up their breakfast followed. He deposed to leaving the breakfast tray in the room, when they appeared well and cheerful. It must have been about ten minutes later that the bell was rung violently and he hurried upstairs. He found the young man in an armchair and the young woman lying on the bed, both of them evidently in great pain. He immediately went for the manageress. The young woman kept on crying out that she had been poisoned, and the young man's distress at her suffering was such that it was impossible to get anything out of him.

The evidence of the widow and the manageress followed. Then came the doctor, and the court grew tense with interest.

It was undoubted, he said, that death was due to aconite, taken apparently in a cup of tea. When he arrived at the hotel they were both dead. Death had been singularly rapid. The other medical man corroborated.

The case had a distinct element of mystery, but in the absence of evidence of motive it seemed that a verdict of suicide was inevitable.

The inspector strengthened this presumption by the intangible insinuation which he managed to convey in his evidence. The jury obviously thought it curious that in reply to a question from the foreman he explained that nothing which could be shown to have contained the aconite was to be found.

Still, the coroner summed up distinctly in favour of suicide, and such was the decision of the jury, a verdict which caused Mr. Gascoyne the greatest distress.

Immediately after the verdict he took his son's body back to town, leaving instructions, as I discovered, that the girl's funeral was to be at his expense unless the relatives wished otherwise, and that he personally would attend, a display of feeling I had hardly thought him capable of.

I returned to town late that night and reached my house at Clapham in the early hours of the morning.

As I opened the door it was as if the voice of an unseen presence pervaded the emptiness of the house, whispering: "Murderer!" and when I awoke the next morning it seemed as if the heavy grey light of dawn wove itself into haunting, opaque shapes. With a shudder I realised that never again should I be alone and at peace.

CHAPTER VII

AFTER such a brilliant success I felt that I required rest. It would not do to set to work again until my nerves were thoroughly restored, and the period of excitement I had passed through had left them a little unstrung. It took me nearly a month after Gascoyne Gascoyne's funeral to recover from the haunting terror that I had left a clue, and that sooner or later someone would come across it. I had scoffed at the maxim 'Murder will out.' I found myself living in company with it. It had a way of springing into my head when I woke in the morning, and the letters danced in front of me like devillings. It repeated itself in my brain rhythmically for days, and it required the strongest effort of will on my part to silence it.

It must be remembered that I was very young, and that what I had done was irrevocable; further, I am not naturally callous. I remained indoors smoking a great many French cigarettes, and accustoming myself to the consciousness of guilt. Grahame Hallward called one evening and, declaring that I looked too ill to be left, offered to spend the night with me. I was about to accept, but refused hastily on recollecting that in my sleep I might fill the house with confessions. No man can be answerable for himself in the silent watches of the night. It gave me a distinctly weird feeling when I reflected that till my dying day I must lie alone o'nights with locked doors.

Grahame Hallward, unaware that I had chosen my profession, threw himself with all the loyalty of his nature into the question of my future. He could not understand my indifference, and, considering that I had borrowed a fairly large sum from him, it probably appeared a little unfair. He loved me too well, however, to give the least indication that he considered I was not behaving quite straightforwardly.

He suggested that I should go to South Africa, but I pointed out that without capital I could not hope to obtain work that was not mere drudgery. I explained also that I had some plans which I would tell him of later, but that at present they were not dependent on myself, which was perfectly true. I was fully aware of how important it was that I should secure some means of obtaining a regular supply of money, and at the moment I had not the least idea as to how this was to be done. It must obviously be something which would not occupy my whole time. I regretted my wasted capital every day. I might have made a small income out of racing. It would not have been very difficult provided I contented myself with small profits.

Whatever happened it was imperative that I should not sell my house. An insignificant, semi-detached villa in Clapham was an ideal lair. I thought at one time of seeing if I could obtain a footing on the stage—that refuge of the vain and derelict—but I decided that it might bring me into such prominence as might even cause the Gascoyne family to take notice of me, the last thing to be desired.

Day after day I racked my brains for a solution of the difficulty. I believed I could carry through any feasible scheme, and my Jewish blood taught me to rely on my powers of application.

While I was deciding on a good method of providing for my current expenditure, I was also deciding on which member of the Gascoyne family my next blow should fall, and I consulted the chart daily.

It was highly improbable that the father of young Gascoyne would have any more children unless his wife died and he married again, and although her grief at the death of her son was extreme, she was not made of the material that succumbs under sorrow.

It was with a weird sense of shock that one morning I received the following letter:

"DEAR SIR,

"Some time ago you wrote claiming relationship to the Gascoyne family, and asking me to help you to some situation in which you might earn your living. I must apologise for my unsympathetic attitude on that occasion. Should you still be in need of a post I shall be glad if you will give me a call.

"Yours very truly,

"GASCOYNE GASCOYNE."

The letter, together with the morning paper, was lying in the hall when, half asleep, I passed through it one early spring morning on my way to the kitchen to cook my breakfast. I was at the moment doing such housework as was necessary. I made myself a cup of tea, toasted some bread and boiled an egg before I opened it. Having read it I sat still as if mesmerised by its contents. I thought I must have misjudged the man, till I reflected that had it not been for the blow my hand had dealt him his nature would have remained hard as before. I was on the borderland of remorse, and it was the aim of my life to keep out of that ghostly territory. I had from the first made up my mind to regard the whole matter of the Gascoyne family from a purely business-like point of view, and so I turned to the practical side of his letter, which required consideration.

Was it possible to make use of him in any way? That was the essential consideration. The first thing to decide was whether it was likely he would recognise me as having been at Lowhaven. As far as the inquest was concerned I had no fear. I had kept well out of his sight. On the other hand, even supposing he had not seen me, was it good policy to conceal the fact that I had been there—always supposing that I decided to make use of him? At any moment someone might turn up and betray the fact, and a reason for the concealment would not be easy to find. Perhaps some idea of putting me in his dead son's place had entered his mind, and thus the question of finance would be settled. I pondered over the pros and cons for nearly a week. One day the pros carried all before them and the cons were in full retreat. The next day the retreating objections had entrenched themselves, impossible to dislodge. The cons had behind them the full force of a nervous objection to facing Mr. Gascoyne, an objection well to be understood. Still, the solving of the financial difficulty was all important. I was near my last sovereign. I could always refuse any offer he made me should it threaten to clip my claws too completely, or smother my freedom of action in a London office. I waited till the sovereign was broken into before I made up my mind. In fact, I waited till my last half-sovereign was eighteen-pence to the bad, and all my boots showed signs of wear. Then I decided to risk it, and I wrote saying I would call on Mr. Gascoyne at his City address at noon the next day. I received a telegram saying that he would prefer it should be one o'clock, from which I deduced that he proposed to give me his luncheon hour, and would possibly ask me to share that meal should I be presentable. I have always had a rare instinct for deducing correct conclusions from the faintest suggestions, and it has been invaluable in acquainting me with the peculiarities of fields on which imminent battles were to be fought. Evidently Mr. Gascoyne was inclined to be friendly, therefore modesty and frankness were the weapons with which to make the victory decisive. He was a business man, and, considering my circumstances, nothing was to be gained by outward display. Indeed, a plain dressing for the occasion—blue serge, blue foulard tie with white spots, and a bowler—was absolutely right, and did not necessarily suggest a Bond Street wardrobe in reserve, rendered temporarily useless for lack of good boots.

I was as nervous as I have ever been when I mounted in the lift to the second floor of the tall block of buildings in the City where Mr. Gascoyne's offices were situated. I could not help reflecting that young Gascoyne must have ascended in the same lift times without number.

It was not for me, however, to indulge in such reflections, and I shook off any morbid cobwebs from my thoughts and stepped into the outer office with a subtle and affected consciousness of innocence which I was by constant practice enabling myself to assume at will.

The clerk took my card and noted the name with a look of intelligence.

"Oh yes, Mr. Gascoyne is expecting you, but there are two gentlemen with him now. Please take a seat. I will tell him you are here."

He went to a speaking-tube and informed some one at the other end that Mr. Rank was in the office.

"Mr. Gascoyne will see you in one minute." And he returned to his papers.

In a moment Mr. Gascoyne opened the door of his inner office, showing out two elderly men. Whilst listening to their last words he motioned me to enter with a grave smile.

In a minute he joined me and closed the door of the office behind him.

"Please sit down, Mr. Rank." He seated himself on the chair behind his desk and motioned me to the one opposite. I could not help noticing how much he had aged in the two or three months that had elapsed since I had seen him last.

"You are not like the Gascoynes," he said, with a smile, "and yet there is a something."

"My father was a Jew, and I think I am like him."

"To be frank with you, I have taken the trouble to find out exactly the relationship in which we stand."

I felt alarmed. It was distinctly unpleasant to hear that he had been making inquiries about me.

"This is my mother's photograph," I said, handing him a small likeness of her. He looked at it with interest.

"It is a very sweet face. She is dead, I believe?"

"Yes, I have no nearer relative than Henry Gascoyne."

"Ah, poor old man, I am afraid he does not know anyone. He is quite childish."

"So I understand."

"Have you ever seen the family portraits at Hammerton?"

"Never." I was determined to deny any particular knowledge of the family.

"Your mother is extraordinarily like some of the women. I do not know the present Earl, but I have visited Hammerton as an excursionist."

"I have never been there."

"And now will you come and have some lunch? I am a busy man and cannot afford to waste time." Either he was wonderfully softened, or the letter he had written me when I first applied to him was utterly unlike himself. I was unable to make out which was correct, but I inclined to the former conclusion.

"I have been wondering," he said, when we were seated over some cutlets and a very good bottle of wine, "why you were so long in answering my letter."

I replied, with every appearance of frankness, that it had taken some amount of thought before I could decide to put my pride in my pocket and swallow his former snub.

"I thought it was that," he answered. "I must frankly admit that my reply to your application was very uncalled for, but when I wrote it I was smarting somewhat under the ingratitude of a young man I had taken into my office a short time before."

"It is forgotten," I said. "After all, men in your position must receive a host of requests for favours that you are unable to comply with."

"That is true," he said, "quite true; but still, from one claiming relationship—however, let us forget it. Tell me about yourself."

I was perfectly candid, and told him the story of my life. It was all inexpressibly strange; this man bending forward with every appearance of interest and sympathy listening to the life story of his son's murderer. I was amazed at the way I could pose, even to myself, as a perfectly innocent person, and was secretly vain of a great artistic success. I found myself filling in the picture which I was painting for him with numerous little touches, all deliberately designed to heighten a carefully considered effect. I told no lies, however; indeed, it was quite unnecessary. Without that part dealing with his own son the simple story was very effective. I did not hesitate to hint that there was the memory of a woman troubling me. He was sympathetic at once but did not urge further confidences at the moment.

"Perhaps one of the other reasons why I was not particularly drawn by your being a member of the Gascoyne family," he said, when I had finished, "was that I am not on friendly terms with any of them. My wife was of humble origin, and such of them as I know were very uncivil to her, and, to tell you the truth, the name of Gascoyne had become somewhat distasteful to me."

We were strolling back to the office and he had laid his hand loosely in my arm. He had evidently taken a fancy to me. So much for the voice of Nature. Indeed, all my life I have noticed that the voice of Nature is a somewhat misleading guide; very apt to call the listener to follow over all kinds of dangerous and quaking bogs. People have a way, too, of labelling the shrill scream and tuneless croaking of their own pet conventions and prejudices as the voice of Nature, if the occasion suit them, and their shallow consciences do not imperatively demand correct definitions.

"Before I make you the offer that is in my mind," he said, when we again reached his office and I was once more seated opposite to him, "I wish to ask you whether you heard that I lost my only son a few months ago under somewhat tragic—circumstances."

"I was at Lowhaven," I said gently.

He looked at me in unfeigned surprise.

"You were at Lowhaven?"

"I did not mention it before, but I was staying in the same hotel."

"I don't remember you."

"I kept out of your way. I was naturally unwilling to intrude at such a time."

He buried his face in his hands, and something between a groan and a sigh escaped him. It was evident that the memory of his bereavement was inexpressibly poignant.

"I am glad you knew him, if only by sight. Did you ever speak to him?"

"A few words in the hotel smoking-room, that is all. He was a splendid looking fellow."

"He was. It has broken his mother's heart. It was strange that you should have been there."

"I did not even know his name, till—" I paused.

He uncovered a haggard face.

"Well, it is over; the past cannot be recalled. Would you care to come into my firm?"

He made the offer hurriedly, as if anxious to escape from painful thoughts.

He then laid his plan before me. I was to come into the firm and learn the business of stockbroking. Further than that he was not prepared to go, and he made no promises.

He looked at me steadily as he said this, and I gathered that if I were satisfactory I might hope for all things. A glance at his face convinced me that he was not the man to recede from any promise, no matter how much his sympathy with me became a diminishing quantity, providing my abilities were sufficient. I accepted his offer. It might be possible to use the situation as a lever. It certainly put an end to the obscurity which I had considered so strong an asset. I have often wondered before and since the trial whether my original plans might not have been more successful. I believe that they would have furnished more adventure and excitement. At the same time, the difficulties would have been almost insurmountable, and—well, I chose my methods and I failed, although I have consolation in the brilliance of the failure.

I was to have two hundred and fifty pounds a year to begin with. It was decidedly a princely offer, considering that he would be paying for the trouble of teaching me.

"Later on, Mr. Rank, it would give me pleasure to present you to my wife. At present I am afraid that you, in the plenitude of your youth and manhood, might rouse sad thoughts."

He drew me a cheque for twenty pounds, and, taking me into the outer office, introduced me to his manager, chief clerk, and the staff generally, and, asking me to be at the office at ten o'clock the next morning, dismissed me.

I walked all the way back to Clapham thinking deeply. Financially I was evidently out of danger for life, and I had good warrant for dreaming of myself at the head of Mr. Gascoyne's firm. It was proof of how entirely the Gascoyne coronet had become an obsession with me, that the prospect of a permanent income, with wealth, even, in the perspective of middle life, did not in any way suggest that I should relinquish the glittering prize on which I had set my heart. Perhaps if Mr. Gascoyne's offer had come before my first success I might have abandoned my purpose, but it would have been obviously absurd to burden I had almost said my conscience—so strong is the habit of conventional thought—with a murder abortively. I could not help smiling ironically on recalling Mr. Gascoyne's evident liking for me. According to all rules of accepted psychology I should have had something unpleasant in my personality which he should at once have detected. It was extraordinarily remiss on the part of instinct that it should not have been so.

Grahame Hallward came in to see me that evening and was over-joyed at my news. He was evidently impressed when he learned that it was my relationship to the Gascoyne family which had secured me such an advantageous situation.

"So after all, Israel, what you used to tell me was true."

"Did you ever doubt it?"

"Not since the day you gave me your word of honour that it was so."

It may appear strange, but I have always been singularly fastidious about my word of honour.

Grahame then broke to me some news which came as a staggering blow. Sibella was engaged to Lionel Holland.

"The one thing I really like about Holland," he concluded, "is the way he has stuck to Sibella."

I could not simulate indifference, and Grahame saw that his announcement had been a shock to me.

I stood looking out on the little garden with its soot-begrimed walls which the sunset had drenched in scarlet, trying to control the tempest of feeling which surged within me.

Grahame understood, and came over, putting his arm round my neck.

"I am so sorry, Israel. I quite understand. Really, I'd sooner it were you."

I smiled somewhat bitterly.

Grahame's preference for me was hardly a consolation, fond as I was of him.

"I'll come over on Sunday," I said.

"Do." He understood my anxiety to impress Sibella with the idea that I did not care. I wondered whether things would have been different had Sibella known of my altered prospects. I was convinced that I held at least an equal place with Lionel Holland in such affection as Sibella was capable of. It was Thursday; by Sunday I might possibly have conquered the first sting of chagrin sufficiently to conceal my feelings. The excitement of my new venture in life was entirely lost in the night of despair I passed. Equally with the Gascoyne earldom, Sibella was my ambition. She was the kind of girl to whom the position of Countess Gascoyne would have come quite naturally. In common with her brothers and sisters she had that which would have enabled her to carry off any dignity, frivolous and superficial as her real nature was. I had dreamed of the joy of placing her in a position so very much above anything she could have expected.

Still, the battle was not over. I believed in my power to conquer her in competition with Lionel Holland, if I were given equal worldly advantages, and it seemed as if such advantages were coming my way.

The fact that I was unable to idealise Sibella never cooled my love. I burned for her, and frankly confessed it. For the rest, she had spirits and special magnetism enough to make her a delightful companion. A great many of her faults matched my own weaknesses. I sympathised with her desire for beautiful clothes at any cost, as well as with her yearning for the right of entry to that society which the middle classes exalt by envying and imitating.

I made up my mind to fight, and went for the first time to Mr. Gascoyne's office somewhat comforted by the mere determination to give battle to my rival.

I discovered very speedily that the work suited me admirably. The rest of the clerks evidently gathered that my being taken into the firm had been made a special feature of, for they treated me almost with deference.

I had by this time fixed on the next member of the Gascoyne family whom I intended to remove. It was Henry Gascoyne, the orphan son of Patrick Gascoyne. He had a sister, but all intervening females yielded precedence to my mother, as heiress to her father. It was therefore not necessary to consider her. Her brother was about twenty-two years of age, and by a little inquiry I learned that he was at Oxford, where he had already gained a reputation as one of those who might do wonderful things if he chose to apply himself, but who preferred to be content with the reputation of his potentialities and the cultivation of as much muscle as was consistent with nights spent in hard drinking. I inspected his father's will at Somerset House, and learned that he and his sister had been left some fifteen thousand pounds apiece, which capital, however, they could not touch till Henry Gascoyne was twenty-five. His sister was entirely devoted to him, and spent her own income in keeping up a small house in the New Forest which he had inherited from his father. He would have been content to let the whole place go to rack and ruin, but devotion to her father's memory, and a desire to have a place which her brother might look upon as home, induced her to support the establishment entirely out of her own resources. So much I had learned from two or three visits paid at irregular intervals to the neighbourhood.

CHAPTER VIII

THE Sunday after Grahame had brought me the news of Sibella's engagement I visited the Hallwards. I managed to get through a conventional speech of congratulation, stung to self-possession by a certain radiance and exhilaration in Sibella's bearing. Grahame had told them of my good fortune, and there was a distinct change of manner towards me on the part of the other members of the family. They had never wholly believed that I was related to the Gascoynes, or had thought that if it were true I was making the most of a very remote connection. To them I had been the object for as much patronage as they dared display towards one not prone to endure condescension. I could see that Sibella looked at me with a new interest. She was growing into a truly beautiful woman, and all trace of the slightly suburban minx was becoming rapidly obliterated by a crescendo of style and distinction. It was quite evident that she would have the manners and self-possession of a thoroughly well-bred beauty, and she had acquired a facility for putting on her clothes with an altogether overpowering effect of distinction. It seemed to me a little curious that a character which I knew to be somewhat small should have achieved a certain impression of breadth and ease in her personality. Probably it was the result of the unquestionable fact of her extreme beauty. At any rate, she was rapidly learning the secret of predominance, and she showed, captivating and delicious, in distinct relief to her surroundings.

Mr. Gascoyne's twenty pounds had enabled me, through the purchase of decent boots, gloves, etc., to bring my wardrobe into play again. I had dressed as rakishly as possible, determined that Sibella should have no satisfaction in the dejection of an unsuccessful lover. I knew her character and the pleasure she would have derived from it. I simulated the best of spirits, and Grahame loyally helped me to sustain the illusion. I was inwardly consumed with jealousy whenever my hungry eyes fell upon her, but I roused myself for a *tour de force* in acting and succeeded. Lionel Holland came in later. I saw him through the large drawing-room windows coming up the path, supremely confident and jaunty. He was evidently surprised to see me. We had not met since the evening of my humiliation. I greeted him cordially, however, and he was obliged to be civil, but I had the satisfaction of feeling that he was by no means at his ease. He was so perfectly assured that, being poor, I was an interloper in a well-to-do house, that he would have liked, I am sure, to ask me what the devil I meant by intruding. I on my part was galled by the attitude of superior intimacy he assumed in a house where I had been intimate when he was a stranger to it. I was perfectly determined that he should not dislodge me, and that nothing he said or did should interfere with my visits to the Hallward establishment. He was staying to supper as a matter of course, and I detected a shade of annoyance on his face when Mrs. Hallward, in consequence of an aside from Grahame, extended an invitation to me to do likewise. I accepted, although I was compelled to submit to the disappearance of the lovers to the schoolroom for fully an hour previous to the meal. I sang and played to the others as I had been in the habit of doing, and worked hard to make myself agreeable. I was so far successful that Mrs. Hallward asked me why I came so seldom, and discussed the Gascoyne family in a corner of the drawing-room with me after supper. She was herself the great-grand-daughter of a Nova Scotian baronet and never forgot it, although she had saving perception enough not to allude to it directly. As a rule she brought it in with some such remark as—"There is I believe a baronetcy knocking about in our own family somewhere—where exactly I don't know—but it is there," a remark subtly framed, so as to convey the impression that, being no snob, she forbore to mention how very near the said baronetcy was, in fact, that it was knocking about so very near that it was quite possible a collision might occur at any moment.

She was most decidedly a snob, but not of an objectionable kind. As a matter of fact, I have always considered well-bred snobs rather pleasant people, and have often wondered whether they would have been as well-bred if they had not been snobs. People who love the pleasantly decorative in life have at least taste, and the preference for titles, fine surroundings and social paraphernalia may be a form of art.

"Do you and Lionel ever see each other in the City?" asked Sibella, who, I had already remarked, was not so much in love that she could refrain from teasing her lover.

"Never," said Lionel shortly.

"For eighteen months I hardly went near the City," I answered.

"Doing other things?" asked Lionel, in an unpleasant tone.

"Living on my capital," I answered airily, giving him a keen, steady glance of daring. "It was the most beautiful time I have ever had, and I don't regret it. It will never come again, and I might have spent it in a dingy City office."

"Earning your living," put in Lionel.

"There was no necessity," I laughed.

Grahame gazed at Lionel in haughty inquiry as if desirous of knowing what he meant by being rude to his guest.

In fact, Lionel's airs of intimacy and general at-homeness obviously irritated Grahame not less than the constant use of his Christian name.

I declined to be drawn into displaying the least sign of annoyance, although Holland seized every opportunity to deliver innuendo or satire, the latter weapon in his hands becoming more often than not mere clumsy facetiousness. I made a point of being gay, and without talking of my prospects in Mr. Gascoyne's firm took very good care to leave the impression that it was their promising nature that accounted for my good-humour. I managed by judicious circumlocution and tact to bring the conversation round to reminiscences, throwing them far enough back to prevent his joining in, and slyly flattering Sibella on the subject of her childish achievements so that she revived memories with zest, and became engrossed with the recapitulation of events and bygone adventures in which I, and not Lionel Holland, appeared as her cavalier.

"I believe Lionel is getting jealous," she remarked towards the end of supper, noticing her lover's sulky taciturnity.

I had been secretly sure of that fact for the last twenty minutes, and had been enjoying a discomfiture which the rest of the company had not appreciated. He had also, as I perceived, grasped that whenever I chose I was quick and dexterous enough to leave him conversationally a laggard every time.

Not that I relied on these qualities to pass him in the race for Siberia's appreciation. My instinct in female psychology was too sure. Certainly, if such superficial qualities could have dazzled any woman, they would have dazzled Sibella, whose mind was prone to skim airily and gracefully the surface of things. Even the most transparent of women, however—if there be such things as transparent women—elude analysis when the exact qualities which attract them in their lovers come under consideration.

Sibella was hardly the character one would have imagined overlooking the pinchbeck in Lionel Holland, and yet she had accepted it with a most surprising ease. Such a surrender seemed to negative all her leanings, at any rate in surface matters, to the well-bred and socially ascending scale. True, he would be rich, but Sibella had other admirers who would be richer. He had personality, and perhaps this wins with women more than anything. With all his faults he was not insignificant, and he was undeniably a very beautiful young man, notwithstanding his obvious veneer.

I had taken my courage in my hands and stayed and smoked with Grahame in the library, knowing full well that Lionel and Sibella were in each other's arms in the schoolroom. It is strange how we manage to endure the things which in anticipation were to slay us with their mere agony.

Mr. and Mrs. Hallward were lax in their supervision of the engaged couple, as they had been about everything else in connection with their children. Sibella and her lover remained undisturbed when her father and mother retired for the night, and it was passably late for a young woman of respectable family to be letting her lover out when the front door closed behind him. She evidently heard our voices, for she came into the library.

"You two still here?"

She seated herself on the club-fender. She was wide awake, and I remembered that as a child she had never betrayed sleepiness at children's parties—she always expressed her capacity to stay up to any hour. Her family complained that she never could be induced to rise in proper time in the morning.

"Isn't it lovely, Israel, for you to have had such a piece of luck!"

"Oh, I shall always fall on my feet," I answered, easily. "You see, I was born lucky, and that is better than being born rich."

"How do you know you were born lucky?" she asked with interest.

I was not to be questioned out of my pose. "It's like genius. An instinct teaches the genius to know himself, and something of the same thought instructs the lucky man."

I spoke with such perfect good spirits and conviction that I could see she found herself believing me. She perched herself on the edge of the great desk which occupied the centre of the library and asked for a cigarette.

"Don't smoke, Sibella," said Grahame. He was the sort of man who would not have objected to the female belongings of anyone else smoking, but who objected to his own doing so, on the ground that it was his business to see that they suffered no material damage in the eyes of the world.

"What nonsense, Grahame! Of course I shall smoke—as much as I like—well no, not quite as much as I like because that would spoil my teeth, and I don't intend to do anything that would injure my personal appearance."

"That is a very patriotic resolve," I laughed. "There is some beauty so striking that it becomes a national property."

Sibella made a face.

"Thank you. I'm nothing of the kind."

"For goodness' sake don't flatter Sibella," said Grahame. "She is vain enough already."

"So long as she is vain and not conceited it does not matter."

"The difference?"

"Well, vanity is a determination to make the best of our superiorities whilst frankly admitting them; conceit is a morbid desire to enforce the fact on other people."

"Subtle," murmured Grahame, who never spoke above his middle tones, "but I am not convinced. Sibella thinks a great deal too much of herself."

"It is better than thinking too little of one's self," said Sibella, blowing rings of smoke and pursing up her lips deliciously, till I could have cried out on her for heartlessness.

"Very much better," I assented. "People who think too little of themselves generally end by a mock humility which is a form of conceit infinitely tedious. No, believe me, the vanity you decry has in it something of virtue."

Grahame turned to Sibella.

"Haven't you noticed, Sibella, how much older Israel has grown of late?"

"Not in looks," cried Sibella. "To-night he looks like a boy."

This idea pleased me. The author of the secret that lay in young Gascoyne's grave looking almost a boy savoured of the incongruous, for which I had developed an appetite.

"I didn't mean in appearance," said Grahame. "Israel looks as if he had never had a trouble."

The idea pleased me even more. Grahame's criticism showed that I was playing my game with the right effect, and that the weeks of prostration following on the successful *coup* at Lowhaven had left no effect. Sibella, from her very nature, could not forbear giving me one or two glances with just enough of feeling in them, to fill the atmosphere with a vague suggestion of sentimentality, but I behaved as if the very air she breathed was not to me love's own narcotic. I fought fiercely against myself lest I should give the least sign that her power over me was supreme as ever.

"What lovely chocolates you used to bring me, Israel!"

I laughed buoyantly.

"Ah, but you remember the first Lionel brought you. They cost more."

"As if I cared for that!"

Grahame laughed in his turn.

"As if, Sibella dear, you ever cared for anything else."

Grahame had the most incomparable way of pointing out people's faults to their faces without offence.

Sibella, however, looked angry.

"No one can say that I am mercenary."

I was at some pains not to join Grahame in the roar of laughter provoked by this remark. Sibella knew of old how impossible it was for her to cope with Grahame, so she turned the batteries of her anger on me.

"I believe you quite agree with Grahame."

"What about?"

"About my being mercenary."

"I am sure I don't."

"Then why did you laugh?"

"I didn't."

"Well, I'm not mercenary, am I?"

"Of course not." I smiled.

She detected the irony.

"Lionel never says such things to me." For one instant I felt the lash and smarted. I was half inclined to retort "Lionel is the prince of good manners," but that would have given her the satisfaction she was waiting for, and most likely she would have gone to bed.

Grahame at heart was very proud of Sibella, but he, like myself, was under no delusions about her. His special fondness was also partly a result of their having been so much together as children. Mr. and Mrs. Hallward's other children were much older, and with the exception of Miss Hallward, an unmarried spinster verging on forty, were either married or out in the world. Miss Hallward, who must have been singularly handsome in her youth, and who as a matter of fact was so still, had devoted her whole life to her brothers and sisters, and was particularly fond of Sibella, who made use of her in every possible way. Miss Hallward had always been singularly kind to me, and I liked her.

I could well remember an incident which occurred on the occasion of one of my first visits to the house. Sibella had been asked to do something by Miss Halward and had refused, and, working herself into a rage, had told her sister, who at that time could not have been more than thirty, that she was a disappointed old maid and that nobody had wanted to marry her because she was so unattractive. Miss Hallward had grown very white, and had turned on Sibella with a fierceness I never saw her display before or after. The occurrence was unimportant, except that it served to frame her, as it were, in the past of an unhappy love story, and she was always the more interesting to me because of it.

When I said good-bye to Sibella I felt sure that she was more interested in me than she had been since as a boy of sixteen I had declared my passion and had been granted the privilege of kissing her when opportunity offered, little love passages of which Grahame had remained in entire ignorance. I also saw that I had succeeded in giving her the impression I was aiming at—that I was wholly freed from her spell. To a girl of Sibella's temperament this is at all times amazing, and so far from being glad at her rejected lover being in spirits she was at pains to detect the unhealed wound. Still, she was in her way really in love with Lionel Holland, and was not prepared to invest more than the smallest superfluity of coquetry and fascination in bringing me again into her net. I verily believe it would have given her some pleasure to see Holland and myself at each other's throats. Then she would probably have been content to leave me to some other woman. Had she known how near I was at times to seizing her in my arms and kissing her, with or without her will, she would have been satisfied—more, I think she would have been frightened.

She had a peculiar and unexpected effect on me. I found myself wavering in my purpose, and returning once more to the question which I had thought decided as to whether the risk I ran was worth the prize. I even found myself troubled with scruples as to the taking of life, and for some weeks was in serious danger of abandoning my undertaking.

And yet I cannot say that Sibella had any direct influence for good upon me, and it would have been hard to define why she should have exercised a restraining influence upon me at all.

I continued my visits to the Hallwards and saw that her pique at my apparent indifference to her engagement grew.

She might have been content with the number of admirers to whom it had obviously been a matter of some moment, but Sibella wanted the one admirer to care who was apparently indifferent.

I evidently pleased Mr. Gascoyne at the office, for his cordiality towards me increased daily. I threw into my manner towards him just as much of the filial attitude as I could without suggesting the least desire to usurp the place of his dead son.

After a few weeks he asked me to come and dine and meet his wife.

"By the way, Rank, my wife does not know that you are a relative of mine, and for certain reasons I would sooner you did not mention it—at least yet."

He was evidently nervous lest his wife might think he had been quick to fill their dead son's place.

"I have my reasons, and I am asking you to oblige me," he added cordially, noting the faint look of surprise I thought it policy to assume; it would never have done to let him think I could be treated unceremoniously.

I dined at the house in South Kensington, outside which I had so often watched. It seemed a quiet and sad household. Mrs. Gascoyne possessed the feminine capacity for filling the house with the presence of her dead, and turning a home into a tomb. Mr. Gascoyne was pleased that I managed to make her smile once or twice, and said as much as we sat over our wine.

"I am afraid there is very little to amuse you here, but I should be glad if you would dine with us now and then. I think my wife likes you. You have dignity, and she always likes people with dignity."

I laughed.

"You have been very good to me, sir," I said.

"I see in you excellent qualities, Israel." It was the first time he had ever called me by my Christian name. I was obviously progressing in his esteem.

He was right. I had excellent qualities. I always had. I am affectionate, naturally truthful and kind-hearted. My secret deeds have been an abstraction, in no way in tune with the middle tones of my character.

Mr. Gascoyne was essentially a business man, and it was my business qualities which appealed to him most. I had a natural gift for order and method, and although he was not given to praise, I detected a look of pleased surprise when I displayed some unusual perception of what was wanted in a particular situation. Lionel Holland, who at least seemed to have imbibed a wholesome fear of irritating me when we were together, could not witness my progress in the scale of prosperity without making an attempt to injure me in the eyes of my employer.

It appeared that he knew a fellow-clerk of mine, a youth who considered that I had ousted him from the place which should in time have been his. I had not been in the office a couple of hours before I grasped this fact. He was a pleasant fellow enough in an ordinary way, but his disappointment had brought out—as far as his relations towards me were concerned—his worst points. He had a slight acquaintance with Lionel Holland. This acquaintance the latter improved upon, and I was not a little surprised to find Harry Oust one Sunday afternoon sitting in the Hallwards' drawing-room. He was staying with Lionel from Saturday till Monday, and I think it gave his host infinite pleasure to introduce him where I had been known from childhood—though what particular satisfaction it was to him I could not quite see.

I soon realised that my life's history was in the possession of my fellow-clerks. I was too much in favour with Mr. Gascoyne for them to venture to show the contempt they felt because my mother had let lodgings. I would have been glad if one of them had had the temerity to throw it in my teeth, for an insult to my dead mother would have found me a perfectly normal person with an absolutely primal sense of loyalty.

CHAPTER IX

I MISSED no opportunity of finding out every detail of young Henry Gascoyne's college career. From all accounts he must have been surprisingly lazy, for no one ever spoke of him without giving him credit for great abilities. He was at Magdalen, had just scraped through his Mods at the end of his second year, and had then apparently given up any idea of serious work, for in a few months his devotion to pleasure and his defiance of college rules became so acute that he was ignominiously sent down. A few days after this auspicious ending to his career as a student, I met him riding in the neighbourhood of his New Forest home with a most cheerful countenance, and humming a tune. I was on my bicycle, and later I came across him again in a by-lane down which I had turned with the object of smoking a pipe. My appearance was quite unexpected and a little awkward. His horse was tethered to a gate, and folded in his arms was a remarkably pretty girl of the cottager class. I wondered if all the human obstacles between myself and the Gascoyne earldom were engaged in surreptitious love affairs.

The girl drew back hastily and hid her face, but not before I detected that she had been crying. I was walking my bicycle, and was a little annoyed that Henry Gascoyne had had such a good opportunity of seeing me. He was evidently thoroughly wasting his time from the worldly point of view, though I should probably have agreed—had he put the matter to me—that he was making the best of his youth.

He was not exactly handsome, but he had a colouring which, despite his dissipated life, gave assurance of clean blood. He was well made, and had hair the colour of ripe com. Notwithstanding, however, his eminently healthy appearance, his self-indulgence had absolutely no limitations except such as were prescribed by good form, and he was prepared to leap even this boundary if he could do so without danger of being seen.

He had the misfortune to be cursed until seventy times seven with the forgiveness of his friends; Harry Gascoyne was not a person they could be angry with for long. He had been known to steal a man's mistress and yet retain his friendship, and as I saw him that summer morning, booted and spurred, playing with the little cottage maiden as a cat might have done with a mouse, the indulgence he managed to secure for himself from his fellow-men was not difficult to understand.

I knew that his next move would be London. A young man with means and no one to control his actions is as sure to gravitate towards London as the lizard is to seek the sun. His sister, who should have been the man, urged a profession, suggesting the army, but Harry Gascoyne kicked at the mere idea of a life of routine and discipline. This much I had gathered at the tiny little inn half a mile from the Gascoynes' house, which was much frequented by the old man who combined for them the office of indoor and outdoor factotum. The keeper of the public-house itself had been placed in his present position by Harry Gascoyne's father, so that the establishment quite partook of the character of a feudal outpost. In addition, the landlady had been cook at the Grange.

"'E'll never do no work, won't Mr. 'Arry," said the old factotum, as he smoked his pipe on the wooden seat by the doorway and surveyed the pines etched black against the crimson flush of the setting sun.

"Not 'e, not 'e," agreed the landlord, taking in the prospect with as little poetical refreshment as his companion.

They were very proud of being able to converse with intimate knowledge of the gentlefolk living hard by, and conducted their conversation like inferior actors, casting side glances at their audience to watch the effect of the performance. Their audience was myself, seated on the wooden bench on the other side of the doorway and regaling myself with cold beef and pickles. Vanity has always kept me from drinking alcohol in any form, otherwise I verily believe I might have been a drunkard. I think, perhaps, that being unaccustomed to spirits, a glass of strong brandy on a certain grim morning that draws nearer and nearer will not be amiss.

But for this great matter of vanity, how many more drunkards would there not be! Not many with a weakness for the bottle are restrained by the immorality of voluntarily surrendering the gift of reason, or the prospect of declining in the scale of prosperity. The first objection appeals to them not at all, and the second is not sufficiently apparent in its immediate effects for it to act as a deterrent. An immediate coarsening of the features and a general degradation of appearance are different matters. Few people care about being repulsive, and to the real drunkard this fact soon becomes apparent.

The two old men found the Gascoyne topic most absorbing, and talked incessantly, till the crimson light behind the pines changed to a faint opal, and the stars were alight in the heavens.

"'Is feyther, 'e never done no work," said the landlord.

"That be true," said the other, as if he were bearing witness to some virtue of the late Mr. Gascoyne.

"'E spent a deal of money too," said the landlord.

"'E wur generous with 'is money," answered the other.

"And none 'ave cause to know that better'n we."

"That's true enough."

"Miss Edith be more like 'er mother. A nice lady but a bit close."

"It was as well one of 'em wur close or there wouldn't 'ave been much left."

"True."

There was a whole family history in these few remarks. A man born rich, but a rake, and possibly a profligate—a long-suffering wife enduring the slur of meanness in her efforts to save something from the wreck. Indeed, it appeared a wonder that she should have saved so much.

Evidently young Gascoyne took after his father. I gathered afterwards that the reason there was anything in the nature of estate left was because the money and house had been largely the property of Mr. Gascoyne's wife, and it was through her forethought that the boy and girl had been left equally well off.

"A girl's natural protector is her brother," her husband had said when he and his wife were discussing the matter. "It is natural the boy should be better off than his sister. If it is otherwise it puts the lad in a humiliating position." Mrs. Gascoyne, however, did not think so. She had absolute confidence in the girl's affection for her brother, whilst from early boyhood she had detected a singular likeness between the lad and his father. Yet although she trusted the girl, it was possible that she loved the boy more. Indeed, it was her very love that caused her to make provision for him in his sister's affection and rectitude.

All this I learned by degrees.

I learned also that the girl I had seen in his arms was something better than a cottager. She was the daughter of a blacksmith who was fairly well-to-do, and it was a tribute to young Gascoyne's courage that she possessed not only a father, but half a dozen stalwart brothers, who would most probably have killed him at sight could they have witnessed the embrace that summer morning in the lane. As I sat smoking my pipe in the perfect summer night, with the fragrant perfume of pine and tobacco mingling, I heard someone coming along the narrow strip of white road bordered with grass, whistling.

It was young Gascoyne on his way home.

It was evident that so far satiety had not begun to knock at the doors of conscience, for a more careless, happy creature it would have been impossible to imagine.

He paused outside the inn in the middle of the road, hesitating. I think I gathered what was in his mind. He was trying to decide whether he should go straight home to his sister, who was probably waiting for him, or stay and drink more beer than he would have cared for her to know of. Already the rose of his youth was coarsening slightly through the habit he had inherited from his father.

He came to the opposite seat and sat down. He was the incarnation of the born lounger. There was a careless ease in his carriage, and a just perceptible touch of exaggerated fashion in his clothes, which betrayed a pleasure in personal appearance, something beyond that merely incidental to youth.

At first he barely noticed my presence on the other seat, mistaking me in the gloom—for I was sitting in the shadow of the house—for some village yokel having his fill before going on his way home to a scolding wife. Gradually, however, it dawned upon him that the occupant of the other bench was not one of the stray labourers who patronised the place. As for myself, I was wondering whether I should retire before he entered into conversation with me, or run the risk, and see if matters turned out to my advantage.

"Quiet place, this," he said, tentatively.

"I'm glad to say it is," I answered, lazily.

Always answer lazily when a well-bred Englishman addresses you for the first time. It impresses him.

Young Gascoyne gathered from my voice that he was presumably talking to an equal. He became friendly.

"I suppose you mean," he said, laughing, "that you came here for quiet, and that you mean to get it."

"No, I don't quite mean that. So long as I can sleep where it is quiet, I don't care very much about absolute silence."

"Then I may talk to you? The evenings are so beastly dull down here." I made a very shrewd guess at the way he had been spending the earlier part of that evening. The possibility of six brothers to fight must have been exciting enough, but then Harry Gascoyne belonged to the class that wants amusing all the time.

"The stillness of the nights here is awful—especially depressing if you've been used to keep it up till the small hours of the morning."

"I should have thought that it would have been a welcome relief."

"I don't find it so."

"I suppose you're too young to feel the need of rest."

He laughed. Evidently he thought it a good joke.

"Oh, I say, you're not much older than I am, if at all. Of course I can't quite make out in this light, but—"

"I've seen a good deal," I interrupted.

"You've come from town, haven't you?"

"How did you guess?"

"Oh, one can always tell."

"Sorry I look such a cockney."

"Everybody who comes from town isn't a cockney. It would be rather awful if it were so."

"Then how could you tell?"

"Oh, the best of people get a bit careless in the country. It's something in the way town men put on their clothes. Fellows who live in the country will tell you that it isn't quite good form to wear your clothes too well, but that's all rot. They're jealous because they know they're slovenly."

I liked the way he talked, and, finding me companionable, he showed not the least desire to move. A new friend always interested me, so I put away any unpleasant reflections as to our future relations, and abandoned myself to the pleasure of a novel and pleasant companionship. My cousin chattered on, and gradually, as will almost invariably happen when two young men are talking together—the more especially over the bowl—the eternal feminine dominated. He was obviously neurotic, for all his healthy skin and philistine view of life in general.

He talked of women incessantly, but without any reference to their share in the higher things of life.

He hinted vaguely of the existence of the cottage maiden, but declined to be drawn when I encouraged him to take me into his confidence.

"It's a ripping thing to be in love; in fact, it's the only thing that reconciles me to stopping in this beastly hole."

"Romance is life," I murmured, lilting agreeably to the rhythm he desired. "I don't understand how people get on without it."

"I suppose there comes a time when everyone wants to settle down," he said, echoing the usual concessions of profligate youth to the demands of a period so very far ahead that there appears to be little inconvenience in confiding all promises of reformation to its keeping.

"When we are tired," I assented. "Perhaps that is the truest definition of virtue, not to run any race with excesses we are not equal to."

"I say, that means a pretty long rope for young people, doesn't it?"

"Yes, the rope will give out with youth, and then they can conveniently hang themselves."

"I say, for goodness sake don't talk like that. I shan't dare to walk home."

"Are you afraid of the dark?"

"Yes, I believe everybody is more or less."

"You are frank, at any rate. What a time primeval man must have had of it! I should say that when night fell these woods were alive with ghosts. I suppose the man with muscle was the only possible romanticist in those days. It was romance under its most healthy aspect."

"You mean that men had to fight for their women?"

"Exactly; so much muscle, so many women."

"The women must have feasted on the sight they love best—men at each other's throats."

"On the other hand, the woman must now and then have lost the weakling on whom she had set her heart." From primeval woman we wandered by easy stages to woman, beflounced, befrilled and perfumed—woman on the path to supremacy.

"I don't know," said young Gascoyne—the glamour of his cottage romance upon him, "but I don't think I care about the sophisticated sort. You never know when they are telling the truth. There was a girl at Oxford—"

Then followed a long story of a rather stupid romance of his college days, ending with, "And that put the finishing touch, and I got sent down."

"Sent down?" I murmured casually, as if it were news.

"Yes, frightfully unfair. The other chap got off scot free on the ground that he was a hard worker and that there was nothing against him. Said he loved the girl and intended to marry her. Silly ass!" Young Gascoyne asked me to lunch the next day. I refused, but he announced his intention of walking over in the morning to fetch me.

"It'll be quite a relief to have someone to talk to. I've got one or two fellows coming down next week, but at present it's deadly."

He bade me good-night again and again but each time sat down and commenced a new conversation.

"I'm coming up to town in the autumn to read for the Bar. Then I shall have as good time as is possible for a man with no money."

"What do you call no money?" I asked.

I knew the amount of his income to a penny.

"Eight hundred a year. A fellow can't do much on that."

I laughed outright. "Eight hundred a year is a fortune to a man with no encumbrances, especially in town."

"Well, I can't exactly say I haven't got any encumbrances. There is this place to be looked after. Not that I do much towards it, I'm bound to say. I should like to sell it, but my sister likes it and as she lives here she does most of the keeping-up."

I strolled down the road with him. He was rather the worse for the amount he had drunk, and hiccoughed slightly as he affectionately bade me good-night and assured me that he would be round the first thing in the morning.

Leaning out of the little inn bedroom I considered the question of accepting his invitation to lunch.

So far I had withheld my identity. If I went to the house on the morrow I could no longer conceal the fact that I was a relation.

When they knew who I was, it might or it might not make my task more difficult, and by this my action must be guided entirely.

I finally came to the decision that I could not expect to gain any access to young Gascoyne unless I followed up the acquaintance.

It was quite possible that when he discovered who I was he might drop me at once. I was a relation, certainly, but my comparatively humble origin on my father's side would not, I imagined, make me very acceptable. Besides, I had gathered that Miss Gascoyne was very proud. She was of good family on both sides, and the villagers spoke of her as being cold and haughty. She hardly sounded like the kind of woman who would forgive a Gascoyne a mésalliance. It was obvious that I must make her brother thoroughly understand who I was before I accepted his invitation. There was another point to be considered. Mr. Gascoyne was their uncle, and I knew that his brother had not been on good terms with him because he had married a tradesman's daughter, although from what I had seen of Mrs. Gascoyne, she had seemed to be quite fit to take her place in any family. Mr. Gascoyne might be offended if I became acquainted with his nephew and niece. I knew from one or two chance remarks which he had let fall that he bitterly resented the fact that they had never made any sign of wishing to become reconciled. I was a little astonished at this, because, after all, Mr. Gascoyne had money to leave, and I should not have thought that Harry Gascoyne was the sort of youth to allow scruples born of family pride to stand in the way of a possible access of riches. Perhaps I should discover more in the morning, that is, if my very distant cousin did not forget all about his invitation, given at a moment when he was not quite sober.

By twelve o'clock he had not put in an appearance, and I concluded that he had forgotten me. I waited till one, and was just about to ask for my bill and ride away when he appeared.

He gave me a swift glance as if to satisfy himself that the favourable opinion he had formed of me the evening before was correct. Apparently the verdict was favourable, for he insisted on my going with him.

I pleaded my attire; but he would hear of no excuse. "Well, perhaps you ought to know who I am."

"You're not a criminal, I suppose?"

"Not exactly, but I'm a cousin of yours."

He looked at me blankly.

"A cousin?"

"Yes, we had a mutual great-great-grandfather—George Gascoyne. My name is Israel Gascoyne Rank. My mother was a Gascoyne. My father was a commercial traveller."

"Oh, I say, that doesn't matter."

"I didn't suppose it would, but all the same it's just as well you should know."

He talked gaily enough as we went along. I watched him keenly, and every now and then I noticed a shadow cross his face. I could make a fair guess at the cause of it. He was wondering how he should tell his sister that the offspring of a mésalliance in the family was her guest. He would no doubt have liked to ask me to say nothing about it, but was too well-bred to do so. His chance came, however, when I informed him that I was in his uncle's office.

He turned and looked at me in amazement.

"I say, there's plenty of time—let's go down this path. It's a longer way round, but I want to talk to you. It's all a bit sudden and interesting, isn't it?" We turned down a side path where the white loose sand was strewn with pine needles.

"You know," said young Gascoyne, "my father and my uncle Gascoyne were not on speaking terms."

"I gathered as much," I remarked.

"When my cousin committed suicide I wanted to write and say how sorry I was, but my sister said she thought that it would look as if we were after his money, so I didn't."

I began to wonder if perhaps the desire to throw a very poor relation in the teeth of this independent young couple might not have had something to do with the action of Mr. Gascoyne in taking me into his business.

"My sister has curious ideas. She thinks that if a Gascoyne went into business he should have changed his name."

"There are heaps of stockbrokers of first-rate family."

"Oh, I don't agree with her in the least. I think it's all rot, and I should rather have liked to be taken up by Uncle Gascoyne, but once my sister gets an idea into her head you can't move her."

"Perhaps she may not care about entertaining me."

"Oh, she'll be civil."

"I'll go back if you like," I said. "I shan't be offended. You could not know who I was."

He stood still and thought deeply.

"No," he said, shortly, "come on, you'll oblige me by doing so. It's beastly rude of me to have hesitated. I like you, cousin Israel. You are quite different from anyone I have ever met."

I laughed. "You forget. There is my point of view. Mr. Gascoyne may not at all like my having struck up an acquaintance with you."

"Well, you can always say you didn't know."

"What, and drop you?"

"Not that, old chap." He linked his arm affectionately in mine. "We'll be great friends when I come to town, and damn it all, I'll be friends with Uncle Gascoyne whether my sister likes it or not."

I was not particularly pleased at the idea of this attractive and well-bred nephew getting into his uncle's good books; at any rate, not until Mr. Gascoyne had made me a definite promise as to my future.

I was very curious to see Miss Gascoyne. It was obvious that she was a strong character. After all, if she were distant it could not do me much harm, and I could leave soon after lunch.

We came upon the house suddenly. It was an old-fashioned place which had evidently been added to by degrees. Unexpected gables arose at every turn, and the red brick and ivy, clinging creeper, and gorgeous trails of passion flower and purple clematis were exquisitely mellow.

The place looked fairly well kept considering the limited means of the owners, and that very little of Harry Gascoyne's eight hundred a year went towards its upkeep.

"We haven't any horses since the guv'nor died—at least, that is, I've got a hack."

"You were riding the first day I saw you."

"When was that?"

I laughed. "I hope you won't think my excellent memory bad taste, but I think I saw your horse tethered to a gate one morning while you were otherwise engaged."

"By Jove! Was that you? I thought I had seen your face somewhere before."

"I wonder you did not recognise me."

"I say, don't breathe a word. It might get about. I can't keep away from her, she's so awfully pretty."

"Who is she?"

"Her father's a blacksmith. You'd never think it to hear her speak, though. I've often thought of taking her to town, but I should never be able to show my face down here again."

"It would be very awkward for your sister."

"It would be awkward altogether."

A figure in white appeared on the veranda. It was Edith Gascoyne, tall, fair, quite beautiful.

She greeted me courteously, her brother looking on nervously the while. He then hurried me off to get a brush down, and left me in his bedroom murmuring that he would be back in a minute. I was perfectly aware that he had gone to tell his sister who I was. In a few minutes he returned and I saw at a glance that his short interview had not been altogether pleasant. There was a determined look round his jaw that was somewhat unusual, and I guessed that he had been putting his foot down. If, however, he had been compelled to insist on his sister welcoming me, she certainly showed none of the chagrin of defeat in the perfect courtesy and queenliness with which she advanced to me when I came down into the drawing-room.

"My brother says we are cousins, Mr. Rank."

"Yes, it is strange my coming across him in this way, isn't it?"

"Very. I do not know my Uncle Gascoyne, but we were extremely sorry to hear of his son's tragic death. You knew him?"

"Barely. I had spoken to him once."

She waited as if expecting me to talk about young Gascoyne, but I held my tongue.

"Was my uncle very much affected?"

"Terribly. I don't think he or his wife will ever get over it."

"I am afraid he must have thought me very heartless." She evidently felt somewhat guilty at their neglect.

We went in to lunch. Everything was wonderfully well done, and I could see that she was determined to make the Grange as attractive as possible to her brother, and to give him no reason for keeping away from it. I recall that quiet Sunday lunch most vividly. The long, low dining-room with its panelled walls hung with pictures of dead and departed ancestors, the stretch of green lawn with the blue depth of the pine-wood beyond. From somewhere came the scream of a peacock, that perfect discord which only nature could have attempted. On my left at the head of the table sat Miss Gascoyne, beautiful and white, in a condition of stately and armed truce.

She managed most perfectly to import into her expression every now and then something which might remotely have laid claim to being called a smile. For the rest, she listened to me during the greater part of the meal with every appearance of attention, answering me with no vulgar or obvious intention of a desire to snub me, although her disapproval of my presence was patent.

I made her laugh, however, as soon as I had discovered the vulnerable point in her armour of gravity. Finally, I ventured an appeal to her snobbery; for I could see that she was a snob, although in her it was a vice trained and cultivated by breeding into what might have passed before the world as a virtue.

I thought that I might venture to mention Hammerton, and did so, a little fearful that she might give me to understand that it was high presumption in me to consider myself in any way interested in the feudal home of the Gascoynes.

She was, on the contrary, frankly interested.

"I have never been there," she said. "I have only met the present Lord Gascoyne once, when I was a child. My brother and I were invited to his coming-of-age, but my mother had died only very shortly before, and we did not care to go."

I shrewdly guessed that had the decision been left to her brother he might not have found his sincere grief at his mother's loss an insuperable bar to his enjoying himself at Hammerton.

I continued, watching her carefully, prepared to beat a hasty retreat should she show the least sign of disapproval at the channel into which I had directed the conversation.

"Directly I saw you to-day I noticed how very like you are to some of the portraits at Hammerton. I was only there once, but I remember one distinctly."

"I should like to see the family pictures. Do you know Lord Gascoyne?"

"Oh, dear no, not at all. I went there quite as an excursionist. It was rather quaint going round as a tripper. The remarks of the people I was with were most amusing."

The suspicion of a shadow crossed her face. She was not pleased to think of the mob tramping through those ancestral halls for which she had an almost Chinese reverence. I detected her disapproval, and hastened to add:

"They were in no way irreverent; far from it, I think they were most impressed."

"I suppose," she said, "it is good for that sort of people to be put in mind of those who have been chiefly responsible for making England what she is."

I had considerable trouble to forbear smiling as I recalled the career of some of the Gascoynes.

"That sort of people had something to do with the making of England. It was not the aristocracy who used the bow and arrow at Crecy."

We both turned with some surprise to young Gascoyne. It was a deeper remark than he usually gave vent to.

"The people are nothing without their natural leaders," Miss Gascoyne replied.

"You think the aristocracy are the natural leaders of the people?"

"Surely."

"It seems to me," I answered, for I saw that it did not flatter her to agree too readily, "that the people got very little done for them till they chose leaders of their own."

"Perhaps I ought to have said that the aristocracy are the natural leaders of the nation, and not of the people. There is a difference, is there not?"

I appreciated the concession in civility implied in the appeal. I was evidently gaining ground.

"I quite see the distinction, and it is a true paradox."

Young Gascoyne, who had seemed anxious and fearful during the first part of the meal, feeling that I had conquered and entered the outer works of at least acquaintanceship, grew happier, and said:

"Rank is afraid that Uncle Gascoyne will hardly be pleased to find that he has made friends with us."

"I am not afraid," I interposed hastily, for I saw that Miss Gascoyne had stiffened perceptibly.

"You said he was sure to be annoyed."

"That is quite a different thing. He has been very kind to me, but he can hardly expect to veto my acquaintances." I was about to say "friends," but checked myself in time and added: "Besides, I don't think he would wish to do so."

"He seems rather a jolly old chap from what you say."

"He is everything that is generous."

I made a point of always speaking enthusiastically of Mr. Gascoyne. Someone was sure sooner or later to repeat what I said.

"We should be sorry to do anything to injure your prospects, Mr. Rank." Miss Gascoyne spoke with just the faintest suspicion of stiffness.

"I don't think that is likely," I laughed.

After lunch she left us alone to smoke. Young Gascoyne wheeled two armchairs to the window, which was delightfully shaded, and, giving me an excellent cigar, seated himself opposite with a pipe, and began to talk of his love affair. Since he had discovered that I knew of the secret meetings he had been only too anxious to make a confidant of me.

"She absolutely prevents my thinking of anything else. I ought to be working, you know, but I can't. Every time I settle down to do anything I think of her—she's in my head and she stops there. The whole day long I wonder what she's doing. She's an absolute servant to those great big lubberly brothers of hers. Of course, they are kind to her in a way, but they want her to marry some lout out of the village. I don't know how it will end, I am sure."

"Oh, these things have a way of deciding themselves."

"Yes, but not always satisfactorily."

"Why, you don't think—?"

"No, I don't mean that, at least I hope to goodness not."

"You had better make up your mind to forget her and come to town."

"I couldn't do it. It isn't in me. It would take a will of iron. If my sister were a man she would do it, but then Edith couldn't have fallen in love with anybody beneath her."

This was so obviously true that it required no comment.

I was busy thinking while young Gascoyne babbled on, quite happy that he had a listener. I reflected what a very useless person he was in the world. He was quite right when he accused himself of a lack of will. The probability was that at forty he would be a confirmed toper. He was a pleasant companion enough, but had evidently as little capacity for true friendship as for anything else.

His sudden affection for me was purely fictitious. I was the nearest thing to hand, and an ordinarily amusing companion was a godsend amid his present dullness. In town he would have seen nothing of me at all, unless I could contribute to the gaiety of his life; in which case he would no doubt give me a proportionate amount of his attention. The poor girl whom he had honoured with his affection was likely to have a very bad time of it should any mischief accrue. He was lovable enough in his way, but he was of no particular value to mankind in general.

He was living in danger of at least a very sound thrashing from the girl's brothers if not from her village suitor, and it was most probable that should matters become acute he would—although not deficient in courage—leave the situation to settle itself without him, and the girl to take care of herself. Perhaps the brothers might not find out; young Gascoyne might ride away; the girl might dry her eyes and in time wed her village admirer, who would remain in ignorance of the guilty little episode in her life. If the brothers found out, were they the sort of men likely to take a violent revenge, and if they were not was the lover such a man? It was worth ascertaining. I decided to spend the next week-end at the village where the girl and her relations lived.

Later, young Gascoyne showed me over the Grange. There was not very much to see. It was a fairly roomy house, commenced in the Tudor style, and completed, or rather building operations had ceased, in the early Victorian. The latter age was marked by a hideous oblong, stucco wing devoted to servants and kitchen premises. Every other age had given the building something fairly picturesque, but the early Victorian era had given something worthy of itself. The semicircular porch with its white columns, unmistakably Carolian in character; the Elizabethan red brick and mullioned panes, the Georgian drawing-room, and low-ceilinged hall, all made a delightful jumble, and hardly deserved young Gascoyne's contemptuous remark that it was a 'ramshackle old place,' true in actual fact as such description was.

The room which had been his father's sanctum was now his; a delightful room with a south aspect and the only view which was not to a certain extent impeded by trees. Through the half open door of Miss Gascoyne's bedroom I caught a glimpse of a prie Dieu and a large crucifix above it. Evidently Miss Gascoyne was High Church and devotional.

We joined her in the garden for tea. The sun was yellowing through the pines, with here and there a faint suggestion of evening crimson, ere I rose and said good-bye. She evidently liked me, for she asked me to come again, and seconded her brother when he pressed me to run down from Saturday till Monday whenever I liked. For a Hebrew youth to have travelled so far in Miss Gascoyne's estimation in so short a time was an achievement.

Young Gascoyne walked back as far as the inn with me, talking volubly of when we should meet again and of what a lot we were to see of each other in town. I rode back thinking a good deal of Miss Gascoyne. I hold—what to the female mind is a heresy—that a man may be in love with half a dozen women at once.

Miss Gascoyne occupied my thoughts a great deal after I returned to town, and for the first few days I even thought that Sibella had been superseded. This I found not to be the case after a visit paid to the Hallwards, in the course of which Lionel Holland succeeded in rousing my jealousy to a high pitch by his ostentatious airs of proprietorship. I was in love with two women: with Sibella ecstatically as always, and with Miss Gascoyne. I was vain enough to think that the rapid change in the latter's demeanour towards me had been in spite of herself. There was between us a decided sympathy. She stood for all that, socially, I most admired.

My taste was always catholic, and her coldness and reserve attracted me immeasurably, although I was also a slave to Sibella's triviality and butterfly gaiety. The picture in each case was complete, the composition harmonious; and from the point of view of charm that is everything. Dull people may derive credit from their very dullness if they be consistent and hold their tongues; consistency achieves character and interest, but an ignoble desire to imitate some garrulous acquaintance will inevitably lead to disaster. In fact, social prominence can only be achieved by the expression of the self in its own peculiar way.

Miss Gascoyne's stately, lily-like personality had also a peculiar attraction for my Jewish blood. Her curiously vivid auburn hair, the almost marble pallor of her skin, the enormous dark blue eyes, full of a peaceful queenliness, were so alien to my own type as to subjugate the opposite in me. In my polygamous scheme I could see her nowhere except on the throne itself. Sibella might have the jewels, Edith Gascoyne would inevitably demand a share of real power. Miss

Gascoyne made me proud to have a half right to the name she bore. She inspired me with the same feeling of pride in relationship as the turrets and battlements of Hammerton had done. For some days I indulged in dreams in which she and I walked hand in hand through the social pageant, eminently the right people in the right place.

I said nothing that week to Mr. Gascoyne of my having made the acquaintance of his nephew and niece. I waited to see how matters progressed. As I thought things over I came to the conclusion that he would dislike it more than I had at first imagined. After all, it was not he who had been insulted, it was his wife, and that was the difficult thing to forgive. The young Gascoynes' opportunity had been their cousin's death. It was undoubtedly an aggravation of the estrangement that they seemed to have completely ignored the event.

I went down to Copsley, the village where Henry Gascoyne's romance dwelt, to reconnoitre. It was a fair-sized place, a village in the proper sense of the word, and not a mere hamlet.

Janet Gray's father was the blacksmith of the place, and he and two of his sons drove a thriving trade. Three more of his sons were well placed in the neighbourhood, and the sixth was a soldier, a lance corporal. Janet and her mother kept house, and from all that I could hear a happier or better managed establishment it would have been impossible to find. There was something patriarchal in the way the old blacksmith ruled his household. I have seen him, when his younger son proved rebellious, enforce his decree with a strong, effective clout. He was what would be described as an honest, God-fearing man; that is to say, he lived strictly within the conventions of his class, and would have scouted the idea that the rights and wrongs of almost every subject on earth were not to be easily grasped by a well-intentioned mind.

His daughter was his joy and delight. He was proud of her looks, which like those of all of his children were out of the common. When he stood on Sunday evening in church surrounded by his family, a more moving spectacle of physical health and primal beauty it would have been difficult to imagine.

He was also proud of his daughter's housekeeping capabilities, and not only he, but his wife and sons, looked forward with dismay to the time when some stalwart lover would claim her. Mrs. Gray almost hoped that her sons would marry and settle down first in order to avoid the desecration of her household arrangements by the unheard-of innovation of a servant.

Mrs. Gray had a sister, a spinster some years older than herself, who, having entered the service of the Gascoynes many years before, had never left it, but had become an institution in the family. The two sisters were devoted, and it had long been their habit to see each other at least once a week. Sometimes Janet accompanied her mother, and when Mrs. Gray was unable to go, for she suffered somewhat from rheumatism, her daughter went alone.

It was on one of these expeditions that she had met young Gascoyne. He had related the circumstances to me a dozen times.

"She was coming back to the station through the pine-trees, and I was struck all of a heap, bowled over first time. I don't know how it all came about, but we talked about her aunt. It was something to go on with. It took me a long time to persuade her to meet me, though."

Judging by the character and determination in the faces of old Gray and his sons, it did not appear that the man who trifled with their womankind would have a very pleasant time of it. It was the identity of her rustic suitor, however, that I was anxious to discover. I was not long in doing so, for he haunted the Gray threshold. Personally, had I been in Janet's place, I should not have hesitated a moment between the magnificent specimen of manhood who was anxious to make her his wife, and the spoilt and vicious youth, who, if her ruin could have been accomplished with safety, would have regarded it as a mere pleasurable and excusable incident in his life.

Nat Holway was in every way a splendid fellow. His occasional violence of temper was a part of the general strenuousness of his character. He was slowly conquering this failing, however, and was likely to make the same sort of man as Janet's father. He had never known any other sweetheart. It had, at least as he thought, been an understood thing between them since they were children. He delayed speaking just a little too long, and it was after young Gascoyne had appeared on the scene that he asked her to be his wife. To his amazement and the no little surprise of her friends she refused him. Ignorant of the existence of Harry Gascoyne in his relation to Janet, they looked around vainly for a cause.

Was there anybody else in the village? True, young Tom Applin had come round with an obviously serious intent, but Janet had very soon shown him that she did not care for him. There were others, but, as she had never encouraged them in any way whatever, they did not suggest themselves as a reason for her refusal of Nat Holway. The only excuse she would give was that she did not care sufficiently about Nat to marry him.

"But, Janet, you've always given us to understand—" commenced Mrs. Gray.

"Oh, but that was when we were children."

"No, Janet, that is not quite true. It's not so long ago that I was talking of you both settling down, and it didn't seem but what you favoured the idea."

Janet did not answer, but shut herself in her room and, unlocking a drawer, took out of it a little jewelled trinket which young Gascoyne had given her, and kissing it passionately, burst into a flood of tears. The poor girl vaguely realised, if she refused to confess as much to herself, that her romance was doomed to a dismal ending. Though she loved Harry Gascoyne she had some dim perception that the glitter of his charm was largely pinchbeck. She also realised with true feminine instinct that she had thrown away the only weapon with which she might have won her battle, and induced him to raise her to his position by marriage. She was already terrified of what might happen, and lay awake at nights possessed by the fear of an approaching presence. She was haunted by the singing of the wind in the pine-wood where they had first kissed, and stronger and stronger through the sad, sweet music came the wailing of an infant.

Young Gascoyne was almost as frightened as she at what he had done, and his true character asserted itself. He positively throbbed with selfishness. He poured out his woes to me at length. He would begin with some stereotyped recognition of the girl's position, thrown in for the sake of mere decency, but after that it was all about the awkwardness of the affair as it would affect himself.

"I'm not a coward, old chap, and I don't mind a good stand-up fight. I can take a licking as well as any other man, and bear no grudge."

This I doubted, and set it down as merely the boastful jargon learnt at a public school.

"But I don't quite see having to fight the whole lot of them."

"They look awkward customers."

"Why, have you seen them?"

I had made a slip. I had not informed him of my visit to Copsley.

"I was passing through on my bicycle, and I just thought I would have a look in at the blacksmith's shop."

"My sister will never forgive me. You see, Janet is old nurse's niece. By Jove, it is a muddle."

He spoke as if the whole affair were not of his doing and as if he were the victim of a conspiracy.

It was the occasion of my spending a week-end at the Grange.

He discussed many ways of solving the difficulty.

"I shall take her away. There's nothing else to be done."

"You will be followed."

"Not if we go abroad. That'll be the thing. Edith will come round in time. I shouldn't wonder, once Janet were away from that common lot, if she didn't improve till one wouldn't mind taking her anywhere."

I was surprised to find that he was in earnest about eloping, but his was not a nature to look very far ahead, and he talked of being able to get along at some quiet foreign town as if he were not the sort of person in whom such an existence would bring out all the worst qualities. At any rate, I was determined to run no risks. I had made too many inquiries about Nat Holway not to be able to predict with some certainty what he would do if he discovered the truth.

I posted an anonymous letter from the next village to Copsley written in an illiterate scrawl. It informed him of Janet's stolen meetings, and hinted the worst.

CHAPTER X

I HAD by this time informed Mr. Gascoyne of my acquaintance with his nephew and niece. At first he looked hurt.

"They are very heartless, I am afraid, Israel, very heartless; when my poor boy died neither of them wrote a line."

"I am afraid, sir, that young Gascoyne has not much depth, but his sister seems to me a fine character."

"What is she like?"

"Beautiful."

Perhaps something in my voice betrayed what I felt, for he looked at me keenly.

"She is a little cold. Difficult, I should say, to rouse to enthusiasm, and she appears to have a will of iron."

"She hardly sounds alluring."

"She has charm."

"Ah! Then everything else falls into line. I should like to see them, but I can hardly make the advances. You see, my poor brother chose to quarrel with me for two reasons; first, because I went on the Stock

Exchange; secondly, because my wife's father happened to have made his money in trade. It was all very foolish, but year after year reconciliation grew more difficult, and what had been a breach which I thought could easily be bridged any moment widened imperceptibly, until it was impossible to make advances. If Miss Gascoyne would write to my wife the thing would be done."

Inwardly I thought it would have been just as easy for Mrs. Gascoyne to write to her.

"What is Harry like? His father was good-looking."

"He is handsome enough."

"Fair?"

"Very."

"So was his father. Dear me, it seems only the other day that we were boys together. It is all very sad, very sad indeed. It is incredible that people should drift apart so."

"I've never had anyone to drift apart from."

"You have your friends. There is young Hallward. He seems to be very devoted to you, and, do you know, I have sometimes wondered whether you appreciate his devotion."

"Oh, I'm very fond of Grahame."

"We must see if something can't be done to bring my nephew and niece and my wife together. You say you are going down there this week?"

"I thought of doing so."

"Then you might spy out the land and see how my niece would be likely to receive advances."

"I think Miss Gascoyne would welcome them," I said, with simulated warmth.

I now felt not the least hesitation in praising the young Gascoynes. I had complete confidence in my position with their uncle. He was not the sort of man to commit an injustice, and what he had made up his mind to do for me he would do; perhaps more, certainly not less.

It may perhaps be wondered why, having a comfortable position and fairly assured prospects, I did not rest content. That I did not do so was due to a consistency of aim which has always been my chief characteristic. In removing young Gascoyne from my path I had burnt my boats, and there did not appear to be any particular reason, except that of cowardice, to prevent my pursuing my original purpose. A middle-class position with moderate wealth in no way represented my ideal. I had dreamed from early childhood of a brilliant position, and if possible I intended to achieve one.

I found also that I was a person of a multiplying ambition. I had begun to meet certain people in a very good set. My musical accomplishments here stood me in very good stead—as they have done many another idle young adventurer. Lady Pebworth, who was an amateur vocalist who would not have been tolerated at a tenth-rate pier pavilion without her title, was singing at a charity concert at which I was assisting. Her accompanist failing her, I took his place. She declared that no one had ever accompanied her so sympathetically, and asked me to call. I was not of the order of modern youth who gives some great lady the use of his inferior baritone voice and other services in return for social protection, but Lady Pebworth had the tact to treat me with dignity, and I found her extremely useful. I paid my respects one Sunday afternoon. The drawing-room of her house in Bryanston Square was crowded, and I at once realised that I was in the society of people of quite a different tone from anything I had hitherto come into contact with. Fortunately her invitation had not been merely formal. She had evidently been anxious to see me, for she welcomed me with a swift glance of pleasure and came from the extreme end of the long room to meet me.

"How good of you to come so soon!"

"It was good of you to ask me."

Then she introduced me to a pretty, dark-eyed woman, whose beauty was just giving signs of approaching wane.

"Mrs. Hetherington, Mr. Rank." And she left us.

Mrs. Hetherington talked incessantly, but I replied in monosyllables. I realised that Lady Pebworth was interested, and my vanity was flattered that a woman, so evidently admired and courted in a first-rate set, should be attracted by me. I could see that she was very much aware of my presence whilst seeming to be engrossed by the conversation of a man of distinguished appearance suggesting diplomacy. A feeble-looking young man with rather a pleasant laugh joined in the conversation between Mrs. Hetherington and myself. He was evidently inquisitive as to who I might be, and threw out one or two baits which I avoided.

Mrs. Hetherington droned on about Lord this and Lady that—if she mentioned commoners at all they possessed double-barrelled names—until there was a general movement to go. I rose with the others, but Lady Pebworth with the greatest cleverness managed to avoid saying good-bye to me till everyone else had gone and we were left alone. Mrs. Hetherington, who was the last to leave, looked at me with the insolent curiosity of good breeding as she was making her farewells, evidently fully conscious of her hostess's manoeuvring.

"Are you in a great hurry?" asked Lady Pebworth, as the door closed behind Mrs. Hetherington.

"Oh, no."

"Then sit down and let us talk. I must have some fresh tea, and you will have something stronger."

I explained that I seldom drank anything stronger than tea.

She looked at me curiously.

"Dear me! You don't look a puritan."

I laughed. The expression as applied to myself sounded quite comic.

"I am afraid my virtue has its origin in vanity. I confine myself to champagne, and that only occasionally."

"You are quite right. It is dreadful the objects young men make of themselves with drink—and women, too, when they cease to attract."

"Do they ever realise when that time has come?"

"Yes, most women are philosophical enough for that."

"Women with charm need never cease to attract."

"That is very true, but you are young to have found it out. It is usually a discovery of the middle-aged."

"Age is not altogether a question of years."

I found Lady Pebworth a mental tonic. She made me talk as I had never talked before, indeed, as I had never known myself capable of talking.

I realised that I had made a distinct impression, and found myself calculating how far she might be useful to me.

She evidently knew everyone worth knowing. She could undoubtedly launch me in the great world if she cared to do so, and I was quite confident of my ability to keep afloat providing I had a really good introduction. I could not help smiling as I reflected how envious Lionel Holland would have been could he have witnessed my *tête-à-tête* with Lady Pebworth.

Later Lord Pebworth came in. He was the personification of the elderly well-bred. It was not probable that he had ever possessed many brains, but he had the amount of conscience which causes a man highly placed to do the right thing at the right moment. He was devoid of enthusiasm, and being eminently safe had even achieved a second-rate position as a politician, which he was quite persuaded was a first-rate one. He treated his wife's young men friends—and I discovered afterwards that they had been a numerous procession—with kindly toleration, and even went out of his way to give them a good time when it lay in his power.

He seconded his wife's invitation to dinner with great cordiality, and accompanied me as far as the front door, an attention which was so unexpected that I began to wonder whether he regarded me as a suspicious character. He gave me an excellent cigar, and I walked down Park Lane in the red light of a Sunday evening in summer, feeling that socially, I had moved on.

Lady Pebworth took me up feverishly, and introduced me to a great many people who seemed quite pleased to know me. Nevertheless, I realised that I should have to make hay whilst the sun shone, for unless I persuaded my new acquaintances to accept me as an intimate I should very soon be dropped. Great ladies have a way of carrying young men into the vortex of society to which they have not been accustomed, and then, when weary, leaving them to be slowly slain by general indifference, till they are only too glad to find themselves back again in their proper middle-class element.

I did not consider the middle-class my element, and I was determined that Lady Pebworth should keep me afloat as long as I chose and not as long as she chose.

As I was engaged in snaring young Gascoyne, I was only able to give her a divided attention. This turned out to be as well, for she concluded that there was another woman, and her interest in me was fanned by jealousy. She tried all manner of arts in order to discover who claimed my attention, arts which she imagined were undetected, but at which I was secretly amused.

Mr. Gascoyne used to chaff me good-naturedly about my smart acquaintances. Some employers in his position might have resented one of his clerks spending his spare time among people who would most probably lead him into extravagance; but Mr. Gascoyne, well born himself, hardly saw the incongruity of it to the extent that an ordinary middle-class commercial man would have done.

At the time I met Gascoyne my affair with Lady Pebworth was in full swing. That is to say, I was getting tired of her, for she had never really meant anything to me. She was beginning to reproach me with neglect, and to take exception to my Saturdays and Sundays being occupied.

I knew how far Lady Pebworth could be useful to me, and I was certainly not going to drop the solid substance of a position in my own right for the shadow of her social introductions.

It was quite extraordinary how ready people were to accept and make use of a young man who carried no other credentials than the good word of a pretty Countess with a reputation for being rapid. I found myself dancing every evening with the peerage. I cannot honestly say that I received many invitations to dinner, or to those more select entertainments which argue any great degree of intimacy. My keen instinct warned me of the unreality of my position and of how necessary it was to make ties of some kind to enable me to retain my hold on society. The men were civil enough, but I had little in common with those who talked nothing but the jargon they had learned at a public school or at one of the 'Varsities.

I had the extreme satisfaction of being seen in a box at the Gaiety by Lionel Holland and Sibella while I was with Lord and Lady Pebworth and Sir Anthony Cross, a friend of theirs.

"What a very beautiful girl," said Lady Pebworth, as I bowed to Sibella.

"Quite lovely," said Lord Pebworth.

Sir Anthony Cross said nothing, but I repeatedly caught him looking at Sibella when Lady Pebworth was not using his opera glasses.

"Who is the man with her?" asked Lady Pebworth.

"Lionel Holland."

"Is he a friend of yours?"

"I know him. I went to school with him."

"I see you don't like him. He looks a bounder."

Lady Pebworth had in her conversation just that amount of frankness which may be permitted to an obviously well-bred woman without its giving offence.

As we were going out I found myself by the side of Sibella for a moment.

"You hardly ever come and see us now," she murmured.

Sibella never lost her charm for me, and the sound of her voice—always a little sharp and unmusical, even when she made an attempt at modulating it, which was seldom—played upon my temperament in the most subtle manner.

I promised to visit them quite soon.

"Next Sunday?" she asked.

"I am going out of town next Sunday."

Lady Pebworth's carriage drew up, and, murmuring something about the Sunday after, I left her.

"Your friend, Mr. Rank," said Lady Pebworth, "is decidedly pretty."

"One of the prettiest girls I have ever set eyes on," said Lord Pebworth.

Sir Anthony Cross still said nothing, but I had a shrewd conviction that he was more impressed than either.

On Saturday I bicycled down to stay with the Gascoynes till Monday, having promised my employer to do all which tactful diplomacy might accomplish to find out how they would take an effort at a reconciliation.

I went a certain part of the way by train, and sent my bag on. I had written to say that I should not be at the Grange for dinner, and found myself riding through a crimson summer evening with a sensuous enjoyment in the perfect peace of the rural scenery through which I was passing. According to the received notion of a man with a murder on his conscience, external objects, however beautiful, should have been unable to convey any sensation of peace to my inner being. So far from this being the case I was immensely soothed, and rode leisurely on with as much moral quiet as is enjoyed by most folk. After all, the degree of power of the conscience is entirely a matter of individuality and force of character. A weak man, hypersensitive to received social obligation, may fret himself into a fever over the merest trifle of a moral lapse. I do not believe the aged Cenci slept the less well for—in the world's opinion—his awful crimes. I have no doubt his affectionate family found him in a comfortable doze when they came to bring him a deeper sleep. The rate at which one great crime will develop a man's intelligence is curious. It is a wonderful grindstone on which to sharpen the intellect. New values, hitherto unsuspected, develop themselves on all sides. An acute and sardonic appreciation of society's laws presents itself, together with an exhilarating sensation of being outside them, which assists in forming an unbiassed and comprehensive view. I could never have belonged to the anarchical type of man, because I never had any comprehension of or sympathy with those who starve in a land of plenty. I could not understand the intellect which could live in a dream of a society regenerated by revolution in the future, and which was yet unable to help itself to a crust of bread in the present. My abilities were essentially practical, so I removed those who were immediately in my way and left the dreamers to remove those whom they esteemed to be in the way of society.

I was indulging in such reflections as these when I passed the lane down which I had turned the day I had discovered young Gascoyne's love affair. The sun had almost set. Already the greater part of the landscape was in shadow. The song of the birds was silenced by the chill of coming night, and they slept. On the horizon the crimson blaze had sunk, and an expiring streak of amber marked where the day had passed. The evening star shone solitary, a little pale for the moment, a faint flame set in a ghastly pallor. I turned down the lane of the romantic memory; why, I could not have said, unless, perhaps, some occult informing power gave me a premonition of what I should find there. The actual road track was quite narrow, there being a wide expanse of grass on each side. I had not gone very far before I saw a figure lying in a curiously huddled heap close to the hedge. I knew it was young Gascoyne at a glance. The expected had happened. My heart almost leapt into my mouth. How seldom schemes carried as well as mine had done! I got off my bicycle and looked stealthily around. There was not a soul in sight. The growing dusk of the lane gave birth to one or two shadows which somewhat startled me as I went towards the body. As I turned him over to look at his face a low groan escaped him.

He was not dead. This was awkward. His face was covered with blood, and there was a terrible wound in the side of his head, while his jaw hung loose as if it were broken. An idea struck me. I lifted his head. I almost fancied that I saw his eyes open, and that even in the gloom he recognised me. I hastened to put my idea into execution. I pressed my fingers gently to the veins behind his neck. I knew that this would produce an absolute insensibility which must inevitably end in death unless succour arrived within quite a short space of time.

After a few minutes I laid him back an inert mass on the turf, and, mounting my bicycle, reached the main road without meeting anyone.

I could not help regretting as I rode leisurely on to the Grange that it was Miss Gascoyne's brother whom I had been compelled to dispose of, but I agreed with the writer who warned the ambitious that they must subordinate their affections to their aims in life if they wished to succeed. It is curious how affection can be subdued. For instance, I loved Sibella, but I was able to subdue my infatuation and keep it out of sight when necessary.

It was quite dark when I reached the Grange, and riding through the fir plantation I was entirely dependent on the light thrown from my bicycle lamp. Suddenly I received a weird reminder of the figure I had left behind me lying half concealed in the fern and bracken by the roadside. Perhaps I was a little more affected by what had happened than I imagined, for I am not superstitious, and only by reason of having young Gascoyne's image vividly in my mind can I account for what happened.

Half-way through the plantation the light of my lamp fell full on a white, human face dabbled in blood. It was young Gascoyne's face, and the blue eyes were wide open and glazed in death. I saw the head and trunk to the waist. The rest of the body appeared to be beneath the ground. So strong was the illusion that I swerved aside in order not to ride over it, and in doing so fell from my machine. When I picked myself up my lamp was out and I was in total darkness. I was about to hurry forward with a mad haste to get out of the wood when I pulled myself up short. Deliberately I remained where I was, picked up my bicycle, lit my lamp and mounting leisurely rode slowly out of the plantation. With such a career as I had planned it would never do to give way to fancies.

There was a light in the drawing-room as I wheeled my bicycle up the drive of the Grange. I could see Miss Gascoyne sitting by a small table with a lamp on it. At first I thought she was reading, but as I drew near I could see that the book was lying in her lap, whilst her eyes were fixed on the ground in deep reflection. She came out into the hall when she heard my voice. I thought there was an unusual animation in her appearance as she welcomed me.

"Have you dined?"

"Well, not exactly, but I had an enormous tea at a wayside inn."

"You look very tired."

Evidently I still looked somewhat agitated by my adventure in the pine wood. No doubt for want of another explanation it must have struck her as fatigue.

"I have had rather a busy week."

We moved towards the dining-room chatting freely and pleasantly, and I could not help contrasting her present friendliness with the hauteur and strictly formal manner she had displayed at our first meeting.

We sat and talked while I ate sandwiches.

"Harry said he was going to meet you."

"I rather thought he might do so, and I looked out for him."

"It is very rude of him not to have done so, or not to have been at home when you came. I shall scold him severely."

She began to talk of her brother and his future. She wanted him to read for the law. Did I not think it would be the best thing?

"Do you really want my candid opinion?"

"Of course. You know I say what I mean."

"I think it is about the very worst profession he could follow."

"But why?"

"Well, apart from the difficulty of the examinations, which in our days is no small matter, it is a profession in which patience is the most important factor. There is no other profession like it for encouraging a naturally lazy man with a small income to idle."

"I should have thought application was altogether necessary."

"Absolutely, but it is optional. He cannot get on without it, but there will be no one to see that he uses his time well. Besides, men in the law are as a rule strenuous, earnest people with all kinds of ambitions, and Harry will hardly meet sympathetics."

"Then what is he to do?"

"I know you will think it rather a curious suggestion, coming from me, but I give my vote for the Army."

"The Army? But Harry is poor."

I inwardly smiled at Miss Gascoyne's notion of poverty. I knew what she thought the Army should mean for a Gascoyne:—a crack cavalry regiment and unlimited private means.

"An inexpensive line regiment."

"Oh dear!"

I laughed. "It's the thing, depend upon it. He will be in a profession he likes, among men who take their profession seriously. After all, he will have a better average of gentlemen than he would have in a crack regiment, even if he does not have the high nobility of exceptions."

"I see what you mean, but I don't think Harry would ever consent."

"I believe you could make him do anything."

I was inwardly congratulating myself on the perfect conviction with which I was discussing the future of one who by this time was most probably solving problems in theology.

We talked on till Miss Gascoyne grew anxious.

"I really wish Harry would come home."

"Shall I go and look for him?"

She knew what was in my mind. His late homecoming meant as a rule that he was to be found at the inn.

"Was he at home to dinner?"

"No. He has some friends living a few miles off whom I don't know, and he rode over in the afternoon and proposed to stay to dinner. There he is."

We both listened. Along the hard road came the sound of a horse's hoofs.

Miss Gascoyne rose in alarm. Either the horse was riderless or it was no longer under control. It was not necessary to listen for more than a few seconds to be convinced of that.

We both went out on to the lawn. A figure came round the corner of the house and hastened on to the road. It was the groom.

"Oh, Mr. Rank, what can have happened?"

"I will go and see."

But she went with me to the gate. The mare had evidently come to a full stop just outside, and was now held by the groom. She was steaming with sweat and gave every evidence of the greatest distress.

Inwardly I was wondering how it was the animal had been so long in reaching the Grange. It must have wandered on slowly feeding by the wayside till it had taken fright at some passing object and started at full gallop for home.

Miss Gascoyne looked around in dismay for her brother.

"She wur alone, Miss," said the groom, blankly.

"It doesn't at all follow that your brother was on her back when she bolted," I ventured.

She looked at me, grateful for the suggestion. She was very white, but her character asserted itself. She turned to the groom.

"Baker, take Jenny round to the stables and make her comfortable as soon as possible. Mr. Rank and I will walk as far as the inn and you can follow us."

"Very good, Miss." The man did as he was directed.

"I will go as I am," she said, "though after all I may be alarming myself unnecessarily." She was not the woman to treat the situation hysterically if it could possibly be avoided. I was genuinely sorry for the grief that was coming upon her. I would have spared her if possible, but I either had to abandon the object of my life or to put up with such unpleasantnesses as were involved with the course I had laid out for myself.

We started to walk rapidly towards the inn.

"I dare say Harry missed his stirrup and Jenny bolted."

On the way her spirits rose. The fact that we met no one seemed to her a proof that nothing much was the matter. Sounds of drunken revelry reached us long before the inn came in sight.

"I will wait here," she said, as we reached the broadening of the road. I left her and went on.

"We'll all be merry,
Drinking whisky, wine, and sherry,
If he can't come, we'll ask his son."

The chorus was trolled forth in disjointed snatches, showing the singers to be very far gone indeed. The door stood ajar and I went in. So convinced was I of the necessity of playing my part thoroughly that I looked carefully round to see if Harry Gascoyne were present. The half-dozen or so roysterers looked up stupidly with open mouths. As a matter of fact, they were none of them drinking whisky, wine or sherry, but had very substantial mugs of ale before them. The atmosphere was thick with tobacco smoke and heavy with the reek from peasant limbs. The landlord, with a figure that threatened apoplexy, surveyed them from the other side of the bar with an approving smile as if he were presiding over an assemblage of highly well-behaved infants. To me he suggested a genial but relentless ghoul, callous to the feelings of the mothers and children who were to welcome home these repulsive sots as governors and lords of their lives and welfare.

They sat waiting for me to speak.

"Has Mr. Gascoyne been here to-night?" I asked.

The landlord looked round the room, and, having as it were satisfied himself that none of the others knew of the young man being concealed unknown to himself, answered slowly:

"I ain't seen 'im."

"No more ain't I," came in phlegmatic chorus.

"Are you quite sure?"

"Quite."

"Thank you." I withdrew.

Miss Gascoyne came forward out of the dusk into the light which streamed from the front door.

"He's not there," I said gravely.

She looked at me in dismay.

"Shall I tell them?" I asked.

She reflected for a moment.

"Yes. He may have fallen from his horse. We must look for him at once."

I turned towards the inn.

"I will come with you," she said, and we passed through the low door.

The song had not been resumed. Evidently my errand had given food for conversation. The landlord paused in the middle of something he was saying and got down off his stool.

"Mr. Gascoyne's horse has returned home without him, and we are afraid he may have been thrown and hurt." I spoke in a loud tone.

At the sight of Miss Gascoyne the whole assemblage had risen. She was looked upon by the cottagers around with not a little awe.

"Will some of you oblige me by helping to look for him?"

The landlord, who had had more than one passage of arms with the justices of the peace as to the way in which his house was conducted, became officiousness itself. Anything to prove to the gentry what an estimable and respectable character he was.

"It ain't like Mr. Gascoyne to get into trouble on horseback," he said, with a laudatory shake of his head, as if to conciliate Miss Gascoyne by conveying to her what a very high sense he had of her brother's horsemanship.

He evidently had an idea of offering her some refreshment, for he looked from her to the bottles of spirit and coloured cordials on the shelf, and from them back again to her, but apparently without being able to make up his mind to so hazardous a proceeding.

As we were all standing outside the inn debating how to conduct the search, a dog-cart drove up.

"Let me see, I am right for the Grange, am I not?" asked a voice.

"Yes," I answered, "but whom do you want at the Grange?"

"Miss Gascoyne."

"I am Miss Gascoyne."

There was a silence. The man in the dog-cart was evidently somewhat taken aback. He was saved from further awkwardness by the character of the woman he had to deal with.

"I am afraid something has happened. What is it?"

"Your brother has had an accident."

"Is he hurt?"

"I am afraid so."

The answer was inconclusive, and it was obviously intended that it should be.

"Seriously?"

"I am afraid so."

The answer was still lacking in finality, and Miss Gascoyne guessed the worst.

We all stood round, the men looking stupid but concerned.

"Will you take me to him, please?"

"I came to fetch you."

"Will you come too, Mr. Rank?"

"Of course." I turned to the landlord's wife, who had now joined us. "Can you find a shawl for Miss Gascoyne? She has no hat."

The landlady disappeared, and returned with a white woollen shawl, which she was taking out of tissue paper.

"When was he found?" asked Miss Gascoyne, as we drove rapidly away, leaving the little group outside the public-house to discuss the matter.

"About two hours and a half ago."

"Where!"

The doctor explained, throwing into his account as much insinuation as he could of the worst. I don't know at what particular moment Miss Gascoyne grasped that her brother was dead, but it was apparent before we reached our destination that she had realised the truth.

He had been carried to a farmhouse, from whence they had sent for the doctor.

"I am afraid he was kicked by his horse. I cannot for the life of me imagine how it could have happened to so fine a horseman."

The doctor ended a little lamely. Young Gascoyne's propensities were too well known for miles round his home for anyone to be ignorant of them.

I felt somewhat uncomfortable as we turned down the lane where I had left Harry Gascoyne. The doctor made no remark as we passed the spot where I knew he had been found.

I was full of curiosity as to how his sister would behave.

As we descended from the dog-cart, the doctor turned to her.

"I hope I have made myself clear."

Miss Gascoyne stood silent for a few seconds, struggling for self-control. Then she answered quietly:

"Quite. You mean that my brother is dead?"

The doctor nodded his head gravely.

It was curious evidence of the apartness of Miss Gascoyne's character that the woman of the house, a buxom, garrulous body, made no attempt at comfort. She at once realised that it would have been an intrusion.

Miss Gascoyne went upstairs with the doctor. She was not away long, and when she returned I saw that she must give way soon, or a mental catastrophe would ensue. Her features were rigid.

I went upstairs at her request.

All signs of violence had already been removed, and he lay as if asleep. Any indications of vice and intemperance had disappeared, and he looked very boyish and beautiful. The doctor was in the room.

"I don't quite see," he said, in a low voice, "how a mere kick or two could have inflicted such injuries. I don't mean, of course, that kicks could not have caused his death, but the blows seem as if they had been struck by a blunt instrument, directed with less velocity than would have been the case with a horse's hoof. I am waiting for a colleague, and then we must make a serious examination."

I murmured that I was no authority. I could not help reflecting how much Harry Gascoyne had been the gainer by dying when he did. Instead of growing into a debauched, worn-out old man, his physical casket lay before us in all the freshness of its youth and beauty. He would leave beautiful instead of ugly memories.

Yes, it was well he had died. His sister might continue to worship him and to preserve her illusions.

She returned to the Grange, and I, having left her to the care of the old housekeeper, went to the inn, though it struck me as being somewhat ridiculous to observe the conventions at such a time.

I did not believe for one moment that the blows which had struck young Gascoyne were from the horse's hoofs. Before leaving the house, however, I went round to the stables. There was no one about, and the mare was by this time as quiet as a lamb.

I examined her hoofs carefully. There was not the least trace of blood—at any rate, not observable to myself. If there were any traces, they must be microscopic.

I sat down on an upturned pail and reflected. I should like to save Nat Holway—that is to say, if he had not already given himself up, which with a nature such as his was quite possible.

Would it help him to smear the horse's hind hoofs with blood? It was worth trying. Where was I to get the blood from? There was only one source, and that was myself.

I am not brave about blood, but the occasion demanded urgent measures. I took out my pocket-knife, and deliberately drew the blade across the little finger of my left hand. I then smeared the hoofs of the horse and, binding my finger, left the stable. The dawn was just beginning to lay ghostly hands on the garment of night. The stars trembled and burned pale in the growing light.

Through the firs the coming day gave almost the effect of an expanse of water beyond. In the cheerless air there was a touch of clamminess which suggested rain, whilst heavy, sulky-looking clouds were driven slowly towards the east.

I walked with a melancholy step along the sandy path that led through the plantation. What would poor Janet Gray do? I made a point of letting my sympathies have as much play as was compatible with my own interest. As a matter of fact, her situation was slightly bettered, excepting that her lover was dead—than which no greater grief can come to any human being. But at the same time she would receive a much larger meed of pity than would otherwise have been her lot.

If Nat Holway were fool enough to give himself up it would be unpleasant, although I could not forget that even if he had not actually accomplished his purpose, it had been his full intention to murder Harry Gascoyne. Still, he was a fine fellow, and it was not nice to think of lives unnecessarily wasted. The next afternoon I would go over to Copsley and reconnoitre. I must confess that I found the whole thing very exciting, especially as I myself stood in absolutely no danger.

On returning to the inn I found the landlord waiting up for me, a great feat for a man who was usually somewhat heavy with alcohol. He plied me with questions, and appeared terribly shocked at the sad catastrophe.

"Such an open-handed young gentleman, sir, and his sister doting on him as she did. Well, there, you never know. The Lord has His own way of doing things."

He sighed and looked as if to say that were it not for this undeniable fact he might be prevailed upon to take a hand in the management of the universe.

I lay open-eyed, tossing from side to side. Miss Gascoyne stood between myself and sleep. Although I could put an irrevocable fact like death out of my mind I could not dismiss a living grief so easily. I knew that she was capable of terrible suffering. Her brother had been her all. At the same time, while feeling acutely for her I could not help reflecting what a much better match she would now be. Sixteen hundred a year was not great wealth, but when combined with a woman like Miss Gascoyne it was a prize worth having.

I believe there is not the character, however elevated, which does not at a moment of supreme grief calculate the particular degree of benefit or disadvantage it will obtain from it.

It was noon when I walked over to the Orange to ask how Miss Gascoyne was. The servant said her mistress particularly desired to be informed of my arrival, and I went into the inner hall and waited. She came down almost immediately. I was shocked at the change in her appearance. She had evidently been weeping bitterly, and for a moment I would have given anything to restore her brother to her. The weakness was only momentary, however, and after all it would have been doing her a very bad turn.

She appeared to derive a certain degree of comfort and help from my presence.

"It seems a little sad, Mr. Rank, that although we have so many relations there is hardly one to whom I could write at this emergency."

This was a great opportunity to please Mr. Gascoyne by obtaining her consent to send for him. There were also other schemes in my head, nebulous as yet, which such a reconciliation would assist materially.

"I should have thought," I said gently, "that your father's brother would be the proper person to send for under the circumstances."

She looked at me in surprise. The idea had evidently not struck her, and she became thoughtful.

"I am afraid he would not come."

"I think he would. I know it hurt his feelings somewhat that when his son died neither you nor your brother wrote to him."

"He told you so?"

"Yes."

"I will send a telegram."

"Let me take it."

She went to her desk and wrote several.

"The groom can take them," she said, as I rose.

"No, let me. I shall be quicker on my bicycle, and it will be something to do."

"It is very poor entertainment for you."

"Anything I can do to serve you. Your brother and I were great friends."

Most of the telegrams were conventional intimations of the news to relatives and friends. That to Mr. Gascoyne ran:

"My brother has been killed by an accident. I am in great trouble; would you come to me?"

My plan was that Miss Gascoyne should make friends with her uncle and aunt and that we four should form a harmonious quartet, and that finally I should marry her, and Mr. Gascoyne should leave us his money.

I fully realised all my own disabilities in Miss Gascoyne's eyes. The Semitic taint in my appearance could not possibly be a recommendation, and my parentage would certainly be a bar. There was no disguising the fact that my father was not, to the world's way of thinking, a gentleman, and from what I could remember I was inclined in strict honesty to agree with the world.

I was not so far even the adopted heir of Mr. Gascoyne, and I was running a grave risk in introducing a considerably nearer blood relation bearing his own name into the house. I did not fear that Mr. Gascoyne would do anything less for me than he had intended, but he might do considerably less than I had intended. He was just the sort of man to admire Miss Gascoyne. Still, should I fail in my scheme, she already had an ample fortune, and was no claimant for relief. I sent off the telegram, but did not return to the house. I gathered that Miss Gascoyne would wish to be alone, and contented myself with sending over a message that I was at the inn should she want me, and that I should remain there till Mr. Gascoyne arrived. She sent back a grateful note thanking me, and asking me to come over in the evening.

In the afternoon I mounted my bicycle and rode to Copsley.

The little village lay still as death in the burning sun. The boys and young men were probably lounging about the adjacent lanes and fields, whilst the older people were taking their Sunday afternoon rest.

The blacksmith's shop was shut, the great worm-eaten doors barred with a massive piece of iron. The house next door, with its trim garden and green shutters, which evidenced the prosperity of the Grays, was in silence.

Or was I mistaken?

I was wheeling my machine, and I paused with my back to the house and bent down, ostensibly to set something defective right. There was the sound of faint sobbing in the house behind me. At the same time I heard footsteps coming along the street. I looked up. It was Nat Holway. His face was impassive, but his features were set. Almost at the same moment the door of the house opened, and Mr. Gray came out.

Apparently he was expecting Nat Holway. They went into the forge together. Old Gray's face was white and stern.

I guessed that they had an appointment, and were keeping it there in order that they might talk undisturbed. I wondered if by any chance Nat Holway was offering to take Janet's shame upon his shoulders. He was the sort of man to do it. Really, if such a thing did happen, and the murderer were not suspected, what a convenient settlement it would be. I should have obtained what I wanted, Janet Gray would in time be happy, and Miss Gascoyne would remain in ignorance of her brother's peccadillo. It is certainly rare that matters move so easily along the ways of common-sense.

I rode back to the inn to find a telegram from Mr. Gascoyne to his niece which she had sent over for me to see. It was to say that he would come by the evening train. There were only four trains to Copsley Station on Sunday—two each way—and the London train did not arrive till ten o'clock. I saw her in the early evening. She seemed worn out with grief, and there was, I thought, a quite tragic loneliness in her appearance.

It pleased her to talk of her dead brother, and, sitting there saying all the nice things I could about him, and full of a real and genuine sympathy for her, I could hardly realise that it was I who had knelt in the dusky lane with my fingers on the dying youth's throat.

"He had a great admiration for you," she said, with a faint smile. "He thought you the cleverest person he had ever met."

"His was one of the sunniest natures; no one could help loving him."

"He was spoilt, of course. My father spoilt him terribly. It was not to be wondered at if he was a little wild."

I allowed her to talk on till I rose to go and meet Mr. Gascoyne.

"I don't know why," she said, as she came out into the lane with me, "but I have always imagined my uncle to be a very hard man. I read 'Nicholas Nickleby' when I was a little girl, and I could not help drawing a comparison between my father, who was like Nicholas's father, and lived in the country, and my uncle, who, of course, represented Ralph Nickleby."

I smiled. "You will find Mr. Gascoyne very different from that. He is much softened of late, but I don't think that he has ever been a miser, even if at times he has carried the principle of justice to the verge of hardness."

I was thinking of the circumstances of my first appeal to him.

When I left her I went at once to the station, and, as the train was late, had some time to wait.

There were one or two yokels in the tiny waiting-room, and the station-master addressed one of them as he passed through from his little ivy-covered cottage to the ticket-office.

"Sad thing, this, about Mr. Gascoyne, Edward." The young man in question answered slowly:

"Yes. They say as 'is 'orse kicked him to death."

"That's strange—very strange. Was the horse bad-tempered?"

"Not that I know of, and I've shod the mare often enough."

"They say as Miss Gascoyne is powerful cut up."

"That's very likely; yer see, she doted on him."

I scrutinised young Gray, the last speaker, narrowly. His manner betrayed no indication that he was in any way aware of his sister's condition.

As Mr. Gascoyne descended from the train he pressed my hand warmly.

"This is very terrible," I said—"very terrible."

"Tell me, how did it happen?"

As we drove towards the Grange I detailed the event as well as I could.

"You think the horse kicked him to death—a horse that was fond of him? That is somewhat strange."

"I don't say it is so, sir. That is what has been surmised."

"When do they hold the inquest?"

"To-morrow."

"My wife is shocked beyond measure. If my niece had expressed the least wish for her to do so, she would have come too."

I did not answer. I could not say how Miss Gascoyne would welcome the idea of her aunt assuming the role of a near relation.

"I am very touched at her sending for me—very touched indeed. Is the body at the Grange?"

"No; it is at a farmhouse some miles off. It will be brought home after the inquest."

"Quite so."

We reached the Grange.

"If you don't mind, sir, I will get back to town. I would sooner. I don't think I can be of any further use."

He did not press me to remain, and I went back to town carrying messages for his managing clerk. I did not witness the meeting between Miss Gascoyne and himself, but it must have been quite satisfactory, for he stayed away over a week, and I learnt that Mrs. Gascoyne had joined them.

I fancied that Miss Gascoyne would be rather surprised at the dignity and well-bred restraint of the tradesman's daughter, and would find it a little difficult to account for her father's prejudice; in fact, his objection could not fail to strike her as having something in it of unreasoning snobbery.

I would have given a great deal to be at the inquest, but although there was no particular reason why I should not be, I thought Mr. Gascoyne might deem it a little officious. Neither did I go down to the funeral, but wrote a sympathetic note and sent a wreath. I let it fully appear that my reason for not going was diffidence, and a desire not to assume too intimate an attitude.

The morning of Mr. Gascoyne's return he called me into his office.

"Close the door, Israel."

He motioned me to a chair.

"Did you see any account of the inquest?"

"No, sir; I have been waiting for you to tell me." As a matter of fact, I had followed the case most carefully in the papers.

"It appeared that there was a serious doubt as to how my nephew received his injuries."

"Really?"

"Yes. In the first place, both doctors were a little surprised that they should have caused death at all. The whole case became quite complicated. There were distinct traces of blood on the horse's hoof, and yet one of the doctors absolutely refused to admit that the injuries could have been inflicted by the horse at all."

"How very extraordinary!"

"Did you at any time exchange confidences with my nephew on love affairs?"

I swiftly reflected. Had he the least proof of our having done so? It would not do to give a direct answer.

"I dare say we did, sir, but I cannot remember anything definite."

"Some letters were found in his pocket."

I almost started. How was it that it had never occurred to me to search young Gascoyne's pockets?

"Were they love-letters?"

"Yes."

"It is not very unusual for a young fellow of his age."

"No, and I am afraid that what they contained is also not unusual. It appears that he had accomplished the ruin of a girl in a neighbouring village."

I looked thoughtful. "Do you mean to suggest that there is a mystery?"

"I am afraid there is. I cannot help thinking that the doctor who refused to accept the theory of his having been killed by the horse was right."

"Why did they not call in a third doctor?"

"They did, and he was evidently under the influence of the man who believed in the horse theory."

"What was the verdict?"

I had forborne to satisfy myself on this point in order to be able to ask the question with easy unconcern.

"Accidental death."

I was astonished, but the country bumpkins on the jury had, I imagined, made up their minds before the inquest that he had been kicked by his horse.

"Were the letters read in court?"

"No. They were considered unnecessary, and no one thought they bore on the issue."

"Do you think they did?"

"Decidedly I do," answered Mr. Gascoyne. "Depend upon it, there was foul play. I talked to the doctor who would not admit the horse theory, after the case was over, and he was quite positive the injuries could not have been inflicted by a horse's hoof."

"Who was the girl?" I asked.

"Well, I do not think it is quite right to disclose her name. I had a talk with her father, who was very distant and said the matter would be best settled by saying nothing more about it. I don't know what he meant."

"Was the girl's name by any chance Janet Gray?"

Mr. Gascoyne looked at me in surprise.

"That was her name, but how did you know?"

"Harry Gascoyne spoke to me once or twice about her, and I wondered at the time from something he said whether he had not made rather a mess of things."

"Yes, I am afraid we men are very selfish, that is, until we have wives and daughters of our own. The possession of sisters does not seem to instil the same sense of responsibility to woman-kind."

"Does Miss Gascoyne know of this?"

"No; unless the matter develops further I do not think it necessary to inform her."

"What did the police think of the affair?"

"I fancy they are quite prepared to accept the horse theory."

"Then the matter is settled!"

"Except for the trouble of the poor girl. It appears that he actually promised to marry her."

"He was generous-hearted enough for anything," I answered, with calculated impulsiveness.

"Her father asked me to give my word that the matter would not go any further, so you will remember that you hold a secret that affects three human beings at least."

"I shall of course be as silent as the grave."

He began to open his correspondence, and I rose to leave the room.

"Oh, by the way, my wife and my niece have struck up quite a friendship. My wife remains at the Grange, and I shall go down there again for a few days next week."

I looked pleased.

"I believe," he added, smiling, "you have been indulging in some diplomacy at our expense. Don't you think my niece is a beautiful woman?"

"I think everyone would admit that."

"I expect she will make a very brilliant match."

I went out. I knew quite well why this last remark had been made, and smiled inwardly. Mr. Gascoyne had thought gently to dissuade me from indulging in hopes which were improbable of fulfilment. He could not know how carefully I had calculated all the obstacles that stood in the way of my success.

As I returned to my desk I found myself murmuring the word *two*. I had the most difficult part of my task still before me, but so far the two opening campaigns had been brilliant successes. I wondered if the Gascoyne family in general realised how much nearer I was to the succession. Probably with the exception of Mr. Gascoyne and his niece they had no idea of my existence.

I took out the genealogical tree and studied it carefully, although there was little need of this, as I could have passed an examination in the entire history of the Gascoynes up to date at any moment.

There were now four lives between me and the object of my ambition.

My great-uncle Henry, who was now very nearly ninety years of age, lived somewhere in the North of England. It was not necessary to consider him in any way. He was a widower without children. There was Ughtred, the uncle of the present peer, still a man in the prime of life. He might yet marry and have a family. He was devoted to good living and had a reputation as a dilettante. I had never seen him, but he had held office at Court, and was altogether rather an important person.

My difficulties would come when I arrived at the main branch of the family, and I reserved them for the final stroke. I should then be obviously near the succession and might be suspected of motives. A great many eyes would be upon me, and there would probably be a young baby and his perfectly healthy father to deal with. I began to realise that so far I had merely nibbled at my task.

It was advisable to give myself rest for a few months, as I discovered that after each campaign my nerve was apt to be slightly affected. I had proved to my own satisfaction that the dictum, 'murder will out,' was invented to frighten mankind, and had in fact been set up as a perpetual bogey. Nat Holway's guilt might be discovered, but the tracing of my anonymous letter would be an almost impossible task.

I was very anxious to know how Janet Gray's affair was progressing, and rather hoped I might be asked to stay at the Grange for a day or two. I gathered as time went on that the friendship between Miss Gascoyne and her aunt had grown stronger and stronger. Mr. Gascoyne told me that their attachment was a great relief to him, that the companionship of her niece had to a great extent dissipated his wife's melancholy, and that having a common sorrow they were very much in sympathy.

"They admire each other, and it is the dignified and warm friendship of two women to whom respect is essential. By the way, Israel, the girl Janet Gray is married."

"Indeed?"

"Yes, to a young miller called Nat Holway. He is very steady and very well-to-do. I almost wondered—" He pulled himself up abruptly.

"Yes, sir?" I queried.

"Nothing, nothing."

I knew what he had intended to say, and fervently wished that he would get rid of his vague suspicions.

I was glad, therefore, when he continued: "I have often wondered whether my nephew may not have had a fight with some admirer of Janet Gray, a fight that ended unexpectedly in a tragedy."

"Do you intend to pursue the matter?"

"No," he answered, energetically. "I think when a man undertakes the seduction of a girl he must look for violence from those whose feelings he outrages or from those whose hearths he pollutes. I could not if it were my own son bring the avenger to so-called justice. I may be wrong, but I believe that if my niece were asked, she would agree with me."

I breathed a sigh of relief, for they were not precisely the sentiments I had expected from him.

CHAPTER XI

I HAD reached quite a new phase of my career. The boy who had set out in life from the little house at Clapham with a distinctly suburban appearance was now hardly recognisable. I was twenty-three years of age. I knew that I had a certain romantic distinction of appearance, for I had been constantly reminded of the fact by women of society who made it their business to secure as good-looking cavaliers as possible. Someone had once said in my hearing that I was like the young Disraeli. Poor Lady Pebworth, in beginning what she conceived to be the patronage of an obscure youth, had been caught in her own trap, and had thrown modesty and virtue to the winds in an overmastering infatuation; she would likewise have discarded prudence had I been in the mind to allow her to do so. I am quite aware of the charge of coxcombry which will be made against me for writing in such a way about my conquests, but when a man sets forth to tell the history of his life he must make up his mind to be impervious to two accusations which are sure to be thrown at the head of the truthful memorist, namely, those of vanity and exaggeration. When we reflect that no novelist or diarist has ever yet dared to paint a truly analytical picture of a human career it is evident how amazingly difficult such a performance must be, and there are few who would be willing to risk the fury of mankind by giving an accurate description of their lives and actions.

Jean Jacques Rousseau certainly made a pretence of doing so, but we read his incomplete memorials with a solemn wink and our tongue in our cheek. His dissipations and weaknesses, which he parades with such an ostentation of candour, he knows are not such as to bring down any great obloquy. Perhaps there is philosophy at the foundation of such an attitude on the part of society at large. An absolute ingenuousness on the subject of our failings might breed too broad a tolerance to suit the present views of humanity. I myself have no intention of admitting the public into the inner sanctuary where dwell my most esoteric emotions. The philosopher wisely avoids the company of those who, indifferent to the opportunities of learning, are ready to practise the habits of street urchins at a sight foreign to the daily life of the streets. Jean Jacques' drama was always legitimate.

Lady Pebworth undoubtedly was the victim of a great passion. Fortunately, she was possessed of a lord and master who was of an unsuspicious nature, otherwise I am afraid that in spite of all my discretion she would have landed me in the Divorce Court. The Peeress and the stockbroker's clerk would have made a meal for many a prurient appetite.

My income was three hundred pounds a year, more or less, and with the instincts of my race I had begun to speculate in a safe, quiet sort of way.

I made no boast of the nearness of my relation to the Gascoyne family in such society as I obtained entrance to. I was anxious for the matter to remain unknown.

I woke one morning to read in the social intelligence that Lady Gascoyne had been safely delivered of a son. The news was not the shock it might have been, as I had known for some time that she was in an interesting condition. The child would have to be removed as well as his father.

It was a task that might well tax the ingenuity of any man. I thought the matter over carefully, day after day. I knew their house, which overlooked the Green Park, and sat for hours gazing at the windows as if they might be expected to furnish inspiration.

Lord Gascoyne was now twenty-six years of age. Without being in any way a prig—in fact, he was a man of some gallantry—he had a great sense of his responsibilities, and was leaving the Guards in order to manage his huge estates the better. He and his wife were little heard of. Despite the fact of her American birth, she was the genuine great lady as opposed to the pinchbeck imposition. Her happiness was not measured by the amount of social noise she could make. Everything about her and her husband was correct, and with the exception of the extreme good looks of both probably somewhat dull.

They belonged to the inner sanctuary of English aristocracy, and I could not at the moment see how I was to scale the fortress of their exclusiveness. I knew that they had been perfectly ready to entertain and make much of the young Gascoynes. Harry Gascoyne had told me as much, but this was a very different thing from welcoming the son of the Hebrew commercial traveller. They might not be so easy to conciliate as Miss Gascoyne.

Lord and Lady Gascoyne's entertainments were not made a feature of in the newspapers. It was a privilege to attend them, and the entrée to Lady Gascoyne's drawing-room was a passport to any society.

Lady Pebworth, I knew, visited them, and had been a guest at Hammerton, but I did not think it very probable she would be able to introduce me, and I was not quite sure that I cared about owing my introduction to her.

CHAPTER XII

ALTHOUGH I had from motives of policy given up the idea of making Sibella my wife, I was none the less somewhat overcome at receiving an invitation to her wedding. Grahame Hallward and I had lunch together in the City the day I received it.

"What do you think, Israel? Lionel has asked me to be his best man," he said.

"Are you going to?"

"Well, I told him that I thought it was rather silly for the bride's brother to be best man, and I asked him whether there was not some-one else. He got quite annoyed, and so did Sibella. He was angry, I believe, chiefly because he could not think of a friend as a substitute. As a matter of fact, I don't think he has many friends."

"I don't understand him," I said. "He goes about a great deal, and knows some very decent people, and yet the men don't like him."

"Women do, though, don't they?"

"I suppose so."

"I'm sorry for Sibella, Israel—I am really. Of course, she won't suffer so much as other women might when she finds him out, because she has no heart."

"Do you really think that, Grahame?"

"Sorry to say I do. Of course, I would not say such a thing to anybody else, but you're almost like one of us."

I gave him an affectionate glance. I was certainly very fond of Grahame.

"You should ask him if he would not like me to be his best man," I said.

We both laughed.

"I should think he rather objects to my coming to the wedding at all. I'm coming, all the same."

Grahame said nothing, and I guessed that there had been some discussion on the subject. I knew that Lionel Holland was not by any means above the vulgarity of showing temper should I be asked against his wish.

"Come and see us on Sunday. Lionel won't be there, and Sibella particularly told me to ask you."

"I'll come," I said. I wondered why Sibella was anxious to see me. "You'll be awfully dull at home without her," I added.

"Yes; she may not have much heart, but at the same time she's jolly good company."

"Yes, that's exactly the expression. Even when we were children she always kept things going."

We both grew a little quiet and thoughtful. I had had delightful times in the Hallward schoolroom with Grahame and Sibella, but I had travelled far since then. I was fighting also against a great and torturing jealousy. I was by practice enabled to keep this feeling well under control, but it had a habit of having a hasty nibble at my heart-strings when I was not on the alert.

Sibella received me with more subdued sweetness than I had ever known her display.

"You are getting on, Israel, aren't you?"

"Oh, I don't know; I'm just making a living, that is all."

"Why, you know that you are quite an important person now."

I was surprised to find that no one else came in, and more surprised when she proposed that we three should spend the evening round the schoolroom fire, as we used to do. I began to gather from Sibella's manner that she was not looking forward to her marriage without misgivings. That she was in love with Lionel in a sort of way I had no doubt, but the price that was to be paid for a few months of ecstasy had begun to dawn upon her. Woman-like, she could not forbear to count the cost. She had never been ignorant of my feelings towards her, and from the day Lionel first entered the house there had been a constraint whenever we were left alone. Such a constraint fell upon us when Grahame, having remembered that he had a message for a friend who lived a little way off, left us for half an hour.

I believe it was at that moment that Sibella began to develop a vague feeling that from every point of view she had made a mistake. In fact, the unexpected happened, as it always does. The absolutely—from the worldly point of view—immoral and incongruous came about as if swiftly driven forward by some occult forces, and she was in my arms sobbing hysterically and erotically, without either of us quite knowing how it had happened.

I had thirsted for her lithe, sweet figure and the caressing of her golden hair so long that I was swept away and found myself murmuring:

"I have not given you up, Sibella."

She hardly gathered what I meant, and I put her arms round my neck. Her mouth had always been to my mind her chief charm, and when I found my lips pressed against its large, sweet lines—which should have ciphered a broad, generous nature—I lost my head—that is, if I had had any desire to keep it.

Old Mr. and Mrs. Hallward dozed away in their armchairs by the drawing-room fire. Miss Hallward was writing her interminable Sunday letters in the library. I have no doubt the house outside looked just as respectable and unemotional to Grahame when he returned to it as when he went out of it, but, all the same, I was wondering when he rejoined us if Sibella would think it necessary to break off her marriage at the last moment rather than marry a man she had betrayed. She might do so, although in my wildest delirium I had kept some vague powers of caution and calculation, and had concluded that morality with Sibella meant self-interest.

I drove home to my rooms in St. James's laughing with triumph. Poor Lionel Holland would have all the appearance of victory with none of its reality.

Had Sibella been a woman of ordinary susceptibilities, I might have received a letter from her the next morning imploring me to bury the incident, accusing herself wildly, and vowing to make a model wife; but the elusive one—as I had named her to myself—was too clever to commit herself to paper, and if her marriage took place she would have it conducted without risks.

The marriage did take place, and I went as a guest. If it was bad taste on my part, it was entirely a question between Sibella and myself. She certainly betrayed no resentment. She had the grace to be very pale and subdued, which gave indications that there might be a certain leaven of conscience somewhere. Holland took my congratulations civilly enough. I think he was feeling really happy, so much are human beings capable of being imposed on, and so little can we make sure of appearances.

They evidently both looked forward to emerging from suburban society, for they were to return from their honeymoon to a flat in Mount Street, although Mr. and Mrs. Holland had wished them to settle down close to their house at Clapham.

"I was not going to agree to that," Sibella had said. "I want to say good-bye to Clapham for good and for all. If it had been Hampstead, I should not have minded so much, but Clapham—ugh! it gets more and more sordid every year."

I did not suppose I should have the entrée to their establishment if Lionel could help it, but I meant to make an attempt, all the same. Sibella was necessary to me.

I suffered a good deal from jealousy the first few days of her married life, but there is a merciful dispensation of Providence which blunts the keenest pangs of wounded love very rapidly when the inevitable has taken place, however sharp they may remain when sustained by hope.

CHAPTER XIII

"MY NIECE is staying with us, Israel," said Mr. Gascoyne one afternoon as he was leaving the office. "Will you dine with us on Friday evening?"

I said I should be delighted. Mr. Gascoyne and his wife had stayed at the Grange till the summer was almost over, and I knew that Miss Gascoyne was going to shut the house up for the winter, and that there was a possibility of her selling it in the spring.

She looked very stately and beautiful in her deep mourning, and was evidently glad to see me. We were together for fully a quarter of an hour before Mr. and Mrs. Gascoyne came down, and she talked quite freely and unconstrainedly of her brother.

The more I saw of her, the more I was struck by her absolute lack of pose in any small acceptation of the word. It positively gave me a sense of personal dignity to be with her.

"I am thinking of selling the Grange," she said. "So long as there was my brother it seemed to me a certain sort of duty that the offshoots of a great family should keep up an appearance and have a fair country residence." Then she smiled. "I am afraid, however, that my views are changing. I don't look upon the Gascoynes as quite such great people as I used to do, though I still think that if one bears a great name one owes it a duty."

"I am half a Jew," I said, boldly, "and as an Oriental I have a great respect for caste and authority."

"Do you think that is why the Jews succeed so well?"

"Yes; their chief aim is to remain at peace with the powers that be, and as Orientals they are satisfied that authority in this country abuses its privileges very little. They have no craving for more liberty."

"They are a curious race."

"I am not a Jew by religion, you know. I was baptised a Christian."

She smiled.

"I don't wish to be rude, but is that as far as your Christianity has reached?"

"My mother was a very religious woman. That is, she tested everything by her conscience, and always held that that was an unfailing standard."

It was really quite wonderful on what a high platform I could conduct a conversation.

Mr. and Mrs. Gascoyne came in, and we went to dinner. The affection that had arisen between these two women was quite extraordinary, and it was surprising to see Miss Gascoyne yielding to her aunt something of the deference of a daughter, although I am certain she would have rejected the insinuation that she could ever put anyone in the place of the mother she had idolised.

The conversation turned on the Gascoyne family.

"Do you know," said Mr. Gascoyne, "I was quite astonished to find how near our friend Israel is to the succession."

It was an awkward remark, and Mr. Gascoyne evidently felt it to be so as soon as he had made it. The subject was allowed to drop at the moment, but Mr. Gascoyne revived it when we were alone.

"I can't think how I came to make such a foolish remark, Israel. It cannot have failed to remind them both of what you have gained by their loss."

This was exactly what I feared.

"I cannot be said to have gained much. Lord Gascoyne has a son and heir."

"Let us consider. If Lord Gascoyne and his son were to die, you succeed as heir to your mother; that is, of course, when the two Henry Gascoynes, Ughtred, and myself, are out of the way—and none of us count for much. You see, the succession does not reach the female heir till it has been carried down to the last male heir. Rather hard on the women of the female lines, but so it is."

"I am afraid, sir, it will be my lot to drudge along in the City all my life."

"You are not the sort of person who ends as a Judge, Israel. Besides, go on as you are doing, and who knows what may happen."

I guessed by the intonation of his voice that he was considering whether he should tell me more of his intentions.

When we returned to the drawing-room I played and sang to them till late, and left the house high in the good graces of both women. From that moment my position in the house at South Kensington became a much more intimate one. Even two women as independent by nature as Mrs. Gascoyne and her niece found it pleasant and convenient to have a young man about who was ready to take so much trouble off their hands. This was, of course, not so apparent till the first months of mourning were over, but when Miss Gascoyne, who was devoted to music and art, began to go to concerts and picture-galleries I was very useful.

I learned that Lord and Lady Gascoyne had called on Mrs. Gascoyne and her niece, and that the three were going to dine with them.

I sincerely hoped that my name would not be mentioned, as I had no wish for the head of the family to know of my existence till I had decided on my plan of action.

I had been inquiring cautiously about Ughtred Gascoyne, and had made a point of coming across him several times in the districts he haunted. He was a very good-looking man, with apparently no such mentality as provoked restlessness. He enjoyed his life thoroughly, for all I could see. He had been in the Guards. He had also sat in the House of Commons for a limited period, and had utterly declined to repeat the experiment. In fact, the two ventures, together with a short period of Court life, had in his own eyes been activity enough, and he had settled down to a life of ease. Having a good income of his own, and being welcome at Hammerton as often as he chose to go there, existence was altogether a pleasant affair. Still, fifty-five is young for a man nowadays, and he might very well marry and have a whole family of children. Selfish and apparently confirmed bachelors do very often in middle age perform a complete right-about-face, and end up as the benignant fathers of a whole troop of boys and girls. Ughtred Gascoyne had now arrived at that age when a man may by some such shock as hearing himself described as "that old bore" be driven into matrimony.

At present there did not seem to be much chance of it. There was a woman in his life, however. She was an actress, Catherine Goodsall, a woman of birth, who moved in very good society, and who, being neither a great tragedienne nor a great comedienne, managed to earn a salary larger than could be achieved by cleverer and more legitimate artistes on account of the extraordinary *chic* and distinction she could import into the delineation of smart society women. She was so much the real thing, so entirely free from the metallic artificiality of the usual impersonator of such characters, that managers sought her continually.

She had a husband somewhere, poor soul, a man who had been in the Navy, a blackguard who had been untrue to the dearest traditions of the British tar by laying his hand on a female otherwise than in the way of kindness; in fact, he had beaten her, and Ughtred Gascoyne had thrashed him, and, strange to relate, the wife had been grateful.

The husband had then disappeared. She had been unable to obtain a divorce, but society, recognising the plucky way in which she had managed to earn her own living, accepted her intimate friendship with Ughtred Gascoyne for the innocent affair it pretended to be.

Her position, perhaps, had also something to do with the fact that she had a keen tongue and a ready wit. Her tongue would have been a weapon to be dreaded had it not been that she had the superlatively rare quality of using it with discretion. Her somewhat unique social position earned her the envy of her fellow artistes, the majority of whom retain such footing as they have in society on sufferance, their insecurity by no means being caused by their profession; for, were it not for their calling, the majority of the theatrical sisterhood, even of the higher ranks, would still be moving in their own proper slatternly or suburban circles.

Perhaps it would be possible to reach the Honourable Ughtred through her. She was not above the weakness common to most women of fashion of possessing a craving for new male friends. I chose an opportunity when Ughtred Gascoyne was out of town to obtain an introduction to her. This was not a difficult matter. I kept my eyes on the advertisements of charitable performances and bazaars to which she was very generous in contributing her services. A bazaar would be the thing, being the sort of entertainment at which it was fairly easy to force an introduction.

I had not long to wait. She was announced to hold a stall at a fashionable bazaar. The particular object of it I forget, but I remember that it was at a town-hall a mile or two from Piccadilly Circus. She had charge of a photographic stall, and I had my photograph taken in such a variety of positions that long before the operation was over, and aided by the mention of one or two mutual friends, we had become sufficiently acquainted for me to remain and help her. Nothing, as I had calculated, could have been more likely to bring about a rapid intimacy, and before I left I had been asked to go and see her.

She had a small house on the north side of the Park, and I made up my mind to call on Sunday afternoon, but before that day I received a note asking me to come to lunch.

"A great many people drop in on Sunday afternoon in the winter," she said when I arrived. "I should probably see nothing of you, and new friends always interest me. People think that a bad trait, don't they, whereas it is nothing of the kind."

"It certainly is not. It shows a progressive mind—that is, if there is no premature protestation."

"Exactly. New friends should have just as many fresh points of interest as, say, a picture-gallery. I love to watch new temperaments; they blaze and change like sunsets."

"You are quite right; but I hope this does not infer that you tire of your friends easily."

"Not of the residuum. The majority pass, of course. One would miss an immense amount of good comradeship if everything which cannot be lasting is to be avoided."

"You are not fickle?"

"Not in the least. We all have our inner sanctuary, and consequently we have our esoteric and exoteric friendships, and the lookers-on make mistakes as to which is which."

"That is very true. There is nothing in which people are so much deceived about each other as in their emotions. Human nature is so much more many-sided than the world is willing to admit."

"You believe that the good are not as good as they would have us believe, nor the bad as bad?"

"Exactly."

She was a woman worth talking to, and I roused myself.

"It can be demonstrated. Goodness is largely a question of having aptitude for the latest conventions."

"Demonstrate," she challenged, and then added: "Personally, I feel it, but have not the proof to hand." I took up the challenge easily.

"For instance, in ancient Sparta, thieving was a virtue and coward-ice a crime. Nowadays, a coward may get along very well, but a thief would probably come to grief very soon. So it is with many other things."

"You think that a criminal may make a charming member of society, a good husband and father?"

I winced. The conversation was extracting opinions from me which were just as well concealed, but I answered frankly:

"I am sure of it."

"So am I."

I continued whimsically:

"Don't you think society would be much happier if, instead of these horrible punishments and immurings, people who had been convicted of a crime should be compelled to wear some outward sign that they were not to be trusted in that particular direction? It should be treated as a disease, not as a disgrace."

"A little difficult to enforce, eh?"

"Not at all. We should all be up in arms if Brown came to lunch without the governmental mark that he was not to be trusted with forks and spoons, and without the least acrimony we should call in a policeman who would correct the matter."

"It might be carried still further, and people might be obliged to wear the evidence of their particular moral failing."

"Everybody would lie, and which do you think would be the most popular hypocrisy?"

"In England, drink; because in the eyes of the average citizen of this country it would carry with it the least shame."

"Well said; but to my mind there is no vice which is not preferable, and yet people will shake a drunkard by the hand when they would shrink from a criminal of the emotions."

We both agreed that this was ridiculous. I had not been in the house an hour before I realised that she was a very charming woman, and that she was sincerely in love with Ughtred Gascoyne.

She harped a good deal on friendship, as if to exaggerate her sense of its value, and send the hearer away with the notion that a pure friendship between man and woman was her ideal.

I have, however, always had a keen instinct for the subtleties of female deception, and I was fully alive to the trend of her dissertations on friendship. They were the weapons she kept constantly in use for the defence of her character. She need not have been so careful, for the attacks and insinuations on her reputation were far fewer than she imagined. She was one of the chartered exceptions to the general demands of propriety. These exceptions exist to a certain degree, even in the most straight-laced society. She made some witty remark about the suburbs, that never-failing topic for the jests of those who consider themselves the elect of the social citadel of Mayfair.

"I am a suburban," I answered. "I was brought up in Clapham."

"You hardly suggest the suburbs," she answered, unabashed.

"Oh, believe me, there are people of distinction in the suburbs."

"Of course; only, one must have one's little joke about them. Personally, I always tell my friends that they must not be too sure that they are free from the parochial because they dwell within hail of Piccadilly Circus."

"Still, I think that, after all, the Londoner has a quickness and intelligence denied to the provincial, don't you?"

"Yes, to the provincial, but not necessarily to the inhabitants of greater London. The guttersnipe of Manchester is a very stupid creature after your Cockney urchin."

We went upstairs and talked until her regular coterie dropped in.

Sir Anthony Cross, whom I had met at Lady Pebworth's, was one of the first to arrive. He did not like me, but, to my surprise, drew me into a corner.

"Do you remember, Rank, that evening the Pebworths and ourselves went to the Gaiety?"

"Perfectly."

"You bowed to an awfully pretty woman in the stalls. She was with a good-looking bounder."

I knew perfectly well whom he meant, of course; but, as he paused for me to refresh my memory, I looked puzzled.

"You must remember—an extraordinarily pretty woman."

I still looked blank.

"Surely you must remember. A fair woman with fluffy hair and enormous blue eyes, but not a bit dolly, like most fair women. Rather a large mouth."

"Oh yes; I think I remember."

"Well, I fancy she's married to that man."

"If it's the girl I think you mean, she is married to him. Her name is Sibella Holland." It was not very well-bred to call Lionel Holland a bounder without first finding out if he was a friend of mine.

"What a ripping name! They've got a flat below mine. I should very much like to know them."

"Do you want me to introduce you?"

Considering that Sir Anthony had gone out of his way on more than one occasion to be rude to me, I could not help thinking that there was a certain insolence in his obvious readiness to make use of me. If he intended doing so, however, I should certainly return the compliment.

"I am obliged to hurry away now, but that's my address. I am usually at home between six and seven."

I gave him a card and said good-bye.

I had promised to spend the evening with the Gascoynes. I was making immense strides with their niece, and I fancy that both Mr. and Mrs. Gascoyne were a little surprised at our having so much in common.

CHAPTER XIV

IF I WAS to have access to Sibella at all, it was necessary to make friends with her husband, and the only way to make friends with him was to be useful to him. I knew quite well that my continued success—and success in his eyes was a question of moving in a higher grade of society—had annoyed him beyond measure. He believed that money ought to be able to buy anything. Money is a thing the power of which the vulgar are always over-rating and the cultured are always under-rating. He and Sibella had a large income, with the prospect of a very much larger one, therefore the doors of good society should fly open. They knew people who had been her friends before marriage, and who moved in what a celebrated English lady novelist would have called "genteel circles," but her husband, having neither the atmosphere of good breeding nor the tact which might have taken its place, was ambitious of forcing the most select assemblies.

If I could be of use to him in this way I was sure that he would be content to waive his dislike for the present, especially as he imagined himself to be in sole possession of the prize we had contended for. It was, of course, just possible that Sibella herself might now object to my coming to the house. She might have fallen passionately in love with her husband, as wives often do after marriage. Lady Pebworth was still ready to do anything for me, and if Sibella was still ready to receive me, I must persuade her ladyship to call.

I met Lionel on his way home from the City one evening, and somewhat to his surprise stopped to speak to him. He was a little cool at first, but I was careful to start a conversation about himself, and he warmed to the subject at once.

He talked of being sick of the City. His father was very ill, and he expressed his intention of selling out and giving up the business should anything happen to the old gentleman.

"I shall go and live in the country, and get as much hunting and shooting as I can manage."

"Still, a man ought to do something," I suggested.

"Oh, cut that; don't preach."

"I wasn't thinking of it from a moral point of view. You're a rich man. You ought to furnish the powers that be with sufficient excuse for giving you something later on."

"What do you mean?"

"A man with twenty thousand a year may aspire to anything."

"What am I to do?"

"Go in for politics. The losing side, of course. They'll be having their spell of office in a few years."

"I don't know anything about politics."

"No, but you've got intelligence; you'll soon learn."

He looked flattered. Inwardly I smiled at the idea of his being in the House of Commons.

"How does one begin?"

It was strange that Lionel, who was heir to a couple of newspapers, should know so little.

"Oh, you get to know all the right people. Let them know that you are ready to drop a certain amount of money. Lady Pebworth was saying only the other day that their people want money. She's rather a power in the political world, you know."

He looked vacant, and had the frankness to ask:

"Who's Lady Pebworth?"

"Well, her husband was in the last Cabinet. Your wife ought to know her. Lady Pebworth admired her immensely the only time she saw her."

"Have they met?"

"No, but do you remember one evening when you and Sibella were in the stalls at the Gaiety, and I was in a box with some people?"

"Yes."

"That was Lady Pebworth. She has been very civil to me. I don't suppose I should have had such a good time if it had not been for her."

This admission of my own indebtedness to someone else for the entrée to certain houses that he had envied me made him quite genial, and broke down the barrier between us, while a little more flattery judiciously laid on accomplished what I desired.

"You haven't been to see us yet," he said, quite graciously.

"I haven't been asked," I laughed.

"I'll get Sibella to write and ask you to one of our Sunday lunches."

We parted quite amicably, and I think I left him under the impression that I was most anxious to be friendly with him.

Sir Anthony Cross delayed coming to see me, as I thought he would, but evidently he could think of no other way of making Sibella's acquaintance, and one evening when I was drinking tea—a habit to which I am addicted—he was shown in.

"No thanks, I never drink tea. I don't know what people see in it."

There was a perceptible patronage in his manner. He assumed the usual attitude of an Englishman of birth when brought into familiar intercourse with a man of whose caste he is not sure. There was no superficial fault to be found with his manner, but it was obvious to a keen perception that he presumed a gulf.

"Not tea as they make it in this country," I answered languidly. "Tea drinking is an art. It is one of the most extraordinary facts of the latter part of the nineteenth century how readily the country exchanged China for Indian tea, and yet it is like preferring cider to champagne." I pushed the cigars towards him. "Most men cannot appreciate tea because their palates are ruined by alcohol."

The cigar put him in a good temper; I knew that it was something exceptional.

He was not interested in the subject of tea, but at the same time, being a gentleman, he hardly liked to make it too patent that he had come about an introduction to a woman, and that further than obtaining that introduction he was not prepared to consider our acquaintance.

"You've got a jolly little place here," he said, looking round. I knew that in his heart he considered it somewhat overdone.

"I am a Jew, and as an Oriental I defy the canons of Western good taste in order to get the amount of colour necessary to my appetite."

He did not quite follow, and I did not intend that he should. It was of no account. There were limits even to my adaptability, and I am afraid I never could have adapted myself to the idiosyncrasies of Sir Anthony Cross. I don't think he had a single delicate sentiment in him.

After a time, and when I considered he had listened to me long enough to be sufficiently subdued, I said: "Oh, by the way, I met Holland, Mrs. Holland's husband, you know, a few days ago."

"Yes?" He made a valiant effort to conceal his interest.

"They are only just married, and of course very much in love."

"What is he?"

"Well, as far as I know, he is something in his father's business. His father is enormously wealthy—owns a couple of newspapers. I don't think he'll hold out much longer though, and then the young people will come into everything."

Riches did not mean much to Sir Anthony Cross. He had eighty thousand a year, so report said.

He was evidently too obsessed with the idea of Sibella to be turned aside by a husband.

"Of course," I continued, "her brother is my greatest friend; we were at school together. She and I used to be sweethearts when we were children, but when Lionel Holland came on the scene he cut me out."

"She looks a charming woman, and I should very much like to know her."

"I can introduce you to Holland if you like. I'll ask them both to dine and meet you."

Sir Anthony hardly disguised his joy.

"I shall be delighted," he said.

"Then I'll let you know when I've fixed things up."

I gave him the opportunity of departing, but he stayed on, talking incessantly of Sibella. He was so infatuated as to be unable to appreciate how obvious he was making it that he was seeking an introduction to a married woman because he was in love with her.

I knew that Sir Anthony was a friend of Ughtred Gascoyne's, and it might so happen that he would be useful to me in that direction.

"Have you known Mrs. Goodsall long?" he asked.

"A few weeks."

"Don't know Gascoyne, do you?"

"Who is he?"

"Ughtred Gascoyne; I thought everybody knew him. He's a great pal of hers. People do say things, but I don't believe it myself. I mention him because I've heard a rumour that her husband is dead, and that she and Gascoyne are going to be married."

"Indeed?"

"Of course they've always been thick, but it isn't often the man does the right thing."

I laughed.

"No, there's all the difference in being able to go and see a woman when you want to and being obliged to see her when you don't want to. Such a prospect immediately subjects her to a new test. I know a great many women who are delightful companions, but I should not care to live with them."

He went away at last, after making me promise again that I would arrange the dinner and let him know.

I was determined, if possible, to persuade Lady Pebworth to be of the party, and called on her a day or two after. She had just returned to town, and received me rather coldly. She had been away for three months, and she protested that I had written to her but twice during her absence. I pointed out that she was blaming me for a too zealous care of her reputation, and that it was one thing for her to write to me when the chance of her letters being seen by anyone else was practically non-existent, and quite another thing for me to write to her, and that I had only done so when I was certain that Lord Pebworth was out of the way. It took me some time to soothe her, inasmuch as she informed me that she thought our friendship had better cease, and I really believe she was in the mood to take a great resolution. This roused me to an effort. It was not convenient to quarrel with her at the moment. I regret to say that in the course of our interview her ladyship so far forgot what was due to good taste as to throw my obscurity in my face, and to make a scarcely veiled insinuation that had it not been for her I should not have been acquainted with anyone of consequence. At this I dignifiedly rose, and, telling her that I had no wish to intrude where I was considered an adventurer, moved towards the door. Then she begged my pardon, said she could not understand how she came to be so rude, and professed her undying readiness to do anything for me. A weaker diplomatist might have seized the opportunity to mention the dinner-party, but I cautiously paid court to her for some days before I asked her if she would come and meet Sibella and her husband. I explained that Lionel was quite ready to be of financial use to her political organisation, putting it in such a way that it was impossible for her to take offence. Finally, she said she would be very glad, so I made up my dinner-party, which was quite a little social triumph.

I fancy Sir Anthony Gross was surprised when he heard whom he was asked to meet.

I entertained them at the best restaurant in town. Sibella's manners were perfect—they always were when she chose—and Lady Pebworth took an immediate liking to her, I of course being very careful not to show the least partiality for her.

The Hollands thus found themselves taken up by a woman who could probably launch them better than they could, in their wildest dreams, have expected. To do her justice, I do not think Sibella would have run after anybody for the purpose of getting into better society.

She had enough of the Hallward pride and egotism to save her from vulgarity. At the same time she was quite prepared to swim with the tide and hold her own.

Sir Anthony managed to keep his admiration within bounds, and the evening was a great success. We finished up by spending an hour at a famous theatre of varieties. Lionel Holland from this time attached himself to me much more than I cared about. He was amazingly proud of Sir Anthony's friendship, and I fancy that exclusive gentleman had to pay somewhat dearly for the privilege of being near Sibella so much. He became quite the friend of the house, however.

Sibella's dazzling beauty was not long in making its way. She was noticed at a brilliant social function by exalted folk, and as a consequence was presented by Lady Pebworth. Lionel was selected as a forlorn hope for the next General Election, and Mr. Holland was so pleased that he appreciably increased their allowance.

It may be asked what good this was all doing me. As a matter of fact, it is an instance of how impossible it is to generalise about character. I was perfectly sure of my power over Sibella, and enjoyed seeing her admired and sweeping everything before her.

They could not get away from the fact—and I don't think Sibella had any wish to—that it was I who had launched them. Of course, people tried to shatter Sibella's reputation by way of putting a speedy stop to her upward climb, but nothing could be said which was in any way susceptible of proof.

I had not since her marriage treated her with anything except the most ordinary friendliness. I was certainly not going to risk a snub. I was convinced of one thing, that had I made a more strenuous effort to win her from Lionel Holland I might have done so. Perhaps some intuitive feeling warned me to suffer, and not to risk my own ultimate profit.

Whilst engaged in trifles I was not neglecting the main business of my life. I had not been able to avoid an introduction to Ughtred Gascoyne, who somewhat inopportunely took a fancy to me. It was rather awkward, as it would have been far more convenient to have remained unknown.

By degrees it leaked out that Catherine Goodsall's husband was dead, and that she and Ughtred Gascoyne were going to be married. She told me the news herself, with tears in her eyes. I am sure I should have been glad if the words of congratulation I spoke could have been sincere, and I really hoped that things could at least be so arranged that they might have some time of married happiness before Ughtred

Gascoyne was removed. But this was not my business; and, further, it might result in another human obstacle being placed in my path.

Their wedding was fixed for a day in Christmas week. It was now October. I had therefore not much time to lose. Of course, neither of them was young, and it was improbable that they would have any children, but it was possible. I had so managed to make everything in my mind subservient to my main object that the prospect of Catherine Goodsall's disappointment only raised a momentary pang.

I racked my brains by day and night, trying to devise some new and entirely original way of starting Ughtred Gascoyne on his way to a happier world.

Being known as a friend of his, it would not do to use poison. Pistols and daggers, although they have their uses, both in melodrama and out of it, did not commend themselves. They suggested danger, blood, and noise. I had early grasped the cardinal principles of my undertaking; firstly, that I must be absolutely relentless; and, secondly, that the word horror must be eliminated from my vocabulary.

As I lay awake one night in my room in St. James's thinking the matter over, I heard the cry of fire, the galloping of horses, and the jingle of the engine as it swayed along Piccadilly. I have always been fond of fires: even as a small boy they possessed a weird fascination for me.

I lay debating whether I should not get up and see the fun. It was evidently not far off, for I could hear the hiss of the water as it shot through the air, and the shouts of men. Suddenly an idea came into my head. Fire was apparently used as a rule in the clumsiest way by murderers. How often may it not have been used successfully and with complete secrecy?

It was important to keep in mind that successful crimes do not as a rule come to light.

Arson to the average mind always conveys a sensation of horror that is perhaps wanting in all other crimes. Suffocation or burning were neither of them pleasant methods, but I was not to be deterred by a sentiment.

The idea, once in my brain, became fixed. I found it impossible to dislodge it. I should have liked to go to the British Museum and read up all the details I could obtain of crime by arson, but this would have been a risky proceeding, and might in the never-to-be-forgotten contingency of my falling under suspicion be exceedingly damning.

I should have to trust to my own invention. Ughtred Gascoyne had asked me to call on him, and early one Sunday morning I did so. He occupied an upper part in Albemarle Street. There was a side door and a flight of stairs leading to his rooms. I immediately grasped the importance of the fact that there was no porter or lift. He had a manservant who slept on the floor above his own, and a woman who came in in the daytime. The establishment was thus conveniently miniature. On the first floor he had a sitting-room that led into his bedroom, with a bathroom beyond. Above this was his dining-room, which was seldom used; also a kitchen and a very small bedroom for his servant. The place was old, curiously so for such a smart quarter of the town, and, I imagined, highly combustible.

The rooms were too solidly furnished for my purpose, but they had muslin curtains and a fair number of knick-knacks. I quite realised that it was an off chance, but at the same time I believed it could be carried out with little or no personal risk. What I particularly wished to do was to enter his rooms with him at night without anybody being aware of it, and to leave them unnoticed.

The Sunday morning I called on him he was, I fancy, a little surprised to see me, but evidently quite pleased.

"I am very fond of young people, and I like to have them about me. Mrs, Goodsall and I agree on that. I cannot understand old people who are content to vegetate with their faded contemporaries."

"It isn't everybody who gets on with young people."

"It is merely a question of mood. You must feel young, and you will get on with them well enough."

"To feel young. Therein lies the difficulty for most people."

"Yes, most people eat and drink and sedenterate themselves—if I may coin a verb—into premature old age."

Whilst he talked I was wondering how long it would take to suffocate a human being, and what density of smoke was necessary, and whether he was a heavy sleeper, a fact he was good enough to enlighten me on.

"Youth is merely a question of spirits, and spirits are largely if not entirely a question of sleep. No, I have never missed a night's sleep in my life that I can remember, not even"—he lowered his voice—"when my mother died."

"You are lucky. I wish I could say as much."

"Directly my head touches the pillow I am asleep, and I don't wake till I am called."

This was indeed good news, that is, if it could be relied upon. It is amazing how people will lie about their own habits. They are a matter of personal delusion to a great extent, and people talking about themselves will, in good faith, deny idiosyncrasies of which their intimates are fully aware.

For aught I could be sure of, Ughtred Gascoyne was a martyr to insomnia, although he certainly did not suggest it.

His bedroom was a light, airy room with very little furniture, and a severe, narrow bed such as is affected by the average English gentleman, and is to me an abomination.

At any rate, this was the room it was my business to set on fire with such completeness as might ensure the passing of Ughtred Gascoyne.

It is the usual habit for those with a weakness for arson to empty paraffin oil over a quantity of furniture, and then set a light to it, a method of procedure that nearly always leads to detection. I remembered when thinking over my plans that Ughtred Gascoyne's rooms were lighted by lamps and not by electric light. Would this help me in any way? It might. I already foresaw that my nerve and courage would be called into play in this enterprise far more than had hitherto been the case.

October passed and some part of November, and nothing had been done, except that I had grown more and more friendly with Ughtred Gascoyne. He was very musical, and liked to hear me sing and play.

Sometimes I made a point of meeting him late at night on his way home from the club, and went in and smoked a cigar with him. I could not help reflecting how very much those whom it was my unfortunate duty to remove seemed to like me. Perhaps it was a premonition that I was about to do them a good turn or what might prove to be so.

His servant was usually in bed when I returned to his rooms with him at night.

Both Catherine Goodsall and he were always talking of the time they would have me to stay with them at the little place they were taking in the country.

"Quite small," said Ughtred Gascoyne, "but altogether delightful, isn't it, Catherine?"

"You know, dear, I'm in love with it. I am looking forward to having a little vault in that dear old church with a stained glass window, to the memory of Ughtred and Catherine Gascoyne of this parish."

"I can't say that that is a very cheerful way of looking forward."

"Well, it's only when that happens that a woman can be said to have her husband to herself."

We laughed. It was really quite delightful to see how happy they meant to be, and after all if "man never is but always to be blest," and the pleasure of all things is a question of the imagination and lies almost entirely in anticipation, they had had as much pleasure out of it as could be expected.

I knew the time Ughtred Gascoyne usually went home, and my meetings with him, looked upon by him as accidental, were by no means so.

November went by, and it was the first week in December, and, strangely enough in this perverse climate of ours, the weather was bitterly cold. It was the sort of weather for my purpose, for Ughtred Gascoyne was a great stickler for fresh air, and it was only in such weather as this that he was likely to shut his windows He was turning into Bond Street one night when I passed him. I laughed as we met.

"You won't be allowed to stay out as late as this soon."

"No, penal servitude is upon me. Coming in?"

We went up to his room, where there was a bright fire burning.

"Now, this is comfortable. By the way, I met a cousin of mine to-day. He says you are in his office."

"I told you I was in a stockbroker's office."

"Yes, but you never told me he was my cousin, and that you are also a cousin."

"I always leave the Gascoynes to find me out themselves. You see, my mother was a Gascoyne, and she was left to keep lodgings in Clapham."

He looked at me kindly.

"You don't feel bitter?"

"Oh dear no, only it isn't a great encouragement to push myself forward, is it?"

"He tells me that there is another cousin of mine staying with him and his wife. He describes her as beautiful. What do you think?"

"I agree. I knew her brother."

"Poor Harry Gascoyne. Killed by a fall from his horse, wasn't he?"

"Horse kicked him."

"Strange, must have been a brute."

I talked to him as he undressed. He was inquisitive about the South Kensington household.

"Hardly know Gascoyne Gascoyne myself. Always heard he married badly."

"He married very well, only her father happened to be a linen-draper."

"Good heavens, that's nothing in our days. Lord Southwick's father-in-law was a grocer, and a very distinguished old gentleman, too. A damned sight better bred than ever the Southwicks were. They all look like stable-boys. Sort of family in which you'd think the women had been going wrong with the grooms for generations. Southwick married groceries and manners at the same time."

"Mrs. Gascoyne is a very charming woman."

"My dear fellow, I can quite believe it. A man like Gascoyne Gascoyne does not retain his polish undimmed if he has been living for years with a woman who isn't a lady at heart."

"I don't think Miss Gascoyne would be devoted to anyone who was capable of offending the canons of good taste."

"They are great friends?"

"I should think so."

"Well, when I am married we must have a nice family party. Don't mind my getting into bed. You can let yourself out, can't you?"

"Easily."

I stood and talked to him while I put on my coat, and then I said good-night.

"Oh, do you mind shutting my bedroom door, the woman makes such a beastly row doing it if it's left till the morning."

"Good-night."

"Good-night. Mind you come to my wedding."

I shut the bedroom door. I was in the outer room alone. I went to the door, and going outside shut it. Then I ran downstairs, opened the front door and banged it, leaving myself inside. I sat down on the stairs and waited. After a while I stole upstairs again. The darkened room with the firelight playing over it looked very comfortable. I gently took the glass off the reading-lamp, and, unscrewing the burner, poured the contents over the foot of the curtains near which was the only wicker chair in the room.

I had to close the old-fashioned shutters so as to screen the room from any policeman on his beat as long as possible. One of my original ideas had been to put a large piece of coal on the fire and lower the register, leaving the room to fill with smoke.

The lowering of the register, however, would make noise. Things were better as they were. While I was completing all these arrangements I was on the alert for the least sound from the other room. Again and again I paused, ready to make for the door and be out of the house before he could reach me. I had placed a chair in such a position in front of his door that he would be bound to trip over it if he came out in a hurry.

Lastly came the most difficult part of my task. I had to remove the chair and open his bedroom door slightly. I listened long and carefully till a snore assured me that it was safe. I leant across the chair and opened the door a little way. The heavy breathing in the bed stopped. For one moment I felt terror; the next moment he had snored again. I removed the chair.

The striking of a match might have betrayed me. I lit a piece of paper at the fire and held it to the soaked curtains. Then I was out of the room like a shot and downstairs. As I glanced back the room was already full of flame.

When I emerged into the streets I looked carefully up and down. There was not a policeman to be seen. I reached my rooms and went to bed. I wish I could boast of such a nerve as would have allowed me to sleep through the night.

The next morning I started for the City at the usual time. I scanned the morning paper, but there was nothing about a fire in Albemarle Street. At lunchtime the first thing that met my gaze as I left the office was a placard issued by one of the earlier and cheaper evening papers:—'Gentleman suffocated in Albemarle Street.'

With an extraordinary calm I read that about three a.m. a fire occurred at the chambers of the Hon. Ughtred Gascoyne, resulting in the death of that gentleman, who was well known in social and sporting circles. His servant, who slept on the floor above, was awakened by the smell of smoke, and getting out of bed and hurrying to the top of the stairs to arouse his master was driven back by the flames and smoke. He was subsequently rescued by a fire escape from the top storey.

On the fire being extinguished the unfortunate gentleman was discovered in his bed. He must have been suffocated in his sleep.

I put down the paper with satisfaction and ate a good lunch. I had at any rate not inflicted any great physical suffering.

Mr. Gascoyne came back from his lunch looking very white.

"It's a most awful thing, Israel. There seems to be a curse on our family."

"Why, sir, what is the matter now?"

"You know my cousin Ughtred?"

"Yes."

"The poor fellow has been suffocated in his bed."

I appeared horrified. "You don't mean to say at his rooms in Albe-marle Street?"

"Yes."

I looked terribly concerned.

"He was to have been married quite soon."

"So I understood. Mrs. Goodsall, the actress, wasn't it?"

"Yes."

"Curiously enough, I met him yesterday at the club of a friend of mine. I hadn't seen him for years."

I called a hansom directly I left the office and drove to Albemarle Street. A small group was watching the house from the other side of the road. The windows were boarded up and the stonework round them blackened with smoke. I knocked at the door, and it was opened by Ughtred Gascoyne's servant. He had reason to remember me with gratitude, for I knew that servants are the adventurer's staunchest allies or greatest enemies.

"Will you step inside, sir? Lord Gascoyne has been here most of the day. He's just gone."

I did not wish to meet his lordship.

"When do you expect him to return?"

"Not till to-morrow, sir."

I went in. There was a gruesome smell of charred wood and stuffs. I followed Mason upstairs.

"This it where it must have begun, sir." He pointed to where the wicker work chair had stood.

"What I can't understand, sir, is how the shutters came to be closed. I never knew Mr. Gascoyne to shut them, and he gave me particular instructions to the contrary. There was no need for them, you see."

I looked towards the bedroom.

"They took him away to the mortuary, sir, to await the inquest. No man could have been a better master."

"He was a splendid chap, Mason. You know how I looked up to him." I spoke in my most ingenuous tones.

"And very fond he was of you, sir. He was always at home to you."

I pressed half a sovereign into his hand.

"Did he come home alone, Mason?"

"No, sir—at least, I fancy I heard voices. Oh yes, and I heard the door bang. I don't know who it was, sir, I'm sure."

The front room was quite burnt out, and there could be absolutely no trace of the oil with which I had started the conflagration.

I had apparently succeeded in a very risky undertaking.

I left a card at Mrs. Goodsall's with my deepest sympathy. The servant informed me she was quite prostrated, and I was made somewhat uncomfortable by hearing sounds of sobbing from the second storey of the tiny house.

At the Gascoynes', where I was to dine, I found the household in the deepest gloom. The tragedy seemed to have brought back something of the bitterness of their own grief. It was too similar in its horror to the death of the two young Gascoynes to be much discussed. We avoided gloomy topics with an almost hysterical earnestness, but it is extraordinary how matters of that kind will obtrude themselves when they are desired not to do so. Left alone with Mr. Gascoyne, however, the constraint passed and we talked freely.

"Just one of those things that are quite inexplicable. The fire brigade authorities do not agree with the theory that a live coal must have dropped out of the grate. They think the fire originated at the other end of the room, and that it must have been a cigarette or something of the kind."

"It doesn't matter much what it was, does it?"

"Of course not; only one cannot help travelling round a case like that and looking at it from every point of view. I called there this afternoon."

"And I was there this evening."

"Did you see Lord Gascoyne?"

"No."

"He was there when I called, and seemed terribly upset. He kept on saying, 'Poor Uncle Ughtred!' and 'He was the life and soul of everything.'"

I could not see that these remarks of Lord Gascoyne's were very illuminating or helpful, but it is curious how little people trouble to be sensible when they are talking of the dead.

Miss Gascoyne pressed my hand as I said goodnight.

"What a friend you are! You are always cheering us. You knew him, too, which makes it all the nicer of you to be so cheerful."

"Good-night," I said, and then threw into my glance a confession of admiration for which I had been months preparing the way. I was sure that had I ventured on such a thing a year before she would have felt anger, born of injured pride, but now her eyes fell, and I knew that I was on the road to success. She had taken me at my own valuation, as I had intended she should.

CHAPTER XV

I WAS glad to discover that Ughtred Gascoyne had left all his little fortune, excepting such as did not return to the Gascoyne coffers, to Catherine Goodsall, and that she would be quite well off. She looked very woebegone when I saw her again, but she was not a pessimist, and soon pulled herself together; not that I believe she ever forgot him. She gave me a tie-pin that had belonged to him, because he had been very fond of me, and had often talked of me to her.

A Sunday or two afterwards I lunched with Sibella and her husband. The old hunger for her was beginning to grow on me, and impel me towards her.

They were for a wonder alone, and Lionel looked discontented. He had evidently reached the frame of mind peculiar to vulgar folk, who think that unless they are living at high pressure and constantly entertaining or being entertained by those they consider great they are dropping out of it. Great folk can afford their holidays, but such social climbers as Lionel Holland can have no respite from the treadmill of entertainment.

I think he was verily too stupid to see that it was his wife's beauty and charm, lacking in depth though they were, to which they owed their improved position.

Sir Anthony Cross—who I knew was with them constantly—must have played a very clever game, a much cleverer game than I had imagined him capable of. To do Lionel justice, he was not the sort of man to play the complaisant husband for the sake of any position, and he had evidently not grasped that Sir Anthony's presence at their house was solely and entirely due to admiration of his wife.

I was certain that so far Sir Anthony had not even been permitted to declare himself. Sibella was vain enough of his attention to keep him dangling after her, but she had no notion of making herself cheap to the men of a society the women of which she was anxious to propitiate.

I suppose Lionel thought that an old lover like myself, who had been discarded for years, was no possible danger. Possibly—for the minx was clever—he had absolute confidence in Sibella.

At any rate, after lunch he left us together. It was the first time we had been alone since her marriage.

It was a little awkward, but I exerted myself to free the situation from constraint.

"Things have changed," I said, lighting another cigarette with a languid feeling of enjoyment at being alone with her, and conscious that the ménage I had contemplated had begun.

"You are wonderful, Israel. It is quite extraordinary how people talk about you, and quote what you say, and yet—" She paused, and I laughed.

"And yet I began life in a third-rate Clapham lodging-house, and am still only a clerk in a stock-broker's office."

"As far as that goes, I can't quite see why people make such a fuss of us."

"Can't you? Then look in the glass."

Sibella rippled with laughter. She loved flattery, and expected it.

"My dear child," I said lazily, "everything finds its level. We were bound to rise. You and I, Sibella, are very wonderful people."

"And Lionel?"

"Lionel is not in the least wonderful. He is good-looking, but by himself he would never have wheeled the shortest flight above the ordinary."

"I won't have you talking against my husband."

"I am not talking against him. I have rather an affection for Lionel. He is your husband."

"It is sometimes borne in upon me, Israel, and I cannot say why, that you are extraordinarily wicked."

"What makes you think that?"

"There is something mysterious about you. There always was even as a boy, and it has grown with you."

I did not like to hear this. Above all people, a secret murderer cannot afford to suggest the mysterious.

"Do you remember what a pretty little boy you were?" she asked.

"Perfectly."

"Do you know, I've got a lock of your hair that I cut off at a children's party. It's such a dear, silky little curl. Quite black."

"Let me see it."

She rose and left the room. Returning, she unwrapped the covering of tissue paper and showed me the curl, as soft and sweet as the day it was cut.

"My hair is coarser than that now," I laughed.

"It's very nice hair, Israel."

And then I took her in my arms and kissed her, which may seem rather premature, but there had been that in the conversation which had led up to the situation. Of course, Sibella would not have been a woman had she not declared that she would never forget that she was now Lionel's wife, and that on a former occasion she must have been mad. She repeated that she always knew I was wicked, and that I had gained an ascendancy over her. She then proceeded to tell me that I was in love with Lady Pebworth, with whom she had lately had a coolness. That lady evidently thought that she had purchased by her introductions a perpetual right to the subservience of Sibella and her husband. She was now experiencing the utter callousness of Sibella's disposition towards her own sex, a callousness she was exceedingly clever at masking till she had obtained what she wanted.

It was difficult to say where the weak point in Sibella's armour came in. She was, of course, vain, but as a rule her vanity was not allowed to interfere with her interests. She was dominated to a great extent by looks. It was this passion for beautiful people that had made it a perfectly safe proceeding to introduce Sir Anthony Cross to her. I was sure that no man so destitute of pretensions to physical charm could ever win her suffrages. In fact, I was pleased to know that he was always to be seen near her, for his case was hopeless.

"Perhaps it is a very good thing we did not marry, Sibella. A strict barrier should always be preserved between the official and the sentimental roles."

"My dear Israel, Lionel is much more sentimental than you are."

"Women are amazingly quick. Perhaps sentiment is the wrong word; I should have said romantic."

"What is the difference?"

"There is all the difference. The sentimentalist has no sense of humour. The romanticist generally has too much. A romanticist may possess the salt of cynicism; a sentimentalist seldom."

Sibella had something of an intellect, and I think, perhaps, that was also a weak point, for inasmuch as it was a poorly developed sort of affair it was easily dazzled, and she would at the merest flicker from an opposing mind credit it with much that it did not possess.

I had led the conversation away from Lady Pebworth, but she brought it back again, and flattered me by insisting on learning from my own lips that I had no affection for the lady.

Fortunately she only knew of Miss Gascoyne's existence in a vague sort of way.

"What would you do, Sibella, if I married?"

"Forbid it."

"You think that would be effective?"

"If it were not I should never speak to you again."

"Ah, unfortunately it is forbidden to a discretion like yours to take such extreme measures."

"Why?"

"Lionel would want to know why we had quarrelled." How she would act when it came to telling her that I was engaged to Miss Gascoyne—which I hoped would shortly be the case—I could not say. Miss Gascoyne's extreme beauty and distinction would not help the matter.

I had my hands quite full, for I was working very hard at the office, and making myself as indispensable as possible to Mr. Gascoyne. The rest of the staff had ceased being jealous when they saw that I was determined to get what I wanted. Such remarks as "one of those damned Jews again," unintentionally overheard by me, I ignored with the sublime cynicism of my race. Nothing was to be gained by being aware of them, less was to be gained by cherishing resentment. Jews are not good at revenge; it is not business. Shylock's case was exceptional, and, given time, his common sense would have reasserted itself.

I was even treated as the natural heir to the business, for I had wisely thrown out veiled hints of a partnership to the managing clerk.

I was about this time somewhat scared by a suitor appearing for Miss Gascoyne's hand, and such a suitor as must have made any mere business man tremble for his own chance.

I knew that Miss Gascoyne was constantly receiving the very best invitations, which she seldom accepted. I also knew that she and her uncle and aunt had dined with the Gascoynes, and I had heard mentioned, not, however, as a matter of any great consequence, that they had met there a Mr. Hibbert-Wyllie. I was therefore a little astonished on calling one Sunday afternoon to find Mr. Hibbert-Wyllie, a young man undeniably handsome and well-bred, in the drawing-room. I could not stay long, but even in the short time I was there it was obvious that the object of his visit was Miss Gascoyne. He was evidently rich, for outside the door was an exceedingly luxurious motor. I looked him up in the landed gentry, and found that he was one of the untitled nobility. He had a huge estate, and was related to half the peerage. His sisters were a duchess and two countesses, and his younger brother was already a distinguished member of Parliament. He was Lord-Lieutenant of his county, and altogether a notable person. It seemed as if, granting any inclination on Miss Gascoyne's part, my fate was sealed.

The next time I called Mrs. Gascoyne said to me when we were alone:

"I am afraid my niece will not be with us much longer."

"Indeed?"

I think she must have had some notion that I had dreamed of Miss Gascoyne as my wife, for there was an accent of kindliness in her voice.

"You have met Mr. Hibbert-Wyllie?"

"Oh, yes." I almost gasped. Surely she was not going to tell me that Miss Gascoyne was engaged to him already.

"It will be a splendid match. She is quite the woman to take her place at the head of county society."

"They are engaged?"

"Oh dear no, but anyone can see that there is a mutual attraction, and it is altogether so exactly suitable that we hope it will take place."

I had never before considered Mrs. Gascoyne a fool.

Mr. Gascoyne came in soon after, and she began again. I think she believed it the kindest thing to do.

"I have just been talking to Israel about Edith and Mr. Hibbert-Wyllie."

Mr. Gascoyne looked astonished, and gave me a side-long glance.

"Indeed? Don't you think, my dear, we are a little premature?"

"There is no harm in discussing it."

In a few minutes Mr. Hibbert-Wyllie and Miss Gascoyne came in.

I had never met Mr. Hibbert-Wyllie anywhere except at the Gascoynes'. He had all the unfailing and general courtesy of the absolutely exclusive. He was not a man who, as far as I could gather, went out much, but he entertained Royalty a good deal, having some of the finest shooting in England.

Of his manner to me I had certainly no reason to complain, but I think he was a little astonished when Mr. Gascoyne very pointedly introduced me as a cousin. I suppose my Semitic appearance had hardly prepared him for the news. Since, however, I was a relation he could not doubt my general authenticity.

Personally I would much sooner Mr. Gascoyne had not been so ready to insist on my being of Gascoyne blood.

I walked home wondering whether after all Mrs. Gascoyne was not mistaken.

I had studied Miss Gascoyne very carefully, and I could not detect any indications that she was likely to capitulate to Mr. Hibbert-Wyllie. At the same time, she was outwardly an impassive woman, and appearances might be deceptive.

I admired and desired her even beyond Sibella, certainly beyond Sibella now that I was sure of the latter. I was not in the least conscious of any absurdity in arranging my affections so as to dovetail with my love for two women. Even theoretical polygamy comes quite naturally to me, for all Jews are polygamists at heart, even if as a nation they find it convenient to disown it. King Solomon, with his enormous female collection, remains their typical domestic character.

I desired Miss Gascoyne, and was determined to run the risk of asking her to marry me, though I was perfectly aware that it was after marriage that the battle would begin. She was not a woman to endure tamely any insult to the conventions, and she was not likely to agree with Dr. Johnson's dictum: 'Why, sir, a wise woman does not trouble herself about her husband's infidelities.' Domestic life would be a different matter if this were a recognised rule, which woman was brought up to regard as a principle of life. It is a fact, however, which a wise woman learns early, that a man's infidelities need not in any way affect his supreme devotion to a particular female. The objection that in that case a woman should have the same privilege is childish, and can of course be refuted on the most elementary utilitarian grounds. If she desired such liberty, a fact which I doubt in the case of the normal woman, I think matters would have been differently arranged, and a more elastic scheme of rearing the young in civilised communities established. I certainly was prepared to sustain my passion for both women, and if society made it difficult, why, I must meet society with its own weapons. I was not going to agree to forego one woman because to a slightly greater degree I desired the other.

I might find out when matters settled down, as I hoped one day they would, that I loved Sibella the better. At present she was at a disadvantage, as the woman possessed always must be, by the side of the woman unpossessed. It was not perhaps brains that lifted Miss Gascoyne above Sibella; it was character. Miss Gascoyne would have sacrificed everything for principle. I could not imagine Sibella sacrificing much, even for prejudice.

I lived for the next few weeks in the greatest suspense. Mr. Hibbert-Wyllie was constantly at the Gascoynes', and I was startled by a false report that the engagement was arranged and about to be announced. I heard it at Lady Pebworth's. Her ladyship was a sort of cousin of Mr. Hibbert-Wyllie's. It turned out to be a false rumour, but I spent a sleepless night. I spoke to Mr. Gascoyne about it the next day at the office.

"I hear that Mr. Hibbert-Wyllie and Miss Gascoyne are engaged."

"Good gracious, I've heard nothing about it."

In my relief I laughed gaily. "Then there can't be any truth in it."

"Who told you?"

"I heard it at Lady Pebworth's."

"Then it is evidently expected. If it takes place it is a match of my wife's making, but I shouldn't wonder if after all she were disappointed."

"It would be a splendid match," I said, hypocritically.

He looked at me keenly.

"You are very clever at disguising your feelings, Israel. I had no idea you were so subtle."

I had made a mistake, and appeared before him for one moment in my true character.

"Where a woman is concerned men discover unexpected attributes."

"That is true." He was too tactful to pursue the subject of my admiration for Miss Gascoyne further, and continued: "No one has a greater respect for rank and its obligations than my niece. At the same time, I don't think a throne would tempt her to lie about her feelings."

I was lunching with Grahame that day. We had not seen each other for some time, but his steady blue eyes met mine with no diminution of friendship. He was at the moment slave to a romance of a most inconvenient type. He had fallen in love with quite a common girl, and was unhappy when she was out of his sight. Luckily there was no question of his marrying her. Had it been necessary I verily believe he would have done so, for his heart compelled all sacrifices.

"We never see each other now, Israel."

I knew how to appeal to Grahame.

"Does that matter with a friendship as strong as ours?"

"Of course it does not affect our friendship, but still one likes to see one's friends now and then."

"Has it been altogether my fault?"

"Well, I suppose not," admitted Grahame.

"I'll put you to the test. Let us go out of town from Saturday till Monday. I know a ripping little seaside hotel, and I love the sea in winter." He coloured and looked confused, and I added quickly: "You can't come?"

"Well, I—"

"Don't prevaricate, Grahame. Of course you can't come. In the first place, you have promised to take her to a theatre on Saturday evening. You are lunching with her on Sunday. You are driving her to the Star and Garter at Richmond to tea in the afternoon, and you are coming back to dine somewhere very luxurious with her in the evening."

He laughed. "That's very near it."

"And in two years' time, or even sooner, her face won't stir a passing emotion in you."

"Don't, Israel, you hurt."

"I'm sorry, but if you did come away you would be thinking of nothing but her the whole time."

"I am afraid you are right."

"You are a sentimentalist, Grahame, only, thank goodness, not a maudlin one, and sentimentalists are only possible during the *entr'actes*."

"Thanks."

My liking and friendship for Grahame were a proof of how sincere I could be if people did not stand in the way of my great design. I suppose I ought to have felt some remorse, considering that Sibella was his sister, but after all such relationships are purely accidental. The fact remains that Grahame might have asked for almost any sacrifice that did not interfere with my slow subterranean tunnelling to the Gascoyne peerage.

CHAPTER XVI

Miss Gascoyne refused Mr. Hibbert-Wyllie. I was first made aware of this fact by the announcement in the *Morning Post* that he had left London, and proposed to go for a six weeks' yachting cruise in the Mediterranean.

I hastened to call on Mrs. Gascoyne when I knew she would be alone.

"So very extraordinary, Israel," she said. "I had almost looked upon the thing as settled, but she refused him point-blank. It's my first and last attempt at match-making. I think Mr. Hibbert-Wyllie in his inmost heart was a little surprised. He took it very well, poor fellow, although I believe he felt quite broken-hearted. It's very strange, for it's not like Edith to lead a man on and then throw him over."

"Did she lead him on?" I asked.

"Surely you must have seen that?"

"Well, I can't exactly say that I did."

"But they went everywhere together, picture-galleries, concerts, theatres, lectures."

"Who asked him?" I interjected, slily.

Mrs. Gascoyne was one of those straight-dealing folk to whom it was perfectly possible to point out a mistake in judgment without creating an unfriendly atmosphere.

"Do yon mean to suggest that the mischief has been of my doing, Israel!"

"Dear lady, I mean to say that in your unselfish anxiety to marry your niece brilliantly you imagined a state of things which did not exist."

"Exactly; you mean that I'm a dreadful old mischief-maker."

"You know I don't mean that."

I always adopted in my attitude towards Mrs. Gascoyne a touch of ingenuousness which I found eminently effective. It impressed her, with a strong belief in my sincerity; in fact, talking to her I have known myself believe in my own sincerity, so free from guile was her manner of thought and speech.

A conviction, the result of some reflection, had forced itself upon me that with my secret inevitably striving to write itself on my face and manner it would be well to cultivate as much as possible the society of the simple-minded, in order to borrow something of their mood. Mood is everything in influencing surroundings. I am still unable to see why a murderer should not go through life with a perfect inward peace, providing his associates are the right people. Apart from a certain love of secret romances, I prefer the society of the simple-minded and the good; just as in order to preserve a proper balance of mind so much time should be spent in the country and so much time in town:—a constant going from the artificial to nature and back again from nature to the artificial. A right proportion of light and shade is a great factor in human happiness.

"I trust Edith means to marry," continued Mrs. Gascoyne. "It would be a crime if so much charm and character were wasted."

"Do you think it is necessarily wasted because a woman does not marry?"

"I am old-fashioned, Israel, and I think a woman's vocation is marriage."

"A great many women must be without a vocation," I laughed.

"That is no reason why as many as have the opportunity should not fulfil it. Now, when you marry, Israel—"

At that moment Miss Gascoyne entered the room. She was a little embarrassed, as if she were aware that I knew all about Wyllie's proposal and her refusal.

She was not the woman to dismiss a lover lightly and with a mere sensation of triumph at her own conquest. She had, I was sure, suffered in a way which most women would not have done.

With most women the dismissal of a lover brings with it a certain feeling of power. It is the one moment at which their sex can be truly said to rule.

Miss Gascoyne's manner had in it a trace of sadness, probably, I thought, expressive of regret that she had been unable to accept as a husband a man whom she thoroughly respected and who perhaps she even felt was in many ways her natural mate. Perhaps the event had led to a certain amount of retrospection and analysis of her own feelings. Lovers are modest, yet at the same time I fancy a favoured lover has as a rule a very fair impression that he is not distasteful, however fluttered he may be before he has made sure of his prize. So by some curious undercurrent flowing between us I gathered that Miss Gascoyne was more interested in my visits than she had ever been before. I had nothing very tangible to go on. There was no sudden development of coquetry, such as a smaller-minded woman would have displayed. She showed towards me the same even friendship, and we did not see more of each other. Perhaps I gathered the increasing warmth of her feelings from a certain relief and gladness at my arrival which even she could not conceal, or it might have been from a certain deference to my opinion.

To the ordinary observer it would have appeared almost incredible that this queenly, beautiful creature of good birth should prefer a stockbroker's clerk to Mr. Hibbert-Wyllie, one of the richest men in England, and connected with half the peerage. Busybodies would have argued that her pride, her sense of family, had always been stronger than her affections; which would have shown how very wrong busybodies, who are necessarily limited to a judgment based on the superficial, can be.

I had taken Grahame Hallward to see the Gascoynes, at Mr. Gascoyne's special invitation. The latter had met him with me in the City, and had conceived a great liking for him.

"You can always tell a man by his friends, Israel," he had said to me, "and young Hallward seems an altogether delightful fellow."

I could not forbear smiling. As a rule, it may be true that birds of a feather flock together, and that a man can be judged by the company he keeps, but at the same time it is curious what a man will put up with in the friend of his heart. The friendship of Grahame Hallward and myself was not dependent on any strong community of tastes and interests. It was the outcome of his own loyal nature, which, having made a friend, held to him. Mrs. and Miss Gascoyne liked him from the first.

He grasped the situation between Miss Gascoyne and myself at once, and he was the one person with whom I permitted myself to discuss it. He was enthusiastic in his admiration.

"She is a queenly woman, Israel. Have you known her long?"

"About a year."

"Well, you're a lucky chap."

"What do you mean?"

"Mustn't I discuss the matter? Tell me to shut up, and I will."

"You know I will discuss anything with you."

He gave me an affectionate look.

"Are you struck, Israel?"

"All of a heap." I always adopted a fresh, breezy way of talking with Grahame. I think that is why he believes in my innocence to this day, and also why he is suffering so much. He never saw the corners of my character, although he had known me so many years. I always appeared to him frank and affectionate.

"She'll suit you better than Sibella would have done."

Had I been without the ambitions I was possessed of, Miss Gascoyne would have done nothing of the kind. Sibella's decadent temperament would have furnished me with far more entertainment. But Edith Gascoyne was on the road to my objective. She was the most natural mistress in the world for Hammerton Castle.

"It's all rot my thinking of such a thing," I said, true to the character in which I instinctively appeared before Grahame. "She's got money of her own, and I'm a beggarly stockbroker's clerk with three hundred and fifty a year."

"Judging by Mr. Gascoyne's manner, I should say he meant you to be a little more than that one of these days."

"Oh, I'm not such a hypocrite as to pretend that it doesn't look as if he meant to do something for me. but I may have ever so long to wait till then."

"Don't you make any money on your own account?"

"Oh, a bit—nothing to speak of."

Grahame must have mentioned Miss Gascoyne to Sibella, because the next time I called she asked me why I had never spoken of her.

"I don't know, I'm sure," I answered, carelessly.

I was glad that Grahame had saved me the trouble of breaking the fact of her existence to Sibella. I was on perfectly good terms with the latter now, and she had quite overcome any scruples about deceiving "poor Lionel." She had in fact not known her own decadence till I had exploited it for her. She was revenged by my becoming intensely jealous of her. After all, she was meeting daily a great number of men who were willing to dance attendance on her till further notice, and it was impossible and unnatural that she should not find some of them attractive, and having been taught infidelity she might profit only too well by the instruction. I behaved with the greatest discretion. I had no mind to have all my plans upset by a divorce case. Mr. Gascoyne would inevitably have shown me the door, whilst my chances with Miss Gascoyne would have disappeared entirely. No, if I could not give up so delirious a vice as Sibella it behoved me to be very careful, and I think I can flatter myself that Lionel never had the least suspicion. I suppose a guilty wife must always be in dread of disclosing her secret in the hours of sleep, like the lady in the opera, but I don't think Sibella was sufficiently disturbed by the consciousness of sin to have her very sound slumbers interrupted.

I was jealous of her, and however much I might upbraid myself for such a weakness I was unable to control it. Woman-like, she very soon discovered the fact, and I was somewhat at her mercy.

Sooner or later, she must inevitably learn all about Miss Gascoyne's existence, and I was glad that Grahame had broken the ice.

"She is very beautiful, is she not?"

"I believe she is considered lovely."

"Then I can't understand your not having mentioned her."

There was a touch of asperity in Sibella's voice.

"Why should I mention her?"

"Because as far as I can make out you are there constantly."

"It is to my advantage to make myself agreeable to Mr. and Mrs. Gascoyne, and," I added hastily, for I never appeared as acting from interested motives more than I could help, "I am very fond of them."

"And very fond of Miss Gascoyne."

Sibella's was not the nature to exercise much control over rising jealousy.

"What nonsense! As far as that goes, you would not have much to complain of if I were to marry Miss Gascoyne."

She looked at me with frightened eyes.

"If I thought you meant that—" she faltered.

"Well, you must remember that you and I might have fulfilled our natural destiny and married."

Sibella laughed in a not altogether nice way.

"That would have been a very pleasant arrangement. We should have been so comfortably off, shouldn't we?"

It gave me an advantage to pretend that it was a cause of eternal grief to me that we were not married, so I answered:

"Well, I've no doubt we could have scraped along."

"Scraped along!" And she laughed again, but she was not nearly so amused as I was at hearing myself use such an expression. "I can't imagine either of us, Israel, scraping along. We should have hated each other in a week."

"We should never have done that, Sibella. We have a sub-consciousness of each other's weaknesses, and we know each other's good points better than anyone else could. We should always love each other."

"I think, Israel, if I had not been so sure that you loved me, I should not have risked marrying Lionel. I could never have believed that good looks could bore one so soon."

"I believe that good-looking people who are stupid get on one's nerves sooner than plain people who are stupid. The latter do feel that they must make an effort. The former are supremely well contented, and seldom take the trouble to make themselves agreeable."

"Lionel is not only stupid, he is a little vulgar."

Sibella's frank recognition of the faults of her belongings had always been in striking contrast to Grahame's loyalty, which would allow no disparagement of anyone he was allied to.

"I suppose we shall settle down one of these fine days," continued Sibella. "We shall get tired of scheming for interviews, and plotting and planning our lives so as to make them fit with a secret."

"My dear Sibella, I had no idea you were such a philosopher. I thought your reflections never carried you further than the moment."

"Oh, I didn't think it out myself. I read it in a book, but I feel it to be true, all the same."

"You mean we shall tire of each other?"

"Yes."

"Then we shall be tired of each other, and in that condition of affairs there is no pain."

Sibella's two blue lakes—in which to those who could read there swam any amount of moral fishiness—brimmed over.

"Don't talk like that, Israel. I do love you, although you may not believe it. If I had known all I know now about my feelings before I got married I do not think I could have been induced to marry Lionel." And she wept.

I took her in my arms and kissed the moist rose of her lips and caressed her yellow hair. Most men dislike seeing a woman in tears; to the artist in romance it has its value if he keep his real sympathies well in the background.

"I should like to know the Gascoynes, Israel."

This had been inevitable. I had not the least wish for Sibella and Edith to be made known to each other. Not that in the case of such diverse characters there was likely to be the least exchange of confidences, but they were certainly better apart. I could not imagine Miss Gascoyne approving of Sibella; I could not conceive Sibella understanding Miss Gascoyne, or thinking her other than somewhat of a prig.

I betrayed not the least perturbation at her request, however.

"Of course you must meet," I said, "but you know how I hate premeditated introductions. They are never a success."

Sibella, woman-like, looked unconscious of any reticence on my part on the subject, but I felt that she suspected it. Well, she had been made aware of Miss Gascoyne's existence in as tactful a manner as possible.

"What would you do if I were to marry, Sibella?" This was a question I was very fond of asking her.

"I don't know; it all depends on whom you married, and whether you married for love, or—"

"Or interest, you mean. I could not do the former very well, as I am in love with you, but you must admit it would be foolish not to do the latter."

"I suppose there is something in marrying for love," said Sibella, a little gloomily.

"In the poorer classes I should think it meant everything. In the case of the well-to-do it is nothing like so important."

"I thought I was in love with Lionel."

"Yes, Sibella, to do you justice I believe you did."

"And when I discovered that I was not it was too late to draw back."

Like all people in love we derived a never-ending pleasure from going backwards and forwards over the whole psychological battle-ground of our romance.

Lionel was often out of the way. He aspired to lead the life of a very smart young man indeed. He confided to me that it was somewhat of a mystery to him that in all the years he had been about town he had only lately succeeded in getting into the particular set he desired to mix with. He was a member of one or two extremely select clubs, although the absolute holy of holies he could not enter, despite the fact that Sir Anthony was still as far off Sibella as he had ever been—at least, such was my impression. The infatuated baronet was prepared to thrust Lionel down the throats of his most intimate circle.

Sir Anthony might have a curious pronunciation of the Queen's English, which dispensed with final "g's," and clipped the majority of words in an altogether surprising manner; he might wear checks which to a chess enthusiast would at once have suggested a problem; he might have a partiality for spats and white bowlers; he might even swear occasionally in the presence of women, but in spite of all these things he remained undeniably a gentleman; for being a gentleman has nothing to do with grammar or morals. In time a street urchin may acquire the one, and a Non-conformist parson may have the other, but the fact of being a gentleman resides in the individual's consciousness. Therefore it is useless for those to whom public companies and cheeses and cheap teas have stood for the goose with the golden eggs to watch my lord's peculiarities or the characteristics of even plain John Brown, gentleman. They never can be gentlemen. Their sons may. Their sons' sons surely will be, but they themselves will feel conscious that they are not the right article till their dying day. They may be the best of fellows, the most upright of men, the most polished of speakers, but they will hear it whispered behind their backs every now and then that "Hang it all, the man's not a gentleman, you know!"

And I am convinced that had I, Israel Rank, been completely a gentleman on both sides I could never have penned the above snobbish paragraph. It is the reticence of gentlemen, and their lack of statement of claim, that keeps up all the barriers and holds democracy at bay.

Lionel Holland might have felt more secure if his father had sent him to Eton and Oxford, which he could well have afforded to do, but to old Mr. Holland these were almost mythical places. Lionel himself spoke with characteristic unkindness of his father for not having done so. He was, fortunately for himself, impervious to many slights and snubs which would have driven a more self-respecting youth back into his own circle.

When I had first advised him to go in for politics I did not imagine the matter would have been so easily arranged. Another and a cleverer man, equally rich, might have waited for years for such an opportunity.

The seat he was selected to contest happened, however, to be in that part of the country in which lay Sir Anthony Cross's estate, and what with Sir Anthony's own influence and the influence of the people around with whom he was connected by ties of marriage or of interest, he was practically able to secure Lionel's election. If the latter had the least notion of Sir Anthony's real motive for all this attention he was evidently prepared to accept it, and laugh in his sleeve at the fool who was carrying his pigs to such a bad market. The son of the man who had risen to wealth from the position of a street boy had plenty of shrewd cunning, and could bide his time. Men of high and noble honour and unstainable integrity do not make fortunes, or at least very rarely, and the valuable qualities of those who do are not as a rule lost in a generation.

CHAPTER XVII

MY AFFAIRS stood thus. I proposed to marry Miss Gascoyne if I could, but I had no notion of breaking with Sibella.

All this time I was closely debating which of the obstacles in my way I should remove next.

There had been three Henry Gascoynes. The youngest was gone. There remained two, and one of them, nearly ninety, was scarcely worth considering. He was hardly likely to marry, and if he did so children were almost out of the question, although I had not made myself acquainted with his physical condition and method of life. He lived the existence of a recluse on a miniature estate somewhere in the lake district. None of the Gascoynes that I was acquainted with had ever met him.

The remaining Henry Gascoyne was a parson and a childless widower. He was sixty-two years of age. His cure was in Lincoln-shire, and one of the very few livings still worth having. The eminently spiritual method of selection practised by the Established Church was testified to by the fact that the living had been the gift of his wife's father, and the claims of a curate who had done the work of the parish for thirty years, representing the valetudinarian and octogenarian vicar, had been passed over. Country livings are an appanage of family, not of church. Even that good old-fashioned custom, however, is going with the diminution in the value of tithes. It is no use struggling to retain what is not worth having. Henry Gascoyne must be my next victim if I were not to play the coward and draw back, wasting so much good work already done. The very "if" that entered into my mind warned me that my nerve could not endure for ever. I had thought the preservation of nerve merely a question of self-control, but as I grew older I realised that there were many and complex human emotional developments in perpetual siege of that valuable attribute.

One thing at a time, and as it would not be advisable to try my luck with Miss Gascoyne just yet, I decided to devote myself to inquiring into the affairs of the Reverend Henry Gascoyne.

Each undertaking of the kind became more and more difficult to manage. An introduction to the Reverend Henry Gascoyne would tie my hands. My presence on the occasion of a third Gascoyne dying a tragic death might become the subject of remark, and once the hue and cry was raised evidence might accumulate rapidly enough, and, as is often the case, most unexpectedly. Even Ughtred Gascoyne's death might become a support to suspicion, though there might never be any direct proof that I had had a hand in it. Indeed, it was prolonged reflection on this matter that made me realise that my nerve was not an impregnable fortress.

Still, I could not draw back. What duty is to many people my ambition was to me. It had to be gone through, though hell fire waited for me when it was attained. It was not that I was incapable of rehearsing the penalties of failure, but that I realised that if once I let my imagination loose among such possibilities chaos would ensue.

I took down Crockford's and perused it. The Reverend Henry Gascoyne had been ordained at twenty-three. Evidently the valetudinarian rector was on his last legs at the time, and it had been advisable to have his successor in readiness. On going into the matter it turned out to be as I expected. After spending two years as curate of a smart West End church he had stepped into the living of Lye.

Lye was in Lincolnshire. If I wished to discover further particulars about my reverend cousin there appeared to be no other way than by going down to the village. I was not at the time quite as free as I had been formerly. Mr. Gascoyne had grown to expect me on Sundays, if not to lunch, to dinner, and I think he considered it as somewhat of a slight if I did not appear. I was looked upon as the son of the house, and he certainly had a right to expect something of a son's duty in return for the uniform kindness he had shown me. Not that he was likely to display resentment at my going out of town for a day or two, but it would involve explanations, and explanations involved deception, and deception involved the danger of being found out. To say I was going to one place when I was going to another meant the possibility of being discovered, and so far I had kept singularly clear of petty deception.

I decided that some friends in a humble walk of life might be useful, and invented a family called Parsons, the name suggested by the quarry I was hunting. They had, I explained, been good to me when I was a poor lad at Clapham, and had now gone to live in the country. To avoid committing myself I wrote down every particular about them which I might be questioned on, and learned them off by heart. I introduced their name casually into the conversation at dinner at the Gascoynes'.

Yes, I told them, in replying to questioning, there was Mrs. Parsons and her son and a daughter. Mr. Parsons was dead. His son had always loved the country, and having inherited a small farm from an uncle, he and his mother and sister had gone to live on it. Was the daughter pretty? I did not know. I had not seen her for some years, and girls change so. The son was the same age as I was. No, we had not gone to the same school, and he did not know Grahame Hallward. Our acquaintance had come of our living near each other.

I changed the subject as soon as possible.

Soon after I found occasion to say that I had met young Parsons in London, and that he had asked me to go down and spend a few days at their farm near Norwich. I felt the whole thing to be lamentably clumsy. It would have been better to get to know someone near Mr. Gascoyne's rectory, but it was done, and as soon as I had finished with the Parsons family I intended to ship them all off to Canada, where there are as many farms as the imagination can desire.

When I declared that I must accept their invitation, or Mrs. Parsons and her children would be hurt, I fancy Miss Gascoyne's face lighted. I was sure that she had endowed me with all sorts of good qualities to which I could lay no claim. She was touched at my consideration for the Parsons' feelings. She was a woman incapable of giving love where she could not give respect.

The world only knowing me through the medium of a trial for murder has no doubt made up its mind that anyone who could respect me must have been a very bad judge of character. The world, however, is not itself a very good judge of character. To man, his fellow-creatures are as a rule divided into two classes, viz.: the penny plain and twopence coloured. If Mr. Brown has been found with Mr. Jones's wife, Mr. Brown is a complete and wholly irreclaimable blackguard. That he has been an honest citizen, an attentive husband, and an irreproach-able father hitherto counts for nothing. These virtues only aggravate the offence, inasmuch as they are shown by the nature of his guilt to have been mere hypocrisies. Public exposure is the real guilt in his fellow-men's eyes. The old, old crime of being found out is the unforgivable offence. They know in their hearts that he is rather a fine fellow, that his slip is what might have happened to any of them. They have probably some such little liability still unpaid standing to their own account, but this does not make them one whit the less severe in judging their foolish fellow who has been discovered. It is thus. A man who has been in the dock and has been convicted loses the right to claim any virtues. As for a man who has been convicted of murder! What can be said for him? Just as he has been found guilty of the crime the law holds most wicked, so must he be capable of committing all those crimes which murder is supposed to take precedence of.

Yet Miss Gascoyne was right, and the world was wrong. She had seen the best side of me, and—at the risk of appearing egotistical and conceited—there was much to respect in my character, especially as seen by her, and it was by no means all spurious virtue. I had a sound judgment. I was no snob, and I was not only well read, but I had musical accomplishments, which—strange in a woman of her birth and country breeding—she did not despise. She deemed me loyal, and so I was, with limitations. Above all, she loved me—of that I was now sure—and everything I had to show in the shape of goodness shone, as will do the deeds of her lover in the eyes of woman. She took a much truer view of my character than the public have done so far. I was kind-hearted; this she had discovered for herself, and, curiously enough, without my putting the fact too obviously before her.

I already saw myself married to her, and I could not help thinking of the importance it would give me in the eyes of the world to have been accepted by the beautiful Miss Gascoyne, who had refused almost the finest match in England. People would hardly credit it, and it certainly was necessary to know Miss Gascoyne in order thoroughly to understand her action.

I went on my visit to the imaginary Parsons family, and when I returned was compelled to invent still further details for Miss Gascoyne's benefit. She was interested in everything I did, and asked all manner of questions about them, down to minute details as to what young Parsons grew most on his farm.

"Really," I laughed, "I didn't ask."

"That's not very like you, Mr. Rank. You generally want to know everything. Your capacity for picking up information has always surprised me."

"We were too occupied in talking over old times," I answered, and the conversation was diverted to a good-natured bantering on my inquisitive ways.

I had, however, seen the Reverend Henry Gascoyne, and had even heard him preach. The village of Lye lay right out in the midst of the fens of Lincolnshire. In the autumn—the time at which I visited it— it looked well enough, but in the winter I should think it must have been dreary beyond description. The village itself clustered round the church, a fine old building dating from about the year twelve hundred. It was partly in ruin; indeed, it was a question whether it had ever really been completed. The interior depended for its beauty on the design, for it had all the coldness and inhospitable aspect of the average English country church where the incumbent has been untouched by the High Church movement. There was a Communion Table which might have been anything, but for its position, and a dusty Litany lay on the desk. The walls were covered with memorials to the Hutchins, the family of Mr. Gascoyne's wife, from whom he had received the living.

There was a brand-new bronze tablet—somewhat of a relief after the black-edged marble mementoes of the rest of the Hutchins family— to the memory of Mary Gascoyne, the beloved wife of Henry Gascoyne, incumbent of the parish, with a space for the name of the Reverend Henry when he should be carried, by a power stronger than his own, from the comforts of Lye Rectory to that land, the glories and happinesses of which he expatiated upon every Sunday, but which he was in no hurry to set out for.

The Reverend Henry was none of your new-fangled parsons who carry the teachings of the New Testament uncomfortably into private life. As for testing social conditions from the Book of Books, it had never entered his head. Christianity was an ideal, and you were to get as near to it as possible. As parson, the only difference between himself and his parishioners lay in the fact that it was incumbent upon him to preserve a greater staidness of demeanour than the neighbouring gentry. Not that he was nearly as staid and solemn as his brother-in-law, Sir Robert Hutchins, who sat in the family pew on Sunday mornings and evenings, a monument of respectability and convention.

Neither, judging by the somewhat florid colouring of his face, did the Reverend Henry hold with temperance doctrines. Indeed, I heard that this matter caused some dispute between him and Sir Robert Hutchins, and that the brothers-in-law were not on the best of terms. It pleased Sir Robert Hutchins to hold a sort of informal service in the village schoolroom every Sunday afternoon, when those who were of a Methodistical turn of mind could hold forth and give addresses and so work off their schismatic steam. Sir Robert was of opinion that the Reverend Henry should have fallen into line with his truly statesmanlike scheme, but the Reverend Henry was in the habit of spending his Sunday afternoon with his port, gazing sleepily from his long dining-room windows across the pleasant Lincolnshire landscape, and he informed his brother-in-law that he was not sure that loyalty to the church would permit him to sit and listen to the outpourings of Mr. Butt, the carpenter, or Mr. Shingle, the village grocer; and that a really well thought out and carefully delivered sermon was a greater strain than his brother-in-law had any conception of: He declared that it very often took the whole afternoon before his nerves had fully recovered from the effort. At this Sir Robert murmured something about clergymen being always so ready to take care of those bodies which they taught other people to despise. Then the Reverend Henry grew mightily offended, and replied with cutting sarcasm that he knew that Nonconformity usually had a contempt for the appointed ministers of the church, but that if his brother-in-law wished to show his contempt he had better withdraw to West Lye on Sundays, where there was enough irreverent and blasphemous Psalm-singing and taking of the Lord's name in vain to satisfy the most egotistical of schismatics. But even when he expressed himself in this highly independent and manly fashion he was so completely the slave of convention as to feel that it was highly improper for an incumbent to be speaking to his patron in such a way; the patron of a living standing—in the sort of nebulous hierarchy which he had constructed in his own head—somewhere between the parson and the Deity.

All of this information I obtained at the village inn from general conversation. It appeared to have been conveyed to the community from the servants at the Rectory and the Hall, and had evidently lost nothing in the telling.

I attended the service, and saw my reverend cousin for the first time. I am bound to say I rather liked him, in spite of the suggestion of good living in his face. He looked frank and honest. He conducted the service in a nice, gentlemanly way, and preached an exceedingly good sermon on scandal and tale-bearing. There appeared, from the knowing looks of the parishioners, to have been some special scandal of late in the village, for everyone glanced at his neighbour as much as to say, "I hope this will be a lesson to you for the term of your natural life."

I seated myself behind a pillar so that I could get a good view of the parson when he was not looking, and could disappear from sight when his gaze wandered in my direction.

The service over, Mr. Gascoyne retired through the Rectory garden in the company of a lady and a young girl, who I afterwards learned were his sister and her daughter. He was a great sportsman and an excellent shot, but I suppose in deference to his cloth he drew the line at eating the game he killed. From what I could gather I should think he was quite alive to the humour of this inconsistency.

I wandered about the churchyard and watched the verger lock the great doors and shuffle out of the wicket gate across the dusty road to his cottage. A silence descended over the village. As I walked round and round the church, pretending to be absorbed in the gravestones, I was racking my brains for some means of carrying out my design on the estimable cleric who was at that moment sitting down to roast mutton and claret as a preliminary to his afternoon port.

Two schemes arose in my brain simultaneously. At the west end of the church there were some ruined arches, which were no doubt the ruins of the unfinished north and south transept. I looked at them with interest. The stonework was crumbling woefully, and it would not be a very difficult matter to detach a brick. The decaying masonry also suggested that it would be easy to climb to the top of the arch, where there was a buttress, the shadow of which might at night furnish absolute concealment to anyone bold enough to scale it. A large stone thrown accurately on the head of anyone passing beneath it would be almost bound to kill. It was a risky proceeding.

Anyone coming from a certain part of the village would inevitably use the short cut, and pass under the arch on the way to the Rectory. How was I to know, however, when the Reverend Henry was likely to pass that way, especially as from all accounts he very seldom went out at night? It seemed as if I should have to give this idea up. I had to consider also that the arch would be by no means a very pleasant thing to climb, and that it might come to the ground under my weight. The risks of the stone not falling on the right spot were also great. On the other hand, it would be sure to look like an accident.

The other method was suggested by my seeing the vestry window open. Looking in, the first thing that struck my eye was a table by the window, on which were a bottle and glass. They had stood at the preacher's right hand during the sermon, and the Reverend Henry had more than once had recourse to them. Was it possible to doctor the water? The Rector would at least have a dramatic death in the pulpit. I could not help smiling at the idea of his tumbling down the pulpit steps in the midst of one of his most eloquent periods. It was worth thinking out.

There was no more to be done at the moment, and as I did not wish to become well known in the village I returned to London.

The next time I went into the district I intended to stay at a small place some distance off, and use my bicycle.

On my arrival in town I was compelled, as I have said, to give a minute account of the establishment of the imaginary Parsons.

Sibella was also anxious to know why she had not seen me for three whole days, but I evaded her questions, and did not let myself in for a repetition of the Parsons inventions.

About this time I was, through no wish of mine, introduced to Lord and Lady Gascoyne. They had, since Miss Gascoyne's arrival in South Kensington, called every now and then on Mr. and Mrs. Gascoyne, and had, I believe, taken a great fancy to the household. Lady Gascoyne, dark, brilliantly pretty—the word beautiful would have been out of place—was an American of very questionable birth, and had recognised at once the real breeding that characterised her husband's unpretentious relations. She was very anxious for Miss Gascoyne to visit them. Would they not all come to Hammerton? Lord Gascoyne warmly seconded the invitation. Miss Gascoyne excused herself on the ground of mourning. Lady Gascoyne had herself lost a brother, and her eyes filled. He had been her father's joy and hope. It was for him the money had been made. She would not have been so rich if darling Louis had been alive, but she would willingly give up all her fortune if it could bring him back. I am afraid that if poor Louis had not died and left his sister sole heiress it was hardly likely that she would have been Lady Gascoyne. But they appeared to be a devoted couple, and she talked almost incessantly of the little Viscount Hammerton, and Lord Gascoyne himself talked of the child a great deal. Mrs. Gascoyne, although the most delightful woman imaginable, was, after all, of bourgeois extraction, and was somewhat impressed by the Earl and his lady. She invariably gave me detailed accounts of their visits, and was hoping that Mr. Gascoyne would accept the invitation to Hammerton. Lady Gascoyne was going to bring little Lord Hammerton to see her. At this Mrs. Gascoyne's eyes filled with tears, thinking of her own boy, and I suppose I ought to have felt uncomfortable.

We were all sitting peacefully one Sunday afternoon not making the least effort to entertain one another, the surest sign of a perfect community of feeling. Mr. and Mrs. Gascoyne were dozing on each side of the fire. I was reading a book, and Miss Gascoyne was writing letters, when Lord and Lady Gascoyne were announced.

"And I've brought Simmy," said Lady Gascoyne, placing a bundle of lace in Mrs. Gascoyne's arms. "Our engagements for the afternoon fell through, so we thought we would run over and see if you were in. Very rude, isn't it?"

Mrs. Gascoyne was holding Simeon, Viscount Hammerton, to her bosom. She was a woman who had been destined by nature to be the mother of many children. There is no mistaking the woman who is above all things a mother when she has a child in her arms. She cannot assume anything in the way of attitude which is not protective.

Mr. Gascoyne introduced me, and with characteristic good taste made no mention of my being a distant cousin. I fancy when Mrs. Gascoyne said, "Israel, come and admire the baby," Lord Gascoyne looked a little perplexed, as if it were a surprise to hear the name out of Petticoat Lane. I went over, and was presented to Lady Gascoyne.

She gave me a little bow, very courteous, very distant, full of that exaggerated reserve assumed by American women who have matched themselves with a great position.

"I do not suppose you are interested in children," she said.

"On the contrary, I love them, don't I, Mrs. Gascoyne?"

"Mr. Rank adores them, Lady Gascoyne. He positively rains coppers on poor children."

This was perfectly true. How far my interest went beyond delight in their beauty I cannot say. I sometimes wonder how anyone can love anything but children. Their delicacy and sweetness are so exquisite compared to the faded or grosser beauty of their elders.

I held out my arms, and to Lady Gascoyne's great surprise took the child with perfect confidence from Mrs. Gascoyne. I fancy Lady Gascoyne was somewhat alarmed, but, mother-like, could not help feeling flattered. As for Simeon, Lord Hammerton, he held out a little fat hand, and clutched a piece of my cheek cooing wildly. I walked up and down the room whilst the ladies laughed.

"By Jove," said Lord Gascoyne, "that is more than I care to do, Marietta. I am afraid he has marked your cheek, Mr. Rank."

"Oh, that is nothing."

"We shall never get to the end of your abilities," smiled Miss Gascoyne.

"What a splendid father you will make," laughed Lady Gascoyne, and she held out her arms to the child, but as I placed him in them his infant lordship set up a shrill cry, which was immediately subdued when I took him again and resumed my promenade with him.

There was a chorus of astonishment.

"Really," said Lady Gascoyne, "I shall have to engage you as nurse, or are you mesmerising Simeon? Is he mesmerising you then, darling?"

His lordship did not condescend to answer, but lay in my arms gazing at her placidly. He dozed off, and I returned him to his mother. He woke up, however, as they left, and held out his arms to me to be taken.

"I shall always believe that you are a mesmerist," laughed Lady Gascoyne, as she said good-bye.

And thus it came about that I was introduced to Lord Gascoyne, and had to make my plans accordingly. I began to think it very hard that none of the family would die off naturally. It was really surprising how many people there were to get rid of, and on paper they had seemed so few.

I had by this time made up my mind that if opportunity occurred to propose to Miss Gascoyne I would do so. I had received so many proofs of her liking for me that I had come to the conclusion that I might just as well try my luck now as wait. The evening of Lord and Lady Gascoyne's visit furnished the opportunity. It was after dinner, and Mr. and Mrs. Gascoyne were dozing over the fire. Miss Gascoyne and I had retreated to the billiard-room, where I sat and smoked cigarettes, while she worked and talked to me. I was always very much at ease in her company. The dignified repose which she emanated was eminently to my liking. It was certainly a great contrast to the electrically charged atmosphere of Sibella's society.

"I am afraid I shall not know how to leave my aunt and uncle," she said. "They grow nervous at the mere idea."

"Is there any need why you should leave them?" I asked.

"Well, of course I am very devoted to them, but at the same time I think I am of rather an independent nature."

"You mean that you would prefer an establishment of your own?"

"Well, yes, you see I have been spoilt. I have tasted freedom. Of course it will be difficult to explain to my aunt and uncle that I am quite devoted to them, that I am perfectly happy here, and yet that I want to set up my own house."

I laughed.

"Yes, it will be rather difficult, although at the same time I perfectly understand what you mean."

"I suppose it seems unnatural for a single woman to want a place of her own; at any rate, until she's thirty."

"It doesn't run in the blood. A bachelor takes a private apartment, a spinster goes and lives in a boarding-house."

"I am afraid it is quite true," she answered, laughing, and then, with that perfect frankness about her sex which was one of her characteristics, she added, "But we spinsters—at least, that is, the poor ones—have to get ourselves husbands. It is potential matrimony that fills the boarding-house."

"You consider matrimony a woman's vocation?" I asked.

"I do." And she looked grave.

My heart beat a little faster. I had made up my mind to put the question. I continued: "And do you think marriages are happier if based on a community of interests or on a passionate attachment?"

She looked at me honestly.

"I think," she answered, "it is as impossible to generalise about marriage as about other things. It only leads to false conclusions. Of this, however, I am sure—if, when the flush of passion is past the interests of husband and wife lie apart, their chance of happiness cannot be very great. Don't you agree?"

I did agree, and embroidered her conclusions with even stronger argument. I was never cynical if I could help it with Miss Gascoyne; it made her uncomfortable, and she had once told me that she believed all cynics were rogues with a white feather. At least, she had read so somewhere, and it had struck her as being true.

I went on to the discussion of romance. I talked vaguely of men who had loved women infinitely above them.

"Even," I ended, "as I love you, have always loved you, shall always love you. I suppose I ought to have kept silence, but I believe you are generous enough not to be angry with me for wishing you to know how much I value you above all other women."

I turned away apparently overcome, and watched the effect of my speech in a looking-glass.

She was very moved, and her eyes filled with tears.

"Why should you not tell me?" she murmured, after a pause. From my point of vantage I could see in her face that my cause was a winning one.

"I ought not to have told you. I have hardly a shilling in the world. I owe everything to Mr. Gascoyne, whilst you—" I broke off.

"Do you think women only value love when it is accompanied by worldly advantage? Surely you are doing us an injustice. Won't you believe?"

I turned on her eagerly. Really, now I come to think over the whole scene, I must confess I played it uncommonly well. I was of course in love with her. She did not rouse fire and passion in me as Sibella did, but I was certainly in love. At the same time, I had none of the modest views about myself to which I had pretended, and it is decidedly difficult to play a half genuine love affair with the tongue in the cheek.

I was somewhat afraid to take her in my arms; she had always been so very stately, but I was surprised at the abandon with which she gave herself to me. It was only for a moment, however; the natural dignity of the woman reasserted itself.

"What on earth will they say?"

"I don't think they will mind; they will only be surprised."

I did not think Mr. Gascoyne would be at all annoyed, but I had a sort of idea that Mrs. Gascoyne would not be pleased.

"Shall we tell them?"

I knew that she was a woman who would demand courage from the man she loved even in little things.

"Why not?" I said.

So we walked into the drawing-room, and I said boldly: "Edith has promised to be my wife."

Mr. and Mrs. Gascoyne, awaked from their after-dinner slumber, gazed at us in astonishment.

Mrs. Gascoyne's face said as plainly as words could have done, 'What, refuse Mr. Hibbert-Wyllie, and accept Israel Rank; why, what are you thinking of?"

Mr. Gascoyne looked from one to the other several times before he spoke, saying finally, as he took her hands in his: "My dear, if I had thought of it at all I should have thought that you were the woman to prefer love and the approval of your own conscience to rank and wealth."

Mrs. Gascoyne, woman-like, could not forgive an event of the heart which she had not foreseen.

"Of course you know your own affairs best, but—"

She paused, evidently changing her mind, and, being one of the sweetest women in the world, rose, and kissing Edith, said: "My dear, I hope you will both be very happy, and, after all, as Mr. Gascoyne says, position and wealth are not everything."

I think the dear lady derived a certain satisfaction from the idea that our quartet would not be broken up. Certain it was that her rancour, if it could be called by such a harsh name, was short lived, and she entered into our schemes very heartily.

The next morning at the office Mr. Gascoyne called me into his private room.

"My wife and I have been talking things over, and we think it just as well that you should be told our intentions towards you. I hope this business will be yours one day, and I am sure there is no one we should wish to benefit more by what we have to leave than Edith's and your children."

I stammered out my thanks, for I was really moved, and for a moment could not help thinking of the son he had hoped would succeed him.

CHAPTER XVIII

BUT I had to tell Sibella.

I looked forward to this task with little relish. I had never seen her in a really bad temper, but I was certain that she could be violent. That was not all. She might break off our little affair, and my heart almost stopped beating as I thought of the possibility. It was essential, however, that I should tell her before she learned it from anyone else. A woman can always bear unpleasant news from the man she loves.

I found her alone and in a bad temper, complaining loudly of her woes. She was being dunned for some bills Lionel knew nothing about. They were living too extravagantly, she declared. They knew far too many rich people. Why were old Mr. and Mrs. Holland such a long time dying? She did not suppose for one moment they enjoyed their life. How could they?

She then wanted to know almost fiercely why I was not rich. I ought to pay some of her debts. It was only fair. Other people made money, why could not I?

I explained that I was doing my best—that on the whole I did not think I had done badly, and that I thought I should do better as time went on.

That was just it, she retorted, with some attempt at wit, time did go on.

I explained with almost brutal frankness—for the sooner she knew the longer time I should have in which to conciliate her—that I proposed to marry money in the person of Miss Gascoyne.

I was quite right; Sibella could be violent. At first she did not believe me; then with white, quivering lips she implored me to tell her it was not true. She was sorry she had been angry. She would retract everything she had said if I would only tell her that it was not true. It was intensely flattering to me to see how acutely she suffered. Most certainly the days of misery I had endured for her sake were amply avenged. I explained as gently as I could that it was necessary for my welfare that I should marry. It was such a chance as might not come again, and after all it need not make the least difference to us—although on this point I was in my own mind by no means sure. I saw looming up on the far distant horizon a very unpleasant and nerve-testing state of things.

Poor Sibella realised with feminine quickness that the woman who has the man in her house, and who, figuratively speaking, washes, cooks, and cleans up for him, stands the best chance of securing his heart— that part of a man's body being inextricably bound up with other and less romantic organs. Indeed, there is a community of dependence on the same flow of blood, and an identity of relation to the same scheme of physical machinery, which renders the fact inevitable.

She realised the possibilities involved in my having children, and in the mutual interests which were sure to draw us together more and more as time went on. As a consequence of these deductions, she wept dismally.

She was not philosophic enough to reckon with my plurality of disposition. As a woman, she might be forgiven for not being able to do so. Neither was she philosophical enough to reckon with the time when she would look back with amazement on that period when my presence meant a certain ecstasy, a solution which nearly always comes about if two people do not bind their lives together by a material interest, or that more iron bond, usage. It is profitable to the man who wishes to live by reason and not by mere feeling to reflect how many millions of the couples who think themselves indispensable the one to the other would have got on perfectly well with somebody else. If Mrs. Brown had married Mr. Jones, would she not say in later years, if she met Mr. Brown in the street:—"Fancy that old frump having made love to me!" The sentimentalist fancies she would still look at Mr. Brown with romantic eyes; not a bit of it. She would entirely have forgotten how very slim his waist had been, how very bright his eye. Believe me, we are not the individuals we think ourselves to be, but are fish swimming in a sea of condition and circumstance of which we all partake necessarily as we do of the air, the food, the ground beneath our feet, the whole world around us. Brown, Jones, and Robinson are much the same people, and the differentiation is largely illusory.

Poor Sibella passed from pleading to violence. If I did not at once break off my engagement she would know how to act. Lionel should know all, and if he turned her out she would insist on coming to me. The idea of Sibella's worldly soul playing ducks and drakes with her prosperity in that way out of mere revenge made me smile. Very well, I could smile, but we should see. Miss Gascoyne should know how I had betrayed my friend's wife. I looked at her in surprise, and she corrected herself; if Lionel was not my friend, Grahame was, and to betray your friend's sister was just as bad as betraying your friend's wife. As Sibella had no morals whatever on the subject, this was all very amusing. My amusement, which I could not wholly conceal, enraged her. People should know me for what I was, she declared. There had always been something about me that she did not like, had never liked, even when I was a boy. She had always suspected me of being a fraud in some way or other.

This made me curious, and I encouraged her to go on. It was as well to know what lay at the back of Sibella's mind, especially if it were not very flattering to what I had believed to be my powers of concealment, but after all a woman with whom one has an illicit love affair sees the worst side of one. I had no fear of Sibella telling Miss Gascoyne. She might in a round-about way try and injure me in the latter's eyes, but I did not think she was likely to go further.

It was a trying scene, however. No man likes to see a woman whom he loves suffer, and Sibella displayed a quite extraordinary amount of resentment, considering that physical jealousy cannot in the nature of things be as strong a passion with woman as with man.

"You will kiss her, and make love to her," she moaned.

"My sweetheart," I murmured, taking her in my arms, "you know perfectly well that I do not love anyone in the wide world as well as I do you—but just think what this marriage will do for me."

"I have sacrificed so much for you, Israel; you might at least sacrifice something for me."

"My darling, I will make any sacrifice that you can show me is necessary."

"This is the end of everything between us, you will see. I shall never be happy again."

She was softening; the danger was over. I pointed out that she had made the marriage she wanted to; she might at least allow me the same privilege.

"I did not know that I was in love with you," she whimpered.

I reasoned with her in the most winning way. I would send her a little French novel, one of the most philosophical works I had ever read, although presented as the lightest of fiction, a pill coated like a sugar-plum. In it there were two people who had loved each other all their lives, and kept their romance evergreen because they did not marry. Marriage spoilt so many things. It was the microscope turned on to the apparently limpid waters of romance. It showed a mass of horrid, swirling, swimming, ugly things that there was no need to see. Why use a microscope? She must have learned the evil of the matrimonial microscope from Lionel. Delusions were as good as realities if one were consistent. If we had been rich we might have married each other. Therefore, poverty knew what was best for us, and had been our most sincere friend.

I think I left her pacified; at least, to the extent of not being dangerous. Lionel came in, and I was obliged to go.

I was compelled of course to spend a great deal of time at South Kensington. Edith was radiantly happy, and her romance had brought something into her face which it had hitherto lacked. I was very proud of her. Poor Sibella, who had seen her at some public function, had evidently not expected anything so beautiful, for she declared that I must surely love so exquisite a creature better than herself. As a matter of fact, Miss Gascoyne's beauty, although of a higher type, was not so dazzling as Sibella's, and I could honestly say, "One admires Miss Gascoyne, but one does not love her," which had a very good effect on Sibella. It was put authoritatively, and it convinced her.

I was now the son of the house at the Gascoynes', and there was Satanic humour in the situation. I moved among all these good people as in some measure a substitute for the dead young man. Where ignorance is bliss 'tis folly to be wise, is true sometimes, and what did it matter to them if I were responsible for the son's death? How could it affect my filial attitude, providing they remained in ignorance?

Mr. Gascoyne doubled my salary, and introduced me to the employees of the firm as his successor. He began by degrees to leave the management of affairs to me, and he did well, for he had grown just a little old-fashioned, and the business certainly improved under my care; in fact, it regained ground which it had lost.

About this time I had another piece of good fortune. It was not much, but such as it was it was encouraging. Old Henry Gascoyne died, leaving only the parson between me and the main branch—of course, with the exception of my benefactor, Mr. Gascoyne.

Lord and Lady Gascoyne called in person to congratulate us on our engagement. They welcomed me as cousin, and asked us all to Hammerton for Christmas. Lady Gascoyne wanted to revive the good old-fashioned Yule-tide. As she justly observed, "What is the use of having an old-fashioned hall if you don't use it as such?"

CHAPTER XIX

MISS Gascoyne and I were to be married the following spring. Why people who want to get married and are in a position to get married don't do so at once I cannot understand. I fancy Mr. and Mrs. Gascoyne would have liked us to live with them, but we resolutely declined to accept any hints on the subject, and they were quite generous-minded enough to see the justice of our objection. At the same time, they regarded the departure of Edith from under their roof with no little gloom.

Miss Gascoyne insisted on settling half her income on me. "I might," she said, laughing, "become weak-minded, or go off with some one else, and it is only fair that you should not run the chance of being worse off." I protested, but on this point she was firm. If she had not done this of her own accord, I think I should have found some means to suggest that she should; for if a man marries money he lives in greater style than he would otherwise have done, and it is not fair that he should be left at the mercy of his wife in the event of their parting, or should his own capacity for earning a living be impaired.

With Hammerton mine by right of descent, and Edith, beautiful and stately, my wife and Countess, I should be on equal terms with the great people of the land. It would obviously be stupid, therefore, to stay my hand, and remain as I was. Lady Gascoyne might have more children, and my task might grow more and more difficult as years went on. At present I was devoting myself entirely to the removal of the Reverend Henry. He, poor gentleman, continued to imbibe his Sunday afternoon port and eat game he had not shot himself, all unconscious of the kind friend who was bent on hastening his reunion with the wife whose loss he so deplored. Indeed, I had justification for what I contemplated, inasmuch as the bronze tablet to her memory declared that his chief joy and hope lay in the prospect of their meeting, though he no doubt philosophically reflected that the union was not likely to be less joyful for being delayed a few years.

I had decided to give up the idea of launching decaying masonry at the poor old gentleman's head. A few experiments in this direction taught me that I could not trust to my accuracy of aim. I abandoned the project with a good deal of reluctance, because if successful it would have been quite free from any danger of detection.

There remained the poisoning of his glass of water. How to get at it was the question.

My plans were largely facilitated by the departure of Mr. and Mrs. Gascoyne for Italy, taking Edith with them. They had long wished to make a habit of evading the English winter, which agreed with neither of them. They had intended to do so the following year, leaving the business entirely in my hands, but the doctor suddenly ordered Mrs. Gascoyne south.

She and her husband wished to leave Miss Gascoyne behind, but I declined to hear of such a thing. I was only too glad to have her out of London for the winter. She, on her part, directly she discovered that Mr. and Mrs. Gascoyne wished her to accompany them, insisted on going.

"Israel and I will see quite enough of each other after next spring," she said laughingly, in reply to their remonstrances.

They departed early in October and I was left free to carry out my plans. They intended to be away seven months, and I was to join them at Christmas on the Riviera. The arrangement had another good point. Sibella was delighted at the prospect of a long winter with me all to herself.

The first Saturday after the Gascoynes' departure I went down to Lincolnshire. It was an Indian summer, and as balmy as June. My sensations were very different from those which the moral reader will no doubt think ought to have animated the mind of a murderer. They were entirely exhilarating and happy, and the pleasant Lincolnshire landscape with the sunlit emerald of its far-stretching flats, intersected by the glistening silver threads of canals, filled me with the delight in Nature which only a thoroughly artificial mind can feel. It may seem odd, but I was genuinely appealed to by the quaint, brown barges with their gay notes of colour in green and red, the trampling horses and the towing-line hauled taut, the jerseyed helmsman alternately blowing at his pipe and whistling a tune. These things I loved as much as the veriest Cockney artist let loose for the first time among the joys of Nature with a sketch-book.

I was in a curious mood for one whose mission was death, and when I caught sight of the tower of Lye Church above the stately elms which were swaying in the fresh October breeze I felt almost sentimental. It was not my intention to stay there, however, and I passed Lye Station and alighted some three or four miles further on at a place called Cumber. Here there was a very comfortable little inn, almost an hotel.

After dark I walked over to Lye, and hung round the comfortable Rectory. Once I ventured a few paces on to the lawn, whence I could see the Rector at dinner with his sister and niece. They appeared to live prodigiously well, and it was very diverting to watch their gestures and the process of mastication as they devoured something they particularly liked, or to observe the Rector say something over his shoulder to the butler, who immediately hurried forward to fill his master's glass.

I could not help reflecting that the silver candlesticks, the gilt-framed pictures on the walls, the elaborate dishes, the obsequious servants, were the appanage of one who had given a special undertaking to imitate Christ and do His work by example. I was even led into some no doubt highly foolish and irreverent reflections as to which of us was the greater criminal—I, who at any rate told no lies to myself, or this polished, good-natured hypocrite who had never tested a single action by His teaching.

The meal over, the ladies left the room. Apparently no social convention was omitted in this house of spiritual direction. When the butler had placed a box of cigars on the table, and filled his master's glass, he also withdrew, and the Reverend Henry lit a cigar, and, leaning back in his chair, half closed his eyes in ecstatic enjoyment. At this point a step scrunched on the gravel path, and then there was a ring at the front-door bell. In another minute or two a gentlemanly-looking curate was shown into the room. He was evidently an embryo Reverend Henry, and he was cordially waved to a seat. From the way he filled his glass and accepted the proffered cigar he was none of your blue-ribboned, fasting weeds. Indeed, it is not to be supposed that the comfortable Rector would have tolerated such a one in his parish. On reflection, I think, perhaps, that I must admit to being the greater criminal of the two, for he had the merit of being unconscious.

Later, the Rector and his curate left the dining-room and passed into the drawing-room, from which there had already proceeded the sounds of a piano. A nocturne by Chopin came to an abrupt ending as the two men entered. Tea was then brought in—the taking of tea instead of coffee after dinner always seems to vouch for the respectability and antiquity of a family, recalling the traditions of piquet and spadille. The curate then warbled 'The Message' in a by no means unfinished way. Mr. Gascoyne's niece played his accompaniments, and the two older people slept right through half a dozen of his performances, only awaked by the percussion of a sudden silence.

This was all very entertaining, but was not helping me much, though it was no doubt convenient to be acquainted with details of life at the Rectory.

The next morning I again walked over to Lye, and wandered about the churchyard during the service. This proceeding did not help me more than my prowl of the previous evening had done.

Through a window I could see the interior of the church, the preacher in the pulpit, and the glass at his right-hand. I was coming to the conclusion that poisoning the glass would be the only way, and the idea received an unexpected impetus. Years before, when my great idea had first taken possession of me, I had provided myself with digitalis in powder form. Anxious to discover whether its effects remained, and nervous of seeking the requisite information, I had bought a small dog from a man in Piccadilly. It was a dog of no particular breed, with a blue ribbon tied round its neck to suggest how eminently suited it was to a boudoir existence. I had taken the little thing to Clapham—the proceeding cost me a pang, for I am very fond of animals, and its eyes were like Sibella's—and had experimented, with the result that the little creature was at this moment lying buried in the back garden. If I could smear some of the powder on the glass before the Reverend Henry mounted the pulpit I might accomplish my design.

I returned to town to think it over.

The next week I went down, and put up at a different village, so that my aimless visits might not attract attention.

I arrived on Saturday, and early on Sunday morning strolled into Lye Church. It was empty. The October sun shone through the uncoloured panes, flooding the building with a cheerful light, while here and there the one or two stained-glass windows threw variegated patches of colour across the worn stone and worm-eaten pews. I sat down, and listened intently to make sure whether anyone was about. After a few minutes of utter silence I went up to the chancel, and glanced casually towards the vestry. The door was open, and I peeped in. It was empty, and on the table stood the bottle and glass. In a few seconds I had sprinkled the glass with fine powder from a small phial.

I regained the churchyard without meeting a soul.

Of course, the plan might very possibly miscarry. The verger might wash the glass. The Rector might not use it. The curate might preach and not the Rector. I considered, however, that my luck had been so good that there might be a special dispensation of fortunate events in my favour. I met the verger as I passed through the churchyard, a fussy little man with side whiskers and an abnormal nose, which looked as if it had been specially designed for being poked into other people's business. His air of importance was quite grotesque, and he was a byword in the village for curiosity. Even as I passed he stopped a small boy on his way through the churchyard with a covered dish.

"What have you got there, Freddy Barling?"

"Mutton, Mester Voller."

"With taters?"

"Yus, Mr. Voller."

Having obtained his information with some degree of tact and suavity he became stern.

"And for why are yer carryin' roast mutton through God's acre, Freddy Barling?"

At the change of tone Freddy Barling gazed at the belligerent whiskers in speechless terror, seized with an awful fear that the family roast mutton and taters were about to be confiscated.

"Go round by the road, Freddy Barling, and don't blaspheme against God's acre with profane food." Freddy Barling hurried away, only too thankful at having rescued the Sunday dinner. The conscientious Mr. Voller pursued his way into the church, pausing at the door to take a view of the graveyard flooded with sunlight. He was no doubt reflecting on the pleasant spot in which he had been permitted to live, and the good seed he had planted in Freddy Barling's conscience.

I lingered about the churchyard. Mr. Voller was probably dusting the litany and the Rector's Bible, and setting such things as he had not arranged over night in order. Presently the villagers began to pass across the churchyard path. There was not much greeting interchanged beyond a 'good-morning' or two. The gossiping came after the service. I went into the church, and sat down in a secluded corner and waited for the service to begin. Time went on, and there was no sign of the Rector or curate. Presently the curate with a very white face emerged from the vestry, and going up to a stout, comfortable woman in a front pew spoke to her in a whisper, and they passed out of the west door into the churchyard.

Suddenly a piercing shriek came through the window. The congregation sprang to their feet. What on earth was the matter? Old Mr. Crabbs, the solicitor, after gazing around hesitatingly for a few moments, hurried out, followed at short intervals by the whole congregation. I was one of the last, and was in time to see Mrs. Voller being led through the wicket-gate at the end of the churchyard by the curate and the Rector.

I quite saw what had happened. Most probably, from the mere instinct of meddling, Mr. Voller had drunk out of the glass, and had as a consequence departed on this pleasant Sunday morning for a better land. By degrees the whole congregation, with many Sabbath-breakers from the village street corners, were crowded round the vestry door.

"Annie, take your little brother and sister for a walk," said one lady, who was evidently bent on seeing as much of the fun as possible herself.

"What has happened?" I asked of a bystander.

"They do say as Mr. Voller 'ave 'ad a fit and died, and the doctor be examinin' 'im now."

In a few minutes an individual whom I took to be the doctor appeared at the vestry door.

"Will some of you run and fetch a stretcher and help to carry him home?"

"'e's dead, then, doctor?"

"I am afraid so."

"'ave 'e 'ad a fit?"

"Heart disease, I think," answered the doctor, gravely.

Full of importance, several young men hastened off for the stretcher, and in their hurry to oblige became jammed at the wicket-gate.

The whole thing was a very serious annoyance to me, and I walked off across the fields in a high state of indignation with the departed Mr. Voller.

That such a nobody should have been allowed to obstruct the workings of a great policy was irritating. I only hoped that it would be a lesson to Mr. Voller in his progress through the underworld to be less inquisitive.

I grew more and more indignant with the shade of that estimable gentleman as the day went on.

I walked over to Lye again in the evening, when the Rector preached a sermon on the instability of human hopes. He alluded to the late

Mr. Voller with much feeling. From the gossip in the churchyard after service I gathered that the doctor had quite made up his mind that death was due to heart disease.

This was fortunate, but Mr. Voller had spoilt my plans.

I returned to London disconsolate. If there should be the least suspicion that Mr. Voller had been poisoned things might become very complicated. Although it was quite improbable that I should be suspected, it would be too risky to attempt the same procedure again. It was impossible not to be amused at poor Mr. Voller's ill fortune. When the humour of the affair got the better of my irritation I laughed heartily.

I did not learn the result of the inquest for two or three weeks afterwards. When I ventured into the neighbourhood again I was intensely relieved to find that a verdict had been returned in accordance with my expectations. Mr. Voller was a most respected character, and the only people who might be expected to bear him a grudge were the small boys who misbehaved themselves in church.

If it struck anyone to wonder what a half empty glass of water was doing there they no doubt came to the conclusion that, feeling faint, Mr. Voller had poured it out to drink.

It was now the Rector's turn. I began to feel quite annoyed with the old gentleman. He was giving me a great deal of trouble, whilst if he had gone off at the right moment I should have been on the best of terms with his memory. Things were made more difficult by Sibella, who was a hard mistress to serve, and who took leave to suspect my reasons for going out of town so constantly. She had had a strange instinct about me from the moment she had surrendered. She vaguely felt that something was wrong, although she had not the slightest idea where to look for it. I was obliged to warn her that jealousy will fatigue passion sooner or later.

It was late in November before I ventured again into the vicinity of Lye. Armed with my small phial of digitalis I spent one or two weekends in the district without other results than a little more private information about Mr. Gascoyne's home life. It was the most difficult case I had yet attempted. Nothing gave me any assistance.

One day I was chatting with the landlord of the inn when the Reverend Gascoyne passed the window. It was about half-past four in the afternoon, and I had presumably come over to the village to fish. As a matter of fact, my nature is too fastidious for so brutal a sport. I cannot bear to inflict suffering for mere pleasure, and I am quite unable to understand the brutality and grossness of a nature that delights in it.

I had been careful, however, to master its jargon, and there were two or three shining specimens at the bottom of my basket to give evidence of my prowess.

"There goes the parson," I said, carelessly.

"Ah! 'e be going to take tea with old Mrs. Finucane."

"Indeed?"

"Wet or fine, twice a week, 'e goes over and drinks a cup of tea with 'er, and reads to 'er for an hour or two. 'e be a good man, be the parson."

"Who's old Mrs. Finucane?"

"'Er husband were organist, and when 'e died—though, by the way, 'e were younger than Mrs. Finucane, and they do say were at college with the parson—well, when 'e died it were found that Mrs. Finucane were a pauper, and wur as like as not to 'ave to go to the workus, but the parson, 'e says to the Squire, 'If you'll put down a pound a week for life, I'll put down a pound a week for life also,' and so 'twas done. Sir Robert couldn't for shame's sake refuse, seeing that Mr. Finucane had saved his son's life, and so Mrs. Finucane be comfortable enough, 'er cottage being 'er own. They do say that the Squire wur none too willing to do it, though."

"Does Mrs. Finucane live in the village?"

I knew it was quite unnecessary to ask exactly where she lived, as every villager loves to maunder on, and give any inquirer details concerning his neighbours gratis.

"She lives in the cottage just before you come to the 'ill. You'll know it, for it be covered with red berries."

I went and had a look at Mrs. Finucane's cottage. It was called 'The Glebe,' and had a mass of creeper with red berries over the front. Through the bars of the high garden gate I could just see a little green with the bare flower-beds of winter round it. I inspected the house from every point of view.

Where the yew-hedge which surrounded the garden was somewhat thin I could see through and into the pleasant parlour. On this cold autumn day a bright fire was burning in the grate, and drawn up before it was a little table with a chess-board, on either side of which sat Mr. Gascoyne and Mrs. Finucane. By this table was a smaller one with a cosy-looking tea-urn on a snowy cover, flanked with plates of hot toast and muffins. It was a homely and pleasant sight to contemplate, and reminded me of one of those inimitable scenes of village life which more than one of our lady novelists has depicted with so much spirit and truth. Strange it is, but such literature as Miss Austin's *Emma* and

Mrs. Gaskell's *Cranford* has always charmed me more than any other, on the same principle, I suppose, that a complex character responds to simplicity. Country folk do not appreciate rural sweets as does the knowing Cockney.

It seemed impossible that I could gain admission to the house. It was as secure from any intrusion as if it had been a royal palace guarded at every gate. From my point of vantage I watched the movements of the two inside carefully. I was screened from the observation of the village. In a minute or so they abandoned the attractions of the chess-table for those of tea and muffins.

The Rector was apparently as capable with tea and muffins as with partridge and port. In fact, to see him at any meal was to receive an explanation of his florid complexion and ever-increasing portliness. He was one of those people—and they are legion—who for the want of a little vanity abandon themselves completely to the pleasures of the table. Vanity has its uses, and should by no means be discouraged in the young. Many a man and woman has been saved from a drunkard's grave through the fear of losing a good complexion. In not a few cases gluttony has met its match in vanity when all other remedies have failed. Vanity has made cowards appear brave, and the miser ostentatious. Charity would be an anaemic spinster were it not for her servant, vanity; and she is as often the parent of moderation as of excess. With a little proper vanity the kindly Rector might have preserved a greater measure of youth and sprightliness.

He was nevertheless a pleasant sight as he sat before the blazing fire and chatted and drank his tea with the old lady. I stood and watched them through the gap in the hedge till the light faded. Then a little maid brought in candles, and, drawing the curtains, shut the pleasant interior from my sight.

I was afraid there was no chance of making Mrs. Finucane's hospitable teapot or genial muffins and cake useful to my scheme, for although such luxuries are poison, it is a slow process.

Occupied with these thoughts, I strolled down the village street. I could reach the road back to the inn where I was staying more quickly by passing through the churchyard, and as I reached the church door a sudden impulse urged me to enter. The gloom was rendered more profound by the faint suggestion of fading daylight lingering about the building. I was not at all disturbed by thoughts of Mr. Voller's ghost, but made my way without trepidation into the vestry. There stood the glass of water and the bottle, and I was about to repeat the experiment which had been so successful in the case of Mr. Voller when something shining lying on the floor attracted my attention. I went towards it and picked up a fluted silver cigar-case. I carried it out of the church, and, opening it, found it full. I went back to my quarters for the night before I made a thorough examination of my find. As I had hoped, it proved to be Mr. Gascoyne's. His monogram was on the outside. I turned it over and over in deep thought. I remembered reading, when I was studying poisons in my house in Clapham, of one used by the Red Indians, who, soaking the end of a cigar in it, were in the habit of asking an acquaintance who had offended them to take a friendly weed, with— from their point of view—very desirable consequences.

I had the strongest objections to using the medium of the glass of water again. It might strike someone that it had played a part in the death of the verger.

On arriving in town I consulted the book in which I remembered to have seen the information as to the Indian poison. It was as I thought; the end of a cigar dipped in a decoction of the Grobi root was sufficient to induce stupor ending in death if immediate measures were not taken to rouse the patient. I knew where to obtain the Grobi root, which is also used medicinally by the Red Indians.

Down by the docks there is a narrow street full of shops devoted to the sale of curios from foreign parts. I had gone there during the days when I was racketing about town to purchase a monkey for a chorus girl who demanded its immediate production as a pledge of affection. It was whilst I was in the shop that I had heard the aged proprietor explaining the properties of a small dried bundle of herbs which hung from one of the low rafters. At the first mention of the word poison I had listened intently, whilst apparently interested in the other articles scattered about the shop.

It was possible that the plant was no longer in its old place. At the same time it was not the sort of thing which was likely to be largely in demand, and it might hang there through a generation without being disturbed. I knew that the proprietor was a great dealer in Chinese cabinets and curiosities of all kinds. I decided to buy Miss Gascoyne something very rare, and took my way to the East End in a state of suspense as to whether the business had been moved. As I entered the street, however, I saw the cages and bird-stands outside the door as of yore. So little had changed that it seemed to give me assurance that the magic root was hanging in the old place. As soon as I entered the shop I looked anxiously at the place where it had been, and gave almost a sigh of relief as it caught my eye.

The wizened little old proprietor hastened forward from the back of the shop where he was inspecting some articles which were being displayed for his approval by a sailor. The latter, in no way disconcerted or offended at being left with such scant ceremony, took up a newspaper which lay on his patron's desk and settled himself to read till such time as the proprietor should be free again. I explained that I wanted a Chinese cabinet; something quite new and original. The old man looked around puzzled.

"They're very much of a muchness," he said, "especially, in our days, when we dealers have got to be as careful as the public that we are not cheated. There was a sailor as used to do the China trip twice a year, and he brought back some of the quaintest looking cabinets as ever I saw, but it turned out that he bought 'em all in this country, and that's the way we're took in."

It did not strike the old gentleman that if the articles were genuine it could not matter very much whether they were bought in England or not.

I objected to everything which was shown to me, and made every effort to get him to go to his storerooms upstairs, suggesting that he might have something put away. He denied this, and continued to grope about amongst his treasures, while the bunches of Grobi root dangled temptingly above our heads.

While he was meandering I examined them very carefully, and studied how I could detach one of the bundles in the shortest space of time. Finally, the old man remembered that he had something which might tempt me in his back premises, and he went shuffling away to look for it.

As soon as his back was turned I took my penknife, which I had already opened in my pocket, and, glancing swiftly at the sailor occupied with his paper in the corner, reached up my hand and cut the string by which the bundle of dried root was attached to the ceiling. I thrust it into my great-coat pocket and looked again at the sailor. He appeared to have been quite ignorant of my proceeding. It was some minutes before the old gentleman shambled back into the shop, bearing in his hands a box of some scented wood, from which, where it had lain buried in cotton-wool, he lifted out a miniature cabinet of exquisite workmanship.

"I had forgotten all about this. I've had it by me for years."

I shrewdly suspected that it was one of those things which had been brought to the old man by someone of whose honesty he was doubtful.

I haggled with him a good deal over the price, but finally took it away, having paid a very reasonable sum, and having in my great-coat pocket the Grobi root.

It was a drawback that it was impossible to test the efficacy of the poison taken in the particular way in which I intended.

I made my decoction, and, steeping the end of one of the cigars in it, dried it and returned it with the others to the case. I then went to the village of Lye, and, entering the church one evening, stole into the vestry. Unperceived, I placed the cigar-case on the table behind a pile of books.

I had well considered the disadvantage of my scheme, which was that the Reverend gentleman might hand his cigar-case to some friend, who would have first choice, and might select the prize. It would not have done to place two poisoned cigars in the case, as the fact of two gentlemen lighting up and swooning away could not fail to attract attention and rouse suspicion.

It was with a sigh of satisfaction and relief that I opened *The Times* one morning and read in the obituary notices that the Reverend Henry Gascoyne, Rural Dean, and Rector of Lye, had succumbed to an apoplectic stroke.

CHAPTER XX

THE REST of the winter I was able to devote myself to Sibella, who grew more beautiful in my eyes every day. She was bewitchingly decadent, and her decadence was independent of extraneous aids to beauty. I was careful not to be seen too frequently with her in public, and permitted Sir Anthony Cross to do all the drudgery. Lionel was quite unsuspecting, and inasmuch as I never omitted an opportunity of obliging him I verily believe that the poor fool believed me to be attached to him.

I well remember how one evening, when Grahame was present, Lionel became quite sentimental over our school days, and talked as if we had all three been the greatest of chums. A smile played round Grahame's dignified mouth as his brother-in-law meandered on about "those dear old days."

"Do you remember when I was training for the mile, and had that accident?" Lionel asked.

We both of us nodded.

"That was a very mysterious affair," he went on. "I could have sworn as I went down that I tripped over something which struck me across the leg."

"Imagination," suggested Grahame.

"I don't know, but it has always seemed to me most mysterious."

"I don't think it's possible to account for sensations at such a moment as that," I said, indifferently.

Lionel went on with his reminiscences. He recalled the first day he 'had ever been to the Hallwards', which, considering that he must have remembered how badly he and Sibella behaved to me on that day, was not a brilliant exhibition of tact. At last he concluded:

"And now Sibella and I are married, and we are all jolly together."

Coming from anyone else the remark might have sounded jovial; coming from Lionel it sounded foolish.

"Yes," I said drily, "we are all jolly together."

For one moment Grahame looked at me curiously, but shrewdly suspecting that my liking for Lionel had not grown much with years, put down the emphasis in my voice to that fact.

I was angry with myself for having made such a slip.

Lionel was soon in the throes of an election struggle, a sudden death having removed a well-known party hack to a greater majority than it had ever been his lot to be numbered with on earth.

As much to his own astonishment as to that of the wire-pullers of his party Lionel was elected. It was a political surprise, for the seat was hardly likely to have been wasted on a nonentity had a victory been probable. Lionel took all credit to himself, and the cheers of approval as he was introduced to the House made him quite delirious with vanity. His old father, who was dying by inches, was so delighted that he immediately handed to his son a large slice of the wealth for which he was greedily waiting. The infatuated young man was somewhat sobered by the reception of his maiden speech, which was such as not even the most self-satisfied of beings could have assured himself was flattering. Sibella somewhat annoyed me. She was for the time quite impressed by her husband's meretricious triumph. I believe she thought that she had underestimated him, and that he really was a person of great intellectual attainments. She began to talk to me of conscience, of remembering her duty, and indulged in all the usual female preliminaries to a retreat; but long before she was ready to make an effort, and show me the door, I had managed to demonstrate to her that her husband had gone as far as he was likely to go. In fact, Lionel himself was incapable of playing a serious part for long, and associated himself with the heir to a dukedom whose election to the House of Commons had been an insult, and who was prepared to hobnob with a stable-boy in default of the society from which he had become somewhat of an outcast. His friends had hoped that a political career might white-wash him, and were now only too anxious for him to lose his seat before some irretrievable scandal occurred. Lionel was quite content with his friend's exalted position, and imagined that he was the companion of the very cream of the popular House, a delusion in which I encouraged him on every possible occasion.

Familiarity with political life likewise disillusioned Sibella, and she was too acute not to learn very speedily that to be the wife of a Member of Parliament need not necessarily carry with it social advantages of any kind.

I fancy Lord Gascoyne had been a little surprised at Miss Gascoyne engaging herself to me, for to his aristocratic prejudices a Jew was a Jew, however charming he might be. He was perfectly prepared to be quite civil to the race, and would have denied it nothing but an entrance into the blood circle. I was, however, indirectly a member of his family, and when it dawned upon him that should he and his heir die I was, after Mr. Gascoyne, the heir, he was compelled to change his attitude. I think he determined, if possible, to bar me out by a family of stalwart sons and daughters. Luckily, so far, Lady Gascoyne showed no signs of increasing the obstacles in my path.

I spent the remainder of the winter thinking out the completion of my design. Of course, the Earl would have to go first. It would leave me several years to deal with his heir, and in the vicissitudes of a boy's life there must be innumerable occasions when death may accidentally step in and claim him.

There was at this time a talk of sending Lord Gascoyne to a large dependency as Governor. The rumour threw me into a state of the greatest anxiety. If he betook himself and his family to the other end of the world he might have half a dozen children round him before I could interfere.

Luckily the project fell through for the time being, but his abilities and personal dignity marked him out as a man to whom the offer was certain to be made again.

Lionel Holland had a great ambition to know Lord and Lady Gascoyne. Lord Gascoyne, at all events, was born a freeman of that inner ring which, for all his fine acquaintances, had so far held Lionel at bay. Some of them had been civil to Sibella, for she, like Grahame, had a natural distinction which people were impelled to admit. When, however, it became a question of accepting Lionel also—and he was by no means the person to stand aloof—they drew off.

His vanity refused to admit that he had been snubbed, but inwardly he was conscious that there was something wrong.

He had therefore fixed on the Gascoynes as people who would be able to secure him an introduction to the highest circle of the social heaven. It was in vain that I assured him quite frankly that I was not on terms of intimacy with them or any of their friends, that, so far, I was not married to Miss Gascoyne, and that my Jewish blood made me more or less of an outsider in the family. He looked upon this as affectation.

"Why, you might be Lord Gascoyne! You're as good as any of them."

"I shall be when I am Lord Gascoyne, but so far I am only plain Israel Rank. No, I won't call myself plain, for that would indeed be affectation."

"You've been to their house."

"Once or twice."

"You've dined there."

"Once only."

"People of that kind don't ask a man to dinner unless they look upon him as one of themselves."

"Except for political motives," I murmured.

He was too dense to see the point, and persisted.

"An acquaintance like that wants nursing," he said patronisingly, much as an old hand might have done to a young man just starting in business.

As a matter of fact, he was exactly suggesting what I was doing, but my methods were superior to his, and I should never have thought of describing them with such a lack of taste. His inability to see this was the secret of his non-success with the particular class he was anxious to cultivate.

I heard from Miss Gascoyne constantly, and my letters in reply to her high-souled, dignified, yet tender epistles were masterpieces in diplomacy—an unkind critic might have said in hypocrisy.

I cannot help wondering as I sit here writing these memoirs what her feelings are at the present moment. I am afraid that she is one of those extraordinary characters who literally cannot love where they do not respect. She will have the pleasure, however, of glancing over her letters written to me at this time, for I have left her the task of examining my papers and destroying such as I thought fit to keep. Sibella's letters I always destroyed. This is an act of justice to any woman with whom one is conducting an intrigue which should not be neglected. Not that Sibella had written many letters. As I have pointed out, there was a curious vein of caution in the Hallward family. In fact, much as I know she must be suffering, she has not made the least sign since the law took charge of my affairs. I believe that she still has faith that I shall extricate myself somehow. Poor child! Jack Sheppard himself could not do much inside the condemned cell of a modern prison. I have given the matter of escape thought, but considering how easy it is to cage a human being, it is somewhat surprising that there should ever have been an age in which the escape of criminals was comparatively frequent. I have also wondered whether, if a murderer were to display signs of madness between conviction and execution, the law would carry out the penalty. It might be worth the while of a smaller criminal to make the attempt. In my case I cannot help thinking it would be somewhat undignified to linger in the public mind as an individual who was mouthing through the remainder of his existence with straws in his hair. Besides, it would be a satisfaction for the public—who have been made uncomfortable by such wholesale murdering—to be able to say, "Poor creature! he was mad." On the whole, I would sooner live as the wicked Lord Gascoyne than with a reputation for insanity. Moreover, my simulation might not be effective, and if a report got abroad that I had made myself ridiculous by feigning madness it would be intolerable.

CHAPTER XXI

LIONEL Holland was, of course, mistaken in accepting as genuine my indifference as to whether the Gascoynes were civil to me or no. Since they had asked me to their house it was necessary I should become as intimate as possible, and Lionel could not know how I had schemed and intrigued to make myself acceptable in their sight. I had nibbled all round their circle, so to speak, unobtrusively attempting to identify myself as much as possible with the people they knew. This was a matter of no little difficulty. I was compelled to make it known how near I stood to the succession. This gave me a certain sort of position, and at least tolerance, as more or less one of themselves by the exclusive set in which the Gascoynes moved. They still, however, showed no sign of great friendliness. Of course, the important person to conciliate was Lady Gascoyne. She did not belong to the difficult set by birth, and was naturally nervous of doing anything which might show her as a novice in the art of social selection. Not that she was in any way a snob; indeed, far from it.

She evidently liked me. I was the sort of personality that the heiress of enterprising American ancestors—the wrong word; her forbears could hardly be described as ancestors—would like. I had, however, so far not interested Lord Gascoyne, whose sympathies were limited. He had asked me to the house in a purely formal way, and as a member of the family who had a right to be so asked.

So far I had, as it were, been conducting reconnaissances round the network of his character and temperament in order to discover his vulnerable point. It was extremely difficult. He was one of those self-contained Englishmen whose sense of duty comes somewhat as a surprise in conjunction with an apparently unenthusiastic temperament. The very person to be a royal substitute in a dependency. Enthusiasm is the greatest curse that can befall a reigning Sovereign, and a really sincere, enthusiastic monarch is distrusted by no one so much as by his own subjects. In his presence I at once suppressed the artistic side of my character, and pretended to a reserve and coldness in no way natural to me. Such topics as were discussed I treated with as much pure reason as was consistent with a respect to aristocratic prejudices, an attitude eminently conciliatory to the English noble, who is never so happy as when he flatters himself that he is displaying liberal tendencies. There did not, however, appear to be any likelihood of my being asked to Hammerton, and even my confession that I had visited the place as a tourist failed to elicit the desired invitation. He was, because of his limitations, the most difficult person I had yet had to deal with. At the same time, my being on visiting terms with Lord and Lady Gascoyne, and admitted by them to be a relative, gave me a social status which I had not before possessed.

It was highly necessary to be swift with his lordship. I must say that I had less compunction about removing him than I had had about any of the others. He was so entirely impersonal in his relations with the outer world.

I think his wife was in love with him. He was the sort of man women love desperately where they love at all; for the simple reason that they are never permitted to become really familiar. They are always in the presence of their reigning sovereign. A very wholesome thing for most women, and especially corrective for an American woman. It had been,

I fancy, a great change for her, inasmuch as before marriage she had ruled her father absolutely. It was a little surprising that Lord Gascoyne should have condescended to mingle his blood with what was, after all, quite a plebeian strain. It was the more surprising as he was in no need of money, and I discovered afterwards that at his request her enormous dowry was settled absolutely on her children. I wondered very much if the dowry would revert to the American relations should she die childless; also if, in the case of Lord Hammerton outliving his parents, but dying a minor, the money would pass to the Gascoyne family. It would certainly be amusing were I to inherit the American dollars.

The great thing, however, was to secure an invitation to Hammerton. If I could only render Lord Gascoyne some service, or place him under an obligation to me in any way, it would probably follow as a matter of course.

An idea struck me. There was the portrait of Lord George, the one thing saved from the wreck of my uncle's home. I knew that Lord Gascoyne took the greatest pride and interest in the portrait gallery at Hammerton, and that there was no portrait of Lord George Gascoyne, my own immediate ancestor, among the family pictures.

Finally, seeing no way of approaching the matter as if by chance, I wrote and offered him the portrait for the collection at Hammerton, and he replied asking me to come and see him.

I went, and was shown into his private sanctum. He was, considering his temperament, quite profuse in his thanks, but would at first not hear of accepting the portrait as a gift.

"As you say, it is not by a great name," he said; "but at the same time it is a very good name, and is worth money, and more than money, to me."

I gave him to understand that if he declined it as a gift it would hurt my feelings, as I should conclude that he did not care about accepting anything at my hands. This I conveyed to him in as tactful a way as possible. He saw, however, what I meant, and graciously accepted the picture.

"You must come down and see it hung."

He could not very well say less, but by the expression of his face I wondered whether a vague suspicion of my motive had not, even as he spoke, entered his mind.

However, the invitation was given, and I intended to avail myself of it. I had no intention of allowing the matter to slip his memory.

"It must be a week-end," I said smiling, "for, you know, I work hard all the week."

"Lady Gascoyne shall write and ask you. She is at Hammerton herself at present."

It was quite unnecessary for his lordship to inform me of Lady Gascoyne's whereabouts, for I followed the movements of his household as closely as he did himself.

At Christmas I paid a flying visit to the Gascoynes in the South of France, and was welcomed with a curious quietness of passion by Miss Gascoyne, and like a son by her aunt and uncle.

Miss Gascoyne always exalted me, mentally if not morally, and even in the latter direction she led me out of the limitations I had laid down for myself, and beyond which it would be dangerous for me to venture. I am quite capable of great moral enthusiasm, and it has always been my habit to keep out of the way of those likely to infect me with strenuousness.

She talked of ideals quite simply and earnestly, and without the least suggestion of cant, and I was obliged to find some aspirations suitable to these occasions. Being a woman in love she was content to warm her romance at a very small fire, and, further, to imagine it a very big blaze.

I was terribly afraid of being found out by her in any way. I knew that once we were married she would die rather than admit that she had made a mistake. Her loyalty would amount to fanaticism, but she was a woman who could take strong measures before the irrevocable was accomplished. Her attitude has been that of a medieval saint matched with a Cenci. She has held her peace, and she has professed to believe what she knew to be false; whilst at the same time she has suffered agonies of abasement. Nearly all women, however, are deceived in love. It is their pastime. Some never discover the fact, and dream their lives away from their marriage-day to the grave. If Miss Gascoyne hardly possessed the phlegmatic instinct which would enable her to join the comfortable ranks of the latter, she was none the less dwelling in a fool's paradise during those winter days on the Riviera. Those who considered her cold would have been astonished had they known all. She was a concealed volcano.

I returned to town a little exhausted by the rarified atmosphere of reverential romance in which I had been living, and looking forward with a sense of relief to the decadent fascination of Sibella.

Miss Gascoyne with her Utopian dreams about the life of usefulness we were to lead required the natural antidote, and, strangely enough, the first whiff of the perfume Sibella used, wafted to me across the room as she rose to greet me, banished all sensation of ever having been bored by Edith, for I never admired her so much as when I was in the company of Sibella. In the same way I never longed for Sibella to such an extent as when I was with Edith.

Amongst the letters which I found waiting when I reached my rooms there was an invitation from Lady Gascoyne asking me to give them the following Saturday to Monday at Hammerton.

From the tone of her letter it was obvious that she had been only too anxious to second her husband's invitation. To do her justice, she had no class prejudices, and such exclusiveness as she displayed arose from her desire that her husband should think her in every way fitted to her position.

In my daily letter to Miss Gascoyne I mentioned casually that I had been invited to Hammerton. I knew that there were few things which would please her so much.

It was a bitterly cold evening in January when I reached Hammerton station, and it was snowing fast when we drove across the stone bridge which spanned the old moat and turned in at the gates.

There was just time to dress for dinner, and, getting into my evening clothes as quickly as possible, I descended and found that the only member of the party who had made his appearance was a young American millionaire who was being introduced to English society. I thought him particularly stupid and offensive, and was glad when Lord Gascoyne and the other guests quickly followed and we went to dinner.

We dined in a long, narrow room with a vaulted ceiling and grey antique stone walls covered with tapestry. The mixture of a feudal past with modern luxury was exceedingly grateful to a fastidious taste. The servants came and went through a low arched door, which must have been built during the early days of the Norman Conquest. The walls were covered with antique implements of battle, whilst imposing suits of armour loomed out of the shadows, their polished surfaces reflecting here and there the blaze from the enormous log-fire in the vast chimney-place. The party consisted of about half a dozen people besides myself. There was the young millionaire I have already mentioned, and who, I believe, was destined by Lady Gascoyne for Lady Enid Branksome, a pretty, fair-haired girl, who was staying at Hammerton with her mother. It is surprising, when one comes to think of it, how few young Americans marry English noblewomen. It would be interesting to inquire whether this reticence is caused by a disinclination to live in America—where, of course, precedence and rank would have to be dropped—or whether the American young man does not care to buy anything in the shape of a title which is not hereditary. It would certainly be incongruous for Lady Enid Branksome to degenerate into plain Mrs. Puttock of Philadelphia. It would seem almost a murder. The Branksomes, however, were poor, and Mr. Puttock was a multi-millionaire. He was obviously much taken with Lady Enid, who, on her side, was evidently torn by the convicting claims of love and interest; for young Sir Cheveley Drummond was also of the party. This had been a great tactical error on Lady Gascoyne's part, for he seemed to find greater favour in Lady Enid's eyes than did the fat, unhealthy cheeks and vacuous expression of Mr. Puttock of Philadelphia. At the same time, a glance at Lady Branksome's face impressed one with the idea that the Lady Enid would most probably be made to do what she was told.

I have nearly always found house parties somewhat dull, unless there happened to be present a personality of new and surprising interest, and personalities do not frequent country-houses. But for the work I was engaged on I might have found the Saturday till Monday at Hammerton as dull as anything of the kind. It was, however, of absorbing interest to me to be in the house with two people whom I had decided on removing. The position pleased me. This absolutely modern company in a medieval castle, and with a medieval criminal in their midst, was truly interesting. Lady Branksome was evidently doubtful about me, but noting the Semitic cast of my features, and hearing that I was on the Stock Exchange, concluded that there could only be one reason for my being m such company, and that must be enormous wealth. Having several other daughters just ready to burst from the schoolroom into the ranks of the marriageable, she was tentatively affable. She was the sort of woman I always found it very easy to get on with; of the world, cynical and good-natured, very strong-minded, and willing to live and let live. She was at the same time most intolerant of people making fools of themselves, and had no intention of allowing those who were dependent on her to do so if she could help it. Providing she was assured that I had no intentions, she would be perfectly friendly, even when she discovered that I was comparatively poor. Indeed, I gathered in the course of a conversation with her, that she had quite a weakness for adventurous young men. Probably it was because she understood them so well that she was such an expert in keeping them at a distance. During dinner, however, and pending inquiries which would no doubt be conducted when the ladies were alone, she treated me as a person rich enough to be conciliated. A very different woman was Lady Briardale. However rich a man might be, he was nothing to her unless he could show a pedigree. She evidently thought very little of Mr. Puttock, and less of Mr. Rank, who looked a Jew. She probably regarded it as a slight that she should have been asked to meet two such absolute nobodies. She had never heard of anybody called Puttock, or Rank. They were not names at all. They were merely ciphers by which the lower classes were differentiated one from the other. She would probably have thought it more convenient if the lower classes had been known by numbers like cabs and convicts; and, after all, they were not so interesting as convicts, and not so useful as cabs in her eyes. She was evidently somewhat annoyed that I should talk so well, a fact she might have forgiven if others had not paid me the compliment of listening. Indeed, she became quite civil to Puttock, who, she perhaps felt, showed himself conscious of his inferiority by holding his tongue.

Sir Cheveley Drummond, whom I knew to be entertaining, but who was quite taken up with Lady Enid, completed the party, which did not promise much amusement.

After dinner we all sat in the picture-gallery. The last time I had seen it was in company with the gang of excursionists, and I laughingly recalled the fact to Lady Gascoyne when she was showing me where the picture of Lord George had been hung. Lady Briardale was apparently a little astonished when she heard that Lord George was my ancestor, and that I had presented the picture to the collection. Lady Branksome had evidently recalled my name.

"I have been wondering, Mr. Rank, where I have heard of you, and I remember now that it was from my youngest boy. He met you at supper one evening. I didn't ask where," she said parenthetically, "but he talked of nobody else for days."

I remembered young Gavan Branksome, a nice, fair-haired youth, who had attracted my notice by being somewhat like Grahame Hallward.

"I have not seen him since."

"No; he is in India. Did you like India, Sir Cheveley?" she said quickly, stopping the love-sick warrior as he was making his way across the room to Lady Enid.

Poor Sir Cheveley was forced to pause, and whilst Lady Branksome detained him, Mr. Puttock sank into the seat which Lady Enid had left vacant for Sir Cheveley.

"Charming man, Sir Cheveley," said Lady Branksome, with almost a laugh when he finally moved away. "I've known him all his life, and he was always attractive, even when he was sixteen."

I am sure she was perfectly honest in saying that she liked Sir Cheveley. She probably liked him as much as, in her heart, she disliked Mr. Puttock.

Poor Sir Cheveley's disappointment, however, did not prevent his being excellent company in the smoking-room.

I sat up in my own room thinking matters over till a late hour. Before I arrived at Hammerton I had had vague ideas of pushing Lord Gascoyne down a disused well, or something of that kind, in which an old feudal castle like Hammerton might be supposed to abound. On consideration, however, I came to the conclusion that Lord Gascoyne would be a very difficult person to push anywhere he did not mean to go.

I was naturally afraid of poison in such a case. It would only be possible to use it whilst I was in the house, and that was dangerous. My growing proximity to the succession was bringing me nearer and nearer to the perilous land of motive. Violence, unless I were given an extraordinarily good opportunity, was out of the question. The cigar would not do, either, for, strange to say, Lord Gascoyne hardly smoked at all. Cigars and pipes he never attempted, and I noticed that as a rule he merely lit a cigarette in order to keep his guests in countenance.

I had heard of people being made away with when out shooting, but in my case it would hardly be possible. In the first place, I did not shoot, having always had a disinclination to the brutal killing of animals for the sake of pleasure. There remained as far as I could see only the ordinary means of poisoning, with all their attendant dangers.

An instantaneous poison would be most convenient, as it was highly unlikely that I should have sufficient access to Lord Gascoyne to deal with him slowly.

I rose in the morning with one scheme after another chasing itself through my brain. Dressing rapidly, I went for a walk before breakfast round the ancient battlements. These were quite a mile in circumference, and the climbing of worn steps, hazardous scalings of the walls from whence to get a better view, and a careful examination of the various architectural designs of which the building was constructed, occupied me very pleasantly for a full hour, and it was half-past nine, the time for breakfast, when I turned to re-enter the castle. As I descended some steps which led down to the quadrangle, I was astonished to come face to face with a girl of about nineteen or twenty and a child. She was obviously a lady, but she had not been at the dinner-table the evening before, or in the picture-gallery afterwards. I concluded that she was the little boy's governess, but who the child might be I could not imagine. I detected at once that the girl was beautiful, and when I say I detected I use the word advisedly, because it was not a beauty which would be immediately appreciated. The grey eyes, oval face, threaded gold hair, straight nose, and delicately-cut mouth were almost too frail to impress the casual observer. I saw at once, however, that she was rarely perfect in such a type of beauty as I always imagined Burns' Mary must have possessed. She wore a quaint hood, almost like a child's, edged with some inexpensive grey fur. The little boy looked at me shyly, and I held out my arms. A smile broke over his face and he offered me his ball, inviting me to play with him. In less than a minute we were all three laughing like old friends.

After having made myself sufficiently agreeable, I escaped from the child, who was clamouring to me to continue the game, and ran down the steps. I found Lady Gascoyne in sole possession of the breakfast-table. "I am afraid we are the only early risers, Mr. Rank," she said.

As a matter of fact, I rather fancied I had caught a glimpse of Lady Enid going along the road towards Hammerton woods, and I think I was fairly correct in guessing that she was not walking at such a rapid pace for the pleasure of her own company. Indeed, I would not have minded taking long odds that Sir Cheveley was not very far away.

I, of course, said nothing of this to Lady Gascoyne, but mentioned my meeting with the girl in the grey hood.

Lady Gascoyne smiled.

"Now, isn't she pretty, Mr. Rank?"

"Almost beautiful," I hazarded. It is dangerous to be enthusiastic about another woman, even to the nicest of her sex.

"That shows your good taste. Some people cannot see it."

"It is the sort of beauty which is very rare, and not exactly showy."

"She is to my mind wonderful. It does one good to look at her. I expect you are wondering who the little boy is. It is a sad story. I had a great school friend whose father was enormously rich. About a year after her marriage he failed, and her husband's fortune went in the same crash. Her husband shot himself, and she died six months later, leaving her little boy in my care. Oh!" she added quickly, evidently afraid that my inward comment might be a disparagement on her dead friend, "she did so at my express desire. We loved one another so, that it was the most natural thing she could do."

"He seems a dear little chap."

"He is a darling, and devoted to Hammerton already. Lord Gascoyne is so good about it, and lets me have him here always. Miss Lane is his governess."

Sir Cheveley Drummond, looking a little conscious, came in at this moment.

"How energetic everybody is this morning," said Lady Gascoyne.

Mr. Puttock, who appeared on the scene almost as she spoke, looked anything but energetic. He looked as effete as only a decadent young American can look. Lady Enid, who followed, managed to convey with great art the impression that she had just left her room. Lady Briardale did not appear, but Lady Branksome, unable to trust Lady Enid, arrived in good time, although she confided to me later that she thought breakfasting in public a barbarous practice.

After breakfast, the whole party, with the exception of Sir Cheveley Drummond, went to church. Poor Sir Cheveley hardly saw the point of going when he knew perfectly well that he would not be permitted to share Lady Enid's hymn-book.

I distinctly heard Lady Briardale say, as we were all waiting in the hall:

"I should have thought, my dear, that he would have preferred a synagogue."

At church a thrill passed through me when I found that I was seated next to Esther Lane. It was an infinite pleasure to me to be sitting beside her through the long and stupid sermon. The yellow winter sunlight fell across the recumbent effigies of dead and gone Gascoynes, and made the painted window to the east a blaze of colour.

Her presence and the surroundings filled me with a sense of purity and peace, and I surrendered myself to the primitive emotions. I suppose a less subtle soul would have been oppressed with a sense of past sins, and would in such a building have been filled with despair at the consciousness of irrevocable guilt. I fortunately had schooled myself to control. The sensation of goodness can, like other things, be acquired. When I had obtained the prize for which I was striving I had not the least doubt that I should find it easy to put away from me any unworthy feeling of regret. Why should I not? The harm was after all very questionable. It was not as if, so far, I had made widows and orphans. The amount of suffering I had inflicted was limited, and at any rate I should not leave poverty, the greatest of all ills, in my track. Indeed, under the influence of that Sunday morning service I felt quite regenerated. When we left the church Esther Lane and her pupil went through the great gates of the castle into the woods beyond, and I would have given worlds to follow her, but Lady Branksome told me that she agreed with her son, and that I was decidedly amusing. She insisted on my going for a walk with her. At the same time she took good care to see that Mr. Puttock and Lady Enid were close behind.

In the afternoon I manoeuvred a meeting with Esther Lane. I surmised that she and her pupil would walk away from the castle, and so I kept watch on the drawbridge. Everybody was more or less occupied. I was aware that Lady Branksome had, before retiring for her afternoon nap, left Mr. Puttock in possession of Lady Enid, who had got rid of him with all the ease imaginable, and was now walking with Sir Cheveley on the battlements.

Lord Gascoyne had pleaded letters, and I had arranged to fetch him in an hour or so and go for a tramp.

As Esther Lane and her pupil crossed the drawbridge I was leaning over the extreme end of the parapet in the most natural manner in the world. I pretended not to notice them, and only permitted myself to be aroused from a contemplation of the beautiful scenery which lay below by the child flinging his arms with a scream of delight round my legs.

She blushed as she apologised for her charge. She was evidently a little nervous as to what her employers might think if they saw her walking with one of their guests, and, after a short interchange of commonplaces, tried to get rid of me. I refused to be shaken off, and a couple of hundred yards took us out of sight of the castle.

We dropped at once into a style of conversation which was almost intimate, and although I was with her barely three quarters of an hour she confided a great deal in me.

Not that there was much to confide. She was the daughter of a solicitor who had left nothing but debts. Her mother was dead, and she was absolutely alone in the world. Her only relations were some very distant cousins who were so poor that it had been impossible for them to help her in any way.

"I was very lucky," she said, gratefully, "to get such a good situation, and it came about in the quaintest way. Lady Gascoyne had seen all sorts of people with diplomas and recommendations which I had not got, and she saw me sitting in the waiting-room as she passed out.

I don't think the agent quite liked her engaging me, but Lady Gascoyne insisted that I was just the person she wanted, and here I am."

She smiled contentedly. She evidently considered herself an extremely fortunate young woman.

She attracted me enormously without in any way usurping the place of the two women who already counted for so much in my life.

All too soon I was obliged to leave her and hurry back to Lord Gascoyne, whom I found waiting for me.

It was the first opportunity I had had of really impressing him, and I did not waste my time. I took such an absorbing interest in everything about me that I fancy he was surprised to find himself talking so much and so intimately.

I was perfectly ready to enter into the subjects which interested him most. He was evidently deeply imbued with a belief in the divine right of aristocracy, and with no superficial sense of its responsibilities. He was above all things a serious man, with little sense of humour. I imagined that Lady Gascoyne must find him dull, but his qualities were essentially those which command women's respect and hold them with a certain kind of fear.

As is the case with his class—a class which the popular organs are fond of describing as irresponsible and brainless—his knowledge and grasp of life were very extensive. His individual sympathies may not have been very great, but he had a general sense of justice which marked him out as an administrator, from many who were perhaps much his intellectual superiors. What he knew was of use to him.

I was surprised at my own capacity for conciliating him. I accompanied him with ease into the region of politics. He was evidently impressed, and it was satisfactory to feel him gradually treating me with less and less formality.

"Your race gave us one of our greatest statesmen," he said, "for I do not believe that anyone has understood real statesmanship better than Disraeli."

"Some people seem to think he was insincere," I replied, "but I don't believe it. His cynicism was simply the complement of a mind with a singularly large outlook."

So subtle an appreciation impressed the man whose own nature was all in a straight line. The curves of a less direct character appealed to him as insight.

In listening to him, however, I could not help reflecting that his kind, whatever the moralist may pretend, is far more vulgar than the abnormal. The orchid is the most fascinating of flowers in all its varieties, but it is rare; or do we only call that type normal which prevails for the moment? Which is the more moral man—he who by reason of a lack of imagination ranges himself as the mercenary of tradition and convention, or he who rebels and finds himself wounded and struck at wherever he turns? Not that I can claim to be a martyr to moral restlessness, although at one time I sincerely believe I had in me the makings of a reformer. Nevertheless, there is always something a little vulgar about the man who ranges himself definitely on one side.

We returned to the castle on very good terms indeed. The rest of the party were at tea in the long picture-gallery. I like, even at this unpleasant crisis, to linger over the memory of the picture-gallery at Hammerton on that Sunday afternoon in midwinter. The long, straight windows through which the frosty sunset flushed the gilded frames and old tapestries, the firelight playing on the silver of the tea-table drawn up before Lady Gascoyne—for there were no servants to desecrate the most convivial of all meals—made up a delightful picture, whilst the child Walter Chard, in his sailor clothes, ran from one group to the other as happy and unconscious as if he had a prescriptive right to the enchantment of the castle.

I was delighted on our assembling for dinner to find that Esther Lane was of the party. She was dressed simply in grey, with a couple of blush roses at her bosom. Lady Enid was talking to her when I came in.

It fell to my lot to take her in to dinner, and we thoroughly enjoyed ourselves. She was quite unconscious amongst these great folk, and unaffectedly joyous. I almost fancied that Lady Gascoyne looked at me once or twice with the faintest sign of surprise. I sincerely hoped she would not inform Miss Lane of the fact that I was engaged, although it was more than probable. Esther Lane was one of those women who are, to a certain extent, lacking in the natural defences of their sex as a result of their own honesty and simplicity. That she was prepared to be interested in me was obvious, and I made the most of my time. After dinner she played to us. It was not a brilliant performance, but she was accurate and had feeling, and she touched the keys wooingly and caressingly, making the piano sing, a gift rare even among some so-called finished performers. If people cannot make instruments sing they had better leave them alone. Afterwards I played and sang, and she declared herself ashamed of her own performance. Music had the advantage of giving us an excuse for remaining at the piano together, and later, when everybody else settled down to cards some way off, we were left trying over one song after the other. When I murmured that it seemed as if we had known each other all our lives she blushed.

Later, in the smoking-room, Sir Cheveley said he was quite astonished to find how pretty she was. It was a fact which he declared had grown on him gradually.

The next morning I returned to town, but I had made such good use of my time that I carried with me an invitation to return in a fortnight, and it was Lord Gascoyne who brought it me from his wife.

He had made quite a friend of me. It was not probable that he had ever had a friend with anything of the bizarre about him before.

CHAPTER XXII

THE TIME passed slowly, but in a fortnight I found myself again at Hammerton sleeping beneath the same roof as Esther Lane. I met her again on the terrace on Sunday morning, as I had expected. I could quite follow the workings of her mind. Because she was possessed of great self-respect, she had determined not to be on the terrace that morning, but because she was very much in love she was there after all. Before many moments had passed I saw that she was aware of my engagement. There was a look of suffering in her eyes as she turned them on me. She had the most wonderful way of suddenly subjecting the person to whom she was speaking to their full glance. If she could suffer because I was engaged to another woman, she had enough sentimental interest in me to excuse my going far. She was the character to appreciate the simulation of agony born of a struggle between duty and affection, and I was ready to ring up the curtain on the comedy. She was fully conscious that I loved her. Yes, I loved her quite passionately, and yet it was not altogether passion. It is one of the presumptuous platitudes of conventional moralists to describe a man's love when it ceases to be concentrated on one individual as lust and base passion. Side by side with this contention they will declare that the highest morality is to love your neighbour as yourself, so little are they given to their own boasted virtue of consistency.

I talked to her for some time about the most ordinary matters, but I could see that she was trembling.

"I have thought of you a good deal," I ventured.

She ignored the question, but without a show of indifference.

"I think Walter and I ought to go in." She moved away a little awkwardly.

"I suppose I ought to go in too." I went to breakfast, leaving the impression I had intended.

In the afternoon I saw her again, and before I was quite aware of it, I had told her I loved her beyond all women in the world, and having done so was compelled to anticipate the scene which I had been mentally preparing.

I assured her passionately that I was not the fickle person I might seem to be, that directly I saw her I knew that I had made a mistake, and that I could never be happy with anyone but her.

She was too much in love to do more than make a pretence of forbidding me to speak on the subject.

She walked straight into the carefully-hidden trap, and found herself being made love to without the question of my engagement being discussed, and once she had thrown down the barriers of reserve, with the enemy actually in her camp, it was impossible to replace them. She accused herself vehemently, however, of being unworthy of her trust. She would resign her position. She could never, she asserted, remain, and be guilty of duplicity. I beat down her poor little attempts at self-defence at once. If she threw up such a position I should never forgive myself. I would go away and never see her again. The threat appeared to terrify her. I persisted that the view of such affairs taken by most people was entirely wrong. I showed that, on the contrary, it was wrong to lie and say you do not love a person when you do, that it was quite possible to talk of our love, to cherish it, and to welcome its influences for good, without allowing it to get the upper hand. All of which the poor fluttering little morsel of sentiment drank in with greedy ears, because it was just what she wanted to believe.

The child found us dull, and cried out that he wanted to play, so I left her and returned to keep an appointment with Lord Gascoyne. Esther Lane was included in the dinner-party that evening, and I again took her in. The arrangement was not so pleasant as on the previous occasion, for there was a distinct feeling of strain between us. I surmounted it with ease; but she was without experience, and she suffered. I could see that she had been crying.

"You must not let yourself be wretched," I said, as we stood a little apart from the others waiting for the move towards the dining-room. "It hurts me."

"I had intended to remain in my room," she murmured.

"Why?"

"I feel as if everyone must see that I am an impostor."

I was about to reply lightly, but checked myself, remembering that the heroine of the comedy was an ingénue.

"If you were not so good you would not have a sense of guilt where there is no guilt."

We went in to dinner.

I talked to her incessantly, and inasmuch as her happiness lay in being with me, she was prepared to be charmed out of her misery for however brief a period.

I was myself somewhat astonished at the hold I had secured over her so soon. I suppose in her inmost heart she was dreaming dreams in which all would come right. But even if I were safely ensconced as Earl Gascoyne I could not have made such a sacrifice as to marry her. Besides, in the sense of a mate, to take my name and reign with me, I would not have changed Edith Gascoyne for anyone in the world, not even for Sibella.

There is among modern English ballads one which has always struck me as having a claim to live because of its simplicity and the heart-throb in it. It is called 'For ever and for ever.' It possesses a perfect blending of music and idea, unpretentious, but full of feeling.

As before, we spent the evening at the piano, and I sang this song to her almost under my breath:

> "I would, alas! it were not so
> For ever and for ever."

I could see that the tears were raining down her cheeks as she listened. She held a fan so as to conceal her face from the others in the room.

"We shall see each other again soon," I murmured, as I said good-night.

Lord Gascoyne and I were the last to leave the smoking-room, and he parted from me at the foot of the stairs that led to the bachelors' quarters. My bedroom was half-way down a long corridor, at the end of which there was a solid door, which gave on to the battlements. It was bolted inside, but not locked, and I had more than once used it to take an evening stroll when the inhabitants of Hammerton Castle were asleep. This evening I opened the door noiselessly and walked out on to the walls. It was a clear starlight night and bitterly cold. I did not mind this, for I had on a thick fur coat. I strolled along, thinking deeply, when suddenly I was brought to a standstill by a ray of light that fell right across my path.

I looked in the direction from whence it came, and was astonished to see Esther Lane leaning out of a window a few feet from me. The terrace at this point took an abrupt turn, and a comparatively new part of the castle had been built out at a tangent.

She had not noticed my approach, for I wore house-shoes, which made no noise.

She was looking at the stars as if their ceaseless splendour might be symbolic of an inevitable dawn of happiness somewhere. They could not have been completely reassuring, for she was weeping, and as I stood and watched, a convulsive sob broke from her. The picture of the forlorn little dependent, a frail white figure in the patch of light, with the gloomy towers and battlements of Hammerton looming round her, affected me strangely. I leant forward over the low wall and murmured her name.

"Esther!"

She started and looked round, drawing back quickly as she saw me clearly defined in the moonlight.

"You must not cry. It breaks my heart."

At the moment I fully believed what I said.

Her eyes, full of tears, were turned upon me, and, with a strange look of fear, which haunts me to this hour, she said:

"I thought I should never see you again."

"You were going away?"

She saw that she had betrayed her intention, and tried to excuse herself.

"It will be better."

"Why? If you go away I shall never come here again."

I was upon the low wall, the ground full sixty feet below me.

"Oh, go back! you will fall."

But I had my hand on her window-sill and one foot on a ledge a short distance below it, whilst the other remained on the wall. She was helpless; to have attempted to stay me would have been to send me in all probability to certain death. She clasped her hands and held her breath. The next moment I was in the room and by her side.

"Don't be afraid; only I must speak to you. We must understand each other."

"Oh, go away, please."

She hid her face in her hands, utterly shamed by the presence of a man in her room.

Poor Esther! I think she was happier. I verily believe that every woman is happier for love fulfilled. I knew that once having chosen her path she would follow it unflinchingly, and that she would be true as steel. I had discerned from the first that she was capable of martyrdom. From that day she never mentioned the word marriage. She declared ever afterwards that it was her fault, that she should have closed her window on me, that she had accepted the position of mistress, and that she could not complain.

At the same time, however, it was no easy task to persuade her to remain at Hammerton. She implored me to let her come away to London. She vowed that she would not be an encumbrance, not even an expense. She was sure that she could get work to do, sufficient to keep herself; but I was firm. I had at one time some idea of letting her live at Clapham in my deserted house, but I had always had a superstition about allowing anyone else to live in it, otherwise I should have sold it long before. Besides, I did not see what excuse she was to give Lady Gascoyne for wishing to leave her, and the latter had grown so fond of her that it was not likely she would accept her resignation without a great deal of inquiry. Esther declared that living a lie made her feel miserable, that she was unworthy of her charge, and ought to resign it.

CHAPTER XXIII

I HAD still made no plans as regards Lord Gascoyne and his heir. I must confess that I had qualms about the child, which shows how illogical and unreasoning sentiment is. It is surely a greater crime to kill a grown individual who has a place in the practical work of the world, and who would be missed by hundreds, than to remove an infant whose loss could only affect his parents. It was not easy for me to inflict pain on a child, as my fondness for children is exceptional. The means would have to be sudden and violent, and they were difficult to think of. It might have been made to appear that his death had been caused through some apparent negligence of the nurse, had not the latter been a careful old lady through whose hands two former generations of the Hammertons had passed. I had, unperceived, followed her in her walks with the Gascoyne heir, and I was afraid it would be impossible to find her careless.

I was prepared to make away with father or child first; whichever event came most readily to hand would have to take place. A novice might have been impatient, but experience had taught me that one had only to watch and wait, and the opportunity would come at the most unexpected moment.

It was nearly time for Miss Gascoyne and her uncle and aunt to return to town. I was wondering whether they would be asked down with me to Hammerton. It would be somewhat awkward, but I had infinite belief in my own powers of dissimulation and tact.

In the meantime I concentrated my thoughts on little Lord Hammerton. I had read of a child being smothered by a cat going to sleep over its mouth. For a time the somewhat impracticable idea possessed me of obtaining a gutta-percha baby, which I would fill with hot water and arrange so that it could breathe mechanically, and then train a cat to lie upon it. The weirdness and humour of the idea commended itself to me. The far-fetched nature of the scheme, however, became more apparent the more I considered it.

I thought I might become a proficient with the Catapult, and aim at the child unseen. In such a case the blame would probably fall on a village boy. This, too, seemed rather far-fetched.

I had seen Hammerton's nursery, or rather nurseries. Even a child of his rank seldom has such a suite of apartments:—a night and day nursery of lofty proportions, with rooms for the head-nurse and her assistant opening off. It was the size and loftiness of the rooms that were exceptional. Lady Gascoyne was a great enthusiast on hygiene, and declared that fresh air was the best food a child could have. In fact, I was not likely to be spared my unpleasant task through any neglect of the little Viscount's health.

My objection to inflicting pain upon a child gradually grew weaker. Something had to be done.

I was seriously considering the matter when Providence put a weapon into my hand.

I arrived one Saturday evening to find Lady Gascoyne somewhat uneasy. Walter Chard was not well. Something quite trifling, no doubt, but he was feverish.

I asked if I might go and see him, but Lady Gascoyne said that she would rather I did not. It was always difficult to say how these childish ailments would develop. It might be something infectious, and she had Hammerton to think of. If anything happened to him Lord Gascoyne would be broken-hearted.

"Miss Lane is with him," went on Lady Gascoyne. "She absolutely declines to allow anyone else to nurse him."

I wondered whether Esther Lane had known that her undertaking to nurse the child would prevent her from seeing me. For the moment I was a little annoyed, as even the most supercilious man will be when he imagines the woman he is thinking of very much at the moment has found a duty which she places above her love.

> 'I could not love thee, dear, so much,
> Loved I not honour more,'

is very trash in the case of both sexes. People who say they cannot love where they cannot respect are talking nonsense. Affection is independent of and survives prejudice, which I should surmise is an added terror in the lives of good people.

"You are not afraid of infection, are you?" asked Lady Gascoyne.

"Oh dear no, but what makes you think it is something infectious?"

"I don't know. I had a sort of instinct that it was so directly I looked at Walter."

I thought nothing more of Walter Chard during my visit except to ask how he was.

"The doctor says he cannot decide for a few hours what is the matter with him," replied Lady Gascoyne.

On Monday morning, however, the Castle was thrown into a state of the greatest consternation. The doctor pronounced him to be suffering from scarlet fever, and Lord and Lady Gascoyne were filled with alarm for the safety of their own child.

Walter Chard had been constantly with him, and any moment little Lord Hammerton might develop the complaint.

The sick child was immediately secluded at the extreme end of the castle, and a trained nurse was sent for. From the moment I heard that it was scarlet fever my mind was at work. Supposing Hammerton did not develop the complaint, would it be possible to convey the infection to him?

If I could get near Walter Chard in the convalescent stage it would be easy enough.

Of course, it did not follow that even if Lord Hammerton took the infection he would die, but there was the chance that he might.

Lady Gascoyne talked of removing him from the castle at once, but the doctor decided that it was not necessary.

"Our patient is too far away to do any mischief. He is for practical purposes quite isolated, and if you disinfect the rooms he has been living in you need not be in the least alarmed."

On my return to town I waited a week, and then wrote to Lady Gascoyne, saying that I hoped Lord Hammerton showed no signs of having caught the infection. I displayed so exactly the right amount of solicitude that on meeting Lord Gascoyne in town he greeted me, for him, almost effusively.

"My wife was quite touched, Rank. Naturally, we were alarmed, but I fancy it's all right. The other little chap will soon be on the road to recovery. Come down with me to-morrow if you are not afraid."

It was exactly what I wanted. The chance might not again offer itself to carry out my design. I met Lord Gascoyne at Waterloo, and we travelled down together. It was the sort of travelling that suited me to perfection; a saloon carriage had been reserved for us, and all along the line we were treated like royalty.

I had been a little surprised that when he and Lady Gascoyne attended anything in the shape of a function in the neighbourhood of Hammerton they rode in a chariot with outriders. The effect was singularly picturesque, and appealed to my Jewish love of colour. I determined that if ever I succeeded I would retain the custom.

When we reached Hammerton we found Lady Gascoyne at the station, quite radiant. Notwithstanding that the patient was at the most infectious stage, there was very little danger, owing to the complete way in which he had been isolated.

I was the only guest, and we retired early. I had, of course, seen nothing of Esther Lane. As I walked on the terrace and smoked my cigar I wondered if she were thinking of me. I paused at a spot which was at the extreme end of one of the horns of a semi-circle. At the end opposite to me were the rooms in which she was nursing her invalid. I stood looking at them thoughtfully. I was thinking of what Lady Gascoyne had said as to the disease now being at its most infectious stage. Contact, or the use of the same article, such as a towel or a handkerchief, might convey the infection. I might be doing something to advance my cause instead of idly puffing at my cigar. The invalid's rooms were several hundred feet away, and to reach them I should have to scale a parapet some ten feet in height, but it was no more than I could manage. I walked slowly round the semi-circle. The night was strangely mild, and it was not improbable that the windows would be open.

I knew the apartments. They had once been occupied by a mad Earl Gascoyne, and had in his day been securely barred.

These bars had, however, long since been removed, and I remembered thinking the rooms almost the pleasantest in the castle. They were some distance from the rest of the living part. When I reached the terrace I saw that there was a narrow stone staircase which I had not before noticed. At the top of this was an iron gate which would have to be climbed. Just then I heard steps on the terrace above me, and I had hardly time to draw into the shadow of a buttress when Esther Lane appeared, leaning over the low wall above my head. I threw down my cigar and stamped on it, for it might have been its scent borne on the night air which had attracted her.

She looked about her for a few seconds and went back. I waited for an hour or so until the lights were turned down for the night. I wondered which of the two women was watching by the bedside of the invalid.

After a time I ascended the staircase and surveyed the iron gate at the top. It looked rickety, and it would be difficult to climb over it without making a noise. If the trained nurse found me it would not be easy to explain my presence.

I climbed over the gate and dropped on to the other side. In the still night air it rattled horribly, but no one seemed to have heard. I had on house-shoes, and stole cautiously forward. I knew that the temporary hospital was a large room with three windows opening to the ground. Danger being almost out of the question here, the windows had been left partly open. I stole cautiously forward and looked in. By the dim light I saw the sick child lying on a bed well out in the middle of the room. On a long, low chair by the fire lay Esther Lane, in a white dressing-gown. I thought she looked exceedingly beautiful, if a little worn with watching. Crossing to the window furthest from where she lay, and having quite assured myself that she was asleep, I entered cautiously and looked round. I went first to the door that I knew gave on to the corridor. Luckily, the key was on the inside, and I locked it. There was another door leading to an inner room, which made me a little anxious, as I concluded that it was occupied by the nurse. It had no key, and I quietly placed a chair in front of it. Noiselessly I stole towards the bed. The child's flushed face was resting on his hand, in which was clasped a handkerchief. This was the very thing I wanted, and with infinite care I managed to unclasp the little fingers and draw it forth without waking him. Wrapping it in my own handkerchief, I thrust them both into my pocket.

I had just finished and was turning away when I became aware that Esther Lane's eyes were slowly opening upon me.

Luckily she did not cry out, but rose quickly with a half-smothered exclamation. As I went swiftly but silently to her I heard the boy stir in the bed behind me, and we both stood waiting in suspense to see if he would wake. Luckily he only murmured once or twice, and sank to sleep again. I was near the light, however, and ready to extinguish it at once should he show the least sign of waking. When his regular breathing had reassured me I drew her on to the terrace.

"I was obliged to come," I murmured passionately. "I had to see you."

"You should not have done it," she said helplessly.—"you should not have done it."

"I am very sorry."

I took my cue and passed into the mood of the reckless, love-sick youth. I knew that to feel a passion is the only way to be convincing.

"It is dangerous, and most dangerous now." She began to weep; she was evidently unstrung from watching. I drew her away into a sheltered corner of the battlements, where the moon made it almost as light as day.

I told her that I was only happy when I was with her, and that all my days in London were given up to thinking of her. The poor child believed me. It appeared that she had been attempting to make some expiation for what she considered the betrayal of Lady Gascoyne's confidence by her devotion to Walter Chard during his illness.

I held her in my arms, and we remained perfectly happy and in silence for a long time. She certainly stirred my blood to an extraordinary degree.

She was terrified lest my visit should convey infection to the rest of the household. I reassured her. At the same time, her having seen me was very awkward. Hers was a character which, impelled by conscience, might be capable of all sorts of extraordinary things, great renunciations and burning sacrifices. I held out a vague promise of taking her to London and allowing her to a certain extent to share in my life. This filled her with a guilty delight, and she clung to me with a sigh. Love in its fierce, personal aspect meant more to her than to any woman I have ever met.

The poor little soul went back and procured some strong stuff with which she instructed me to disinfect my clothing.

I returned to my room almost laughing with glee at having the handkerchief from the sick boy's bed with me.

When I reached my bedroom I packed the two handkerchiefs carefully up in several layers of paper and then went to bed. Of course, I had to reckon with the fact that I might take the infection, but I will do myself the justice to say that at no time during my career have I been much affected by a consideration for my own safety. It has always appeared to me that an absolute disregard for my life was the only method on which to proceed.

The next morning I excused myself from accompanying Lord and Lady Gascoyne to church. Lady Gascoyne quite sympathised with me.

"A gallop will do you much more good."

I thanked her, but said I preferred a tramp.

As soon as they had walked over to the church I made my way to Lord Hammerton's nursery. I was no stranger to it, and was a favourite with the nurses. The little viscount knew me quite well, and crowed directly I appeared.

Old Mrs. Howick looked at me indulgently as I took the child in my arms. After a time she went into the inner room, leaving me in possession for a few minutes. I hastily took out of my pocket the handkerchief, which was still wrapped in my own, and let it fall across the child's face. He clutched it with two little fat hands, and I allowed him to play with it, and then thrust it in between his frock and his chest and left it there. I had previously taken good care to ascertain that it was unmarked, and was not likely to be recognised.

When the nurse came back I was still playing with the child, and she took him from me and dressed him for his morning's outing without discovering the presence of the handkerchief.

I then went for a long tramp through the woods, laughing at myself for what I could not help feeling to be a piece of absurdity. On my return to the house I went again to the nursery. The little viscount was asleep, and I managed to extract the handkerchief and lay it where the air he was breathing must pass over it. Then I removed it, and congratulated myself that I had left no foolish clue whereby my action might be identified. Mrs. Howick was delighted at my attentions, and told Lady Gascoyne that she never had seen his lordship take to anyone as he had taken to me. Inwardly I hoped that he might take to the infection with even greater ardour.

There was still the question of Esther Lane to be dealt with, if it were possible to deal with it at all. If the child should fall ill she would be sure to think of me and find out whether I had been to visit him. As is always the case, my romantic susceptibilities had landed me in a position of danger which all my other intrigues had not done. If Esther Lane should tell the truth, my entire house of cards would fall to the ground. The telling of the truth would involve a general exposure. It would mean farewell to Miss Gascoyne, and also the shutting of the gates of Hammerton Castle in my face, which would be a far more fatal obstacle to my success.

I did not bless the day on which I had met Esther Lane, and further cursed my own weakness. This is a habit of men when they have obtained their desire.

I should have remembered the dictum of a celebrated countryman of my own, which prophesies material doom for those who are unable to control their affections. He should perhaps have substituted another word for affections.

There were no measures for self-protection to be taken as far as I could see. My strongest card was Esther's love for me, and if that were not strong enough to prevent her betraying me, nothing would. I had wit enough to see that it was likely to prove a still stronger weapon if I kept away from her.

I waited some days, and read one morning in a halfpenny paper which deals in such tittle-tattle that Lord and Lady Gascoyne were in the greatest anxiety about their only child, the heir to the title, who was suffering from a severe attack of scarlet fever.

I had had several false alarms as to whether I myself had not caught the infection, and having gone to bed one evening feeling very seedy and convinced that I had, was not a little relieved on waking the next morning to find myself perfectly well.

I wrote a note of sympathy to Lady Gascoyne, and the same day received a wild letter of self-reproach from Esther Lane. She accused herself of being a murderess, and of having betrayed Lady Gascoyne's confidence in the most despicable manner. There was only one way out of her misery, she declared, and that was by suicide. I hardly dared hope that she would take any step so drastic, or so convenient. I was much reassured as to my own safety by her imploring me not to write to her, as she did not know what might happen, and if her correspondence were opened it might involve my ruin, and she blamed nobody but herself.

The unexpected happened. Lord Hammerton died, and I was now very near the succession indeed.

This was the time to strike. Whatever happened, Lord Gascoyne must go, and as quickly as possible.

I was asked down to the funeral. Lady Gascoyne wrote me a heart-broken letter, recalling the fondness of the dead child for me.

Mr. and Mrs. Gascoyne and Edith had returned to London the day before the catastrophe.

"It seems, Israel," said Mr. Gascoyne, "as if the direct line were doomed to extinction. I sincerely pray that the title may never pass to me. It would be really very inconvenient at my time of life and with all my other interests. It is not likely, however, for my life is not as good a one as most people imagine."

I looked at him earnestly. This was the first I had heard of his health being anything but exceedingly good.

He interpreted my glance in his own way.

"Don't be alarmed, Israel. Nothing immediate is likely to happen, but my doctor tells me my heart is not the sound organ it ought to be, and that I must be very careful."

"You must leave as much of the work to me as possible, sir," I said feelingly.

"So I do, so I do, Israel; but you don't want to turn me out altogether, do you?"

I looked hurt.

"My dear boy," he continued good-humouredly, "I should not have ventured to take so long a holiday if I had not had you to depend on. Let us go to lunch and talk things over."

I found that talking things over meant that he was anxious to make matters easier for my marriage, and, in fact, he made them so easy that Miss Gascoyne and I were able to fix a date within two months of their return.

Once we were married I did not mind so much what Edith discovered. Nevertheless, I had to admit that if I was frightened of anybody I was frightened of my future wife. I had imagined at one time that it would be possible to live with her on quite a dignified, unfamiliar footing, but I had now realised what I ought to have guessed before, that Miss Gascoyne to the man she loved was very different from the woman the world knew. Perhaps that is a wrong way of putting it. She was English, and a certain self-consciousness towards the world at large was born of a morbid dread of betraying the strength of her nature to the vulgar.

CHAPTER XXIV

ALTHOUGH Sibella had more or less accustomed herself to the idea of my marriage, the nearness of its approach gave her somewhat of a shock. Woman-like, she wanted to meet Miss Gascoyne, but on this point I was firm. After we had been married some time such a thing might be possible, but not till then. Personally, I had no intention of bringing about the introduction. The women with whom one has relations are best kept apart. A chance word or look, unsuspected even by ourselves, might give a clue to the truth. The whole thing would make me too nervous. She asked me whether if Lionel died I would break off my engagement and marry her. I replied that of course I would do so, and though I do not suppose she believed it any more than I meant it, the statement seemed to comfort her mightily.

Mr. Gascoyne and I went down to Lord Hammerton's funeral.

We only saw Lady Gascoyne for a moment. She was too overwhelmed to hold conversation with anyone for long. Lord Gascoyne was wonderfully self-controlled, but he looked very careworn. I had begun to understand him, and I could see that he was much touched by Mr. Gascoyne's solicitude. He mentioned Miss Lane in the course of the morning.

"She is utterly broken down. She seems to have some idea that carelessness on her part is responsible. Of course, it is nobody's fault, although I think we ought to have gone away directly Walter fell ill. However, it is no use saying what ought to have been done."

"What is the doctor's opinion as to how the infection was carried?" ventured Mr. Gascoyne.

"He seems utterly perplexed. From what I can gather from the other doctors he is not to blame. He blames himself, of course. Well, it is a great grief to us, but we shall get over it; and, after all, we are young." I knew what he meant, and I could only sincerely hope that my chance might come soon.

The funeral was extremely stately for so small a corpse. The tiny coffin was borne into the castle church on a bier that had evidently been accustomed to heavier burdens. The church was full. It was quite evident that as regards that part of the country the heir of the Gascoynes was considered an almost royal personage.

Esther Lane was in the church, looking terribly worn and ill. Once I thought she glanced at me almost fiercely, but she wore a crêpe veil, and

I could not be sure. I did not see her, for Mr. Gascoyne and I returned to town in the evening. Two days later, however, when I was dressing for dinner, a note was brought up to me in her handwriting. The lady, the man said, would wait for an answer. I opened it in almost a fever of excitement, fully expecting to read that conscience had won the day, and that she had confessed all, but the note only asked me to see her. Two minutes later she was in my room and in my arms sobbing wildly, but declaring that, however much she was prepared to sacrifice herself, she would not betray me.

She was thirsting for some little display of love. Her loneliness had been more than she could bear, and her guilt had added to its terrors. Poor little soul! my love meant so much to her that in a few minutes she was smiling almost cheerfully.

She had told them at Hammerton that her nerves were on the point of breaking down, and that she must have change; and she was now on her way to spend a few weeks with some friends in the North.

I showed her how we might steal two days on her return and spend them together at a small seaside village that I knew of on the Yorkshire coast. It would be very near my marriage-day, and it was the sort of thing which always held vague possibilities of discovery, but still I am glad I risked it.

Esther interested me enormously. I had never come across quite her type before. That, with her high moral stamina, she should so completely accept any scheme of deception which I chose to propose was extraordinary, but so it was. With me she seemed to have no will but mine.

It was curious that she did not reproach me with the death of Lord Hammerton, but hers was not the nature to blame others for any guilt of which she had to admit a share.

She must have concluded that my visiting Lord Hammerton's nursery the morning after I had been in Walter Chard's sick-room was responsible for the tragedy.

I had expected a torrent of reproaches on this score, and was very pleased that she said nothing. The curious moral numbness from which she suffered when with me seemed to have put the memory of it out of her mind.

CHAPTER XXV

I NOW made the great mistake of my career.

I had so far proceeded with extraordinary deliberation. I had from the first realised the danger of hurry. For a time I forgot caution, and that is why I, Israel Rank Gascoyne, Earl Gascoyne, Viscount Hammerton, am writing my memoirs in a condemned cell instead of living in almost feudal splendour in Hammerton Castle.

As Lord Gascoyne had said, he and his wife were young, and there was every prospect of another heir. I had no time to lose. The way in which all the heirs of the House of Gascoyne had died off was beginning to attract attention. People had discovered that I was very close to the succession, and I was now a welcome guest at many houses which had hitherto been closed to me. Lady Branksome had evidently taken back her remark about the synagogue, for she was sweetness itself. Sibella appreciated my position fully, and began to regret her marriage with Lionel, saying that she had made a great mistake, and that she ought to have waited. She had long since told me that Lionel bored her terribly.

"He isn't even wicked or vicious," she complained; "he is only weak."

I said that I was astonished that she should have taken so long to discover so obvious a fact.

She might have answered, had she been clever enough, that in a woman's eyes the fine animal will stand for a great many virtues, and that the illusion has a habit of lasting a very long while. The truth of the matter was, however, that the thoroughly unhealthy life which Lionel led had quite destroyed any physical charm he had ever possessed. He developed a capacity for middle age which was quite startling. He might have possessed Jewish blood, judging by the speed of his transition from slim boyishness to stale maturity. Sibella, who was extraordinarily fastidious on the subject of physical beauty, noticed it very soon. Considering that she was married to him, the discovery did her credit. I have known so many people marry for beauty and afterwards show the most extraordinary callousness to its decay. I suppose the romantic resource of most people gives out after one attack.

Sibella's was not the kind of organisation to become phlegmatic. Robbed of her essential food—excitement—she would have become querulous and irritable, but she could never settle into the easy-going. It was a proof of her opulent temperament that I verily believe she had been somewhat in love with Lionel and myself at the same time. Lionel now grated on her in proportion to the fascination he had once exercised.

I was only afraid that she might find my divided attention all too insufficient. Sir Anthony Cross had somewhat dropped off. The pertinacity of the most fervid lover cannot withstand perpetual disappointment, and he was beginning to realise that he had set his heart on the moon. I think he realised also that I was laughing at him for the effusive civility with which he had treated me whilst he thought I was playing his game, a civility which had long since given way to marked coolness. This I did not mind, for the time had now passed when he could be useful to me. I should have attempted to conciliate him if I had thought otherwise. I knew that in his heart of hearts he had always disliked me, though at the same time my Jewish blood taught me not to create one more enemy than was necessary.

My marriage drew near, and a cloud of family connections descended on Miss Gascoyne. People who would some time before have denied that I was in any way connected with the Gascoynes, thought it such a nice thing that she was marrying one of the family, and though it was improbable that dear Mr. Rank would ever succeed, still, one never knew; whilst any reference to my Jewish blood was no doubt met with: 'Oh, I don't know; perhaps a very slight strain;' which, considering my appearance, was ridiculous.

I went the length of presenting myself with a wedding-gift from the imaginary Parsons family. It was the sort of thing which I did not like doing. It is always difficult to say how active deception in small things will end, and no wise criminal encumbers himself with a number of petty deceptions. They clog his footsteps, and, besides, the trifles of life should be used to build up a reputation for veracity and good fellowship. It is limiting to play for small stakes. An attention to detail is imperative, but the detail must be essential and not superfluous. Still, considering that I had made so much of the Parsons' devotion to me, it would have looked strange if they had not sent me something, even from Canada.

CHAPTER XXVI

I CANNOT quite decide whether it was the preparations and natural excitement consequent on my marriage, or whether much success had made me careless, but certain it was that I conducted my campaign against Lord Gascoyne, the most delicate affair of all, with a lack of forethought which candour compels me to admit has very justly brought me to this place.

I believe it would have been better if I had dealt with him some time before. Now I come to think the matter over, it would obviously have been better to leave the Reverend Henry alive, and to have waited my opportunity in the case of Lord Hammerton. I should then have appeared so much further from the succession that suspicion would not have been aroused.

In the first place, I was much too hasty in deciding on the means by which I intended to remove Lord Gascoyne. To have decided on vulgar, common-place poison at such a crisis was an error in judgment for which there is really no excuse.

Miss Gascoyne and I were to spend a few days at Hammerton at the conclusion of our honeymoon, and I chose that occasion for the completion of my task. It would then be practically finished, for I had no intention of getting rid of Mr. Gascoyne. A natural feeling of gratitude towards so excellent a man was my first objection, and I did not think there would be any necessity. I should not, I imagined, have long to wait, and a few years in the position of heir would be by no means unpleasant.

I was obliged to ask Lionel and Sibella to my wedding, but Sibella, I was glad to find, had not the least intention of being present. She made herself perfectly ill about it, and my one prayer was that she might not become hysterical. Women in a state of hysteria do such extraordinary things.

We were married somewhat quietly, considering all things. I don't think my wife ever looked more beautiful. Hers was too deep a nature not to take so serious a thing as marriage somewhat sadly. The service, to my mind, was a little cold. My taste for ritual was Oriental, and I could have wished that my wife-elect had belonged to the Roman communion in order that there might have been more splendour. I should have been quite prepared to become a nominal child of Rome had it been necessary.

We spent our somewhat short honeymoon at a place called the Green Manor, a small country-house belonging to Lord and Lady Gascoyne, a fact which quite placed us as a married couple.

I had manoeuvred so that our honeymoon should be a short one, giving as a plea that Mr. Gascoyne's health was far from good, and that I did not care to neglect the business. My wife at once fell in with the idea.

The truth of the matter was that I was anxious for our visit to Hammerton to take place as soon as possible. With my marriage, however, there came a new terror into my life. I was full of fear that I might say something in my sleep which might give a clue to my secret. A chance word might do it. Still, it was a risk I was obliged to take. If I had been in love with my wife to a certain extent before marriage, I cannot say that my passion lasted very long. I fancy she brought to what I had always looked upon as a delirious relaxation too strenuous an ideal. With her it could not have been otherwise. I managed to conceal the fact from her with considerable success, but the truth was that she got on my nerves. She was a great creature, but she was on a different plane from myself, and it made things very difficult. A good woman, however, being without experience, is always more easily deceived. If this were not so the artificial arrangements which are supposed to safeguard society would have disappeared long ago.

The life she was always sketching out for us, to her so beautiful and noble, was to me excessively dreary. Doing good appeared to be its chief entertainment. We were apparently to spend our money—all too little for the wants of a young couple who wished to make a decent figure in society—on other people. I foresaw a very speedy parting of our ways. I was strong, and she was strong, and it was impossible that either should impose views on the other. She was one of those women who are perfectly prepared to follow love to heaven, but who have not the least intention of being led in the contrary direction. Conscience with her was supreme. I was determined, however, that nothing should appear at all wrong during Mr. Gascoyne's lifetime, or until I was in safe possession of Hammerton and the title. Mr. Gascoyne's fortune amounted to close on a hundred thousand pounds. This would, I knew, come to my wife and myself, and if I suffered defeat, it would be a very pleasant addition to our own capital; and though I did not think that, except in extreme circumstances, Mr. Gascoyne was likely to leave his money away from us, it was possible that if he had an idea that I was not making quite the husband he expected he might settle it somewhat too exclusively on Edith.

I set myself, therefore, to study the art of concealing from her that her ideals bored me, and that her outlook on life was too serious. At the same time I bantered her a little, and tried to bring her into an atmosphere of gaiety. She was ready to attempt a greater levity of manner to please me. The effort was somewhat of a failure, for saints off their pedestals never present an absolutely dignified appearance.

Our honeymoon was a success, however. A man of taste and imagination can never be quite dull when in possession of a beautiful woman, not, at any rate, until the novelty has worn off. Serious though Edith was, she did not exhaust herself in a fortnight.

We arrived at Hammerton in due course, to find Mr. and Mrs. Gascoyne of the party. The reception that Lord and Lady Gascoyne gave us was quite feudal and eminently flattering. I inwardly promised his lordship that if it were in my power he should have a magnificent funeral.

It was quite a family gathering. Naturally, we had not expected many people to be asked to meet us, as they were still in deep mourning. It had been very nice of them to ask us at all, considering the circumstances. I had grown so accustomed to pose as one of the mourners at a tragedy of my own making that the situation had ceased even to possess weirdness.

It was a little awkward that my wife took an immediate fancy to Esther Lane. It was surely against all the laws of human nature that Esther Lane should reciprocate the liking.

It seemed to me that from the moment she met my wife her whole manner towards me changed.

I think she began instinctively to distrust a man who could behave so badly—from her point of view—to a woman like Edith. I don't think she entirely believed all I had said about my marriage being one of mere convenience. Before I had had an opportunity of seeing her alone, in the course of a few remarks which we hurriedly interchanged while we were looking over some songs after dinner, she told me that she could not understand any man not loving a woman so beautiful and good. I could see that without saying as much she was a little surprised that Edith and I should have come together. She had a fine instinct and perhaps realised how unsuited we must be.

I was anxious to have a private conversation with her, but she declared that it was quite impossible, that she was not so depraved as I imagined her to be.

When I did manage to get a few words with her alone I found that she was adamant. It was certain that she had changed to an extraordinary degree, and somehow she gave me an uncomfortable and somewhat sinister impression of being a possible danger. She did not deny that she still loved me a great deal too much for her own peace of mind, and I have no doubt that if I had had a free hand as to the time I could spend with her I might have had my own way, but I was occupied with other things, and in particular I was occupied with Lord Gascoyne.

I had decided that after dinner, whilst Lord Gascoyne and I were sitting over our wine I would try, if possible, to carry out the finishing stroke of my policy.

Evening after evening I sat within arm's length of him without the desired opportunity occurring.

Lord Gascoyne was in the habit of drinking claret after dinner. His cellar of this wine was quite remarkable. He was, however, a moderate drinker, and I do not think that beyond a couple of glasses after dinner he ever took anything at all. Sometimes he drank whisky-and-soda in the smoking-room, but very rarely. Indeed, we were a most abstemious couple.

It was towards the end of my visit when the opportunity occurred. One evening as we were sitting over our wine a servant came in and announced that there was a fellow-magistrate in the justice-room who wished to see him, if only for two minutes.

He left the room, saying that he would not be long, and with the usual conventional admonition to help myself. Now was my chance. My courage failed me for a few minutes, and then I made the greatest mistake I could have done. His glass was empty, and so I poisoned what remained in the bottle. As I had the bottle in my hand a servant entered in search of Lord Gascoyne's eyeglasses. He saw me with the bottle in my hand, and noticing that my glass was empty, and knowing I drank port, filled it. As I was wondering what I should do, Lord Gascoyne re-entered and seated himself.

I gazed at the bottle before him, fascinated. I would have given worlds to get rid of it. Just as I was thinking of doing something to upset it, he poured out a glass and began to drink it. I saw at once the whole chain of mistakes. I was the only person in the room. I had been seen with the bottle in my hand. It would be next to impossible to destroy the bottle with its damning evidence. I had also obtained the arsenic from a chemist in the ordinary way. I had signed the wrong name, and if I were recognised that would make the matter worse. I had every motive for the crime—a motive which would stand out with startling clearness after Lord Gascoyne's death. I had felt nervous before. Now I experienced a sensation of acute terror. I must have shown it to some extent, for I turned pale, and Lord Gascoyne asked me whether I was ill. I declared I felt quite well, although at the moment he was taking another glass of claret.

I realised with an extraordinary feeling of depression that I was a clumsy murderer walking about like any ordinary criminal with blood-red hands, and trusting that nobody would notice their colour.

I watched Lord Gascoyne drinking his claret with sinking spirits, and could only pray that he might be one of those people who possess an inexplicable immunity to the poison I had used. It was not our custom to remain long over our wine, and in about a quarter of an hour we joined the three women in a small octagonal room off the picture-gallery. As Lord Gascoyne and I walked along the dimly-lighted picture-gallery towards the little room at the end I felt as if I were in a dream. It seemed as if the presage of a Nemesis, tardy but terrible, were upon me. The dark figures on the canvas stared down upon him as he passed, claiming him as one of their ghostly company; and I almost thought that his own picture, high above the great mantelpiece carved in hundreds of twisted forms by Grinling Gibbons, shivered as he walked below it. I expected every moment a cry of pain or the first moan of faintness. I had to pull myself together, and by the time we reached the others I had regained complete control. Lord Gascoyne always drank tea instead of coffee after dinner, and on occasions like this there were no servants, and it was made in a delightfully informal way by Esther Lane. She asked me to carry Lord Gascoyne's cup to him, which I did and he took it from me with murmured thanks.

I must still have shown traces of my recent agitation, for my wife drew the attention of the others to my pallor. She had hardly done so when Lord Gascoyne's cup fell with a crash to the ground, and he sank back into his chair in a dead faint.

The others went towards him at once, as I did also after the first moment.

Lady Gascoyne said something about brandy, and Esther hurried from the room to obtain it. Lord Gascoyne had somewhat recovered by the time she returned, but very shortly relapsed into another faint. I saw that my purpose was accomplished, and that before morning only Mr. Gascoyne would stand between myself and all I coveted. Lord Gascoyne retired in indescribable pain to his bedroom, and a groom was despatched for the doctor. As for myself, I hurried to the dining-room in the hope of being able to do away with the decanter of claret containing the evidence of guilt. If the decanter were discovered, I should immediately fall under suspicion. It could not be otherwise. Well, I must be as calm as possible. On entering the dining-room I saw at once that the decanter had been removed. My opportunity of destroying all chance of detection was over. In reality it was here that I made the fatal mistake, for I should have obtained possession of the decanter at all costs and destroyed it, or at least have cleansed it. I should have invented some excuse, seeing its paramount importance to me. I was, however, too nervous of arousing suspicion. In fact, I had lost my nerve for the time being without realising it. It is certain that had I been as cool and self-possessed as I am now I should not be here. I allowed the golden opportunity to slip. There was some excuse. Lord Gascoyne was momentarily growing worse. Everyone in the castle was in a state of alarm. I was seldom alone, for my wife hardly left me except when she could be of use. I cursed myself for my stupidity in not choosing a more rapid poison. I might at least have given the foolish doctors an opportunity of declaring death to be due to natural causes. The learned fellows require so little encouragement to commit blunders.

I remember well the electric shock I received when, towards the morning, one of the doctors stopped me in the corridor and said something about its looking very much as if Lord Gascoyne had been poisoned.

"Poisoned?" I asked in surprise.

"Yes; he must have eaten something which was poisoned. One never knows in these days of food adulteration. One is safe nowhere— not even at the best tables."

I felt almost inclined to say that doctors themselves were curiously lax on the subject, but I was too much alarmed at his having put his finger on the spot at once to enter into an abstract discussion on the ethics of the medical profession.

I was drawing him out in order to see how much he had guessed, when his colleague came out of Lord Gascoyne's apartment and called him in. Coming along the corridor I met Esther Lane, seeking for news. I went towards her. Was it my fancy, or did she shrink from me? It seemed to me that she did, but I was in a weak, morbid state of mind, in which I was a prey to fears of my own shadow. It was a dreary trio that met round the breakfast-table. Lady Gascoyne did not appear, and Esther always took her meals with her charge, except when she was specially asked by Lady Gascoyne to join herself and her friends.

One of the doctors came in, but brought only bad news. In answer to Mrs. Gascoyne's inquiries he threw up his hands.

"We do not know what to make of it, and—"

He paused, as if afraid to go on.

"Please tell us," said my wife anxiously.

"Well, of course, while there is life there is hope, but—"

"You don't think—"

"I am afraid we must prepare for the worst."

There was a long pause. The two women were horrified. I rose and went to the window, as I knew not what guilt my face might betray.

Suddenly the end came. A wail shivered down the corridors, and then, from where I was watching the bedroom door, I saw Lady Gascoyne led out by Edith. After a few minutes the two doctors came out, and in answer to my question, explained that all was over. I carried the news to Mrs. Gascoyne. She was terribly distressed, and asked me to wire for her husband, which of course I did. It suddenly struck me that it might be possible to obtain the decanter that evening at dinner. I supposed there would be dinner. There usually is, even at moments of the greatest stress. Curiously enough, the whole thing once over, I began to recover my nerve rapidly, and by the time Mr. Gascoyne had arrived I was quite myself. I did not know that, even at that moment, the junior doctor was conducting an examination into what Lord Gascoyne had eaten and drunk the evening before, and giving orders that everything which had been left was to remain untouched.

I think such a knowledge would have tempted me to buy some means of retiring from the scene on an emergency. I had not even a loaded revolver. It was evident I was not the clever person I had imagined myself to be.

Mr. Gascoyne could hardly believe the news.

"Israel, it is terrible. There seems to be a curse on the family." He was silent for a few moments, and then continued thoughtfully: "Israel, has it struck you what this means to you? Failing male heirs, the title descends through a woman. Your grandfather would have been the last male heir, therefore your mother would have succeeded as his heiress, and then you."

We had talked this over before, but I pretended to think of it deeply, as if it now presented itself to me seriously for the first time.

"Of course, it has struck me, but the possibilities seemed so remote."

"They are close enough now. It would seem as if Fate had been on your side."

I certainly hoped that it was. He little knew that that fate in its concrete form was sitting opposite to him.

"What do you think was the cause of death, Israel?"

"Nobody seems quite to know."

"He looked just that sinewy, tough sort of man who was likely to live for ever."

I was silent.

"There must have been something organically wrong," Mr. Gascoyne continued.

I was still silent, meditating whether I should tell him what the doctor had hinted at as regards poison. I decided that it would be better to do so. It would look very strange if he should discover that the doctor had already suggested such a thing to me, and that I had ignored the fact.

"Dr. Phillimore thinks that death must have been caused by some violent poison."

"Poison? Impossible!"

"So I said. I don't suppose he meant for one moment that anybody had poisoned him."

I regretted this remark. It might rouse suspicions in his brain. The nervous analysis of everything I said was becoming automatic.

"He was taken ill directly after dinner, you say?"

"When we left the dining-room."

"If it had been anything he had eaten you would all have been taken ill as well."

"It would seem so. At least, I don't know. There may have been some dish which we others did not touch."

"It is all very mysterious, but it is quite possible that the doctors may be wrong."

"Oh, quite," I said dryly.

The rest of the drive he spent in asking after Lady Gascoyne, and for other details of the affair.

As we entered the great hall I saw the two doctors at a distant window in earnest consultation.

They came forward and greeted Mr. Gascoyne as the Earl.

They had evidently been waiting for him. Dr. Phillimore, the younger of the two, who had been called in in consultation, said at once:

"Dr. Grange is anxious for a private interview with you when you are at liberty."

I had from the first felt nervous of Dr. Phillimore. He was evidently a man of exceptional intellectual power. He had a massive, square forehead, and a strong resolute face with an expression of great alertness. Even now, although he had had no rest for twenty-four hours, he showed few traces of fatigue. Dr. Grange, on the other hand, looked worn and jaded to a degree, and would, I am sure, had he been left to himself, have retired to rest before taking any further steps in the matter. I did not know that, whilst I had been out, Dr. Phillimore had been making extensive inquiries, and that he had already placed under lock and key everything which had been on the table the night before.

It appeared that he had once before been concerned in a poisoning case. Decidedly my good fortune had been on the wane without my knowing it. I think his previous experience had somewhat obsessed him with the idea that poisoners were everywhere. Only in this way can I account for the unerring ability with which he followed up every clue.

I was beginning to feel more and more uncomfortable, and when Mr. Gascoyne and the two doctors disappeared into the library—I had not been invited to be present—I felt much like the criminal who in a moment of panic betrays his guilt by flight.

My wife came to me once or twice; but she was a great deal with Lady Gascoyne, or rather stayed just within call, for Lady Gascoyne was a proud woman, and preferred to suffer in solitude.

Whilst the consultation was proceeding in the library, I remained in the corridor outside, controlling my agitation with really wonderful success. As I stood in the dusk looking out through the open window, round which climbed June roses and clematis, Esther Lane stole up to me.

So ghost-like and silent had been her approach that I gave a cry as her eyes met mine. On further recollection, the sound I made was a smothered yell. It was a sound which now seems to me to have been full of a confession of guilt.

For a moment she did not even say she was sorry she had startled me. She was evidently too amazed at my display of nerves. I even think that a faintly defined ghost of suspicion floated through her mind. At any rate, the incident seemed to widen the gulf between us.

"This is terrible, is it not?" she said.

"It is terrible."

"And but for me Lady Gascoyne would have had her child to console her." She covered her face with her hands.

"I do not think you ought to put it like that," I said gently.

"The doctors say he was poisoned. It is strange, is it not?"

"It is strange," I answered.

The sunset hour, the knowledge that the three men in the library were hovering over an undetected crime, invested the situation with a deep gloom. The ghostlike figure of Esther at my side, from whom remorse and suffering had taken something of her bloom, seemed to me made for suffering. I felt that Fate had marked her out for some terrible experiment in sorrow; that grief had chosen her for its own, and that I ought to have foreseen it.

I had made the cardinal error of allying myself with a soul that was moving in a cycle of sorrows. It was curious that I should not have detected a fact now so apparent. One should always seek the companionship of the joyous. To walk with those who are wedded by Fate to grief is to play with fire. It is to step within influences that may destroy us. So much of the mystical I can infer. There is hidden meaning in the phrase, 'Let the dead bury their dead.' She seemed to be afraid of her own company, and I think sought mine out of pure loneliness. I was too absorbed, however, in my own danger to comfort her. What had she to fear compared to me? She had lost something which was of purely conventional value, whilst I might be in danger of losing the essentials, life and liberty.

"I am very unhappy," she said, in her low, musical voice, with the curious thrilling vibration that had given it such an appeal for me. "I feel as if somehow I had meant nothing but sorrow and grief to this place, as if I were of ill omen. Of course, it is presumptuous of me to even think of myself as being of so much importance."

"You seem to think very little of me now," I murmured. It seemed unchivalrous not to render her some comfort of the heart.

She was silent for a moment, and then pulled herself together.

"I am afraid I think of you too much."

Even at that moment I was moved in my essential sex vanity, and was prepared to play the lover if it were worth while.

"You have been very unkind lately, Esther."

I touched her lightly with my hand. She drew away from me.

"I think you are wicked, and I know that what has been must be expiated. That is an inevitable law."

I shivered. There was a stern intensity in her voice despite its music.

"Yes," she continued, "I love you still, but I have no joy in doing so. If by dying I could make you better, I would willingly die, but I could never again—"

She broke off abruptly, but I knew what she had intended saying, and I also knew that she meant it.

She moved away, and left me peering out into the dark, mechanically trying to distinguish the features of the landscape as they became more and more blurred by the gathering dusk.

Finally, I heard the library door open behind me, but pretended not to have done so. I started with feigned surprise when Mr. Gascoyne touched me on the arm. The little piece of acting was quite unneeded, but it denoted the nervous necessity that I felt for dissimulation. One glance at his face, even in the dusk, reassured me that, so far, I was not in any way an object of suspicion.

"There will have to be an inquest, Israel. Phillimore is convinced that Gascoyne was poisoned. I think his insistence on the point rather annoys Dr. Grange."

"I concluded that an inquest would be necessary. When is it to be held?"

"Phillimore has wired to London for a specialist in poisons, and the post-mortem will take place directly he arrives. It appears that Phillimore was mixed up in the Greybridge poisoning case, and knows a good deal about these things. Not," he added hastily, "that there is the least suspicion of foul play."

Phillimore was evidently a highly unpleasant fellow, and I would willingly have pushed him over the battlements if occasion had offered. I made myself very civil to him, however. I was told that he had gone into the kitchen and superintended the cooking of everything which was sent upstairs. This had the effect of frightening all the servants into fits, and half of them were already complaining of imaginary internal aches and pains.

I saw the humour of the situation, notwithstanding my alarm, but the others did not. They sat round the table with the conventional Christian look of gloom which is considered suitable when a brother Christian has, presumably, entered into a state of bliss.

After dinner I went and sat with my wife and Mrs. Gascoyne. They informed me that Lady Gascoyne, thoroughly worn out, had fallen asleep.

"I am afraid the most terrible moment of all for her will be when she wakes up to find that it is not a dream but a reality."

Frankly, I thought worse sorrows might have befallen a woman with three-quarters of a million of her own, who still retained youth and beauty, not to speak of being a dowager Countess. No, it was impossible to feel very sorry for Lady Gascoyne. Nobody realises the tragedies of love better than I do, but at the same time one cannot forget that lovers for the beautiful and rich are to be found every hour of the day. She had bought a title and a lover once. She might conceivably do so again.

Of course, grief is always terrible, but the most terrible thing in the whole world is poverty. I do not deny that it may be a vice to attach the importance to wealth that I have done. I have never concealed from myself the fact that my mind is glamoured and decadent. Poverty, it is true, is comparative, but to have to endure that which is relative poverty is a slow torture which has no equal.

The conversation at the dinner-table had dwelt with a mournful decency on the probable cause of death.

"It must have been something in the food," held Dr. Phillimore.

"If that is so, why is no one else ill?" And Dr. Grange looked as if he had effectually crushed his colleague.

"It may have been something of which the others did not partake. I have had all saucepans, cooking-utensils, food, dishes, and wine used last night isolated and locked away."

I stared at him, petrified. It was the first time I had been brought face to face with the hard fact that the claret decanter would be thoroughly examined. I passed a gruesome ten minutes, but managed to maintain my composure and take my share of the conversation.

"Dr. Grange thinks the cause of death may be something quite different from poison," explained Dr. Phillimore, turning to the rest of the company.

I think Mr. Gascoyne, whose instinct for character was not his strong point, also felt that Dr. Phillimore was somewhat premature in his conclusions, that, in fact, he was rather officious and inclined to treat us all like children. With my special knowledge I was, of course, able to appreciate his real value, though, even had I been a mere spectator, I think I should have set him down at a glance as a man of first-class brain-power.

The great specialist arrived whilst we were at dinner. He was a man of opulent, indeed quite princely demeanour. Unlike Phillimore, whose exterior bore a certain ruggedness, his power was concealed by an outward courtliness that might have deceived the unwary. Personally, I felt it at once.

He went into consultation with his brethren, and I learned afterwards that he speedily came to the opinion that Lord Gascoyne had died of a violent irritant poison.

All these details were kept from Lady Gascoyne as much as possible, and it was not till after the post-mortem that she learned what had taken place. I saw by the look of perplexity in the faces of the three doctors that they were puzzled at what they had found. I had already resigned myself to the fact that the poison would be found in the bottle of claret. The wretched thing, with other food which was to be examined, was locked up in a strong room, of which Dr. Grange held the key. Figuratively, I was before that strong room every precious hour that passed, wondering how it might be opened. How wretchedly I had over-reached myself! However, it was done. It was of no use to whine. I must fight until the whole thing was decided against me.

The doctors were quite secret over what they had discovered, but I kept Dr. Phillimore well under observation. He left the house soon after the post-mortem, and drove off in the direction of Gaythorpe, a town about five miles away. I knew what he had done. He had written his telegram before leaving the house, and I read it on the blotting-paper by means of a looking-glass. It was as I thought. The message was a telegram to Scotland Yard asking for a detective. While he was doing this, the poison expert was examining the food.

I tramped the battlements for one hour making up my mind as to what I should do in case the charge should be made against me.

I did not make the mistake of dwelling on those points of the case which were in my favour. I kept my attention fixed on those that seemed most damning. My own guilt, viewing it as I did from the inside, seemed easily susceptible of proof, but I had to remember that a detective, however expert, would approach the matter from a totally different standpoint. He was, after all, an outsider, and I must try and put myself in his position if possible.

It took me a long time to decide my course of action should suspicion fall upon me. I also began to grow uneasy as to whether I had left anything in my house at Clapham which might furnish a clue to my movements during my former operations. I was sorry I had concealed the existence of the house.

If I were arrested the grief of Mr. Gascoyne and my wife would be rather trying, but I had counted the cost of discovery when I originally set out on my adventures.

Mr. Gascoyne was busily occupied in arranging for the funeral.

I was very anxious to discover whether there was any likelihood of a posthumous heir.

I noticed that Mr. Gascoyne did not so far permit himself to be addressed as the Earl.

The inquest was held the next day. The detective, I knew, had arrived the night before, and was making inquiries. In the morning he was standing in the hall as I passed towards the breakfast-room. I knew perfectly well he was waiting to see me, and the swift glance I took at his face convinced me that he was on the right track.

I felt a terrible shock, notwithstanding the fact that I had been steeling myself ever since Lord Gascoyne's death to meet such a situation.

The specialist was the only occupant of the breakfast-room when I entered. I had not seen him or his brethren since early the evening before.

"Have you arrived at the cause of Lord Gascoyne's death?" I asked.

"Poison," he said shortly.

I started, as if immensely surprised.

"Then Dr. Phillimore was right. Something in the food, I suppose?"

He hesitated.

"We don't quite know. We have not finished our investigation yet."

This I knew was not true. The detective had evidently asked him, if his own discretion had not prompted him, to hold his tongue.

The specialist volunteered no more information, and in a few minutes my wife and Mrs. Gascoyne joined us.

CHAPTER XXVII

THE inquest took place in the justice-room.

It was not deemed probable that it would be necessary to summon Lady Gascoyne as witness. The evidence of the others who had been in the room at the time when Lord Gascoyne was taken ill was considered sufficient. The statement I had already made to the coroner's officer was quite simple. I declared that I had not noticed any signs of illness on the part of Lord Gascoyne till we reached the room where the ladies were. There had certainly been nothing to arouse anxiety before we left the table.

The depositions of myself, Mrs. Gascoyne, my wife, and Miss Lane were taken first, and they then passed on to the medical evidence.

Dr. Grange was the first to be examined. He stated that on reaching the castle he found Lord Gascoyne in such a serious state that he immediately sent for the assistance of Dr. Phillimore. The latter seemed to think that Lord Gascoyne was suffering from poisoning, an opinion which he had not at first shared. At the post-mortem, however, a sufficient amount of arsenic was found in the body to have caused death.

Dr. Phillimore's evidence was identical, but it was easy to see that it was he who had guided Dr. Grange's opinion.

Finally, the expert was called, and the detective glanced at me to see what effect his appearance would have. I am glad to say that I gave him no satisfaction. I do not believe that I changed colour or moved a muscle. Indeed, I believe he has had the fairness to say that he never came across a criminal who had such complete self-control, and that it seemed incredible that a criminal so self-possessed should not have found means to get rid of the claret in the decanter. He afterwards declared that he had at one time hoped to trace more than one of the Gascoyne mysteries to me, but in that he failed.

The expert corroborated the evidence of the other doctors, and then stated that he had made an examination of the food.

"I naturally selected the one thing which was most particular to Lord Gascoyne," he said, "and I began, principally for the sake of simplicity and so as to clear the way, on the claret."

I found myself breathing hard. It was a moment of supreme test. Many things convinced me that there was at least some suspicion attaching to me. The detective imagined that I was not looking at him, whereas I was conscious of his least movement. It is indeed a pity that what ought to be a particularly brilliant profession is left to the lower middle classes. It accounts for the comparative lack of scandal in the higher ranks of life, for a gentleman does not find it difficult to hide his crimes and vices from those reared in perhaps the most obtuse section of society.

It was also easy to see that the servant Waters had been questioned about me, for directly the bottle of claret was mentioned he cast a furtive glance in my direction.

"I found this bottle," continued the specialist, "to be full of arsenic—so full, that it would have been impossible to drink any of the contents without succumbing to its effects. To be brief, I found no traces of arsenic in any other bottle of claret taken from the same bin or in any of the other food."

"You are quite sure of that?"

"Yes. The claret was a brand of which there was barely a dozen left. I believe Lord Gascoyne had been heard to regret that there was so little remaining."

After the expert's evidence there was a pause.

Mr. Gascoyne looked terribly worried. He had evidently not imagined that the matter was likely to become so serious and complicated.

The next witness was Gorby, the butler. He deposed to having fetched the wine from the cellar. No one had access to the wine-cellar but himself. He kept the keys. He had been in the family for forty years.

In reply to the coroner, he said that he himself placed the wine on the sideboard, and that it was his duty to pour out his lordship's first glass before withdrawing.

No one drank claret after dinner but his lordship. Mr. Rank usually drank one glass of port, sometimes he drank nothing, but certainly never more than one glass.

"And on this particular evening?"

"Mr. Rank took port, sir."

The coroner leaned forward and put the next question impressively.

"Was it possible for the arsenic to have been put into the decanter between your placing it on the sideboard and the arrival of the company for dinner?"

"I don't think so, sir. I was late with some of the wine, and did not leave the dining-room at all till the company arrived."

"It was possible, however, for anyone to reach the wine while you were out of the room?" persisted the coroner.

"It was possible; but the servants were very busy."

"How many servants were there in the room besides yourself?"

"Two."

"You yourself poured out the claret which Lord Gascoyne drank?"

"Yes, sir."

"What did you do with the decanter?"

"As usual, I placed it in front of his lordship."

"And then you left the room?"

"Yes."

"And the other servants also, I suppose?"

"Yes, sir."

There was a pause. An unaccountable whimsicality made me think of the game which children play, and which consists in sending someone out of the room and then hiding an article which the absent one is to find on his return. I felt almost inclined to cry hot and cold to the coroner as he hovered over the evidence. Not that I felt callous as to what might be going to occur. I had enjoyed life far too much. On the other hand, I had always reckoned the cost, and had never counted my chickens before they were hatched.

Mr. Gascoyne crossed over to me in the interval, and said in an undertone:

"What does it all mean?"

"I really do not know," I said.

"Surely they are not trying to prove that his own servants poisoned him?"

"The poison must have come from somewhere."

"Yes; that is obvious."

He looked at me in some surprise. I noticed his almost startled expression, and began to analyse the remark I had made. Was it what I should have said had I been guiltless? If it had been, Mr. Gascoyne would not have displayed such discomfort—a vague discomfort, true, but an evidently indefinable sensation that something was wrong. He was from that moment uneasy about me, and yet almost unconscious of any uneasiness.

The other servants were recalled, and declared that neither of them had touched the wine. It would have been such an unusual thing that the one who had done so would have been noticed by the other. The claret was in a very peculiarly shaped flagon. By no possibility of means could anyone have mistaken it for the claret which was offered during the meal.

Evidence then followed as to all the wine which was handed round during the dinner. There was champagne, said Waters, but only Mrs. Gascoyne took any. Neither Lady Gascoyne nor Mrs. Rank drank anything. Lord Gascoyne drank nothing but claret—the claret—at the end of the meal. Mr. Rank drank port at the end of the meal.

The coroner persisted. I was thankful to him. His continued examination might make one of the witnesses nervous. The sleek Waters might contradict himself. The other two servants might relapse into a hopeless confusion of ideas as to what they had done and what they had seen.

It was a delusive hope. All three adhered strictly to their statements, and finally there was another pause.

Everyone appeared to wonder what was going to happen next. I thought I could guess the direction the proceedings would take. I was not mistaken. The detective passed a piece of paper to the coroner. The latter looked at it, and an expression of surprise crossed his face.

He mentioned me by name almost with a suggestion of apology, as if he were deprecating the official side of him which insisted on a course of action repugnant to his more social and well-bred half.

I did not look at Mr. Gascoyne, but I felt him stir in his chair uneasily as I rose to my feet. I moved to the foot of the table where the witnesses had stood during their examination.

"You were left alone with Lord Gascoyne after the ladies had withdrawn?"

"That is so."

"Can you recollect his lordship making any remark as to a curious taste in the wine?"

"No."

"He made no remark?"

"None at all."

The coroner paused, and then said:

"Recall Richard Waters."

Richard Waters stepped into my place. For one moment I felt dizzy. A curious unreality seemed to surround the scene and its actors. I saw things through an ecstasy which seemed to remove me afar off. Everybody in the room bore a strange profile expression like great gaunt marionettes. After a few minutes the sensation passed, and I felt myself growing abnormally tense and keen; in fact, the acuteness of intelligence which I felt was in proportion to the recession from realities which had just possessed me. It had been an unconscious recoil, but my perception advanced with greater force because of it.

"You came into the room when Lord Gascoyne and Mr. Rank were alone, I believe, to tell his lordship that Colonel Markham wished to see him in the library?"

"Yes, sir."

"You then returned to the dining-room!"

"Yes, sir."

"What for?"

"His lordship told me to bring him his eye-glasses, which he had left on the table."

"What did you see?"

"Mr. Rank had the decanter of claret in his hand."

"What did you do?"

"I thought he had mistaken the decanter of claret for port, and I took it from him and helped him to port."

"But you say that the claret and port were in two totally different decanters. The claret was in a flagon?"

"Yes, sir."

The port decanter and the flagon were here produced. No one could have imagined that the claret flagon held port; at least, so I thought, but it may have been my guilty conscience.

The coroner continued his examination.

"Please be very careful in your answers."

"Yes, sir."

"When you took the flagon from Mr. Rank, where was the stopper?"

"On the table."

"You are quite sure?"

"Quite."

"Why are you so positive?"

"I cannot say, but I am quite sure."

"That will do."

The coroner looked perplexed. The jurymen gazed at him as if for inspiration. The detective made no sign.

The coroner rose and announced that the inquiry was adjourned.

I realised the grim meaning of his laconic announcement.

It was apparent to everyone that the case had assumed an ugly complexion, and that there was a so far unspoken suspicion of foul play in men's minds. Such a suspicion was not likely to remain unexpressed very long, and it soon rose from a whisper to a crescendo of excitement. Lord Gascoyne had been murdered, so everyone said, and the London papers that came down by the evening train already had the announcement in large letters. They hinted at a mystery, and declared that sensational developments might be expected at the adjourned inquest.

Mr. Gascoyne was in a state of the greatest nervous agitation. He took every care, however, that no suspicion of the dark things which were being said should reach any of the women, and the papers were carefully kept out of their way.

Worried as he was, I do not think that he in any way anticipated the blow which was about to fall.

Edith asked me one or two questions after the inquest as to what had taken place, but it was quite evident that she had not the least suspicion of what had occurred.

Mrs. Gascoyne, on the other hand, who had lived in the world, and had been brought up in a commercial family, had her eyes fairly wide open. I could see when we met at dinner that she was very uneasy.

It was a dismal meal. Lady Gascoyne did not, of course, appear. My wife was sad and preoccupied. Mrs. Gascoyne, with, I am sure, a full premonition of impending disaster, strove to be cheerful, but to little purpose. Mr. Gascoyne hardly spoke a word. When we were left alone he drew his chair nearer to me, evidently prepared for a long conversation.

It would have been amusing, had the subject not possessed such grim significance for me, to notice how very deprecatingly the servants offered us wine.

The castle cellar itself had, of course, been placed under lock and key, and the detective seemed to have disappeared from the premises.

"Israel," said Mr. Gascoyne seriously, "if poison was found in that bottle, someone must have put it there."

"That seems very obvious."

"I could have understood it had there only been a very little arsenic in the bottle, but that it should have contained the quantity it did is amazing."

Why Mr. Gascoyne should have understood it better had there not been so much arsenic in the bottle was not very apparent, but he was in the sort of mood in which people are apt to talk nonsense.

"Have you the least suspicion as to who might have put the poison in the bottle, Israel?"

He looked at me furtively.

"They might say that it was I, sir."

I fancy that he gave almost a sigh of relief. He would never have dared to make such a suggestion himself, and I could see that he was thankful to me for giving him an opening.

"To tell you the truth, Israel, it has struck me that in the absence of anyone else being open to suspicion they might hint at such an absurdity."

I laughed, a highly successful laugh.

"You see, sir, in my case there is motive."

"I am almost afraid, Israel, that people may say unpleasant things. Reading the bare evidence, they may be tempted to come to ridiculous conclusions."

I saw that it was time to affect a serious view of the matter. I kept a close watch on my tone of voice, however, and was most careful as to the light and shade of any expressions I used.

"You don't mean to say, sir, that you seriously think anybody would connect me with the crime?"

"Seriously, no; but I think irresponsible gossip might make things very unpleasant."

"It certainly would be unpleasant."

"You are my heir, Israel. Failing me, the title passes on to the branch of Lord George Gascoyne, whose heir you are through your mother."

"Exactly, sir; as I said, in my case there is motive." I looked a little grave, and continued slowly:

"Someone must have put the poison in the bottle." I was deliberately allowing my gravity to increase in order to emphasise my growing apprehension.

"I notice the detective has left the house," I said.

"Detective!" echoed Mr. Gascoyne in amazement.

"Surely, sir, you knew that there was a detective in the house?"

"My dear Israel, I knew nothing of the kind."

He thought for a moment, and then added: "I think I ought to have been told."

"I thought you knew, sir."

"Are you sure it was a detective?"

"Quite sure."

But even as I spoke I remembered that I only had my own deductions to guide me. No one had told me he was a detective. I searched swiftly in my brain for some excuse, but could think of none.

"How did you know he was a detective?"

"I heard him questioning one of the servants."

"Which servant?"

"Waters."

"What about?"

"I did not quite catch what he said, but it was quite easy to see what he was."

"He may have been gathering evidence for the inquest."

"That is what I suggest."

"Oh! I beg your pardon."

He was evidently a little puzzled.

The next day Lord Gascoyne was buried. It was a beautiful sunlit morning, and as we crossed the courtyard following the coffin in procession I glanced up towards the windows of Lady Gascoyne's apartment. I could see a white hand slightly drawing apart the closed curtains. I was sorry for her, but as matters were going I was a good deal more sorry for myself.

The affair had already attained the dignity of a first-class mystery in the London press, and as the victim was a Lord the sensation was twice what it would otherwise have been.

Most of them frankly admitted that as far as they knew there was no clue. But one halfpenny daily with an enormous circulation, whose consistent unveracity seemed a matter of supreme indifference to its readers, declared that there was a clue, and stated that someone had come forward to show that Lord Gascoyne had been in the habit of purchasing arsenic, that he was a confirmed arsenic eater, and that everything he ate was impregnated with it.

It was very unpleasant to have the searchlight of the entire press turned on the case so soon. It would put Scotland Yard on its mettle, and detective forces are apt to strain matters somewhat when their credit is publicly involved.

That evening I was walking up and down the terrace smoking a cigar with no very comfortable feelings, when I caught sight of the gleam of a white dress in the shadow of the battlements some way off. I guessed at once who it was. Esther Lane was watching me.

Why was she doing so? Was it possible that some suspicion of the truth had entered her brain? It dawned on me that, creature of instinct as she was, she might have arrived at the truth by the clear light of intuition.

I went swiftly towards her.

There was no time for her to evade me, but she shrank back into the shadow as I approached her.

"Why are you watching me?" I said as gently as I could, putting out my hands nervously.

She shrank back, thrusting me from her.

"Don't touch me. Don't touch me."

Her voice was low, tense with a latent hysteria, which must have caused her an immense effort to control.

"Why are you watching me?" I asked again.

She looked at me silently, the terror in her eyes growing.

She began to give me a strangely uneasy feeling.

"Oh, it's horrible, horrible," she murmured, and then stole away, moving along the parapet like a ghost.

I was afraid of her, and of what she might do. She was evidently losing her self-control fast. That she had guessed the truth was obvious.

I went towards her rooms. They were dark. Perhaps she was still wandering on the battlements with her unquiet thoughts.

I found my wife sitting up when I returned. She had been with Lady Gascoyne.

"Such an utter loneliness, Israel. It is terrible. She seems to have lost all interest in life. I have never seen such desolation."

People have a way of being superlative when talking of those in grief. I, too, was very sorry for Lady Gascoyne, but though she had no children, she had everything else in the world to console her.

I comforted my wife and took her in my arms, wondering curiously whether this would be the last night we should spend together, which, indeed, it turned out to be.

The next day the inquest was resumed. None of the ladies of the castle were present. Mr. Gascoyne—or Lord Gascoyne, as he was now called—looked haggard and worn, and, as I thought, avoided my eye. His manner, however, was extraordinarily kindly.

The servants were recalled and closely re-examined. They were still quite consistent.

The bottle of claret had been opened and decanted by Waters. He had placed it on the sideboard. No one else had touched it. The servants were all devoted to their master. There was not the slightest reason or motive for foul play on their part.

I noticed the detective sitting with the representatives of the county police, the chief constable himself being present. I smiled grimly as I surveyed all the materials for a very dramatic arrest.

The coroner then called me.

"After the ladies had withdrawn from the dinner-table on the evening in question you were left alone with Lord Gascoyne?"

"That is so."

"He was called out of the room and a servant entered whilst he was away?"

"Yes."

"Who declares that you had in your hand the claret decanter from which Lord Gascoyne had been drinking."

"I don't remember. The servant took the decanter from me and poured out some port."

It was just as well I admitted this, for the servant's statement received curious corroboration.

"That will do."

The next two witnesses were disconcerting. They were the chemist from whom I had bought the arsenic and his assistant. I was confronted with every proof of my folly.

I shall never forget the awful greyness which came over Lord Gascoyne's face when these witnesses gave their evidence. I noticed that when they had finished everyone avoided looking at me. They seemed afraid. The case appeared so simple that at first it also appeared incredible. Those around hardly grasped it.

The coroner asked me if I would like to explain why I had bought the arsenic.

Perhaps I made a mistake in saying that I used it as a tonic.

"Had I been in the habit of doing so?" was the next question.

"Yes, I had done so before."

"Have you ever bought arsenic from that chemist before?"

"No."

Here the family lawyer interposed, advising me to be very careful of my answers. I was not obliged to reply to anything which might incriminate me.

There was nothing more to be done. Towards the end of the inquest the chief constable crossed to my side, and, sitting down in quite a friendly manner, asked me to accompany him after the inquest into the next room.

The jury, evidently taking into consideration the fact that I was the next heir, that I had arsenic in my possession, that there was every motive, and that I was the only person who could have done it, returned a verdict of 'Wilful murder' against me. In my own eyes I stood convicted as the veriest bungler who ever danced at the end of a few yards of rope.

Lord Gascoyne was inexpressibly horrified, and there was a something in his face which I had not seen before. Was it suspicion? Perhaps he was thinking of the occasion when he learned that I was in the Lowhaven hotel at the time of his son's death. Truly I had made some inexcusable mistakes.

If nothing succeeds like success, it is also true that nothing fails like failure.

I found it somewhat difficult to play a sentimental role which should be convincing. I felt that I ought to take a dramatic farewell of my wife. Scenes of this sort, however, were distasteful to me. I asked Lord Gascoyne to go and explain the situation to her, and when she arrived I received her with a manner which entirely forbade any outward expression of anguish. To do her justice, she was not the kind of woman who was likely to make a scene. She displayed the most perfect self-control, although I could see that she was suffering acutely. It came as a terrible blow to her. No suspicion, I am sure, of the possibility of such a thing had before entered her mind. I don't think anybody really thought me guilty, which was, to say the least of it, peculiar, for it seemed to me as though the evidence were plain enough. From his manner the chief constable might have been driving me over to his place to stay for a day or two, and the first intimation I received of the unpleasant reality of the situation was the passing under the great gates of the county prison and the knowledge that for the future I was not free to go where I liked.

CHAPTER XXVIII

I SUPPOSE I must be thoroughly selfish, for at this moment of extreme depression and misery I was thinking chiefly of myself. Of course, I am curiously constituted, quite artificial from the world's point of view. I cannot say that I was a victim to the agony and woe which I believed would have been the lot of most people in my condition.

I, who had staked so much to win what I coveted, might have been expected to suffer tortures at the reflection of what I had lost. I had always thought that the most terrible thing about shame and imprisonment must be the complete triumph of those who have hated one—the triumph of the 'I told you so.' This and the irrevocable loss of earthly pleasures and the binding hand and foot as if one had no passions or emotions, were the things I had always dreaded. My consolation was that my failure could not be a commonplace one. Ordinary criminals might wear out their lives in captivity and lose their identity through long years of vile slavery, but the law, stupid and sordid as it is, had at least a due sense of the dignity of my crime, and would meet a defiance like mine with the dignified retort of death. Sordid crimes must meet with sordid rewards. Death is never sordid, and it shuts out the derision of a virtuous world.

I was caged, and through my own folly. A little patience and ordinary care would have saved me. To have failed after such triumphs, and to have failed where failure was irretrievable, was maddening. I hated myself more than a converted sinner could have done. It was all quite dreadful. A miserable fiasco, with a tragedy as the result. I turned hot and cold whenever I thought of it—I mean the fiasco, not the tragedy. I felt like an actor who has mangled his part and knows it. The only thing to do was to make the end as flamboyant as possible. There was strong temptation to proclaim my triumphs forthwith. I was certain that for all hope there could be of retrieving the position I might do so. I had, however, thrown away too many cards. One never knows how time, even of the briefest, will deal with facts, so I determined to be wary. I would fight every inch of the ground. It would, at any rate, be an amusement till the end, and my memoirs would keep my fame alive after death. One does not sin greatly to be forgotten, and, after all, the great sinners of history have had their share of posterity, and without the aid of public monuments. The world is always more curious to hear about vice than virtue.

For the first few days after my arrest I was a prey to savage rage, and found it difficult to reduce myself to that condition of mind in which a fighter who wants to make the best of things should be.

The first visit I received was from Lord Gascoyne. I was sorry for him. He looked ghastly, and avoided my eye. I was sure now that suspicion had done its work. Yet I knew he was blaming himself for even wondering how it came about that I was in the hotel when his son was poisoned. He had believed in me so thoroughly that he was trying to drive off the horrid thoughts that would pursue him. My wife's belief in me did not waver. Women like her do not lightly throw down the idols they have once set up. She loved me still, and she was steadfast. I wondered what Sibella and Esther were thinking. I was chiefly sorry for Sibella. It may have been because in my heart of hearts I loved her best. I knew how helpless she would feel. She would be obliged to conceal her grief, and she was the sort of woman to whom repression might mean hysteria. She had nothing to hold on to. The morbid horror of the whole thing would terrify her. I found it better for my peace of mind not to think of her.

I had caught sight of Esther for one moment before I left Hammerton. No one else saw her, but I was sure that she would be about somewhere. She was in the woods as I drove past. Her face was not pleasant to look upon. It was like the wraith of a memory, the pitiful phantom of a disembodied soul. It seemed to me as I sat alone during the quiet summer evenings, with the immense stillness of the prison around me, that sometimes her presence passed into my cell and made it curiously uncanny. I felt as if the arms of her soul had reached as far as my prison home in her agony, and once I even thought I heard her speak to me in a still, small voice.

I am no disbeliever in the unseen world, but curiously enough it has never had any terrors for me. Its concreteness has always seemed to me a difference in kind; a plane on which the idea is shaped with more fluidity; that is all.

I wondered if she would confess our relations. She had, I am sure, a high sense of honour, and her loyalty would probably stand any test. Still, hers was a subtle mind, and might, its white light having once been split, display a variety of tones and colours.

I do not think Lord Gascoyne had confided his suspicions to his wife, for I received from her nothing but the kindest and most encouraging of letters.

So I lay in gaol and waited, and the day for my examination came. The police-court where I appeared was packed. The county turned up in force; they were the same people who would have fawned on me had I succeeded in my object. Perhaps it is unworthy of an artist to suggest so much bitterness as lies in the word fawn. I had been taken by Fate on my own terms, and if I had failed, it was not for me to show a bitter spirit; in fact, it was illogical and small. I had played for their admiration and, having failed, obtained instead their derision.

My wife was in court the first day, and spoke to me in such a way as to impress upon the world her absolute confidence. I had no wish, however, to add to her sorrow, and I told her it would make me happier if she remained away.

The case was gone into most exhaustively, and, despite the fact that my lawyer declared that there was absolutely nothing on which to go to a jury, I was committed for trial.

I am pleased to say that the newspapers were unanimous in noticing my absolute calm of demeanour.

CHAPTER XXIX

A MAGISTRATE'S court is not a dignified place, and I had longed for its sordid littleness to have an end that I might emerge on to a larger platform.

I did so sooner than I expected. Lord Gascoyne, whose heart had never been strong, succumbed under the strain and anxiety of the whole affair, and I awoke one morning in prison to find the dream of my life realised. I was Earl Gascoyne. My child, whether boy or girl, would be the next heir, and whatever happened, I had achieved my purpose.

It had one unlooked-for result. I immediately claimed my right to be tried by my peers.

Judging from the newspapers, the claim came upon the public as something of a shock. In the Radical press there was an outcry for the abolition of such an antiquated custom. They were, however, brought face to face with a law of the land which so long as it stands is good.

This prospect almost reconciled me to my position. I saw myself, a picturesque figure, seated on a dais, with my fellow-peers in their robes before me. Yes, I had just the appearance to carry off such a situation.

I was sure of female sympathy. I was barely twenty-six, and looked younger. I should certainly have obtained something for my trouble.

The question as to whether I was likely to get a fairer trial from my peers did not weigh with me. I would not for a certain acquittal have foregone the scene in the House of Lords.

As far as I knew, the last peer to be tried on a charge of murder was the celebrated Earl Ferrers. I read everything to do with this trial with assiduity. I noticed that, instead of being relegated to the common gaol, he had been confined in his own house. I regretted to discover that this was not a right, or if it were I could not find anything bearing on the subject.

It would have been eminently satisfactory to go under escort from Park Lane to the House of Lords every day. As a matter of fact, I supposed I should have to be taken to and fro, or perhaps I should be lodged in some apartment in the precincts of Westminster Palace. The prospect teemed with interest, and was not a little comic. The papers, which had, of course, talked of nothing but my case for weeks, became trebly excited. The probable ceremonial was discussed at length by all of them. Articles by celebrated lawyers, letters from antiquaries, suggestions from all sides, filled up their columns and tided them over the dull weeks in a way which ought to have made them highly grateful to me.

I was myself in doubt for a short period as to whether my never having taken my seat or the oath would prevent my claiming my privilege. I believe everyone was too anxious to see the fun to press any debatable point. Of course, at the end of all this excitement loomed a not improbable and most unpleasant climax, but I was accustoming myself to think less and less of it every day.

I read the State Trials assiduously, for they teemed with interest for me.

The fact that I was not to be tried with the farce of a jury was a great comfort to me. If there is one thing more ridiculous than another in our judicial system, it is the fiction that when a gentleman has been tried before a dozen petty tradesmen he has been tried by his peers. If a peer were tried by a dozen gentlemen of ordinarily good standing and repute, he would be tried by his peers, but to try a gentleman before a dozen men who can have no knowledge of the conditions under which he has lived is simply absurd. Murder trials, the results of which with our system of capital punishment are irrevocable, should be tried by three judges whose verdict should be unanimous, and the trial should always take place in another part of the country from that in which the crime has been committed.

My perceptions became abnormally keen on matters of legal procedure. I sometimes found myself, when reflecting on such matters, starting with the assumption that I was innocent. It was amazing how completely I could follow a line of argument having my innocence for its basis.

It was decided that I should be taken to the House of Lords the night before the trial and lodged in the precincts, under a strict guard, till its conclusion.

I was uncertain until the last moment whether I should have the escort of military, or mounted police. As a matter of fact, I was honoured with neither, but was hemmed in by detectives.

I did not doubt but that I should have a perfectly fair trial. I can imagine no tribunal where a man is likely to receive more impartial treatment.

I read all the papers, and was disturbed to notice that a suspicion gradually manifested itself as to the real truth. It began to be remembered how speedily the members of the family which stood between me and the title had disappeared, and under what tragic circumstances.

I had always made a point of not having my photograph taken. Unfortunately, the police did this for me, and the proprietor of the hotel at which young Gascoyne Gascoyne had stayed when he was supposed to have poisoned himself recognised me at once. It was flattering as a tribute to my individuality, but inconvenient. I was for at once admitting that I had been at the hotel at the time, but my lawyers would not hear of it. Every inch of the ground, they declared, must be fought. They were a most able firm, and, realising that I was an advertisement such as they could never hope for again, they nursed the case—which in the first place was strong and healthy enough to have satisfied any lawyers—with tender solicitude.

I said that I had mentioned the fact to Mr. Gascoyne, as he then was, and that he might have told his wife. I asked if this would be accepted in evidence. They scouted the idea, however, of its being used, so I forbore to press the question further. The chances that Mr. Gascoyne had told his wife were extremely remote.

Having tracked me to the hotel at Lowhaven, the police were somewhat at a loss. They utterly failed to establish the fact that I had any poison in my possession at that time. They then threw themselves with ardour into the details of Ughtred Gascoyne's death. Here, again, although it was possible to show that I was not infrequently at his flat late at night, their most strenuous efforts could not prove that I was there on the night on which the fire had taken place.

I was sure that suspicion about this began to creep into my wife's mind. Perhaps she had learned that the Parsons were fictitious individuals. It may also have struck her that I must have passed the road where her brother was found dead, earlier on the same evening. These two facts, taken together with my being in the same hotel with young Gascoyne when he died, and as much evidence as could be raked up against me in connection with Ughtred Gascoyne's death, must have forged a chain of implication which could not but shake the most serene confidence. Not that I had the least fear of her acting in a hostile manner. She could not have done anything had she wished to; besides, she belonged to that class of woman who, possessing most of the virtues, would never drag her husband's name in the dust. Her conscience might—had she been questioned—have triumphed, but that she would speak out of her own free will I did not believe.

As the day of the trial drew nearer and nearer without any new charge my confidence rose. I suppose this optimism lies at the back of every prisoner's mind. The possibility of an acquittal probably never disappears till the foreman of the jury delivers the terrible word guilty, a word which has a leaden sound complementary to the deadliness of its meaning.

My wife came to see me the day before the trial, and though she strove hard against the awful horror that I could see was in her mind, the strain was at last telling on her. She was taken away in a dead faint. I was sorry for her. I knew it was the last thing she would have wished should happen. My own danger had driven all three women out of my mind, and it was a psychological point which interested me extremely.

I had loved them so fervently; and I could love fervently, even if not on the highest level. My own position, however, was so enormously important in my eyes that they were quite dwarfed. I could not rouse myself to any degree of emotion over their sufferings. It was not the idea of losing them that predominated in my mind, nor the idea of dwelling in their memory as a thing for pity, the victim of a terrible and gloomy death.

I regret to say that my departure for London, considered as a spectacle, was a failure.

I left the county prison in an ordinary carriage, and was put into a special train which drew up at a crossing in the depths of the country. I remember as I passed from the carriage to the railway-train casting my eye over a mellow, moonlit landscape, and wondering where I should be when they cut the corn. To one of my temperament it was a beautiful world I was perhaps leaving, and it was a dismal reflection that I might not share in the next year's harvest of pleasant things.

The train reached London at an early hour of the morning, and such perfect arrangements had been made that the few porters about hardly realised who it was who was hurried into a private carriage and driven off.

Passing through the streets as dawn was breaking, I could see on the advertisement boards outside small newspaper shops the soiled posters of the evening papers. They bore large headlines with: "Trial of Lord Gascoyne," "Latest Arrangements," etc., etc. There was not a paper which has not displayed it more prominently than any other item of news. This was gratifying. The carriage drew up at the peers' entrance to the House of Lords, for such was my privilege, and in a few minutes I had full assurance that I was receiving the hospitality of gentlemen. I was ushered into two rooms which had been set apart for me, and in one of which was laid a comfortable and substantial break-fast. To this I did full justice. Arrangements had been so made that I was practically alone in the room, although, of course, I was being very carefully watched. It was exceedingly comforting to feel that if they were going to hang me, they were going to do it with tact and breeding.

Parliament being in session, my trial would not take place before the Court of the Lord High Steward. I was glad, for that would have been comparatively a very small affair.

It may be as well to state that the House of Lords is a Court of Justice, of which all Peers of Parliament are judges, and the Lord High Steward the President. It differs from an ordinary court of law, inas-much as all the peers taking part in the trial are judges both of the law and of the facts.

At a very early hour I could hear a great deal of bustling and passing to and fro. I lay down on my bed, however, and had a most refreshing sleep. On awaking I was told that my lawyers wished to see me.

I had an interview with them lasting about an hour. They were both mightily important and very excited. The atmosphere of the place had evidently given them the idea that they were historical individuals, and I fancy that they looked upon me as if I had been accused of High Trea-son, and, in fact, treated me as quite a great personage.

So intense had been the excitement aroused, and so general was the interest displayed, that it had been decided to hold the trial in the roomier accommodation of Westminster Hall. I knew from what my counsel had told me that the peers had begun to assemble at ten o'clock. It was fully eleven, however, before I was summoned.

Although I was guarded to a certain extent by the usual officers of the law, I was nominally in charge of the yeoman usher of the Black Rod, and in his custody I was brought to the Bar.

Just before I entered a note was put into my hands which I was allowed to read. It was from Esther Lane, and ran:

> "Love is always difficult to bear, because of its madness, which overthrows, and its vision, which distorts. Pleasant we deem the kisses of men, though they sting, but the stings of suffering are the kisses of God, and they burn like fire."

Woman-like, though she was thinking of me, she was thinking somewhat more of herself.

It was a brilliant scene which I emerged upon, though perhaps somewhat lacking in the magnificence that would have attended it had it taken place a century earlier.

The Lord High Steward, as President, was seated in front of a throne, and on either side of him were the peers, in their robes, and wearing their orders. In front of the President was a raised dais, on which was placed an armchair, and by the side of which was a table.

Near this dais were tables at which were seated my counsel and other legal advisers. There was a gallery at one side, in which were seated the peeresses, and another gallery at the other side, in which were a number of Ambassadors, foreign royalties and noblemen, semi-resident in England. The difference between such a trial conducted amid a feast of colour and variety from what it must have been had it been conducted at the Old Bailey with its gloom and almost squalid lack of breadth was startling to think upon.

I had thoroughly studied the effect of my entrance. I knew that the scarlet of my peer's robes formed an absolute tone contrast to my Jewish appearance, and I was conscious of making a marked effect on the women present.

As an artist, I had suffered grievously in my own estimation by the blunders I had made in removing Lord Gascoyne, and I was determined that henceforward, whatever happened, I would not do anything which could mar the beauty and interest of the situation.

I waited at the foot of the dais while Norroy, King-at-Arms, called 'Oyez, Oyez.' The letters patent constituting a Lord High Steward were then read.

Norroy, and the Gentleman Usher of the Black Rod, then did their reverences kneeling, and presented the White Staff jointly to the Lord High Steward, who, receiving it, immediately delivered it to the Gentleman Usher of the Black Rod on his right hand. The Purse-Bearer, holding the purse, was on his left.

All these officials in their archaic costumes produced a most picturesque effect. The composition was seen in a sort of half-light, mellowing its garishness and the primary tones of official uniform. Through the windows, which had been veiled to keep out the glare of a brilliant summer sun, a golden light fell here and there, just sufficient to edge the scene with a gilded splendour.

The writ of certiorari for removing the indictment before the King in Parliament was then read. I will not reproduce this legal document, but it is sufficient to say that it charged me with the sole offence of poisoning Lord Gascoyne. I already saw in the faces of those around me that they believed what the press had daily insinuated, viz., that I was a wholesale murderer. Herein lay a great peculiarity and paradox of justice. It would not have been permissible to even hint in a court of law that there was a breath of suspicion attached to me in regard to the deaths of the other Gascoynes; it struck me, however, that it would have been excellent proof as to my innocence had it been argued that so clever a criminal as the alleged murderer of these others had been, would never have blundered so grossly over the murder of Lord Gascoyne.

As I stood and listened to these preliminaries I was being scrutinised by everyone in the Hall. The Lords were freed from the discomfort of trying one who had been born and bred among them. There were no recollections of Eton and Oxford to spoil the abstract drama of the occasion. I was to the great majority a stranger, and to the rest a mere acquaintance. Of course, I was connected with some of those present, but in so distant a degree that it hardly amounted to anything, and for all practical purposes I stood there a stranger. This must undoubtedly have been a relief to them, as curiosity could be given full play.

The clerk of the Parliaments then directed the Sergeant-at-Arms to make proclamation for Black Rod to bring his prisoner within the Bar.

I was led to the chair on the dais which was technically considered within the Bar. The dais had been provided so that I might have, as was only fair, a commanding position, and see and hear all that was going on. I remembered to have seen an old print of Charles I. being tried, and the recollection of it came back to me very vividly, except that in place of the motley crew of fanatics and bullies who constituted themselves his judges I had an assembly of gentlemen, reinforced by English judges, and in place of Bawling Bradshaw, I had a Lord Chancellor who was one of the most cultured men of his day.

Having arrived on the dais, I did due reverence to the court with all the dignity imaginable. I fancy the impression was good, and must at any rate have convinced the peers present, that even if I were unknown to them they had not been summoned to try a vulgarian under the most select form known to English law.

The Clerk of the Parliaments then again read the indictment and asked:

"How say you, my lord, are you guilty of the felony whereof you stand indicted or are you not guilty?"

I pleaded not guilty, and the trial proceeded.

I have come to the conclusion that the case was a curiously simple one, although it entirely depended on circumstantial evidence. The principal witnesses were the chemist, and the two servants. It was a descent from the sublime to the ridiculous when these humble folk stepped into the box, and I shall never forget—by the way, under the circumstances not a prolonged limit of memory—the bewhiskered and perspiring little chemist gazing round on the august assemblage before which he was appearing, evidently not at all certain that he might not be ordered out to instant execution. I almost thought that he would become delirious and be unable to give his evidence, but he pulled himself together, and by the time he left the box was evidently under the impression that he was one of us. Indeed, he replied in quite a chatty way to the Lord High Steward when asked a question by that exalted functionary.

The opening of the prosecution struck me as being vindictive, but it is possible that the prisoner is not a good judge of such a point.

It was lunch-time before the preliminary law questions had been disposed of and the opening speech of the prosecution made. I was led out by a side door before anyone else moved. When I returned the court was already assembled. The remainder of the day was spent in examining the witnesses. There could be no doubt that I had bought arsenic, for I was recognised by both the chemist and his assistant. Not till I heard the story unfolded in court did I realise how very crudely I had acted. The examination of the witnesses was proceeding when the court rose. I spent the evening looking out on the river with some very melancholy reflections on the advantages of liberty. The dark barges, looking like gigantic pachyderms, floated silently past, with their solitary lights shining dimly. The river reflected the city lights in innumerable little splashes of flame, which danced and glimmered with the restless waters. On the far bank I could see figures passing to and fro. In the solitary fastness of a gaol it had been easy to realise the fact of being a prisoner, but in a room which bore no resemblance in any way to a cell, it was exceedingly difficult. Besides, there was the open door, and I almost forgot the watchers in the passage. The windows had been barred temporarily. Otherwise there was an air of comfort, even of luxury, about the room.

I received a long letter from my wife which did extraordinary credit to her sense of justice and her self-control. It was written as if with the utmost belief in my innocence, and evidently she had striven to keep her mind in such an attitude. I answered her at once, not abating any apparent affection, and saying that between us two it was unnecessary to reiterate my innocence, as I knew her trust in me to be absolute.

Towards the end of the letter I worked myself into quite a fervour of sublime confidence that no injustice would be done, and that an unseen Providence was watching over me.

Then I read Lord Beaconsfield's *Vivian Grey* till I went to bed. I slept well, all things considered. I hoped to sleep better when the verdict was given, whichever way the case might be decided.

The next morning I awoke early, and as the law took so little account of individual psychology as to imagine that I might cut my throat, I was obliged to send out for a barber.

The youth who performed the operation was a pleasant young man, whose excitement was so painful that I warned him it was High Treason to cut the throat of a peer of the realm when he was being tried for his life.

I asked him what his own opinion was as to my guilt.

The question took him so entirely by surprise that he sprang away from me fully a yard.

"Come," I said. "What do people say?"

He flushed and was silent.

"So people think I am guilty, do they?"

"Some do, your grace."

"That means that most do. Now, does anyone believe in my innocence?"

"Oh yes, my lord, of course, some."

"I see; very few people believe in my innocence. Who are those that do?"

He smiled. "I think the women do, my lord."

This was satisfactory. I could not have had more practical support.

He told me further that there was a vast crowd outside in Westminster Yard.

I advised him to make his way at once to a newspaper office, and sell them a description of his interview with me. I warned him, however, that he must exaggerate if he wished to be believed, and I gave him full permission to invent any details of the occurrence which he might think useful.

The Hall was perhaps even more crowded than it had been the day before. This showed a proper increase of interest.

The cross-examinations were masterly, especially when it was considered how simple the evidence of the bare half-dozen witnesses was.

My counsel managed to throw doubt on the fact of my having been the man who bought the poison. This doubt, it is true, counsel for the prosecution soon swept aside, but I could not help admiring the dexterity with which my counsel threw a veil of uncertainty over what, when stated by the prosecution, had seemed facts beyond dispute.

The contention of the prosecution was very simple. It was to nobody's interest but mine and Mr. Gascoyne's that Lord Gascoyne should die, and whilst Mr. Gascoyne was in London, the prisoner was constantly in Lord Gascoyne's company. Further, it was pointed out that I was the only person left alone with the bottle of claret, and that the moment I was so left alone was the only one during which the wine could have been poisoned. I was further proved to have been in possession of arsenic for which I could not account. It had been suggested that the poison might have been in the cup of tea which Lord Gascoyne had drunk, but there was nothing to support this view. It was regrettable that this cup had been removed, and washed before it had been examined. Lord Gascoyne, however, was taken ill almost immediately after he had drunk the tea. This made the insinuation that it was poisoned unlikely, as arsenic had, as far as could be proved, never acted instantaneously. My counsel, in the course of his address, made an earnest appeal that everything alien to the case which had been circulated, he could only say in a most scandalous manner, in certain organs of the press, should be put out of mind. He insinuated that in this respect he felt a greater confidence in their lordships than he would have done in an ordinary jury.

He concluded by the usual passionate appeal for the benefit of any doubt which might linger in their minds.

The Lord High Steward summed up the evidence, and a very brief summing-up it was. Then their lordships retired, and after three hours' deliberation I was brought back into court.

I knew directly I returned what the verdict was, for in all faces there was the same look of intense gravity. Over the entire assembly there lay an almost oppressive silence. I noticed that people avoided looking at me, as if it were an intrusion to witness the emotions of any human being at such a moment.

After the verdict was given there passed across the whole place a sort of sigh, followed by a terrible hush.

I stood up and heard the sentence, and then, with the most profound reverence to the entire court, withdrew, satisfied that I could not be accused of having behaved otherwise than with a calmness and dignity befitting the privilege of belonging to such an assembly.

CHAPTER XXX

I SUPPOSE the feelings of a human being awaiting extinction on a near date fixed by the law must vary according to temperament. In this, as in most things, ignorance has its advantages. A chaplain working on a mind incapable of the intellectual effort of scepticism might send a criminal to the scaffold with a distinct feeling that in spite of its other disadvantages, murder plus hanging plus repentance was a short cut to eternal bliss—a view of the question which would no doubt shock the reverend gentleman who had inadvertently been a most effective advocate of murder.

Capital punishment is, of course, a profoundly unphilosophical thing. Only a very ill-informed person would uphold it as a deterrent, and if not a deterrent its only excuse is the selfish one of putting someone out of the way whom it cannot control without expense and trouble. This principle, however, is a very awkward one, and would, stated in its crudest form, astonish some people who mechanically support it.

As soon as I was back—I cannot say comfortably back—in prison, and in the condemned cell, I made up my mind to concentrate myself on a human document which should be a record of my career—a document to be written with as little display of feeling as possible, a statement of facts with well-bred calm and restraint.

I knew, of course, that it must be incomplete. No one has ever .told the truth about himself. I, for one, dislike the yawning gaps in the confessions of Rousseau. Either a man's confessions should have something in them which Rousseau's have not, or they are not very much worth confessing. A few obvious sexual trivialities are not of very great interest when all human beings guess what has been kept back. Dr. Johnson, when told that the unfortunate Dr. Dodd was devoting his last days to literary work, said: 'Depend upon it, when a man knows he is going to be hanged in a few days, it concentrates his mind wonderfully.'.I found this to be true. The learned doctor's point is subtle, and he no doubt was surprised that the concentration was not entirely on that unpleasant event daily coming nearer. Such was my difficulty. I had my human document to finish before a certain date, and that date interfered very largely with my concentration of mind. It had a way of dancing on to the page while I was writing, and of floating, detached and apparent, before my eyes in the growing dusk.

My life began to grow more and more ghostly. My nerves suffered considerably, although I endeavoured as far as possible to conceal the fact from the two sordid figures who kept watch over me. I could not help thinking of what a torture this fortnight or three weeks would have been to anyone afflicted with a terror of death. Personally, I felt the situation more as an offence against good taste than as an offence against humanity. Let anyone reflect what it must mean to be watched morning, noon, and night till the end comes, never to have one moment for solitary reflection or sorrow, not to be able to render to the soul the relief of despairing abandonment; to have the slightest weakness witnessed by careful official eyes, staring with a weird fascination through the long day which is all too short; to feel, in addition, the horror of being caged and held like a wild beast in a trap till the time comes to be led out to die. As I say, I am a singular character, and these things were rather an irritation than an agony. But I wonder that it does not drive the ordinary criminal mad. The man who has slain his wife in a moment of insane jealousy—which is, after all, viewed logically, an evidence of his love, a quality which might still have been turned to good account—is tortured and killed. It is a proceeding which reason condemns as mere barbaric vengeance. Not, as I was saying, that I suffered these horrors. My view of life was too objective for that. True, I had been given a body with which to express myself, and I had done my best for that body, but when that body was condemned to extinction I was able, as it were, to remove myself from it, and view men and their ways from a distance.

The chaplain called on me, sometimes three times a day, and I enjoyed his conversation very much. I led him from the crude vulgarities of attempted conversion to discussions on minute questions of Christian culture. I also dissected my sensations for his benefit. I told him that the reality that the end was so near now and then flashed upon me like an electric shock, and that this sensation was exceedingly uncomfortable, which he said he could well believe. I was not, I told him, afflicted with any very great terror of the mere function itself. This he thought extraordinary, as I was an agnostic. I told him that I thought it highly probable there was a hereafter, but that it was quite possible that it might be so different from anything we could imagine as to confuse our view of ethics, and that I might awake to find myself greeted as a saint. He was a little shocked, and took the joke as an admission of guilt, a point in which I was obliged to correct him.

I think he was surprised when I involved him in a long discussion on the moral aspect of capital punishment. Perhaps he went away and said I was callous. This is the orthodox designation of a man who has strength of mind or courage enough to meet a humanly-devised punishment with indifference. The same quality used in a different field will earn a reputation for valour. The dear chaplain was true to his cloth, and evidently viewed the crime of an English peer with something more of indulgence than he would have felt for the guilt of a member of the lower classes. Indeed, his reiterations of 'my lord' in his religious discussions were so constant as to confuse me with regard to the particular individual he was addressing.

I received a letter from Esther Lane in cryptic language which I could not understand at the time, but which was to be fully revealed afterwards.

I do not care to dwell upon the farewell interviews with my wife. They were curiously and unexpectedly unpleasant. The Dowager Lady Gascoyne—I allude, of course, to the widow of my benefactor—who, strangely enough, had never had the least doubt of my innocence, also came to see me. I think that in a sense the farewell that cost me most was that from Grahame Hallward, the unobtrusive and consistent friend. I do not think that the hopeless agony in his face could have been more terrible had he been related to me by the nearest of blood ties. He assured me that he would devote the rest of his life to proving my innocence. Thus is the tragic often unconsciously allied to the ridiculous.

My mind was fully occupied. The chaplain's visits and those of people who wished to say farewell, in addition to a great deal of time spent with my lawyer, with whom I had to make many arrangements, took up all the spare moments I did not devote to these memoirs. I should have liked to know whether my child was a boy, although in either case it would make no difference to the succession.

I was astonished to learn that there had been an extraordinary revulsion of feeling in my favour. I thought that the facts were really too plain to admit of an outburst of sentimentalism. I suppose the idea of a peer dying a sordid death shocked the British public as much as the idea of slaying a woman gently born had done some short time before. Hanging was good enough for the ignorant and poverty-stricken. The snobbery of the public is easier appealed to than its humanity.

The usual petition which my lawyer had prepared was signed by all sorts of unexpected people, even by some of those who had voted for my guilt.

The Home Secretary could not, however, find any loophole for interfering, and the Governor informed me of the date fixed, in a curious phraseology which was no doubt meant to modify facts.

I was getting a little feverish, as was only natural. I found it necessary to use some effort to brace myself up for the final ordeal. Thoughts of Sibella haunted me, and played upon my memory like the love motive on the lover's brain in Berlioz's *Scarlet Symphony*.

She was the allure beckoning my thoughts back to life, and it was a strange confirmation of what I had always felt—viz., that she was my strongest human magnet. I had not heard from her since the day of my arrest, but two days before the end I received a letter. It gave me infinite pleasure, and I knew it was the one thing I had been waiting for. She did not know, she wrote, how she had managed in her agony to conceal the truth from Lionel, but so far he had suspected nothing; indeed, he was working night and day for me.

I became quite sentimental over this letter. My thoughts wandered back to the schoolroom in the Hallwards' house on Clapham Common. I saw Sibella as a little school-girl with a host of boy admirers. I remembered her as she was that afternoon we came home from football and all had tea together. I remembered the kisses, beautiful and perfumed as roses, which we had exchanged as children, and I remembered the burning kiss, unexpected by both of us, exchanged that Sunday evening when Grahame left us alone. These things returned to me with the dull pain of melodies, associated with wild moments of joy, heard again in moments of desolation, phantoms of music wailing past in the haunted air.

Apart from the ineradicable desire to live, which is the chief vice of human beings, I was not very anxious for my friends to obtain a reprieve. In default of an absolute pardon, my reason taught me that it would be better for them to fail. I did not relish the idea of wearing out my life in chains. Thus, when the eve of the fatal day arrived, I experienced a certain relief.

I retired to rest with an indifference which I saw impressed the only audience I had left. I slept peacefully for several hours, but towards morning I experienced a curious sensation of semi-giddiness, as if I were being rocked in mid-air. The sensation grew more and more rapid, till, suddenly, it seemed as if I were hurtling through space at a terrific speed, as if worlds, stars, and atmosphere were revolving round me at a rate indescribable to human intelligence.

It was as if I were in the engine-room of the universe, and as if the ceaseless terror of its secrets whirled me hither and thither, like a grain of sand. I was in the unlimited, unable to grasp time or space. Then, by degrees, there came a calm; I lay still: and, almost unconscious of having passed out of the sleeping state, I was awake, with my eyes fixed on the Governor.

The cell was warm with sunlight, and it struck me at the time that this was most unsuitable. As, half awake, I looked at the Governor, a somewhat humorous idea struck me. I thought I was late for the ceremony, and that he had come to bid me make haste. I sprang up with a start, and I may have turned a little pale. It was excusable, I think. I then saw that the room was full of people, and not the people whom I had expected to see. The Governor seized my hand, and Grahame Hallward sprang forward and grasped the other.

"Lord Gascoyne, your innocence has been established beyond question. The real culprit has confessed."

It sounded like a speech out of a melodrama. Luckily, I retained my self-possession sufficiently to say something expressive of my thanks to Providence. I think it met the occasion.

Who the real culprit could be I failed to understand.

"I have given instructions," said the Governor, "for you to be taken to a comfortable room till the actual order for your release arrives."

Then I recollected my manuscript on the table. No one had seen it but myself, but if it were noticed it would be awkward.

It was a terrible moment. I expected the Governor as I picked it up to say: "Anything written in a prison becomes the property of the Crown," but I was allowed to walk off with it.

Escorted by a congratulatory group, I was taken to a room which was quite luxurious. Grahame Hallward and myself breakfasted together.

Then he told me all about it.

"You remember the governess at Hammerton Castle?" he asked.

I nodded.

"Well, it is very sad for Lady Gascoyne, but it appears that Lord Gascoyne had made love to her, that she was about to become a mother, and that she poisoned his tea that evening as she had already poisoned the wine. The servants remember now that she had been in the dining-room. She intended at the time to kill herself as well, but she had not the courage. Last night, however, she did so, having written to your wife and to the Home Secretary, your lawyer, and others, so as to make sure of the news arriving in time."

I looked at him, striving to hide the sheer horror which I felt for the first time in my life.

I was not surprised at the sacrifice, for it was the sort of gigantic thing that a nature like Esther's would have conceived and carried out. Nevertheless, the news filled me with a profound gloom.

It was better, however, to be sitting there finishing my coffee and smoking a cigarette than meandering out on to the unknown.

"Sibella has been awfully ill, Israel."

"Did people think me guilty?" I asked.

He avoided my question, and said:

"The revulsion of feeling has been tremendous. Everybody will be delighted."

And so it turned out. People had not at all liked the idea of a real, live lord becoming an unreal, dead lord by such means. The Home Secretary sent the order for my release the same afternoon. The dead Lord Gascoyne became a monster of iniquity, and I was congratulated by everyone on the *dénouement*.

But to this day, there is a sadness in my wife's manner, and although she tries to hide a shuddering aversion for me when we are alone, it shows itself unexpectedly in trifles. In some way she has grasped the truth. Indeed, she must have done, for there can be no other explanation of her conduct. We have two children, and perhaps there is something pathetic in the amount of moral training she gives them. I am sure there is no need for Hammerton to turn out other than well. I have done the work. He has only to reap the benefit and the reward. The second boy is a gentle little creature, Oriental in his nature, and most devoted to his father, as they both are, but the second boy especially so.

Sibella is still—Sibella.

THE END

CPSIA information can be obtained
at www.ICGtesting.com
Printed in the USA
LVHW010750080820
662689LV00002B/354